DISCLAIMER

CW01499268

Heart of Crimson is a dark paranormal romance that contains explicit content, graphic violence, profanity, and topics that may be sensitive to some readers.

Trigger warnings:
Graphic gore/death, torture, threats of sexual assault, and sexually explicit scenes.

This book is written in British English, including spelling and grammar.

Heart of Crimson

CURSE OF THE GUARDIANS BOOK FOUR

TAYLOR ASTON WHITE

DARK WOLF
PUBLISHING

www.taylorastonwhite.com
Official Taylor Aston White Newsletter

SUMMARY

He'll do anything to stop her... and she'll do anything to survive.

Titus is just trying to control his new power without losing himself to the darkness. Already cursed, and now suffering with noxious black magic, he believes his luck couldn't get any worse.

Until an assassin appears, ready to end his life. He never expected such an infuriating woman, and now he's not sure what to do. Kill her before she can kill him, or give in to the intense desire that proves bad luck comes in threes.

Rae is prepared for a typical hit. But when she can't seem to eliminate her target, she quickly realises that it wasn't only Titus who has a price on his head.

Forced to work together, or risk both their lives, Titus and Rae must unravel the mystery of who hired the hits, all while fighting against a dangerous attraction that's a frustration to them both.

Can they trust each other to survive long enough to discover who wants them dead?

Or will they end up killing each other instead?

BREED INDEX

Celestrial - Also known as 'angels.' Can lose their powers and wings, known as 'falling'

Magic class - Unknown

Origin realm - Unknown

Other - Once a celestrial has fallen, they're rumoured to be as weak as humans, but none have openly confirmed (See Fallen Angel)

Daemon - Druids who choose to ascend into black magic. In return for more power, they sacrifice their bodies and sanity

Magic class - Black

Origin realm - The Nether (also known as Hell)

Other - Once imprisoned in The Nether, they now freely move between realms

Druid - Born male, druid genes are inherited from the fathers

Magic class - Natural/Arcane. Can be strengthened with Ley Lines

Origin realm - Earth Side

Other - Breed governed by the Archdruid. When they come of age they must tattoo a syphon, known as a glyph, around their wrists to better control their arcane

Guardian - Druids who were cursed to share their soul with a 'beast.' Their bodies, including their 'beast' form, are designed to battle Daemons, with increased strength, agility and ability to survive severe damage

Magic class - Natural/Arcane. Can be strengthened with Ley Lines and glyphs

Origin realm - Earth Side

Beast - Unknown

Other - The Archdruid made the deal with Hadriel, the Fallen Angel who powers The Nether, creating the curse in return for soldiers

Fae - Umbrella term for anyone from Far Side. Includes faeries, selkies, pixies etc. Split into two castes, light (Seelie) and dark (Unseelie)

Magic class - Wild Magic

Origin realm - Asherah of Far (also known as Far Side)

Other - Never say thank you, and be wary of gifts (Fae stuff seem to have a mind of their own)

Fallen Angels - Celestrials that have 'fallen'

Magic class - Unknown

Origin realm - Unknown, but now reside on Earth Side

Other - Hide themselves amongst humans, always trying to regain their wings

Ghoul - Name for a failed vampire transition. Primal instincts only

Magic class - N/A

Origin realm - Earth Side

Other - Killed on sight

Human - Class themselves as the 'original' species on Earth Side. They have no access to their chi

Magic class - N/A

Origin realm - Earth Side

Other - Make over 60% of the population

Shifter - Born with a animal spirit, able to transform into said animal

Magic class - N/A

Origin realm - Earth Side

Other - Are not infectious, despite rumours. Usually live in groups/packs with a strict hierarchy

Witch - Humans who were gifted the ability to access their chi. Magic originated from the four elements, diluting through generations

Magic class - Arcane (balls of concentrated chi), Natural (plants) and Black (blood/death)

Origin realm - Earth Side

Other - Rumoured that it was Fae royalty who originally gifted humans magic

Vampire - Humans who've been infected by the Vampira virus

Magic class - N/A

Origin realm - Earth Side

Other - Low success rate, resulting in death and/or Ghouls. If turn is successful they must feed from a live source, surviving on proteins found in fresh blood

SHADOW-VEYN INDEX

Shadow-Veyn are wild creatures easily influenced by Daemons. They hide themselves from the general populace with glamour, but lower class cannot hide their shadows (hence their name)

Magic class - N/A

Origin realm - The Nether (Hell)

Other - Along with Daemons, they're no longer imprisoned in The Nether. Feed upon flesh, and as of yet, no evidence that they breed

Classifications -
   A - Small. Weak. Used as scouts.
   B - Venomous. Covered in black fur.
   C - Can heal using dark vapour.
   D - Scales as strong as armour, as well as fur.
   E - Defined by sheer size, and extra bones along spine.

HEART
OF
CRIMSON

CURSE OF THE GUARDIANS
BOOK FOUR

TAYLOR ASTON WHITE

PROLOGUE

TITUS

B*reathe.* Except every breath was excruciating.

Titus had never felt pain like it, as if fire was burning through every vein, slowly burrowing deeper with every agonising beat of his heart. Except it wasn't truly flames, but a thick, blackened tar that he could feel corrupting, changing.

Conversations filtered around him, dissonance that was nothing compared to the roar inside his head, at his beast's rage as it fought against the black magic polluting his body.

Hours. Days. He'd lost count in the eternal agony, and not once had he screamed. Of that he was sure, instead memorising the faces of the Daemons who watched with such fascination, such delight as they forced him through the Rite.

Forced his body, and chi to hold more power than he thought possible, stretching him beyond what he was capa-

1

ble. And yet they continued to push, and he continued to survive.

Breathe.

What felt like lightning had stripped his strength, his arms shaking when he finally managed to settle his weight. Head low, shoulders aching as he gritted his teeth, determined to stand, to answer his brother's call from somewhere in the distance. He couldn't hear, but his beast thundered in response, knowing they weren't fighting alone.

He had to get up. There was no other choice. Get up or die.

A sharp scent, blood that was a hot splatter across his bare flesh. He would've flinched at the sudden touch, except he was no longer in control of his own body. He sensed the Daemon, lifting his head up to meet eyes of crimson. The smile was cruel, a twist of the Daemon's lips as his words flowed over Titus in a wave.

Not once had he screamed.

Until then, the sound forced from his throat.

Breathe.

Except he couldn't.

CHAPTER 1

RAE

Rae broke into the office building as if she'd done it thousands of times before, the security none the wiser. Probably because they were fucking idiots, and didn't know their arses from their elbows. But what could the company – 'Scott Lee Financing,' according to the sign – really expect?

The entire building, which housed around fifteen different business, all sounding as boring as Scott Lee Financing, earned hundreds of millions annually. Yet they only hired a third-rate security firm, whose reviews included such one liners as, *'A ferret would have done a better job,'* and *'Mike's a useless twat.'* Them being incompetent only benefitted her, and in the two days she'd watched the place, she could probably put money down on which security guard was the notorious 'Mike.'

Rae pursed her lips, waiting until she was sure the security guard, who was currently doing the rounds on the thirteenth floor, was gone before she set herself up by the window that faced the Royal Park. Thirteenth floor because it was her lucky number.

She was born on Friday thirteenth. Her father died on

October thirteenth. Thirteen was how many assignments she'd fulfilled, meaning that after tonight she'd only have another eighty-six before she was free. Eighty-six more lives she had to take, before she was given back her own.

Fucking fabulous.

Light swept beneath the doors, a constant movement that didn't linger long enough to be a concern. Rae already knew the building wouldn't open again until 7:30am, where hundreds of men and women in restrictive business wear would start their miserable day. It gave her over seven hours to complete her assignment, and clean up before anyone was the wiser.

Footsteps faded, and Rae finally moved towards the window she'd already picked days before. The glass wouldn't open, not unsurprising on a building that had forty floors, but after a quick tool that cut through like it was paper, she was almost ready, and with time to spare.

I'm getting pretty good at this, she mused to herself.

Planning to murder a stranger wasn't something she wanted to gloat about, but until her one hundredth kill, she had no choice.

The sniper was cool in her hands, familiar as she carefully set it up. The click, click, click therapeutic as she slotted everything into place, the bullets the length of her palm.

Guns weren't her thing, the assassination less personal than she would've liked, even if she was a great shot. There was always a reason for why she was hired, and Rae usually enjoyed piecing together evidence to figure it out if she had the time. Because then, when she finally cornered her target, she got to watch the guilt as she explained exactly why she was the one that straddled their laps. Why she was the one who took their life, preferably with her favourite dagger.

Except her current target was a mystery.

Gently playing with the pendant around her throat, Rae glanced down at the piece of paper, and studied the image of her next hit. His dark blonde hair was pulled away from his angular face, lips parted as he huffed out a puff. Tattoos dominated the skin at his throat, and silver glinted on his lip, and nose. The image was slightly blurry, but it caught the anger in his dark eyes. The frustration.

Assignment No. 638273

Name, if known: Titus Liu Wood
Aliases, if known: Unknown
Gender, if known: Male
Age, if known: Unknown
Undead age, if relevant: N/A
Breed, if known: Unknown – Caution
Preferred method: Gun. Must pierce heart
Other details that may be important to the success of the hit:
Spotted hanging around Riley Storm.

That was it. Her target's entire life condensed to a single piece of paper. Disappointing, and pretty sad really. She'd been given a name, a time frame, and the image.

It had taken her weeks to find him, the man essentially a shadow, and according to records, he didn't exist. It had taken even longer to trail Riley Storm, and she'd finally found her target coming out of a construction site over in the square, dressed entirely in black like some grim reaper wannabe.

Now, Riley Storm was an interesting addition to the growing mystery. Titus Liu Wood may only have existed on paper, but she sure as hell had heard of the notorious bachelor of London. He was a pretty-boy businessman, and Rae had more than once seen his image grace magazines and news articles with words such as 'sexiest,' and 'charitable,' printed over them.

What the mainstream media didn't publish was that he was also rumoured to be so ruthless, that even the nastiest of Lords didn't mess with him, or his dangerous men that were just whispers amongst the Undercity. Speculation, of course. It was hard to believe anything coming from the gossip of those that frequented the Troll Market, especially when many of them were high on ashroot, or that new mist she'd heard about. Not to mention the sheer amount of Fae, who'd made twisting lies into deceiving truths an art form. But one thing she was sure of, was that Mr Storm had money, and power. Two things she didn't need to complicate her life with if she fucked this up.

So she took her time. Planned the hit perfectly.

The early morning sky was dark, the park beyond barely illuminated by the streetlamps along the pavement. It was quiet, just as she knew it would be. There was no residential housing, just boring skyscrapers that held just as equally mundane corporations. A handful of coffee shops, and cafes sprinkled the street with a little colour, but other than that the area was strictly business. Which meant no witnesses.

The sniper nestled perfectly in the little hole created in the window, the surrounding glass starting to spiderweb at the added weight.

"Fuck," she muttered quietly, blindly grabbing for the tape in her bag. One arm held the gun, and the other placing pieces of the stupidly expensive tape along the edges. It would be secure enough for her to finish the job. So now, she just had to wait.

Because for once in her life, she'd found something she was good at. It just happened to involve killing people.

CHAPTER 2

TITUS

T itus groaned as vomit erupted from his nose, the burn causing his eyes to water.

"That stops, eventually," Lucifer said, patting him on the shoulder like a child.

Titus flipped him the finger before he leaned forward, somehow managing to bring up more puke from an empty stomach, splattering against the floor. It burned like acid, his throat raw as he coughed, hoping that was the end of it. "How... how long?" he managed to say between waves of nausea, turning to look at the Daemon, and then Axel who stood beside him.

Lucifer shrugged, the movement overdramatised as it stretched his shredded black t-shirt. "Hundred years or so, I can't really remember."

Fucking, great.

"You've got this," Axel added, his eyes almost sad when they met his. But Titus quickly looked away, not wanting the pity that was the default emotion on most of his brothers for the past three months. He wasn't dying, he was just... he didn't know. He wasn't a Daemon, at least not entirely. But he was no longer what he once was, either.

Only he had the bad luck to be forced into a ritual not once, but twice. First as a child, which resulted in his beast that now shared his soul, and then again as an adult. He was still learning what he gained, or lost, from the Rite. He knew he went through at least the first stage of ascension from a druid to a Daemon. But the memory of the details were hazy.

"You need to try again," Lucy said, crossing his arms with an impatient grunt. "We need to know your limits."

"Limits?" Titus repeated, resting back against the cool brick of the wall as his stomach finally settled, his skin slick with sweat, and Axel's blood. "My limit is fuck you, Batboy." Black magic uncoiled in his chi, like a viper ready to strike.

"At least let me give you a fucking summoning name," Lucifer said. "You need it to balance the magic. It'll help settle the –"

"Fuck off."

Don't puke. Don't puke. Don't puke.

"Lucy's right," Axel said, wrapping a scrap of fabric torn from his own shirt around the cut on his palm. The same cut they'd used to heighten the black magic that now thrummed in Ti's veins. "Kyra said it would hurt, but you'll harm yourself until you learn to control the effluence. Being sick is good, it means you're repelling the bad effects."

"And not letting it settle into your little, innocent soul," Lucifer added. "Us Daemons are a unique Breed, as you're clearly figuring out."

"There's no *us*," Titus hissed, dragging a hand across his mouth, and tasting copper. His attention slid to the hound, a hole in the centre of its skull that was still burning. A hole he'd created. By accident. "We already know I can hold more arcane, my chi responding faster than anyone else's.

That's it, there's nothing else." Except any time he pulled on the new power, he puked his gut's up.

Axel reached as if to touch him, and Ti flinched. "Kyra said –"

"I don't care what Kyra said," Titus growled, chest tightening at the guilt in Axel's expression. "I'm not doing that again."

"But Kyra said –"

"Fuck off," Titus snapped, instantly regretting his anger. "Shit, I'm sorry. I just... I need a minute." He couldn't look at Axel, closing his eyes as he concentrated on every breath going in and out of his lungs, on the distant cars, and general noise of the city. On the wind that teased the strands of hair, and with it the stench of carrion, and rot from the hound.

Axel's voice was soft. "You guys deal with this, I'll go catch up with the others."

Footsteps faded, and Ti swallowed the shame.

Fuck.

Lucy was right, Daemons were indeed a rare Breed. Druid magic was that of the natural ley lines that ran throughout the earth, electrical sockets that enhanced their chis into physical arcane. Both magically stronger, and weaker compared to other magic users, because unless they were standing in a ley line stream, druids arcane was nothing but a trickle at their fingertips. But when they did, their magic was unrivalled in power, until it consumed them. It was the reason his Breed specialised in healing and defensive magic, rather than offensive. And also the reason their ancestors found another way to hold all that magic without dying.

The ritual as a child had already made him, and his brothers, different, their bodies able to call, and control higher amounts of arcane due to the glyphs tattooed on their skin, amounts that would vaporise a normal druid.

Syphons that helped them concentrate the arcane in much the same way the ley lines did.

But the new magic, the one that was alien to his chi, noxious, was something else entirely.

A woman walked past, hand tightening on the strap of her bag when she spotted them both hanging around the darkened florist shop.

"For fifty quid, you can watch," Lucifer purred, and the woman's eyes widened in alarm before she hurried across the road. "What, not into voyeurism?" He leaned beside Titus, an unwanted presence as he waited until the woman was out of sight.

"What's wrong with you?" Titus muttered, ignoring the headache that was beginning to thump behind his eyes.

"Many things, but at least we won't have her calling the police saying we've killed an innocent doggy."

"No, she's just calling them to say there's two fucking creeps hanging around a darkened street, *with* a dead dog."

A shrug. "I doubt she even noticed the dog." Lucifer was pensive when Titus turned to face him. "You're going to hurt yourself."

Titus didn't bother with a response, knowing Lucy would continue anyway.

"You're fighting the black magic," Lucy said, undeterred. "So it's fighting you back."

Titus frowned. "What the fuck does that mean?"

"It means you're going to lose, and when you do, the black magic will consume you. Why do you think the success rate of the Rite is so poor?" Lucy shook his head. "For such a smart guy, you're an idiot."

"Fucking hell Luce, don't hold back, would you."

"The magic doesn't control you, you control it. Accept the power and stop trying to fucking expel it, because trust me, it's not going anywhere."

Titus spat onto the cobbled stones, clearing his mouth from the vile taste. "I'm fine."

"That's my point, you're far from fucking fine. Axel's only trying to help, and yet you push him away. I didn't have anyone when I went through the Rite."

"I'm not *through* the Rite, I'm just..." Titus gritted his teeth, staring at the fresh tattoos along his fingers, ones that were trying to help him control his overcharged chi. "I don't know, I'm not –"

"You, anymore?"

Titus's nod was hesitant. "My chi's different."

"Black magic does that," Lucifer said with a shrug, his powerful shoulders empty of his wings. "Druids can't use black magic, nothing but arcane, which is just an extension of their weak-arse-chi." Lucifer grinned. "It's why the Archdruid has that stick up his arse. He knows even when connected to a ley line, we could destroy him with a flick of our fingers before his own magic poofs him out of existence."

Lucifer's palm erupted into arcane, a deep red with a heart of black. It was hot, the magical flames dancing freely before morphing into a clouded sphere. It was perfect, not a single wrinkle in the shimmery surface.

Titus called his own magic, the once white arcane tainted with flecks of black as he called it to his hand, before quickly extinguishing it. That same magic had killed the hound in a single hit.

"The reason Daemons are so powerful, and have been hunted since the beginning of existence is because, unlike witches, black magic doesn't harm us once we accept it." Lucifer turned his hand, the sphere moving with him. "There's no long-term effect on our body, or sacrifice to our sanity."

"You say this like your body didn't erupt wings and horns."

"I said *long* term." Lucifer closed his fist, the arcane extinguishing. "You try pushing your body through a mountain of black magic at once, and see if you don't grow fucking wings." Lucifer reached inside his jeans pocket, pulling out a joint and lighting it in one, quick movement.

Titus was sure his glare could cut.

"Oh right, you did!" Lucifer clapped him on the shoulder with a chuckle before taking a long inhale, holding it in his lungs before releasing the smoke out his nose. "Fascinating really, shows how connected all magic really is. Druids. Witches. Fae, and even those celestrial twats who think they're better than everyone else. Children of Chaos."

"We're not going to start that –"

"All magic was once Chaos, and then boom!" Lucifer slapped his hands together, creating a sudden crack.

" – again," Titus sighed, refusing the hand-rolled cigarette held out.

"It exploded into what we have now. Three realms, each with their own magic. Four if you count the Nether, which *I* don't." Lucifer took another drag, releasing the smoke like a dragon. It created a haze around his face, drawing attention to the intensity of his eyes.

"You're like a broken record," Ti said dryly, eyeing the joint. Ashroot probably, maybe mixed with some spices, from the scent.

"History's interesting," Lucy said before holding out his cigarette. "You sure you don't want some? It's some good shit."

"I'm cutting down," he explained, and Lucifer nodded in understanding. Axel was still early in his addiction recovery, and getting high from ashroot, or anything else for that matter, while his cousin was suffering, was an arsehole move. "And what you're saying is not history. The Chaos theory's just that, a theory."

"I'm sorry, explain to me how I'm able to drift and glamour myself, the same as Fae, while no other Breed can without the assistance of a charm? Or how both you and I can use death and blood to heighten our magic? The same as a black witch. Or –"

"Ugh, Fates kill me now."

A snort. "Bloody hell, those old hags aren't going to help."

He wasn't sure why he was calling on the Fates, three women his Breed revered. If he'd believed in them as a child, that faith left long ago when he was trained, and tortured to within an inch of his life. What goddesses subjected a child to such cruelty?

No, they didn't exist. And if they did, fuck them.

Titus's gaze wandered back to the hound. *Why the fuck hadn't it broken down yet?*

Lucifer frowned, his attention settling on the hound too. "I think this might be a problem."

Ignoring the surrounding smoke, Titus kneeled. The hound was definitely dead, the vapour that usually floated around their exposed ribs and nostrils long gone. The heart, which was visible at the side, had blackened into a darkened husk. Hounds, as well as all classifications of Shadow-Veyn, usually broke down in death, returning to the Nether within moments of their death.

"How long's it been?"

Lucifer raised a dark brow. "Since what? Since I pissed Jax off? Since I fucked someone other than my hand? Since I –"

"Why are you allowed to hunt with us again?" Ti muttered, pulling out his phone, and clicking Riley's number. He answered on the second ring.

"What?"

"We've got a problem."

Titus waited for the cleaners to finish whatever the fuck they were doing, the spell surrounding the hound making the edges of the scene hazy. If he looked away, his peripheral would show nothing but a shadowed florist, and not the two five-foot witches who both frowned down at the hound.

"Has this happened before?" Viktoria asked, her obsidian gaze so direct when she lifted her head, it was disconcerting. "This creature not 'breaking down,' as you put it?"

"Not that I'm aware." Titus ignored the glare from Viktor, the attention sharp barbs against his skin. He'd been staring since they first arrived at the scene ten minutes ago, only looking away when his wife demanded a second opinion, or when he wanted to glower at Lucifer instead.

Lucy remained uncharacteristically silent in the corner, watching everything with a slightly feral smile. He'd only been joining them on watch the last few weeks, and each time they'd been partnered together. Which meant he was a fucking babysitter. That and his cousin. For a male recently mated, Axel had a lot of time on his hands to constantly hover, as if waiting for Titus to explode.

Viktoria snapped out in Russian, and he frowned until he realised she wasn't speaking to him. Viktor's voice was much softer than his wife's when he replied, pulling out a white handkerchief from his pocket before gently laying it on the ground.

"This is not something we usually take care of," Viktoria said, watching her husband kneel in his perfectly pressed, black suit.

"It's an unusual situation." Titus knew little about the cleaners, Riley usually dealing with the exceedingly expensive service. "But my Sire said you're the best."

Viktoria's expression remained passive, the compliment only causing a subtle shift of her perfectly painted lips.

"And discreet, of course," he added.

Viktor spoke from his position by the hound, his briefcase, a patent black as spotless as his shoes, open beside him.

Titus waited, Russian a language he wasn't fluent in.

"We accept the job," Viktoria said, her accent that of English upper-class. "We will handle this as we see fit." She dismissed him with a flick of her hand.

Titus gritted his teeth, not appreciating the command for him to leave. "Viktoria," he said with a gentle incline of his head. "Viktor. A pleasure." A lie, even more so when Viktor looked up in the reflection of the shop's window, a flash of fear tightening his face before he caught it.

Titus turned, feeling the magic brush against his chi as he passed through an invisible barrier, and he knew if he looked back, he'd see nothing but cobbled stones, and a closed florist surrounded by an arch of pink and purple fake flowers.

"Those two aren't witches," Lucifer said, moving in step beside him. "They're something I've never felt before."

Titus tightened his lips into a thin line. "You see how Viktor watched us? Like he was examining a rat."

"That's because he was testing our chis. Little fucker," Lucifer growled over his shoulder. "You see in his little bag of tricks? There were these vials that looked like liquid metal."

Titus dragged a hand over his face, his body restless. "I'll drop Riley a text and meet you back at the house."

"Wait," Lucifer said with a frown. "Where the fuck are you going?"

Agitation at the interrogation, at being constantly questioned.

"Ti?" Lucifer called after him, but Titus was already moving, needing to work out the relentless energy that never let him rest. Let him think.

The black magic from earlier coiled tightly inside, polluting with every breath. It was pure, undiluted power, heightened when he added blood to the mix. Agreeing to cut Axel had been a mistake, the resulting surge of magic too dangerous. Too unpredictable.

Enough! he thought, ignoring the effluence. Ignoring how easy it would be to accept the power, to let it corrupt him. Control him.

Titus didn't want to think. To feel.

He used to work out in the gym, using the equipment until his body could take no more, and he could finally sleep. But at home there were too many fucking questions. Too many worried glances. So instead, he ran. Ran until his feet bled. Until his legs ached, and his head was empty. Until there were no more thoughts, nothing but the weight of each, mechanical stride.

He crossed Tower Bridge, the early morning sky still pitch black as he welcomed the quiet, the route so familiar he easily slipped into autopilot. There was nothing but the rhythmic pounding of his boots hitting the pavement, of the wind whipping against his face. He finally started to feel the beginning of exhaustion, enough that he may have been able to sleep. To rest without nightmares.

Titus reached the edge of the Royal Park, the streets silent as he crossed a corner, only to feel the air shift a second too late.

A single thought broke through the emptiness of his head, the pain lasting a second as the bullet tore straight through his chest.

CHAPTER 3

RAE

Rae gently kicked her target's thigh, knowing she was about to struggle with his sheer size. Not to mention his outfit of black tight leather, making him look extra bulky.

"They really need to update the questioning," she muttered quietly to herself. "If I'd known he was this big, I'd have brought a forklift."

Folding her arms, she scanned the surrounding area, thankful he'd appeared before the morning light, the area still quiet. The wind had picked up, an audible whoosh as she knelt down and touched his chest, her bullet passing through his clothes and skin with the ease she expected from a sniper. Impersonal, boring. But she also wasn't stupid. Unlike some of her cockier colleagues, she knew there was no way she'd be able to take out someone several times her size. Not with her weak-arse-strength, and zero magic capabilities.

She'd been too eager once, and almost lost her head when a particularly aggressive shifter wolf had decided to swipe his claws across her ribs. It was a warranted response, and she couldn't really blame him when she'd been sitting on his hips trying to cut out his heart. Now if she planned to be up front and personal with the killing, she used drugs before tying them down. If that wasn't possible, a gun it was.

It seemed all those years of her father trying to 'man-up' his children by taking them to a gun range, rather than telling them he loved them, had finally come in handy.

Who'da thought?

"Sorry about this," she said, pulling out her phone to take a confirmed kill picture for the Guildmaster. "Nothing personal." Her hand swept along his shoulders, tracing the tattoos along his throat before brushing across his cheek. His jaw and cheekbones were sharp enough to cut, lips full as they relaxed in death. Kohl smeared along his top lash line, emphasising the slight angle of his eyes.

He was handsome, okay, more than handsome, but she was always a sucker for tattoos, and from what she could see this guy was covered in the most intricate designs. She wondered what he'd done to piss someone off enough to warrant an assassination. She wasn't there to judge her target's life, fuck, she'd done enough desperate shit to probably warrant her own hit. But, from some cruel twist of fate, she was the executioner, and each kill was a step closer to her freedom.

Fourteen done. Eighty-six more to go. Easy-peasy, lemon squeezy.

Her hands skimmed lower, back across his blood-soaked chest to the gun strapped beneath his arm. She hadn't noticed it at first, the strap loosening.

It was heavy in her hand, heavier than expected from a pistol. Except the barrel was thicker than any she'd ever played with, the grip wide enough her fingers were barely able to clasp it, never mind reach the trigger. With a frown she tilted it into the limited light, realising that not only was it one of the most unique guns she'd ever held, but it was also covered in glitter.

Rae couldn't help the smile that tugged her lips.

Everyone needed a little glitter in their lives, even a man who looked like he could kill her with a single punch.

"You need help?" a voice asked from within the shadows.

Rae jumped to her feet, holding out her new gun in warning. "Nathan?"

Nathan's lanky form slinked out from where he'd stood behind a bush, flipping a knife in his hand. "Hey Rae." His green eyes, brighter than her own, snapped to her target's still form, a look of bloodlust sweeping across his features as he licked his lips.

"What are you doing here?" she growled, keeping the gun aimed at his face. "This is *my* job."

Nathan held up his hands, his knife glinting in the light before his attention slid to her with a smile. "Just wanted to see if you needed any help, that's all, Cupcake."

Rae controlled her burst of anger, finally lowering the gun to her side. "I'm not your Cupcake." She wanted to send him away, because she knew as soon as she accepted his help, she'd owe him, and Rae could never be sure what he'd want in return. Nathan was greasy, a snake both literally, and figuratively. He was one of the rarest shifters, and that made him an arrogant prick with severe superiority syndrome.

"Careful Rae," he said, his eyes brightening. "You'll hurt my feelings."

"Your ego can take it." Slinging her new gun in her bag, she felt her phone vibrate in her pocket.

"Souvenir?" he asked.

"Yeah," Rae groaned, rubbing her thumb against the text as if it would disappear. She hated this part of the job, where she was required to take part of the body as proof, as if the photograph of his chest wide open wasn't enough.

"Let me guess," Nathan drawled, rocking back on his heels. "They want his cock?"

Rae sighed, dragging her fingers through the knots of her ponytail before flipping the long strands over her shoulder. "Help me get him into the boot of my car."

Nathan's returning wink was nauseating because she'd accepted his help. "Of course, Cupcake."

She threw him the keys, and before she could tell him where she'd parked, he turned in the right direction. Which meant he'd been watching her for far longer than she'd originally thought. *Bloody hell.*

Drops of rain fell on her cheeks, the wind turning violent as she reached down to brush the blonde strands of her target's hair from his face. His roots were darker, the same shade as the five-o-clock shadow that scratched along his jaw. She found herself mesmerised by the swirls and lines down his throat, wondering how much of his body was actually covered in the beautiful markings. Slipping her fingers into the collar of his t-shirt, she pulled it down to find the lines morphing into something else, a large black and grey piece that –

Headlights flashed, a door slamming before Nathan stood over her with an expression of fury. "What the fuck are you doing?" he snarled, leaning down to grab her arm in a bruising grip. He hauled her to her feet, hand not releasing as he pulled her towards his chest. He was almost a foot taller, having to curve his body down to look her in the eyes.

"Let. Go. Of. Me," she said calmly. "Now, Nathan."

His nostrils flared, his tongue flicking out to taste the surrounding air. It always grossed her out, reminding her that he wasn't just a man, but a reptile too.

"Three."

His grip tightened, pupils shifting into slits. "Why were your fingers down his top?"

Rae released a steady breath. "Two."

"What? You're such a slut that you'll fuck a –"

Her fist knocked against his nose, the resulting crack satisfying as he howled in pain. His hand fell from her arm, and stepping out of his way she waited for him to realign his already relatively flat nose.

"You finished?" she asked, steel in her icy tone.

His pupils remained elliptical, his smile threatening. "Careful, Rae."

"Don't touch me without permission, and it won't happen again." Rae reached her car, popping the boot. "Now, help me get him in here."

Rae grabbed her target's left leg, attempting to pull him towards her car. He weighed a ton, and she'd barely been able to move him an inch by the time Nathan finally helped, and between them they were able to haul him into the tight space.

"That's a problem," Nathan said with a chuckle, their earlier spat forgotten. It wasn't uncommon to fight with her colleagues, especially when everyone seemed to suffer from arse-hole-itus.

Rae bit her bottom lip, trying not to laugh at the sight of her target barely fitting. His long legs stuck out the end, his torso alone taking up the entire boot. "Good thing he's dead, otherwise this would suck for him." Lifting his legs she folded them over his chest, and Nathan quickly shut the boot. "I'll meet you back at the Guild." She didn't wait for Nathan to reply, grabbing the keys from his hand before slipping into the driver's side and hitting the accelerator.

The lights blurred around her, the roads starting to welcome other cars despite the moon still dominating the sky. Turning on the radio, Rae sang along to a popular pop song, thankful to see the city disappear behind her, and with it the tension of being caught.

Hiding a body was a situation even she couldn't talk herself out of, and she knew as soon as they ran her name through the system she'd be in even more shit. Because technically, just like the guy in her boot, she was dead. Not dead, dead. Or even vampire dead. Just registered as deceased, the exact day she'd signed her contract with the Guild in blood.

Slowing down for the speed cameras, Rae drove carefully until she was on the outskirts of London, knowing the likelihood of being pulled over was low, but never zero. The music shifted into a heavier beat, and she sang along pretending she was a teenager again, belting out the lyrics in the tight confines of the cabin. It helped her relax, losing herself in the song rather than thinking about what would happen next.

Because it wasn't just any souvenir the assignment demanded, they wanted her to deliver his head.

Why did people turn their music down to see better? It wasn't as if the music obscured her sight, but she still found herself turning the radio until it was a whisper, her eyes scanning the pitch-black country road.

The only illumination was from her headlights, and

even they didn't make a dent in the vacuum of darkness, the moon hidden behind the rain clouds that sprinkled her windscreen. It made driving the road dangerous, her car jerking over every bump, and hole in the dirt with a heavy thump. The route to the Mirror, a lake named for its perfect reflection on the calm water just north of the city, was hard enough to find in the daylight, with all signs removed to prevent those curious enough to visit.

At night, where she couldn't see more than a few inches in front, and nothing behind at all, it was almost impossible. Nothing surrounded her for miles, the area a dead zone. Rae had read of planning permission to build luxurious flats at the edge of the water, and construction had even been going on until a year or so ago, when workers started going missing.

The company building the flats went bust, and with the negative press surrounding the project everything was abandoned. The missing men were never found, the hollow shell of the partially built structure an eyesore compared to the beauty of the untouched lake. Or it would have been, if she could fucking see anything.

Slamming on her brakes, Rae saw the metal chain link fence seconds before she hit it, her wheels skidding until the front of her car kissed the gate. Handwritten cautions had been attached to the metal, pictures of monsters and anti-Breed slander that would make even a sailor blush. Locals warning about the lake. It was for those same reasons she'd driven for over an hour at almost three in the morning.

Sliding out the car, Rae quickly pulled the gate open, the lock long gone. It was still dark, the clouds finally opening up to let some moonlight reveal the way down towards the water's edge.

Pale skin appeared, heads breaking the wet surface as Rae grabbed the torch she'd hidden in the glove compartment, her new pistol from the seat, as well as the earbuds. The sirens didn't bother with glamour as they pulled themselves from the water, their lithe bodies naked to the night as they easily adapted to two legs. Their faces were beautiful, their hair, although wet, was thick and curled around their shoulders in gentle waves. Three walked over, the moonlight highlighting the jewel tones along their skin, scales reflecting that of their tails that dipped between their bare legs. Nails, long, and sharp as talons draped from their hands.

Rae made sure her ears were secure before she stepped out the car, placing the gun in the thigh holster beneath her short skirt and putting on what she hoped was a friendly face. She'd worked with the sirens before, but unlike their selkie cousins, sirens were a much meaner type of faerie, ones who lived on flesh. Convenient when she needed to get rid of a body.

"We haven't seen you in a while," the leader – Mira, if Rae remembered correctly – said, her voice musical as all three stopped at the edge of her headlights reach. "Thought you may have forgotten about us."

"You bring us a present?" the left one asked, her hair a bubble-gum pink a few shades brighter than her scales. Her cheeks were rosy, lips a similar colour with eyes large enough to belong to a doll.

Rae kept the car between them, not wanting to get too close. "I need the head, but you can have the rest."

Mira pursed her thick lips, her voice taking on a higher note. "You sure you don't want to join us in the water? Come, it's so warm."

Rae felt her body tense at the command, magic, she presumed. Unfortunately, she had no access to her aura, and because of that she didn't have a chi. At least, she assumed she didn't have a chi. Magic, unless blatantly obvious, passed over her like the wind. It was a vulnerability she couldn't have in her line of work, so she tried to keep up to date with the different Breeds she was likely to encounter. There was a lot of lore surrounding the Fae, and as they never confirmed, or denied anything relating to them, she wasn't sure how accurate the information was.

A pain in the arse, but that was what she got for choosing sirens to clean-up for her. Sirens, who according to an old, ripped, book in the small, quaint book shop she'd fallen in love with when she'd first joined the Guild, *sang* their victims to death.

Rae unlocked her muscles, movements stiff as the earbuds blocked the compulsion to follow the beautiful women to the water. Where she was sure she'd survive for long enough to take one last breath before disappearing beneath the mirrored surface. Walking around the car, torch facing the uneven earth beneath her feet she paused, barely able to make out the outline of the open boot.

"Fuck," she cursed, sweeping the torch over the empty insides. Wires that were probably supposed to alert her when the boot was open were ripped, the frayed copper mocking.

"Is there a problem?" Mira purred, appearing around the side, footsteps silent. Her long, white hair draped over her breasts, lips curved into a sensual smile. "Come with us, you'll love the water."

Rae found herself taking a step forward before she locked her knees. "Back off!" she said, voice a sharp bark as she slammed the boot shut, only for the bloody thing to rebound back up, the latch torn clean off.

Mira's smile grew, revealing her terrifying razor-thin teeth. Needles, ones Rae had witnessed on more than one occasion tear and shred.

"I said back the fuck off!" Rae grabbed the gun tucked

beneath her skirt, finger straining to reach the trigger. The shot hit only an inch from Mira's webbed toes, kicking up the dirt. It caused all three women to jump back with a screech, enough time for Rae to throw herself into the driving seat, shove the car into reverse, and get herself out of there.

CHAPTER 4

TITUS

Titus's chest burned, as if every vein was pulsing with magma. His whole torso ached, as well as his spine, and pretty much every muscle possible. Probably because he'd been pretzeled into the boot of a fucking car.

He'd never felt an ache like it, every movement excruciating.

Grazes and cuts marked his arms, his palms bleeding from where he'd used them to catch his fall. He'd expected the driver to notice him missing, if not from the noise of punching through the latch, then from the sheer weight shift as he'd rolled himself out. Except, apparently she couldn't hear above her own, off-pitch singing.

Climbing to his feet with an audible groan, he touched his chest, sinking his finger into the hole with a wince, and felt the metal imbedded. "Great," he mumbled, scanning the area. He could see reasonably well in the dead of night, thanks to his glyphs, but nothing but darkness surrounded him. No road, no signs, or even trees. Nothing but dirt, rocks and tyre marks. If there were buildings, they were miles away, the city not even a silhouette in the distance.

Where the fuck am I?

Reaching into his back pocket, he found his phone, the screen smashed. "I swear to the fucking Fates," he growled, ignoring the glass as it cut into his thumb, scrolling through the contacts.

"Yo, this is Sythe..."

"Hey man, I need a –"

"I can't come to the phone right now... probably because I've better things to do. Leave the secret password, and I may, or may not get back to you."

Titus waited for the beep.

"You're a fucking idiot, Sy." Leaving the message, he scrolled to another one of his brothers.

"What?" Jax answered on the first ring.

"I need a pick up." Ti could picture Jax's scowl, an almost permanent fixture on his brother's face.

"Why?"

"Because I need a fucking pick up." Titus called for patience, the beginning of a migraine starting to pulsate behind his eyes, just adding insult to injury. "Can you track my phone?"

A pause. *"What the fuck are you doing all the way out there?"*

"I wanted to go for a walk," Titus drawled, beginning to move in the opposite direction of the car, his hand slipping down his side. "I have to... Fuck!"

"What?"

Titus's yanked at the holster, ignoring the burning across his chest. "That bitch stole my fucking gun!"

A deep chuckle down the receiver. *"One of your play-dates go wrong?"*

"It wasn't a fucking playdate!" Titus snarled, counting to three in his head before he continued, calmer. "You able to pick me up, or not?"

"I'll be there in the next hour." Jax hung up.

Titus took the stairs two at a time when he got home, unable to relax until he was behind the door to his room, stripping his shirt off with a pained wince. Storming into the bathroom, he checked his chest in the mirror, the hole obscuring the skull tattooed there. It would heal, but he'd have to get the shading done again, or he'd be left with a random patch of bare skin, which was almost as fucking annoying as the stolen gun.

Reaching over to the marble sink, he gripped the edge, the surface cool to touch as he glared at his reflection. His hair was a mess, more brown than blonde from the dirt, and there were little cuts along his cheek where he'd caught some loose stones. Bruises shadowed his left shoulder and arm, the skin of his chest covered in blood, darker than he was used to. Almost black.

But he barely skimmed across the injuries, immediately drawn to his eyes. Eyes that weren't his. Titus immediately dropped his gaze, unable to stand looking any longer. They used to be bourbon, one of the few characteristics other than the shape, that he'd inherited from his grandmother. Now they were a deep burgundy, a constant reminder of the pain he'd suffered. Of the black magic that was slowly changing him.

His beast released a grumble in the back of his mind, just as pissed as he was. Which made sense, as someone had tried to kill him, and if he'd died, he was sure his beast would have ceased to exist too.

Two beings cursed together against their will, destined to be dragged to Hell after one hundred years, to be a slave to the very fallen angel who'd cursed them in the first place, and the only thing that could stop that was to bind his soul to someone else. A chain, for a chain.

Great.

Titus released his grip on the marble, turning just as Jax appeared in the doorway. The pain radiated down every limb, an intense ache that throbbed along with his pulse.

"Sit," Jax grumbled, a man of many words.

Following his brother, Titus sat in the armchair that faced his bed, sitting straight as Jax knelt in front. "I thought you liked to tie your dates down?" he asked, frowning at the hole as he reached for the long tweezers from the first aid box he'd brought with him. "You must have really pissed her off."

"Funny." Titus pressed his lips together, swallowing the grunt as the cold metal dug into his wound, tapping against the bullet lodged deep inside. It caused tendrils of agony to break off in every direction. "You seem to have a fascination with my sex life."

"I have to live vicariously through someone, may as well be you." The tweezers were removed, and Jax sat back on his heels. "Fuck."

"Fuck?" Titus rolled his shoulders, and Jax quickly reached over to grip his arms.

"Stop, that bullet's in your fucking heart!"

Titus stilled, the ache in his chest pulsing with vengeance. "Well, get it out then," he said through gritted teeth.

"Ti, it's fucking shredded. I don't know how you're still moving." Jax frowned, pulling the scar that sliced down his left eye, a few shades darker than his olive skin tone. As kids they used to joke about some great monster ambushing him, which was exactly what had actually happened. Jax had fought, and killed a Shadow-Veyn at only eight years old, *before* he'd been merged with his beast.

30

"If you don't do it..." Titus reached for the tweezers. "I will."

Jax pulled them away, his arms in perfect proportion to his large frame. "Fuck's sake, you can't –"

"What happened?" Riley asked as he opened the bedroom door without knocking.

Titus closed his eyes, trying to calm his racing pulse.

"Bullet to the heart," Jax said with a grunt. "Should be dead."

"Bloody hell." Riley closed the door quietly behind him.

"Can someone just take it out." Titus glared at them both. "Please," he added.

Jax sighed, leaning forward until Titus felt the tweezers inside his chest once more.

Riley folded his arms, head cocked. "How does it feel?"

"Like bad indigestion, how do you think it feels?"

Riley's lips quirked up, but he noticed the worry in the deep set of his grey eyes. "J, how bad?"

Jax continued to prod, tweezers pausing for the barest second. "The heart's healing around the bullet. Fast enough that it's continuing to pump. Pretty sick, actually."

"You able to take it out?"

Pressure on his chest, the pain blossoming out until the surrounding muscles were rigid. A second later Jax pulled the bullet free, dropping it into his own palm. "Looks like a .300 Winchester Mag." Curling his fingers, he dropped his hand to the side. "I'll analyse the shell, and get back to you."

"Look forward to it," Titus grumbled, rubbing the heel of his hand against his chest, as if it could ease the throbbing. "Thanks."

Jax stood, free hand squeezing Ti's shoulder before he slipped out of the room, taking the bullet with him.

"You wanna tell me what happened?" Riley asked, widening his stance.

Titus grabbed the tissues from the first aid box, wiping the blood from his skin. The hole was already beginning to heal, far faster than any of the other Guardians, and from the expression on Riley's face, he'd noticed it too.

"I was shot –"

"No shit."

" – And I think it was a professional hit." Titus threw the tissues down, leaning forward to drag his hands through his hair. His entire body still ached, and for once he felt like he could sleep. At least for an hour, maybe two if he was lucky.

Riley stilled, a vicious predator in human skin. His eyes swirled into liquid silver when Titus looked up, his beast just as raged. "We need to figure this out quick, we're already down one Guardian with Sythe going dark."

Meaning Sythe wouldn't be contactable at all, not until the job was done. Which explained his voicemail. "How long this time?" He'd disappeared for three months before, infiltrating a small gang who specialised in black market body parts. He'd destroyed them from the inside out.

"As long as it takes." Riley's gaze was direct, their beasts calling to one another. "The Guardians don't exist. *You* don't exist."

So how the fuck had he been targeted?

Titus clenched his jaw, pulling out his shattered phone to check the last photograph taken. It was dark, the night mode terrible, but he could just make out the details of the licence plate. It would be fake, he was sure, but every time that particular plate flagged on any camera in the entire fucking city, he'd know. And then he'd find the bitch that had tried to kill him. "I'm dealing with it."

The Guardians were able to withstand damage that would usually kill an ordinary man threefold, their bodies coated with glyphs, the tattoos syphoning the excess powers from their beast. They'd been forced through such training that they were stronger, faster, and more agile than almost every other Breed

But the silence stretched between them, the knowledge that Titus shouldn't have survived a shot to the heart a heavy tension that caused something dark, and volatile to burn in the pit of his stomach. The Guardians may have been able to withstand more damage than most, but they weren't invincible.

Nothing could survive a hit like that.

Except, possibly a Daemon.

CHAPTER 5

RAE

Rae glared at her target's photograph, imagining all the ways she was going to kill him. Painful ways that involved her using her precious knife *before* folding his lifeless body into the boot.

How the fuck did he survive a shot to the chest?

Not even his chest, his heart. Her bullets had been the length of her fucking hand, and she never missed. Okay, she missed sometimes, she wasn't a robot, but her aim was usually spot on. And she'd seen the damage, his wound a bloody mess when she'd checked his pulse. Nothing. Nada. No sign of life. And yet he somehow climbed out of her boot with a mortal wound, and what? Walked away?

Rae rubbed the heel of her hand against her sternum, the dull burn a constant reminder that she was running out of time. One entire week had passed, seven days and nights and she still wasn't any closer in tracking down her target. Titus-fucking-Liu Wood, a man who had apparently disappeared after birth. He'd never had a job, or a parking fine, or even a speeding ticket. And according to the details, he had no other aliases, which made him a fucking ghost.

Her staying alive was reliant on her hunting down a ghost.

Again.

It wasn't uncommon for Rae to feel out of place. Her clothes had been more often than not threadbare, dirty, and covered in holes. Sometimes they'd been missing entirely, leaving her in nothing but a t-shirt in winter. She'd received attention even if she didn't want it, a child who didn't understand why people looked, whispered, and pointed.

She hadn't felt like that since she was fourteen and was forced to live with her aunt, but right then, as she walked into the gleaming skyscraper that was a sharp sword piercing the sky, she felt that familiar attention prickle against her skin. Rae tossed her hair, tied high in a ponytail on her head, over her shoulder, ignoring the sound of her heels on the shiny marble floor. Her pencil skirt and white button-down shirt stuck to her body like a second skin, and even though she'd stolen it from a respectable shop, she knew she stuck out against the expensive business attire that surrounded her.

But she was desperate, enough that she risked walking into the atrium of the one place Mr Storm had to be. In the last few years Riley had been breaking down his empire, giving away more money than she'd ever see in her lifetime to various charities. It was suspicious, to say the least, but people saw what they wanted.

He was generous, smart, and the playboy of the city, or at least he was until he'd married. A powerful businessman who'd graced covers from the top fashion magazines such as Style Icon, to financial newspapers like the Business Times. And yet, he was also feared amongst the Undercity.

His life was available for the world to see, yet Rae would put every penny she had – which admittedly wasn't much –

on it all being a front for something else. Something far more dangerous.

"How can I help you, Miss...?"

"Rae, it's just Rae," she replied, uncomfortable with the scrutiny of the man's – Gary, according to his security tag – eyes.

"How can I help you, Rae?" he asked with a forced politeness. He stood over her, creating an imposing shadow, wearing a suit that looked like it cost more than six months of her allowance.

Rae put on her friendliest smile. "I'm just waiting."

"Well, you've been waiting every day for the last three days straight." Gary's returning smile wasn't as friendly. "You need to move along, Miss Rae. There's no loitering in the atrium."

"Excuse me?" Rae straightened, spine rigid. "I'm waiting for a very important –"

"Then you must sign in." Gary gestured to the front desk. "If you don't, I will have to ask you to leave the premises immediately. This is private property, and you've been spotted lingering far too many times."

Rae felt her temper spike. "Excuse me –"A familiar flash of blue/black hair in her peripheral, Mr Storm walking across the floor with powerful strides, a blonde woman by his side. " – Thanks for your help, Gary! I'll take it from here," she chirped, patting him on the shoulder as she shot to her feet. "Don't worry, I won't tell your boss how you were such a snobbish dick!"

Rae raced after Mr Storm, skidding to a stop just outside. He stood across the street, dark hair pulled back from his face, his face carefully composed as his steel grey eyes met hers. Panic tightened Rae's lungs, freezing her legs until she was pinned in place, the surrounding commotion blurring to nothing but white noise. Two roads separated them, as well *as a crowd of pedestrians, several obnoxiously loud black cabs, a red bus, and a handful of cars.*

Yet, he noticed her. Following him.

Fuck.

With a nod of acknowledgment, he turned, slipping into a waiting car and disappearing into traffic.

Last time, it had taken her weeks of trailing Riley Storm to find her target, but Rae didn't have weeks now. She had a few days, if not less. She wasn't sure how Riley had become aware of her existence, but now he'd be even more cautious.

She'd become reckless in her desperation, and that could well end up being what would finally get her.

"You still haven't found him?" Nathan said, appearing over her shoulder. "Fucking hell Cupcake, you're cutting it a bit fine."

Rae grabbed her notes that she'd scattered on the table. Nix watched from his position on the other side, silently eating his apple, slice by slice, with his pocketknife. She looked up at him, but he barely reacted as he chewed mechanically, his crystal blue eyes just as dead as his personality. At least he wore clothes, the last time he'd decided to hang out in the common room he'd been as naked as the day he was born, hatched, or however one of the Fae were when birthed. He was... impressive, but she didn't want to see it all hanging out while she was eating her cereal.

"I'm sure I can take over your assignment, Cupcake," Nathan continued, sitting himself on the edge, so close his thigh brushed her arm. "We'll just figure out a fun way for you to pay me back."

Rae fought the heat in her cheeks, anger pulsing through her blood. Nix's dark brows snapped together, eyes narrowing when they settled on Nathan. It was an insult to take over another's assignment, which meant Nathan had branded her incompetent not just in front of Nix, but also Galen, and Winter.

"Careful Nathanial," Winter purred, her voice pure seduction edged with warning as she stepped away from the little shared kitchenette. Her white, blonde hair had been pinned into two buns, shorter strands framing her slim face. "That sounds like a threat. Next you'll be trying to *buy* Rae's contract."

Rae froze, dread settling into a pit in her stomach.

Nathan smirked, the smile slimy.

Their contracts were interchangeable, the magic that bound them flexible enough that she could be bought, or sold until she'd met her conditions. The idea that Nathan would essentially own her... Rae couldn't swallow the sour taste of fear quick enough.

"Viv wants you," Galen said, tone a deep rumble. He leaned against the kitchen counter, dark eyes snapping between Nathan and Rae. "I wouldn't keep her waiting."

Nathan hissed, but jumped from the table. His footsteps were silent as he headed towards the Guildmaster's office, the wards that were carved into the walls pulsating. As soon as Nathan was gone, the markings returned to their passive state, runes created by Vivian herself.

They were designed to protect those that were inside, supposedly helping to restrain violence, but not stop it entirely. Apparently they only really initiated if there was a risk of death, and then the aggressor would experience such pain they'd be disarmed. Not that anyone had tried it, that she knew of. But it made sense considering the only way to become the Guildmaster was to be gifted the job, or to kill the old one.

Vivian stayed safe within the walls, rarely emerging

from her quarters unless it involved more money, or meetings with the Syndicate, the organisation that created each individual Guild. Vivian liked money, and they definitely earned her money. Because of Rae's unique contract, she didn't get to see a single Ravyn or pound, unlike her colleagues who were all earning a decent cut from their jobs.

"I guess that witch in the market wasn't any help?" Winter said with her usual sunshine attitude. She was Fae, just like Nix, although she was only half. But while he was night, she was dawn. Calm, warm, and way too happy, but then again, she liked money too. Tucking a few of her loose strands behind a pointed ear, she turned to Galen. "I told you G, they're just con artists. They can't really see the future."

Rae tugged at the strands of her hair. "Nothing I didn't already know... which is nothing." She let out a sound of frustration, reaching for her dagger and slipping it into its sheath beneath her skirt.

"Where do you keep your knife in an outfit like that?" Galen asked, crunching into a slice of toast.

Rae frowned. "Where do you think I keep it?"

Galen swallowed, his Adam's apple bobbling as his eyes dipped between her legs.

"It's not a fucking purse," Winter snorted.

Nix flipped his pocketknife, his tone bored. "Everything's a purse if you try hard enough."

Rae pointed at the both of them. "You see, this is why you're both single."

Galen scowled, and Winter laughed. "You got a backup plan, Rae?" she asked.

"You mean other than to run and hide before you guys come hunt me down like a rabid dog?"

"I'll give you a head start," Nix said, shrugging when

they all turned to face him. "It was a joke." Except his face remained passive, not an ounce of emotion passing across his sharp features.

"*We* won't hunt you," Winter said, glaring at Nix with irises made of lavender. "But you know the rules."

Fail a target, and void the assignment.

Her life would be forfeit, which was ironic considering it was the reason she'd become a contractor in the first place.

Winter bent to grab something from a lower cupboard, and Nix's eyes immediately dropped to her butt, moving quickly away when she straightened. "Stay safe," she said, handing Galen the jar of chocolate spread. "We're here for you."

Rae smiled, knowing she'd need every piece of luck she could muster to complete her job in time. "Thanks, I'll make sure to invite you all to my funeral." She lifted a hand in farewell.

The Guild was situated not far from where she grew up, outside the house a derelict street with potholes, broken lights, and more graffiti than the local governing body cared to paint over. It was a forgotten part of the city, the human side of which was growing smaller and smaller every year. Breed seemed to accumulate together, and London was one of the most multi-specied places in the world. People underestimated her because of what she wasn't, which was something she liked to use to her advantage.

Vivian had bought the entire run-down building years before she'd taken Rae on, only renovating one floor, on which they all lived. The eight floors below, and three above, she'd gutted entirely, leaving nothing but the frames needed to keep the structure stable. There was a single lift, controlled by Vivian alone, and a set of stairs. The floor she'd renovated was split into sections, with each contractor having their own, small room, and bathroom. A communal area which they shared, and her office/living quarters. It wasn't much, but it was more homely than where she'd been before. Even if she had to share it with people like Nathan.

Walking into her bedroom, Rae dropped to her knees and moved the old rug that covered the space directly beside her bed. Making sure her door was still closed, she pried open the floorboard, blindly reaching into the dark hole hidden beneath. Her fingers brushed the crushed velvet box, one of two things remaining of her previous life. Pulling it out, she took a second to stroke across the soft surface, tracing her name in gold thread along the lid. It had been a gift from her mother, the last gift she'd ever received from her. Unable to stop herself, Rae grasped the pendant at her throat, the familiar, cool texture making her feel at ease. The necklace had been hidden inside the music box, along with a note that Rae hadn't discovered until *after*.

Dropping her hand before certain memories could resurface, she opened the lid. Ignoring the little ballerina spinning, the music no more than a broken whine, she lifted the hidden compartment to find... nothing. The space empty, the velvet worn.

Her charms, the ones she'd spent all her allowance on, were gone. Not even the note remained that she carefully kept folded at the bottom.

"Killian!" she shouted loud enough for the entire floor to hear. "Bastion!" *Those fucking twins.* She locked her bedroom every time she left, but the wolves were experts at breaking in to places they shouldn't, and would have likely done it for the shits and giggles. "Have you been in my room?"

Her charms had been there only hours before, she knew because she'd checked. Counted. She couldn't deal with the loss of the note, not yet. Later, when she had the time, she'd allow herself to cry, but not until she was in a safer space. Without judgment and prying eyes.

Closing the music box gently despite the irritation, Rae placed it back beneath the floorboard and rug before jumping up and opening her bedroom door with more effort than needed.

"I swear to fucking God," she continued to scream. "If I find you've been –"

"Killian and Bastion aren't here," Vivian said, her brown eyes taking in her unmade bed, the pile of notes on the floor, and clothes thrown on the dresser in one, quick sweep. Anger bracketed her mouth, and Rae snapped hers shut. "You have less than three days before the forfeit comes into play."

"I know, I'm working on –"

"Sort it." The words came out cold, clipped. "You're making us look bad. If the client finds out..." Vivian let the threat taper off, her long nose reminding Rae more of a rat, than a witch. She wore her usual suit, slim fitted and in a light grey that matched her neatly coifed hair. Pearls completed her ensemble, tight around her throat with a single crystal hanging in the centre.

Rae bit her tongue, waiting for Vivian to walk away in a gust of fresh rain, and expensive perfume before she grabbed her new gun from the dresser. Hiding it beneath her black denim jacket, because it was illegal to carry for pretty much everyone under British rules. It was why she preferred her dagger, the beautiful blade nestled neatly against her thigh.

She closed and locked her bedroom tight, her anger not dampening in her way down in the lift, the old metal thing whining the whole descent, nor when she found her crappy car in its usual spot on the ground floor, the boot closed using duct tape and sheer force.

She had fifty hours to figure everything out, but first she still needed to find the ghost.

Titus-fucking-Liu Wood.

When she finally found him, she was going to make sure he stayed dead this time.

CHAPTER 6

RAE

Rae ran into the shop just before the slight trickle turned torrential, the sky above rumbling. Mystic Medlock's Magic was one of the only remaining independent charm shops left on the high street, the rest taken over by big corporations that bulk bought poorly made charms. She'd tried them once, hoping to save money, but they'd barely worked for more than ten minutes. Which she couldn't really complain about when she compared the prices. What did she really expect when a charm to hide her freckles only cost a few quid?

There were a few more independent shops closer to the Guild, but Rae had wanted to drive, to quiet her anger, and pain of losing the final words written by her mother. She never looked at it, not since the first time she'd found it inside the hidden compartment in her music box, along with the necklace. But she could never throw it away, just leaving it folded against the delicate velvet, the words engraved forever on her memory.

Wiping the moisture from her face, mostly rain, but not all of it, she swept her gaze across the shop floor. It was a place she'd always wanted to visit as a kid, but was never allowed. The rustic outside was once painted black, and Rae remembered the left pane of glass advertising novelty magic tricks for the Norms, in thick, gold lettering. No such adverts adorned the window now, the front recently repainted in a bright red that caught her attention from all the way down the street.

Vines, flowers, and little paper suns garlanded the outside, the shop still decorated in beautiful wreaths of Summer Solstice, despite it having happened several months ago. A plastic box sat in the corner, a fat black cat lazily stretched across the left flap, fast asleep. Inside were grinning pumpkins and silly black witches' hats.

"It's August," Rae muttered, shaking her head when she spotted the Hallows Eve cards in a pile beside it. Samhain months away.

"Erm, can I help you?"

Rae turned at the question, smiling at the young assistant with bubble gum blue hair. She looked bored, her whiney voice matching her expression. "Ah, yes please. I'm looking for the costume charms." She didn't have any magic herself, but she could use the costume charms to disguise herself for short periods of time. Black hair, rather than red. Clear skin rather than dot-to-dot freckles. Little things that made all the difference when she needed to change her appearance quickly.

Amulets offered a longer solution, the glamour working for years rather than hours. Except amulets cost ten times more, and Rae was on a budget.

Bubble Gum blinked slowly, letting out a sigh before pointing to the wall of drawers. "Hair's in the third from the bottom. Sixth from the left. Facial cosmetics can be found in the bottom drawer, third from the right. Physical changes can be found on the top left."

Rae ignored the attitude, simply nodding in thanks as

she opened the correct drawers, scouring the small wooden disks.

Shit.

The prices had doubled since the last time she'd bought any, even the cheapest concealer out of her budget.

"Erm, do you have anything cheaper?"

"Cheaper?" the assistant parroted. "You want something cheaper? They're like thirty quid."

Rae gently slid the drawers closed, brushing the dust from her knees as she stood. "Yeah, as in half the price?" She smiled, hoping it would break the assistant's cold façade. But no, Bubble Gum just continued to blink slowly, lip twisting in slight annoyance.

"Err, let me ask my manager." She didn't let Rae reply before disappearing out the back, the curtain of beads tingling as she passed through. "Al! There's a customer who wants to know if we have anything cheaper?"

Rae waited, about to leave when a slim man with algae green eyes appeared, his smile soft. "Hi, I'm Alistair. Ruby said you're looking for some cosmetic charms?" He cleaned what looked like oil from his hands down the front of his blue apron. Screwdrivers stood up in his front pocket, as well as random shards of metal. An engineer, maybe?

Rae nodded. "I just need –"

"I have a box of unlabelled charms." Alistair frowned, turning towards the old vintage cash register. "It's somewhere... ah, here it is." He picked up a small cardboard box, placing it on the counter.

Rae peeked inside, the charms various shapes and sizes. Some were the usual discs, in generic oak, pine and a few redwood. Others were small 3D shapes, such as stars, hearts and diamonds. Not one was marked, everything tossed together with no information on what charm they actually were.

"These are all cosmetic... I think." Alistair frowned once more, his hand brushing against the contents. "I can sell you them for cheap, because, well, you know." His face flushed, Adam's apple bobbling with his swallow.

Rae picked up a walnut star, feeling its weight in her hand. She had no idea what it would do, whether if she activated it, it would it give her blonde hair, or a bushy tail. "How much?"

Alistair shrugged. "Five for ten pounds?"

Holy shit! For that price, it was worth the bushy tail.

"Deal." Rae grinned, reaching to grab four more charms at random. Two plain disks in oak, a heart in redwood, and a pine shaped like the sun. "Thanks."

"No problem." Alistair accepted the cash she held out, ringing her order up on the vintage register. "Let me know what they do, okay?"

With a smile Rae stepped back out into the street, not caring so much as the rain soaked into her jacket and skirt. Her only lead knew what she looked like, so if she had to activate all five of her new charms to stop Riley Storm from recognising her, she would.

Rae paused, spiders crawling across her spine as she turned, scanning the quiet street. The rain had washed everything out, creating a dull, grey view with pops of colour from the sparse umbrellas. Cars parked along the road, pedestrians walking, and shopping much faster than a leisurely stroll as the rain beat against them. There was nothing out of the ordinary, so after a second she slipped into her car, locking the door before turning the ignition. She may have had the charms, but she still needed the blood to be able to activate them. And unfortunately, hers wouldn't do.

Magic was one of those things that if it worked, it was life-changing. But when it didn't work, it could cause total mayhem. Rae grew up amongst that mayhem, her father a witch, and while her brother had inherited some of his magic, Rae hadn't. Not even a single drop.

Absolute bullshit, but she got over it pretty quickly when she realised that Miles wasn't exactly special. Governed by the witches, but classed so low they had their own specification, Miles had been branded a mage due to the dilution in his blood. He had focused access to his aura – or whatever the fuck it was – which allowed him to create his chi, but other than a few party tricks, he couldn't do much. No spells, no potions, and definitely no arcane, unless creating a flame on a single finger counted. Which was awesome when they were kids, but pretty anti-climactic as adults in a city full of supernaturals.

But one thing Miles had inherited was his blood, because while it was too diluted for the Magicka's stupid standards, it had enough of the special enzymes required to act as a reagent for charms. So he sold it on the black market for people like Rae, his enzymes reacting with spells, and essentially activating them.

Which was exactly the reason why she pulled up outside her old place after almost a year, the familiar brick just as worn as she remembered. The front door had been changed, as had the fascia which stuck out against the rest of the run-down street. Although, the fence had been smashed, creating sharp spikes that matched perfectly with the attached neighbours'.

Her name was no longer on the tenant's agreement, but she still sent her brother what little allowance she received. The townhouse had been split into two flats, with Rae and Miles renting the bottom one since she'd turned eighteen, six years ago. It was in a rough area, so it'd remained reasonably cheap over the years, but they didn't care, because it had given them both freedom and shelter.

The door whined when she opened it, the corridor and staircase that connected the two flats surprising clean, painted in a startling white that she was sure would have been even brighter on a sunny day. Miles' flat was directly to the left, the lock scratched as she inserted her key and stepped inside.

The stench of mould, and rotten food assaulted her nose immediately, the room stuffy as she clicked the door shut behind her. Empty bottles clinked as she knocked them, the floorboards squeaking as she moved to set her bag down on the side table beside the sofa, followed by her jacket.

"Miles? You home?" Thick curtains had been pulled across the front window, and when Rae pulled it back, she accidentally pulled it off the hooks, releasing a cloud of dust. "Shit," she said, coughing, unable to reach the pole to reattach the curtain, so leaving it where it fell in a heavy heap.

The living room looked like it needed a good clean, the floor covered in various crumbs, while glass bottles and beer cans sat on almost every available table surface. The rug that used to be in front of the TV had been rolled to the side, leaving a relatively clean space in the centre of the room. The fabric of the sofa had been burned, cigarette holes spotted randomly on the cushions. She didn't want to know what had happened to the blanket that draped across the back.

She didn't need to see the kitchen to know it was likely in a worse state, and mentally made a note to return with bin bags to clear up the place. Not wanting to linger any longer than she needed, Rae walked past her old bedroom to

Miles's, hoping he still had some stock of his blood left for her to borrow.

His bedroom was unlocked, inside a dark void as Rae blindly slapped against the wall for the light, finally finding it beneath her –

Pressure around her throat, the light flickering on with a dull whine as her back slammed against the door, head knocking back with a crack.

Rae blinked up at the calm face, at odds to the fingers tightening, stealing her breath. Her fucking target stood over her, his expression that of someone entirely uninterested. Which was almost insulting considering his hands were starving her of oxygen.

Reacting in pure panic she reached up to scrape her nails down the arm, not even breaking skin before she lifted her knee, and hit him right between the legs. His oomph of air confirmed her hit, and as she went to knee him again he shifted his hips, fingers loosening a fraction. Her fist hit his jaw next, but his head barely moved while her knuckles seared with pain. He looked more surprised than hurt, but she was able to twist from his grip and scramble beneath his arms.

Her shoes slipped on the wood, heart racing so hard the blood pumping through her ears drowned out everything else. She opened her old bedroom door in a panic, throwing herself beneath the long unused bed. Her hands reached in the dark, silently praying to any God that would listen that her brother hadn't sold the charms she'd left there. Pushing past cuddly toys and old clothes, her fingers brushed against something cold –

She was yanked from beneath the bed, hauled to her feet and slammed once more against a wall. Rae attached the cuff around his wrist, the click loud even against her heavy breathing. It seemed to stop him for a second, his brows furrowing as he stared at the cuff attached, the long chain that connected to an identical one around her right wrist. Pulling it, he twisted her in his arms, using the chain to cut against her windpipe.

"Wait!" she said, barely able to push the words out. "If you kill me, you'll never find out who wants you dead."

CHAPTER 7

TITUS

"If you kill me, you'll never find out who wants you dead," she said, voice rough from where he'd held her. She was already bruising, knuckles swollen, likely broken from where she'd sucker punched him in the jaw.

It took a second for her words to register, his beast's growl quieting to a gentle hum as he waited with a surprised patience at the back of his mind. He no longer called for blood, but instead was fascinated by the women with hair of startling red. She squirmed against his chest, her nails failing to tear at his skin. With a single movement he spun her, releasing the chain that joined them from her throat to press her harder against the wall.

Her face was flushed, breathing laboured as she sucked in a lungful of air. He expected anger, or even fear, not a mutinous expression with only her deep green eyes hinting at the earlier panic.

"Do you know the damage you've done to my car?" she said with an angry hiss, nose scrunching up.

"Excuse me?" Titus blinked, a small laugh dimming the

anger that burned hot in his gut. "You shot me in the fucking chest."

"Exactly," she said, reaching up to stroke the mark he'd left on her pale throat. "You're supposed to be dead."

"Yeah, well I'm a bit harder to kill." *The audacity of this fucking woman.* "Now, who the fuck are you?"

She lifted her head, lips pressed firmly into a stubborn line.

Titus gritted his teeth, his fist creating a dent beside her head when he caged her in. She flinched, but didn't drop the rebellious tilt of her chin.

'If you kill me, you'll never find out who wants you dead.'

"Assassin," he said, finding himself leaning forward, only to go predator still. His stomach clenched, senses on steroids as his beast pushed to the front of his mind. Titus stretched his chi out to brush against hers, expecting a prickly sensation to match her attitude. But instead he found...nothing. "Wait, you're a fucking human?"

Something snapped inside his chest, the sensation strange, a warmth spreading. He would have acknowledged it if a faint blush hadn't darkened her cheeks, bringing out the pale freckles across the bridge of her nose. *This* was who'd tried to kill him?

"You don't need to make it sound so disgusting. And we call ourselves contractors."

Titus didn't care for her reply, eyes drifting over her features with sharp focus. Those emerald eyes pinched under his scrutiny, but for once she remained silent as he studied her.

Humans didn't have a specific look, but he would have bet money on her being anything else. There was just something about her, something ethereal that no human could pull off so effortlessly. Her eyes a fraction too large. Heart shaped face too symmetrical. Her porcelain skin too perfect, not a single blemish marking the soft surface other than a slight scar on her temple.

Titus couldn't help himself as he reached forward to wrap his hand around her throat once more, her pulse doubling in speed as he gently brushed his thumb over it. He didn't tighten the hold, just held. Controlled as her delicate pink lips parted.

"You need me," she said on a breathless whisper.

Fuck the Fates.

A human had tried to kill him, and likely came close.

"Tell me everything." His voice came out harsher than he'd intended, but he continued to brush his thumb against her pulse, feeling it spike. "Who hired you?"

She tried to swallow, feeling the movement with his palm. "It doesn't work like that," she said, fire burning in her eyes. "I only receive the assignment once it's agreed, telling me how long I have for the hit. I don't get the details of who hired the Guild." She tried to shrug, pulse finally calming beneath his strokes. "I sometimes get more information, but your assignment was basic. Literally just a name and a picture."

"Picture?" His growl vibrated through his chest. "Where?"

"I don't have it here." Her brows furrowed, eyes snapping over his shoulder as if looking for some invisible saviour that didn't exist.

Titus dipped his head forward, her sweet, yet tart scent of peaches and cream invading his lungs. "Tell me your name." When she hesitated, he tightened his grip, just a little, enough for her to feel his capability of ending her life. But he wouldn't, because she was right, he needed her. "Tell. Me. Your. Name." The chain connecting them rattled, the weight of the cuff a reminder that she'd fucking trapped him.

"Rae," she finally said with a defiant snarl. "It's Rae."

Rae. His beast repeated her name across his mind, testing it. Tasting it.

He released her throat, stepping back enough that her shoulders loosened slightly. The cuff was heavy on his wrist, the chain so thick he knew he would do more harm than good if he tried to break it. Twisting around he searched for the keyhole, anger pulsing through his veins at the tiny hole. He wouldn't be able to pick it open with only one hand anyway, and no way would he call one of his brothers. They were already watching him like hawks, waiting for something to happen that would push him over the edge.

"Take off the handcuff."

Her large eyes rounded, flicking down to her own wrist. Her gaze took in the thickness of the metal, and then the length of the chain. "I can't."

Titus closed his eyes, praying for patience. "What do you mean you can't?"

"I don't have the key." When he didn't respond, she continued, her words coming out in a rush. "He was beating his wife, and the assignment stipulated it had to look like a robbery gone wrong, so I took it. I thought after that maybe I could sell it, but who wants handcuffs with no key?"

"And you shooting me in the chest?"

"Heart," she added. "I was specifically asked to shoot you in the heart." Her eyes dipped to his t-shirt covered chest, as if she could see through the fabric. "I very rarely miss."

Titus was going to break his jaw, or at least his teeth if he didn't relax. "You didn't."

Rae's eyes dilated, excitement flaring across her irises,

which only made Ti want to wrap his hand around her throat again, and feel her pleasure through her pulse. She enjoyed the thought of hurting him, or at least the praise of succeeding.

"I have this guy, he'll be able to get us out of it."

"You have a guy?" Titus tugged hard on his arm, and the chain yanked her a step forward, hands coming up to slap against his chest. "Do this often, then?"

Rae pursed her lips, rubbing at the skin beneath the metal. It had cut, the scent of blood driving his beast crazy. Violent. Titus forced his beast down, keeping himself perfectly immobile as he articulated his next words with clear precision. "I'm not asking again. Get the cuff off, Rae." He didn't like to not be in control.

Her eyes glowed with resentment, but she didn't step back. "I just said I know someone."

"Then lead the way."

"Not until you promise –"

"Promise what, exactly?" Titus smirked, enjoying her frustration. She wore her emotions on her face, every nose twitch, lip curl, and brow furrow giving away every thought. "Promise to not kill you, like you tried me?"

A fierce stare. "If you kill me, you'll never find out who wants you dead."

"You've already said that."

"I still have a few days before my Guild sends someone else, If I go missing –"

"They'll send someone sooner. I get it." Her lips snapped open, but he didn't give her a chance to respond. "I won't kill you when these cuffs are removed."

"I sense a *but* coming."

Titus glowered down at her, her attitude grating on his last nerve. "Mess with me again, and you'll see."

She licked across her bottom lip, and Titus couldn't help but watch the movement. "I won't kill you either."

A chuckle, his hand reaching behind her back, untucking her skirt. "Like I trust a word from your pretty little mouth. You're an assassin." He pulled out his own pistol, the fucking glitter that his cousin glued as a prank glinting in the light. "And a thief."

"Contractor," she corrected, her smile full of poison. "You need me, remember?"

Titus checked the magazine, counting a bullet missing. "Let's go." He tugged her towards the door, not bothering to turn as he pulled her into the daylight, the earlier rain leaving the pavement wet. Her car had been easy to track, the fake plates the same as when she'd stuffed him in the fucking boot. Shaking his head at the size of the car, he shot her a glare, but she only smirked in response, as if reading his thoughts. He would never have believed he could have fit into that tiny bloody thing, but the aches in his muscles were testament that she'd somehow managed.

"Payback's a bitch," he muttered, reaching for the car door handle when he paused, tingles of warning cascading down his spine.

"What are you –"

He tugged at the chain, forcing them both to the ground the instant bullets began raining down. He threw his body over hers, aiming his pistol towards the trajectory of the rounds and let off one warning shot. The car whined, tyres popping one after another. The stench of petrol floated on the wind seconds before flames licked at his skin.

"Fuck!" He dropped his head, metal and debris hitting his back as the car exploded just inches from them. He grunted, ignoring the sharp shards slicing into his flesh. Thirty seconds, that was how long it took from the first bullet to hit, to the car exploding. And in those thirty seconds Ti knew exactly where the shooter stood, his mind able to calculate the trajectory to within a micron. So without looking, he lifted the gun, and pressed the trigger.

A shout, his shot hitting true.

Flames continued to crackle, and it wouldn't be long before the police would be there to ask questions they couldn't answer.

Rae pushed against his shoulders, moving from beneath him to stare at her car. "I think someone else's already on your assignment."

Titus climbed to his feet, gaze scanning the surrounding area to find them alone. He spotted a puddle of blood, but no body. "Yeah," he said, pulling out a chunk of metal from his shoulder. "No shit."

CHAPTER 8

RAE

She'd panicked. She was always the first to admit when she'd fucked up. Okay, she never admitted when she fucked up, but when the option was either sure death, or to be attached to her target like a dog, she'd fucking bark.

She didn't have a contingency plan, because in what world did someone survive a direct shot to the heart? And then said survivor hunting *her* down. No one could have planned for that, which meant no one could judge her for it, either. If she died before her contract was complete, her brother would suffer the forfeit. If she failed, she would be killed as per the rules of the guild.

Rae checked the grazes along both her arms, the pavement having scraped across her skin when she'd landed heavily. Titus's SUV was much larger than her car, forcing her right arm to drape over the centre console as he shifted gears, pulling her hand away from the gravel she tried to remove her arm. The cuff was a direct result of the panic, but it also likely saved her life. She'd been nervous on her first job, especially considering she had to make it look like a robbery gone wrong. There had been no training, you just got shoved into the deep end and hoped that you floated.

There had been guilt at first, but not for long, not after everything she'd witnessed. She'd never found out, but Rae was sure it was the wife who'd ordered the hit. When going through the house she'd found polaroids, as well as a diary of exactly every degrading thing he'd done to her in vivid detail. Rae could only bring herself to look at one picture, the image taken from above, the woman who she assumed was the wife sprawled on the floor as if just pushed, cord wrapped tightly around her neck. Her arm had been lifted up as if to grab the camera, the other covering her bare breasts, bruises patterned across her stomach and thighs. Her cheeks and chest had been flushed a pink, tears glistening down her face to mix with the blood on her upper lip.

The guilt at what she had to do vanished instantly and never returned. Rae had enjoyed killing her target, drugging his tea and then tying him up with the same cords that had hurt his wife. It was where she'd found the cuffs too, in his little box of pain displayed proudly in his walk-in wardrobe. The toys there were designed to hurt, so she'd taken pleasure in tightening the cuffs on his wrists until his fingers had turned white from lack of blood, and then used those same toys on him.

He'd begged, for hours as she'd played with him, he'd begged, and then when she pretended she would let him go, she'd stabbed him through the eye. Wrecking the house had been fun too, except she was careful to not break anything that looked expensive. It was the same with stealing, she'd taken her target's wallet, his collection of watches as well as his phone, and laptop. But she couldn't bring herself to take anything that may have been the wife's. She'd even posted everything back a few weeks after his funeral, everything she'd stolen except the cuffs.

Rae had learnt a lot about herself that night. Firstly, she was messed up. Whether it was a nature versus nurture thing, she wasn't sure. But she shouldn't have enjoyed killing that man as much as she did. To hurt a person who'd harmed someone weaker than them had been invigorating. Intoxicating.

The cuffs had been an impulse steal, and once she realised she couldn't sell them without the key, she'd tossed them into her old room. It had all been a test, and when she'd succeeded, she'd actually forgotten about her first souvenir in the disarray of being forced into the guild, and officially becoming just another pawn for the Syndicate.

But now the same cuff cut into her wrist, and she still had no key. She just hoped Erik could actually get the bloody thing off, because while Titus-fucking-Liu Wood was drop dead gorgeous, she didn't want to be attached to him for the rest of her, admittingly, short life. Although, it would have been a fun way to go.

Rae sneaked a peek to her right, his movements mechanical as he followed her directions with little acknowledgment of her presence. The picture she'd received along with his name didn't do him justice. A square jaw, sharp cheekbones and a perfectly straight nose that clearly made him God's favourite. A silver ring pierced through his nostril, matching the one through the centre of his bottom lip. Those lips were relaxed, slightly fuller than usual for a man, but soft enough that it only emphasised the masculine angles of the rest of his face, framed slightly with dark blonde strands that had escaped his bun. Even darker brows over golden skin pulled together, and his eyes when he turned were as if they were on fire, a shadowy reddish brown that seemed to glow the more she stared. Maroon, or maybe even burgundy, a colour so unique she'd never seen it on anyone before, not even one of the Fae. Back at the house she could have sworn his irises had been silver, metallic. But that could also have been her brain being deprived of oxygen.

"How did you find me?" she asked when he took a sharp right, pulling her almost across the console and onto his lap. She hissed out in pain, but Titus didn't seem to notice as the metal cut into his wrist. His long sleeves clearly protecting him compared to her bare arms.

"You never changed your licence plate," he said, voice like rough silk. He'd been in a calm rage, even when he'd pinned her so effortlessly to the wall, his fingers wrapped around her windpipe. "Plus you seemed to be friendly with an acquaintance of mine."

She'd made a mistake following Riley Storm. *Fuck.*

"Dangerous move on your part." His eyes slid to hers, a smirk twitching his upper lip. "It was even easier to follow you once we had an image of your face. A few clicks and I could find you anywhere there was a camera."

"That's impossible."

Titus pulled out his phone, clicking a few buttons before handing it to her. It showed a crappy image of the back of her car, the darkened image barely showing the license plate.

"Swipe."

Tensing at his smooth command, Rae grumbled as curiosity won. The next image showed her car over Tower Bridge, and then down another road, and then another. Stomach twisting, she swiped through fifteen images of her car, and then the first of her face appeared.

She was inside Storm Industries atrium, waiting in her business attire with her legs crossed and hands clenched in her lap. The image was as clear as if it was taken on a professional camera, despite the timestamp indicating it was CCTV. The next picture was of her outside, the angle taken from across the street. One from inside Mystic Medlock's on her knees, another outside her brother's flat. The final picture was taken from within the guild, her expression angry as she walked to her car in the underground garage.

Vivian exclusively owned all the CCTV in the building, watching who came, and went from her office. So how did he get access?

"So you're some creepy stalker then?" she asked with more humour than she felt, disguising her anxiety at how easily he'd been able to find her. "Explains the hit. So, how did you do it?"

Without a word he touched the screen, and one last image appeared.

A couple smiled in the foreground, the man's long arm stretched to take the picture. It looked like any other selfie, except right in the top corner was Rae. She was barely a blob in the background, but her face had turned towards the phone, the shape of her features made out against the rain.

Holy fucking shit.

Now that was impressive.

She had to tell Killian, he'd piss himself with excitement at being able to hack someone's personal phone. Might make him a bit more helpful at tracking down targets.

"You can park anywhere here," she said when they'd arrived, any nerves at the pictures disappearing in a flutter as she pulled back the reins. She was in charge. She'd trapped *him,* not the other way around.

Titus frowned, the industrial area she'd taken him to quiet. Secluded. Not at all suspicious.

"Relax," she said, noticing the tension along his shoulders. "What's the worst that could happen?" She smirked at his frown, waiting for him to get out the car before she could crawl over the space. It wasn't exactly dignified, especially in a short skirt. It had been more awkward to get in the car, having her bare cheeks out as she figured how to climb over to the passenger seat, all while her right wrist was attached to his.

"What is this place?" he asked, continuously scanning their surroundings. He'd put the glittery gun in the top of his dark jeans, hidden beneath his black t-shirt. She was pissed at losing a weapon, but at least he hadn't found her knife still hidden beneath her skirt.

Rae studied the warehouses, empty due to being after hours. Everything was a sea of grey. Boring, bland, and exactly why the secret club thrived, hidden beneath the concrete. "It's called Bite."

"Bite?"

"Yeah, It's a dance club." She gestured to a door down the side of one of the warehouses, inconspicuous in its design, it blended into the brick from a distance. An optical illusion that changed depending on the angle. "It's Friday, so Erik should be here."

"So he might not be?" An impatient glare. "Can't you just call him?"

"Erik isn't someone you can just call." He didn't even own a phone, or if he did, he never shared his number with her. "He's a creature of habit." She hoped. It wasn't like she knew his exact schedule, but every time she'd been with Atlas and Winter, Erik had been there. Not that it was often, considering Rae usually only went for karaoke night, which was once every few weeks.

"What exactly is this club?" Titus asked, catching her hand before she could knock.

"One that isn't openly advertised." She shrugged, not sure what to say. "It's a place for Vamps to come and relax, I suppose."

"Relax?" His hand was a brand on her hers, heat fighting against the cool wind. She tried to tug free, but he tightened his grip.

"I don't know? The entire place is designed with vampires in mind. There's a floor with low music, another with loud. The bar specialises in blood infused drinks, and you can get a discount if you're willing to let a Vamp feed from you." The only way for a vampire to get drunk was to drink blood from someone who'd already consumed alcohol.

"Being treated like dinner. Is that a kink, Rae?"

She pulled at his grip again, harder than before. He released her with a cocked brow, and the extra momentum knocked her hard against the wall.

"So you're taking me to a club that's entirely catered to vampires," he said, voice a gentle growl. "I don't fucking think so."

"Look, do you have any other ideas, arsehole? Because I'm all ears." she said in a scathing tone. She'd already watched him try to break it, his frown amusing when he couldn't even dent a single link of the chain.

"Yeah, I could just break your fucking wrist."

"Try it," she snarled. "And you'll be eating soup through a straw for the rest of your miserable life."

Titus froze, his irises seeming to glow before he let out a rough laugh. It brushed across her skin, warming everywhere it touched.

His fist knocked against the metal door, his eyes alight like flames. "If you fuck me over, the person who owns that dirty flat will pay. It won't be hard to find out who, you've already seen what I can do. Understand?"

Rae bit her tongue, blood a roar in her ears.

"Use your words." Titus punched every word carefully. "Do. You. Understand?"

"Yes," she pushed out, her smile masking pure rage. "Just as you understand that without me, you're fucked."

They glared at each other, the cool wind picking up to twist strands of her hair around her face. Titus watched her, his gaze so direct, unwavering. He was a man of pure stone, always studying his surroundings with a feral intelligence. Except when he watched her, it was as if she held his entire attention. And right now he was furious, even if he didn't really give his emotions away.

Her lips parted, but before she could speak the door slid open, and the heavy thrum of the techno music escaped. "After you."

Titus paused for the barest second before he tugged her along.

"Welcome to Bite, have you been before?" The receptionist danced behind the desk, body swaying as she looked between the two of them, and then at the chain. Her pupils were blown, blonde hair teased into two buns on the side of her head like flattened horns. Small shorts bared her long legs, and while she wore an electric green crop top, it didn't cover much.

Rae hoped her smile was softer than before. "We're just looking to watch, not participate."

The receptionist continued to dance, hips shaking perfectly to the heavy beat. It vibrated the floor beneath their feet, and Rae knew it was only going to get louder. "You're overdressed," she said. "And you're wearing *the* no-no colour."

They both wore head-to-toe black.

"You registered with us before?" she continued, tapping the square on the desk, waiting until Rae placed her palm face down on the surface before clicking a button. The light around her hand hummed red, and then after a second turned green.

Rae flinched, pulling her hand back to reveal a hole in the middle of her palm. A single pearl of blood appeared, and the receptionist swiped it away with a fresh tissue.

"You're clear, but you won't be chosen for the cage unless you've consumed at least four drinks. We will be checking." She turned her attention to Titus, who didn't hesitate to place his palm on the same square. The green light around his palm immediately turned pink, and before the receptionist could wipe him clean, he'd clenched his hand and pulled away.

"Now *you're* ready for the cage," she purred, lips kicking up seductively. "Your blood must be delicious."

Titus tensed, lips pressed together.

Rae cleared her throat. "Is Erik in?"

The receptionist nodded her head, the movement tilting her neck to the light, and revealing the scars there. "He's around." Blood Kiss, an addiction to the euphoria some vampires could create from their bite. One of the many reasons she stayed away from anyone who had fangs.

She'd attended Bite a few times with Atlas, the only vampire in the guild, and had always enjoyed her experience. She came to dance, to drink, sing, and enjoy herself without the chance of being harassed. If she entered any of the floors without a glow-in-the-dark wrist band, she was off limits, and after a rumoured incident where a Vamp took an unwilling drink was staked right in the middle of the dance floor, no Vamp dared approach. It still left all the other sleazebags, but after dancing with someone like Atlas, or sometimes even the twins, they usually left her alone too.

Rae pushed Titus gently towards the heavy steel door. The music amplified until it rattled her bones, the limited lighting causing her to stumble. Titus caught her arm, his hand a brand. "Thanks," she mumbled, her voice drowned out as she waited for her eyes to adjust to the dim lighting.

Titus released her as quickly as he'd caught her, pausing at the edge of the rail and looking down to the floor below. The entire club was designed with concrete and steel, not that you could see much of the industrial design. It was dark, uncomfortably so, with only the UV lights brightening pale clothing, and the reflective paint on the sharp edges.

"Why do you think your friend will be able to help?" Titus had to repeat himself over the music.

Rae pressed herself closer to him, his body rigid at her touch. "He's into this stuff." She lifted her arm, the chain clinking against the railing.

Titus's brows pulled together. "Into what?"

"You'll see."

The mezzanine looked down on to the loud bar and dance floor, a strip painted around the top. The bartenders all wore glow sticks around their wrists, the rest of their bodies hidden in shadows. The dancers were just a distortion of bodies blurring together, their features hidden but for flashes of teeth against the UV. It was the appeal of the club, the darkness something people could lose themselves in. Except the club was designed for vampires, and vampires could see perfectly fine in the pitch black. It went back to the basic instincts of predators and prey. Making vampires the hunters, and everyone else the vulnerable sheep, while remaining in a safe, consenting space.

The adjoining building housed the quiet bar, identical to the loud bar, but with the music at a more comfortable volume for superior healing. It was connected by a short concrete tunnel, and the majority of the Vamps preferred the area. Rae had always thought it was awkward to watch so many bodies dance to music she could barely hear.

The cage the receptionist mentioned was still in its high position on the ceiling, but Rae knew that it wouldn't be long before it slowly descended, the owner choosing a sacrifice from the all too willing patrons. People danced for hours, hoping to be selected as the next meal.

The chosen one was stripped naked and displayed for all to see, the cage held just above the dance floor. Vampires paid to take a single sip from any place on their body, and more often than not it became sexual. Blood and sex went hand in hand, and the one time Rae had watched, it'd become a full-blown orgy.

Which was why she'd never stayed long enough to watch again.

"He should be on this floor."

Titus's lips brushed the shell of her ear. "Lead the way." His breath was hot, intimate against her cheek, and when he pulled back their eyes locked, the air thickening. Tension twisted, an abrasion that was heightened by the threat of death hanging above them both. It throbbed against her skin, and she hated the fact her pulse kicked in anticipation. In excitement.

"Rae?" His voice was deep and velvety. "The cuffs." His eyes dropped, and Rae finally remembered what the fuck she was doing.

Jesus Christ.

"Yeah." Rae cleared her throat. "Come on."

Her eyes had finally adjusted to the limited light, and it was enough to notice Titus's mouth twist into a smile for the barest second, before quickly returning to his usual impassiveness. A marble statue had more emotion.

"This would be more help if I knew who you were looking for."

"We're looking for a Viking."

The top deck was slim, with only the walkway towards the stairs, and strategically placed tables that overlooked the activities below. Rae passed each table carefully, the tops painted bright for safety, as were the chairs, but it was still hard to make out shapes when not everyone, or everything was reflective. The entire floor was quiet, much quieter than she expected as she searched.

Shit.

If he wasn't there, he might have been on the dance floor where he'd be almost impossible to find amongst the crowd.

"In the corner."

Rae paused at Titus's voice, turning her head when she spotted a burst of colour in the distance. Moving closer she realised it was glow sticks fashioned into a crown, one that perched on the very person's head she was after.

How did Titus see Erik from over there?

Even standing a foot away, Rae struggled to make out the details, only the woman really visible with her lips painted, as were her hands, and the thick choker around her throat. A chain, not too dissimilar to the one on Rae's wrist, was attached to the front.

Rae blinked, her eyes struggling against the bursts of random light amongst the black. Erik's silhouette moved, and a lamp on a table hidden beside him burst to life. The light was low, likely undetectable from even a few feet away, but enough to make out his distinctive facial features. His nose was strong, dominant on his slim face, with large bushy eyebrows held low over pitch black eyes. Pure white hair was braided from the fringe, curling around to drape over his shoulder in a thick rope long enough to reach his waist. His beard too was braided, just a single line in the centre, the sides left in a dishevelled mess. He was striking, in a curious, unusual way. She imagined him as a warrior, bearing an axe and shield from an era long gone.

What looked like chain mail draped over his heavy shoulders, more chains criss-crossing over his chest in heavy ropes.

White lines were displayed on the mirrored table, as well as a selection of coloured pills and a few cigarettes. Leaning over, the woman licked along the glass, catching a pink pill on the tip of her tongue before curling it back into her mouth. Her eyes closed in bliss, body draping over Erik's lap.

"Erik," Rae said in greeting, mouthing her words slowly, clearly. "You look well."

He smiled, revealing descended fangs stained with blood. His attention settled on Titus, pupils swallowing the rest of his whites. His tapped the women's head, and as she lazily slipped back, his hands lifted in front of her face.

"Erik wants to know," she said in a soft, dreamy voice that somehow carried above the heavy music. "What delicious feast have you brought him?"

CHAPTER 9

RAE

"He's not for you," Rae said, watching as the woman translated in sign, her hands moving slowly between each word.

Only for Erik to respond, voiced by her faraway tone. "Unless you're here to accept my offer, fuck off."

Titus widened his stance, violence threatening the air.

"Hey, come on Erik," she said quickly. "I thought we were friends?"

"We're not friends." Erik's laugh was silent, his mouth wide open and head thrown back. "Not since you stole my dagger."

"That was Atlas," she shouted above the music, the lie easily falling from her tongue. It had been a dare between Atlas, herself, and the twins. She couldn't remember much of that night, not after the amount of vodka she'd consumed, waking up with Erik's famed skull dagger on the pillow beside her. It was hers now, and she wasn't giving it back.

"I'll trade a favour."

"Favour?" Erik brushed his fingers across the woman's collarbone, tracing each and every scar there. "The favour would be to allow me to feed for the night."

"You know I would never agree to that." Rae's eyes flicked to the chain attached to the woman's collar, ending beneath Erik's boot. "Can you just take a look?" She lifted her wrist to better show her cuff, only for Erik to jump to his feet, hand curling around the solid metal.

Titus stiffened beside her, but said nothing as Erik gently turned her hand, studying each groove in detail before stroking his fingers over every link.

"The cuffs," Titus grunted. "Can you get them off?"

"I think they were made by J," Rae added, Titus's head whipping to face her.

"The precision and detail is beautiful, even down to his delicate signature hidden on the eighth link." Erik grinned, all teeth and fangs made even more eerie by his words in such a gentle voice. "But no one meets J, not even me. I can't help you."

Titus's hand curled around the back of her neck, the chain hard against her spine. "Are you telling me J made these?" He pressed himself closer. "You've got to be fucking kidding me."

"Surely you can do something?" Rae ignored Titus at her back. His presence just a reminder that she was on a deadline. "Come on Erik, can't you just break them?"

Titus didn't wait for a reply, dragging her back with the fucking chain.

"Hey!" Rae turned and shoved at his chest. "What was that? I was handling it."

He pointed to the bathrooms, giving her no choice as he pushed into the men's, her forced behind him. "Fuck off," he growled at the single man there, his body bent over the sink snorting a line. "Now!"

Rae pressed herself to the side as the man scrambled back through the door, the music quiet enough they could speak at a reasonable level. Wrinkling her nose, she waited until Titus had checked the two stalls before pinning him with a glare.

"This is the men's room."

"No shit, I need a piss." He lifted his arm, and she staggered against him.

Fisting his shirt, she tipped her head back to better look him in the eye. "I'm not holding your dick."

Titus's eyes gave nothing but indifference away, his face schooled into complete boredom. Yet he was angry, she felt it in the slight tension beneath her hands.

"I bet you get into trouble for that mouth."

"Daily." Her eyes dipped to the tattoos that just beneath his jaw, at the line and curves that reminded her of runes. "What are you?"

His head cocked to the side, brows lowering over his eyes.

"A Witch?" she continued when he just stared. "Faerie? Human with a druid fetish?"

"All of the above." He turned her, the sink digging into her back. "Now tell me everything said on my assignment, because clearly you don't even know what Breed I am."

"So you are Breed," she said, grinning as if she'd won. Not that she ever thought he could be human. He was just too much... everything. "And we've been through this, I've told you everything I know."

"I think you're lying."

Irritation prickled her. "Why would I lie?"

"Because you lied so easily to your vampire friend back there." He dipped his head, and Rae refused to move even a millimetre. "Keep holding out on me, and see where it gets you."

"Sounds like a threat, Mr Liu Wood. You need me, rememb –"

"I'm aware," he growled. "But that doesn't mean *you* don't need me, either."

Rae smirked, Titus's eyes dropping to her lips. "You think so highly of yourself." She knew she should fear him. He was dangerous. But so was she. "Tell me, Mr –"

"It's Titus," he said. "You're so formal for an assassin."

"Contractor," she bit out, smoothing over her irritation with a flirtatious smile. "Tell me, *Titus.*" She purred his name, her free hand slowly slipping down the side of her body to slip beneath her skirt. "Who did you piss off to warrant an assassination?"

His eyes narrowed, but she'd already reached her dagger, the blade kissing his throat before he'd caught her wrist so fast his movement blurred. Blood was a thin line along the sharp edge, his skin barely grazed.

Rae let out a sound of frustration, her right hand pinned with the bloody fucking chain, and her left in his iron grip, stronger than the cuffs even. With little effort he broke her hold on the dagger, studying the skull on the pommel.

His lips curved, the air between them electric. "Is this you flirting with me?"

"I want that back," she said, hating the way her pulse jumped at his velvety tone, even with the underlying threat. His eyes traced over her face lazily, moving slowly down the column of her throat. Her pulse kicked once more, his attention zeroing in on the delicate movement.

"I could kill you so easily." No arrogance in his words, just the cold, hard truth.

"Truce," she said when his eyes cut back to meet hers. "I call a truce."

He didn't hide his smile this time. "I don't even think you know what that means."

"Of course I do." Frustration made her voice sharp. "You've proven your point, you're faster, bigger and stronger." She purposely eyed where he still held her. "I won't try again."

"Such pretty lies you tell," he muttered, but released his grip. "Now, be quiet." He reached into his back pocket for his phone.

Annoyance sparked.

"Yes, sir," she mocked, only for a hint of desire to darken the red of his eyes.

TITUS

He wasn't sure whether it was the fact she'd tried to kill him. Again. Or the way she called him 'sir' with a throaty rumble. He knew she was being sarcastic, but his cock didn't seem to care. It had hardened instantly, the fucking traitor.

Fuck the Fates.

He didn't have time for this, his beast on alert from the second he'd first stepped into the place. The entire club was wrapped in black magic, subtle undertones that were an abrasion against his chi. He suspected it was in the drinks, or maybe the drugs that seemed to be everywhere he looked. He shouldn't have been able to feel it, and yet it sang to his blood.

"Well?" she asked, raising a brow in challenge. "Are you going to give me back my dagger?"

Titus released a growl before he could stop himself, attention dipping to those fucking lips, quirked up in a smirk. He wanted to push her limits, to punish her for being a disobedient little bitch who had the audacity to try and kill him.

He pinned her legs with his own, dipping his head until

her breath mingled with his. He knew the instant she felt his physical response, her eyes widening, and smile dropping from her smug expression. He wasn't sure what possessed him, but when arousal carved carnal lines across her face, nipples hardening beneath the thin t-shirt she wore he knew he wanted to push her further. Sex was always a great tension release, and he had a lot of fucking tension.

Yes, sir.

Fuck. If only she had been on her knees, begging him for –

"Are you broken?" she asked, her voice hoarse, despite the attitude. "I asked for my dagger back."

Brat.

"Why would I do that? You'll only try and kill me again."

"I'll try a lot faster if you don't give it back." A spark of impatience. "It's mine."

She really wanted the fucking dagger, the blade small in his hand. It even had a skull on the pommel, as well as two more on each side of the guard.

"Truce," she reminded him, holding out her unchained hand.

He flipped it, catching it on the flat. "Be a good girl and keep it in its sheath."

Titus didn't care for the anger that darkened her skin, finally stepping back to release some of the tension between them. His cock ached, its first reaction in months, begging for attention that wasn't going to happen. She was a fucking assassin, a thief, and as soon as he received the information he needed, she was going to be dead.

She was just another head fuck in his already fucked up existence.

"Two calls in a week, I'm honoured," Jax's sardonic

voice echoed in his ear, pulling him from Rae's teasing, defiant face.

"I need you to get to my place."

"When?"

No questions, a reason to love Jax's brashness.

"In the next hour," he replied, watching Rae strain to hear the conversation. "Also, since when did you make handcuffs?" Jax specialised in weaponry, not chains.

A snort at the end of the line. *"Told you to be careful with those females."*

"Just fucking be there." He hung up, not wanting to listen to Jax's brutal laughter.

CHAPTER 10

RAE

Being attracted to your target was a big red flag. Huge. Gargantuan, even. It was fucked up, because how could she imagine all the dirty things she wanted him to do to her when she was only days, if not hours away from separating his head from his shoulders?

She hadn't had sex in months. That was it, just her body's natural response to a suppressed orgasm. Because no way could her core clench at just one look, as if he was ready to devour her whole.

Except there was no way she'd give in to her need. She didn't mind teasing a little, but anything more was a step too far, even for her.

Titus had been silent on the drive to his place, the building sleek in its design as she waited beside him in the shiny lift. If he owned the lease, his name wasn't on it. She would know, she'd had Killian try and find a single digital crumb of the notorious Titus-fucking-Liu Wood. Except there was nothing.

"You going to tell me what exactly's happening?" She hadn't heard the entire conversation on the phone, but she understood enough. "Remember you promised not to kill me."

"I don't remember promising anything."

"You – " Pain across her sternum, Rae lifting her hand to rub the heel along the mark beneath her bra. *Fuck*. How long did she have before the forfeit came into play? Fifty-something hours?

Titus shifted his head, but she refused to meet his gaze as the ostentatious black chrome doors opened to reveal dark red carpets and panelled walls.

The chain jingled between them as she studied the keypad to his apartment. She knew the place was expensive from when he'd parked in the street level garage, everything accessible by key cards and pin codes. But she didn't just realise how expensive until Titus unlocked his door using his fucking handprint.

"This is..." The front door lead straight to the living room, with the kitchen to the direct right, and two doors to the left. The space was taken up by a dark oak table, large leather sofa, and a TV. There were no pictures, or personal effects that gave her an insight into his life. It looked like a show home, everything new, pristine and decorated in various shades of black. "Do you have something against colour?" she mused, itching to look around.

"Like you're this Rae of sunshine?" He clicked a few buttons on a keypad beside the door, the locks initiating with an audible click.

"Ha ha, so funny," she said dryly. "Like I haven't heard that one before."

Titus's lip curved. "Come on, he'll be here soon."

"He?"

Titus didn't reply as he pulled her towards the door to the left, opening to reveal a bedroom just as dark as the living room. "Jesus Christ, I think you have a problem."

His bed was made to perfection, the black satin sheets without a single crease. The armoire, wall length mirror, and chest of drawers were all in matching dark mahogany, not a single item on top of the polished surface. A computer desk with three monitors was set up on the right, bare other than the screens, a mouse and a keyboard. Even the cords were pinned perfectly straight, and mostly out of sight. Nothing seemed disturbed, everything having its place.

"What do you do for a living?" she asked as Titus moved his mouse, the middle screen flashing white before returning to black. "Computer stuff?"

"You could say that."

Rae pursed her lips, sweeping her gaze around his room once more. "So you're not even going to try to elaborate? I'm trying to help you figure out who hired the Guild to kill you."

Titus turned to sit against his desk, crossing his arms. The simple movement forced her a step closer or having to risk injury to her wrist, and she was so ready to get the cuff removed. "I specialise in cyber security."

"Okay." She wasn't one hundred percent confident what that was. "Maybe a rival ordered the hit?"

"I have no rivals," he said with a smooth arrogance.

"A dissatisfied customer, then?"

"Possibly, except any customers I take on know nothing about me. I don't exist."

Rae flicked her hair over her shoulder. "Hate to break it to you, but you do, in fact exist."

His right brow arched, unusual eyes darkening with impatience.

"I found you, didn't I?"

"I wouldn't hold your breath," he muttered. "You're a pretty shit assassin."

"Contractor." She pinned him with a glare, his voice so

fucking relaxed, as if entirely bored with the conversation. "Also, I shot you from the thirteenth floor, across the street in almost pitch black."

"Killing me is literally your entire job." Titus laughed, the deep rumble at odds with his expression. "And you failed."

"Fuck you, arsehole! You're the one with the hit on your head!" she snarled. "Maybe it's because of your chipper personality."

"I don't know what you're talking about," he said, the laughter devoid of humour. "I'm a loveable guy. Now are you going to behave? Or am I keeping your pretty dagger?"

Rae clenched her fist, swallowing her acerbic comment.

The centre monitor flashed white at his back. "Come on, my brother's here." Titus slipped off the desk, silent as he moved them both back through his apartment to the front door. They keypad glowed, only unlocking once he'd placed his palm against it.

Rae frowned, the pendant that set between her breasts heating up until it almost scalded her flesh. "Shit." She pulled it away from her skin, cursing low beneath her breath before looking up to face the man somehow even taller than Titus. His dark navy eyes were hard, yet curious when they met hers, his frown tugging at the thick scar that sliced down his left eye, a few shades darker than his warm skin tone.

"And you are?" he asked, staring at her.

"She's no one," Titus said, opening the door further.

Wow, Rae thought. *Story of my life.*

TITUS

Jax watched Rae with an intense concentration, and Rae moved slightly behind him, the first sign of intelligence in hours.

'You're hiding something.' Jax's voice was just as serious when it brushed across his mind. *'Who is she?'*

'She's mine,' he said almost instinctively, and Jax's eyes snapped to his, the mental connection as easy as breathing.

'Yours?' A glint in the blue depths.

'Until I get what I need, yes.' Titus clenched his jaw, grinding his teeth.

Jax's eyes narrowed. *'And what exactly do you need?'*

'Right now, I need her.'

Jax paused, looking like he wanted to say more. "I'll set up on the table," he said aloud, attention settling back on Rae. "This shouldn't take long." He didn't wait for an answer, pushing past them both to place a heavy bag onto the pristine oak.

"That's your brother?" Rae whispered against his back. "Different fathers?"

"And mothers."

Rae frowned, but she remained plastered to his side as he guided them to the table. He was surprised considering her earlier bravado, but then again she'd survived long enough in her industry to know when to shut up, and not poke someone bigger. Unless that someone was him, apparently.

Jax stood an inch or so taller than Ti, the tallest of the Guardians along with Lucifer. He was intimidating with his large frame, permanent scowl and scar.

"You sure you don't want to keep it?" Jax said in his low baritone, his humour subtle.

"Get this shit off me." Titus placed his wrist on the table, watching his brother brush his fingers across the metal before his fingers glowed, arcane licking at his skin.

"Stay still," he said, brow furrowing with concentration. Pulling a weird, pointed tool from his bag he pressed it against the cuff, gently scraping against the cold surface. *They're part of a set of three made for a certain high spending client. Was my biggest customer until I found out he was trafficking women for the Vipers.'* Jax's movements were rigid. *'Tried tracking him down a while back, but he went missing not long after Kace destroyed their den.'*

'I think your client's dead.'

A raised eyebrow. *'How would you know that?'* Jax's beast rumbled through his chest. At Titus's silence, he continued. *'That information got anything to do with your little redhead?'*

'Maybe.'

Jax paused what he was doing, looking like he wanted to push further. *'What did you find out?'*

Titus risked a glance at Rae, her gaze flickering between them both. *'She's connecting me to the person who hired the guild.'* Not technically a lie, but he couldn't risk him knowing who Rae was exactly. Jax would have killed her without hesitation, as would any of his brothers.

'Guild?' Jax pressed his lips into a thin line, his tools working quickly across the cuff. *'Cloaks and fucking daggers, then. At least with an independent you could torture them directly. You really think she knows anything worth keeping her around?'*

'Better to keep your enemies close and all that shit.'

'So she's an enemy?' Jax looked up for the barest second before returning to his work. *'Lucy said you missed training with him and Kyra.'*

Titus narrowed his eyes. *'You keeping tabs on me, J?'*

'Someone has to.' Even mentally Ti could hear the acerbic edge. *'You know why you shouldn't miss training.'*

Titus pushed Jax from his mind, closing the connection down tight.

"It's important," Jax continued aloud. "It's a..." He caught himself, flicking his gaze to Rae with a frown. "You need to speak to Lucy. Stop making excuses."

"I think I have a decent fucking excuse, don't you think?" he said between gritted teeth. "Besides, it's my shit to deal with. Not yours."

The cuff opened gently on Titus's wrist. "You've been helping all of us for so long, you're neglecting yourself."

"What exactly are you trying to say, J? Spit it the fuck out."

Jax's irises swirled, the edges teasing silver. "I'm just saying be careful." He blinked, pushing his beast back. "Because right now, you're lying to yourself if you think you're okay."

Titus paused, an argument at the end of his tongue. "Fucking hell."

He remembered little of the Rite, of the magic that was forced through his body, changing him, corrupting him. His brothers had witnessed some of it, knew what he'd been through, or the direct aftereffects.

Fuck.

He needed to fucking sleep. Just an hour. Maybe two if the stars fucking aligned.

"You guys are saying a lot, and yet nothing at all," Rae muttered, the chain hanging limp from her arm. "So I know you're like this weapons god or something, and in any other situation I'd fan girl and stuff. But can I get this thing off now? Pretty please?"

Jax patted the table, silent as he worked on her cuff. Her shoulders were tight, her wince small as he tugged on the metal. It opened just as gently as his had, but beneath, her skin was bruised, broken.

"Thanks, brother."

Jax's voice was detached when he moved towards the front door. "You're supposed to be on rotation tonight, but I'll cover you." His lips were tight. Jaw too. "You need us, you call. No exceptions."

"I'm fine, I'll –"

"Maybe you should speak to Eva. She understands –"

"She went through much fucking worse than me." Titus's head jerked, needing to look away from his brother's penetrating gaze. "I'm fine, I'm dealing."

Jax's movements were rigid as he returned his tools to the bag. "Then Lucy."

"I don't need a fucking babysitter," Titus said with a scowl.

Jax's reply was instant. "If you think we're babysitting you, you're a bigger idiot than I realised." He didn't add more, turning to leave with a slam of the door.

Titus pressed his palms against it, for just a second as exhaustion beat heavily against him. He would have stayed there, head limp until the scent of copper drifted, his beast forcing him to move. Reminding him he wasn't alone.

"You didn't tell him who I was."

He'd expected Rae to leave, to run. Instead she remained at the table, her delicate fingers studying the cuffs that had been locked around them for the past few hours. Her right wrist wasn't a pretty sight, the skin several shades of black and purple, with a few marks deep enough that they bled.

"If I'd told him you were the one that tried to kill me, you'd be dead." Titus leaned on the table, hands planted flat on the surface.

She didn't believe him, her expression smug.

"I didn't tell him, because you're mine to deal with." He made sure to move closer, to force her to lean back. Except she didn't, his nose almost touching hers. "And trust me, I'm going to fucking enjoy it." Without another word, he turned towards his room, knowing she'd follow soon enough. She wasn't one to not have the last word.

It wasn't long before he heard a chair squeak, and just as he's predicted, she'd moved to sit by his desk while he searched in the top drawer for the well-used first aid kit. The rest of the drawers were virtually empty, a few spare clothes and toiletries, but nothing else.

The apartment wasn't his home anymore, but he'd still kept it. A sanctuary from when he needed a break from his brothers, or for when he needed a release. Sex was always cathartic, a game that involved pushing boundaries, whether that was pleasure, or pain until his partners begged. And they always begged, turning the women that willingly climbed into his bed into nothing but creatures that craved his touch, their brains empty but for the pleasure he'd forced through their bodies. It was addictive, that control.

Except he found he wasn't interested in the softness of women anymore. Or anything at all, for that matter.

"What are you –" Rae's eyes landed on the first aid kit in his hands. "Oh."

Titus was silent as he pulled out the antiseptic cream, holding out his hand for hers.

"I can do it," she said, her scowl pinching her face. It highlighted the little sprinkle of freckles, the thought that his assassin was a cute little doll with freckles was enough to curve his lips.

"Sure you can."

His fingers were gentle as he brushed the cream across her skin, the grazes stinging as she winced. Her left arm done, he silently asked for her right arm, only for her to hiss, jerking her hand back to cradle against her chest after a little pressure.

"It may be sprained, you'll need to wrap it." Searching the contents, he found what was left of the bandages, the roll almost at its end. "You want me to do it now? Or after you've cleaned yourself up?"

Her scowl deepened. "Cleaned myself up?" The comment seemed to disgust her, or maybe it was because *he'd* suggested it.

"Do whatever the fuck you want, but I'm going to shower." His t-shirt was itchy, back aching as he rose to his full height. "Do I have to remind you what happened last time you tried to kill me?"

"Where do you think you're going?" The chair moved as she stood, fire in her expression. "We need to discuss what happens next, and you still need to give me back my dagger."

Titus tensed his muscles. "What happens next is we figure out who hired you. Which means you stay with me."

Rae ignored his clearly stay back vibe, closing the distance between them. "Wait a god damn minute –"

"You run and I'll hunt you down, and we both remember how fucking easy that was."

She barely hit the height of his shoulders, but she didn't seem to care as she glared up at him with tightly coiled rage.

"But you won't leave, because you won't risk it," he continued when she remained silent. "What is it Rae? Is it the fact you're waiting for the right moment to kill me? Or is it because you're too scared to go out on your own and get shot at again."

A little squeak of temper escaped her parted lips. "I'm not scared. I'm not the one who has a target on their –"

"Those bullets weren't aiming for me." He was sure of

it. The car had blown up too easily, as if something had been planted inside.

Doubt widened her eyes. "No... I still have over fifty –"

"It looks like we need each other," he interrupted, just to see her face glow with resentment. "So be good." Her little snarl was beautiful, but he didn't stay long enough to watch her explode, needing to rip the fabric from his back, and burn his skin beneath scorching water. To distract his beast from the infuriating woman that seemed to awaken something inside him that he'd thought he'd lost.

Fuck the Fates.

CHAPTER 11

RAE

"Be good?" she growled at the closed door, the shower starting seconds after he'd entered. "Be fucking good?" What was she, a dog? Rae lifted her middle finger, facing it against the door for long enough her arm ached.

Titus was wrong, there was another contractor hunting him, not her. There was no other explanation. She still had time to kill him, except, she was beginning to realise, that it might be more difficult than simply stabbing him when his back was turned. If he'd survived a shot to the heart, maybe he could survive other stuff?

"Fuck. Fuck. Fuck!" she whispered, rubbing the heel of her hands against her eyes. She had to kill him, she had no choice unless there was a way to get out of the assignment without initiating the forfeit. And while it pained her to admit it, but he was right, she did need him. Because no way was she going to just let him wander off into the sunset when it had taken her weeks to fucking find him in the first place. She was sticking to him like glue.

Jesus Christ. How the hell did she get into this position? She'd been good, counting down her kills one at a time, enjoying her restricted life as much as she could. And now she was essentially stuck in an expensive apartment with a man who seemed to have the emotional maturity of a potato. One who was currently stripped naked, completely wet and –

Rae squished that visual dead.

Stress. That was the reason for her impure thoughts. Stress-induced madness.

Deciding to explore rather than think about Titus naked behind such a thin door, she moved through to search the kitchen. "You've got to be kidding me." There were no knives, and only a few long-life crackers that tasted like cardboard and did nothing to quell the rumble of hunger. It was as if the kitchen had never been used, the marble so clean she could probably have eaten off it. A show home.

Leaving a few crumbs just to piss him off, because their weird truce was still standing, she continued to look through the apartment. The living room was just as clean, the wood immaculate and without a single scratch. The ridiculously large TV didn't have a speck of dust, but there was no remote in sight. The window was almost the size of the entire back wall, a small balcony too skinny to really accommodate Titus comfortably, but enough for Rae to step on and study the city she called home. It was late, the moon high in the sky and yet the city was awake, the mixture of old, and new architecture glistening against the dark. The street below was clean, cobbled, and far too pretentious for her tastes. Even the streetlights looked expensive, tall, black structures that looked more at home in a different century, but somehow worked against the townhouses opposite.

With a sigh, Rae stepped back into the bare in comparison living room. The door on the right looked to be another bedroom if she went by the large shadow on the carpet, but the entire room was empty, as was the adjoining bathroom.

The fixtures had been ripped out, a blackened mark crawling up the wall to the ceiling as if there had been a small fire.

Returning to the main bedroom, Rae brushed her fingers against the tall armoire, the wood an intricate design. The handle was thick in her hand, heavy as she opened the door. "Holy shit!"

Inside was an array of sex toys. Plugs, dildos, paddles, and some stuff she'd never seen before, and wasn't sure how to even use, sat displayed along the shelves. Wipes, bottles of lube, and other cleaning supplies rested at the bottom. Rae cringed at how loud the door slammed, glancing towards the bathroom where she could still hear the steady sound of the shower.

He'd been in there a while. Long enough that Rae was agitated at being stuck waiting, her legendary patience nowhere to be seen. The need to figure out a plan pushed her forward, lifting her hand to knock against the door.

"Titus?" she called, knocking again. "I know you can hear me, we don't have time for this." If she could hear the shower, he could hear her. Probably. "Fuck it," she mumbled quietly, hand grasping the handle to find it unlocked.

Steam billowed from the slit in the door, the bathroom much larger than she had expected. The open aired shower took up the majority of the back wall, the mirrors facing it obscured from the condensation, the top half covered with a towel. Titus's head was thrust back, eyes closed with his wet hair draped down his back. Water cascaded across his skin, the tattoos that covered every inch glistening. It took her a second, the lines and curves intricate around the Chinese dragon that seemed to wrap around his arm, before she glanced down to watch his hand move rhythmically beneath the stream.

"Can I help you?" he asked, not stopping the languid movements of his fist over his thick cock.

Oh. My. God.

Rae felt her mouth snap open, forcing her eyes up to his face. "I... you weren't answering me."

"I'm a little busy," he grunted, stroking himself faster, his thumb brushing across the head.

She ignored the slight burn against her cheeks. "When you're done playing with yourself, we need to talk."

She risked one more glance down, and she swore there was a glint of metal. *Jesus Christ.*

"Just..." Why was her voice so hoarse? "Hurry up or you'll go blind." Not particularly interested in seeing the end to his little show, she stumbled backwards to the door, the cool air welcoming against the sweat at her nape.

Well, she thought. *That was...*

Rae kept walking, deciding she didn't want to be anywhere near his bedroom while he finished himself off. Passing straight back to the kitchen she pulled herself up onto the side, reaching for the dry, cardboard crackers to distract herself from visions of Titus all naked and wet. It wasn't long before he appeared, stopping to hook his hands up on the doorframe, scowling at her feet on the counter.

She'd taken her shoes off at least. She wasn't a monster.

"What did you want?" he asked, brow furrowing at the crackers she was shoving into her mouth as if she hadn't eaten in years. He wore no shirt, his tattooed skin on full display with thin, grey jogging bottoms covering his legs. A skull, that was what shaded the majority of his chest and stomach, the details so well done it looked like runes had been carved into the bone. The dragon curled around his left arm, just as intricately detailed as the skull, with the rest of the visible skin covered in those strange swirls and lines. "Rae?"

"Did piercing your nipple hurt?" she asked around a mouthful, forcing herself to keep her eyes above his waistline. "Do you know what? Never mind." She dismissed the question with a flick of her hand. "We need to keep moving, it's not safe."

"We're surrounded by some of the best security money can buy. It's secure. " The doorframe creaked beneath the pressure of his hands. "We should rest, we'll leave in the morning."

"I'm sorry, but I don't trust your definition of safe." Rae jumped from the counter, bare feet slapping against the cool tiles. She slammed the rest of the crackers against his chest, forcing him to grab the packet or risk a mess on the floor. "Guess the shower's mine then?"

Rae didn't wait for him to reply, her stomach cramping from the bloody crackers that she'd eaten dry. She made sure to twist the lock to the bathroom, pulling at her clothes with a grimace. Her wrist ached, but other than the slight swelling, it was fine. Flexing her fingers, she carefully checked her movements, happy that it wasn't broken. The cuff had been tight, the metal cutting into her skin with every tug.

Rae scrubbed her left hand across the mirror, removing the condensation and towel to study the mark between her breasts. The bottom half of the stylised moon was darker than the top, a literal hourglass filling up with every passing second. She knew if it ever darkened to black entirely it would be over, and she'd have broken her Guild contract. It proved she still had time, the assignment active. She wasn't sure about the exact hours, but she had at least a few days to figure it out.

Her mother's pendant sat just above it, usually hidden from sight beneath clothes as per her mother's last request. She never understood why she had to hide it, the necklace beautiful with its design, holding a blue stone in the centre. One side was solid silver, the other a series of white stones that glistened even without light. But still she found herself keeping the chain long, the pendant usually nestled safely away beneath her t-shirt. She'd never taken it off, ever.

For you to wear until your last breath, my love. Never remove it from your skin, for it will guide your soul to the old gods when the time comes.

Her mother had babbled gibberish, if it wasn't alcohol that loosened her tongue, she would blame the voices inside her head. She was sick, Rae understood that now, but as a child she'd listened to her mother's wild stories with curiosity, even when her father screamed at her to stop. And when she didn't, he'd make her.

Her mother had needed help, medication, therapy or even hospitalisation. But no, that would have looked poorly for her father, the respected detective, and retired SAS sniper. So instead she'd suffered for years, those voices slowly eating away until there wasn't much left.

Rae shook the memories of her childhood away, not wanting to dwell on the past. They were both long dead, her mother no longer hearing those voices, and her father no longer using his fists.

Her shower was quick, just a wash with the masculine scented soap to get off the rest of the dirt. What happened to pretty scents like honey and lavender? Or vanilla and jasmine? Why did men want to smell of musk? What even was musk?

Rae eyed the clothes on the floor, her t-shirt slightly ripped and covered in filth from her earlier fall. Smoke was still faint in the fabric, as well as burning rubber.

Not wanting to put dirty clothes back on if she was

staying the night, she slipped out of the bathroom in just a towel, thankful Titus was nowhere to be seen. Brushing her fingers through the long strands of her hair, she found the drawer she knew had some clothes in, stealing one of the three t-shirts inside.

He definitely didn't stay there permanently, or if he did he clearly needed very little. Padding barefoot into the living room, his t-shirt long enough to hit her just shy of her knees she found him on the sofa.

"You can take the bed, I'll stay on the sofa," he said, keeping his back to her. Tattoos patterned every inch of skin there, vertical lines in symbols and patterns that she wanted to study closer. He'd pulled his hair back up on the top of his head, just a few strands loose to brush against his nape. "I'll order some –" Titus turned, eyes hardening. "Take it off."

Rae blinked at the hostility, his nostrils flaring. "I don't have anything else to sleep in."

"Take. It. Off," he growled, the cold steel of his voice melting the further his eyes dropped, devouring her bare legs.

Rae ignored the heat pooling between her legs. "Or what?" Her tone remained light, but then tension between them electrified, vibrating her blood.

Titus climbed to his feet, all hard muscle and delicious tattoos. "Test me and find out."

"Don't say I didn't warn you." She pulled from the hem, tugging his t-shirt off in one, quick movement, and simply dropped the fabric to the floor.

CHAPTER 12
TITUS

Titus was known to be quiet, even reserved, but never speechless. Until Rae took off his t-shirt, and revealed *nothing* beneath. Absolutely nothing, her fair skin bare to his gaze.

Fucking brat.

He hadn't said a word, instead locking his legs from stepping closer, to test whether her skin was as soft as it looked. Whether her nipples peaked because of the cool air, or because of him. The fabric had hit the floor, his beast a roar inside his head and she'd simply shrugged, turned on her heels with a *'good night,'* and left with what he was sure was an extra wiggle to her hips. And now he was suffering with the most painful erection, despite relieving himself only hours earlier.

"Fuck," he grunted, palming his cock through the fabric, only to immediately let go. The idea of touching himself to the image of a certain redhead pissed him off. He'd been so fucking close to just taking her, to tease and edge until she was a wet mess on her knees, begging him to allow her to come.

He could envision it, her pretty lips crying out, eyes glazed over in pleasure as he thrust his fingers in the perfect rhythm that would drive her mad. *'Yes, sir.'*

It was the first time he'd been aroused since... before. He'd had no interest in sex, not when the jagged memories from the Rite still haunted him. He hadn't had much interest in... anything. He might not have recalled what had happened except for bursts of colour and sound, but his body sure remembered. He'd shake, every inch of skin slick with sweat as he sunk to his knees, dread coating his tongue. There were no triggers that he could figure out, no reason for his response. He would be sitting there, and the next moment he'd find himself on the floor.

A weak, pathetic mess.

He'd hidden his reactions from his brothers, locking himself away as much as possible, only emerging when he was on rotation. He couldn't stomach their concern, their constant worry that he was going to break, to explode.

Titus counted his stomach crunches, gritting his teeth from the tightness against his cock. All he wanted to do was sleep, to reset the creeping anxiety that set him on edge, but even as his muscles ached with exhaustion, he couldn't. Not because of the nightmares, nor the dark magic that never slumbered. No, it was because his beast was so attuned to the human woman who slept next door. In his bed.

Oh fuck!

Titus reached for his phone, dialling his cousin.

"Hey, where are –?"

"When your beast chose Sam, how did you know?" Titus's stomach tightened at the pause.

Axel's concerned rumble crackled in his ears. *"What happened?"*

"Just... what was it like? Was it instant?" Titus gripped

his phone so hard the case creaked. "Can the beast change his mind?"

"Are you talking about your beast choosing? Or the actual mating bond?" Rustling, Axel's voice muffled as he held the microphone. *"We already know everyone's bond's very different. I know with Kace his beast pushed the mating, binding them both without permission. But you know Kace, his beast's always been volatile."*

"And you?"

"I guess my beast chose Sam, yeah. But I wouldn't say it was instant, the mating bond snapped into place a few months of me being clean." More static, followed by whispering. *"It's difficult to explain, but it felt right."*

"Fuck." Titus dragged a hand down his face. "Fuck. Fuck. Fuck."

"Are you saying –?"

"I've got to go. Just... don't worry, I'm fine." A lie, one he'd told so frequently recently he'd believe it himself soon enough. "I'm staying out tonight. I'll be home soon."

"Wait, Ti!"

Titus clicked off his phone, and then silenced it when Axel immediately called back. He had to deal with one thing at a time, his beast choosing a mate, choosing the fucking assassin that had tried to kill him was the least of his worries. He needed to figure out who the fuck had ordered the hit, deal with them before he could even consider... no. Rae wasn't his mate. He didn't even fucking want a mate.

His beast was wrong.

Mine.

Titus groaned at the growl echoing across his mind, a thought that wasn't his own. His control over his beast wasn't as strong, not since the black magic that had entwined like vines around his chi. He felt the weight, effluence as Kyra called it. It was thick, like a blackened sludge impossible to remove. It wrapped around him, suffocating every breath with more power than he'd ever asked for. Had ever wanted. He had no idea how Lucifer dealt with it, or Kyra, for that matter. How they slept so easily while it wriggled and curled, keeping him awake.

Titus brushed his fingers through his hair, scraping hard against his skull. No bumps or horns, the confirmation releasing some of the tension that held his muscles. Turning his head, he stared at the fabric still crumpled on the floor. He'd been an arsehole, but the sight of her in his clothes had made him violent. A reaction he sure as fuck hadn't expected.

A whimper, Rae letting out a delicate cry. Without thought he'd moved towards the bedroom on silent feet, to find her face creased, body twisting in the black satin of his sheets. The duvet had slipped off, revealing bare legs all the way up to the bright red thong and her dusty, ripped t-shirt. She twisted some more, flinging herself on her back, arms spread as her legs scissored, pushing the rest of the duvet to the floor.

Bright pink kittens decorated the bottom sheet, the same design he'd bought Axel as a prank for mating with a leopard. *Fuck's sake.* Rae already thought he was weird, and now she thought he slept on cute cartoons of kittens playing in fluffy clouds.

Another whimper, her fists clenching, gripping.

The strange warmth spread through his chest, but he ignored it. "Rae?" he whispered, fingers brushing down her arm, soothing. "Rae it's –"

A beep, Titus jerking his head towards the centre screen of his computer.

This time he yanked on her leg, the movement jolting her awake. "Get up, we've got company."

Her sleepy green eyes blinked up at him, his words taking a second to register. "Company?"

"Get dressed." Titus slipped out of his jogging bottoms and quickly pulled on his jeans while Rae scrambled for her own clothes. Why the fuck didn't he keep fighting leathers there?

"I thought you said this place was secure?" she hissed, pulling up her skirt.

Clicking a button on the keyboard Titus brought up the CCTV of the entire building, watching as one by one the screens went dark. "Recognise him?" A male dressed in black walked through the corridor, a sword strapped to his back. He seemed to be speaking into the collar of his jacket, which meant he likely wasn't alone.

Rae frowned, nose wrinkling. "No, should I?"

Titus clicked a few more buttons, the screens running thousands of random letters and numbers as everything corrupted. "Step back." As soon as Rae had moved, he punched through the computer tower, holding his fist inside as arcane melted what little was left.

"Was that really necessary?" Rae asked. "Who's that man?"

He didn't answer her, instead pushing her towards the kitchen. "Stay here," he demanded. "Don't move."

"Stay here," she mocked in a deep voice. "Don't move."

It took him seconds to grab the discarded t-shirt from the floor, pulling it over his head in one tug, and then yanking his boots on over bare feet. Rae had already laced up her own shoes, standing ready, her face no longer soft with sleep.

"Stand there." He pushed her so her back was to the cabinets, concealed from view of the front door. Titus placed himself on the opposite side. He pulled out his phone, clicking the security measure Kace had installed.

Rae had scraped her hair into a crude knot, pulling it from her face. "I grabbed you this." She held out his gun.

Titus eyed his front door, the wood trembling, straining against whatever was happening on the other side. "I thought I told you to stay there?"

"The correct phrase is, 'You're welcome.'" She didn't blink at his glare.

"Fuck... here." He reached into the bread bin, handing over her skeleton dagger.

Rae grinned, slipping it beneath her skirt. "You think they were tailing us?"

Titus pursed his lips, but grabbed the gun before returning to his position, hidden. "It's possible." Which made him a fucking fool. "When I say run, you run. Understand?"

A sharp nod, head turning towards the loud bang as the front door flew open.

"Three," Titus counted down.

Rae tensed, but stayed where she was.

"Two." A loud pop, directly above the kitchen's doorframe.

He reached for Rae's arm. "Run."

A thick billow of smoke erupted, encompassing the entire space in a blast of white powder and sparks. The force smashed the assassin across the room and onto the oak table, the legs giving out to crash against the floor. His once black suit was entirely covered in the white, itchy powder, his face too as he wiped across his eyes. With a snarl he threw himself at Rae, catching her around the waist and launching them both out into the hall. Titus shot after them, fist landing hard on the attacker's jaw.

Teeth clattering, his grip loosening on Rae as she twisted, the palm of her hand shooting up to break his nose.

Titus grinned at the crunch, at the blood that turned pink against the powder before a knee knocked against into his side. Something had cracked, probably a rib from the ache inside his chest.

"Fuck's sake." Titus lifted his gun, letting out two shots.

A neighbour opened their door. "What the hell is –" Only to slam it closed seconds later.

"Titus!" Rae screamed, but he'd already felt the air shift.

He leaned back seconds before the assassin's sword swung over, millimetres from where his throat would've been. The blade sliced into the wall as if it were butter, moving so fast it hummed through the air in a silver blur. The two bullets Titus had shot had hit him in the chest and head, and neither had slowed him down.

Great.

Titus ignored the growing urge to scratch across his torso, the powder working its way to irritate his skin. The assassin hissed, fangs descending past his lips while dark eyes swirled black, fury carving sharp lines across his face. He took a step forward, sword glinting through the smoke as he lifted for another swing.

A flash of red hair. "Here." Rae pushed something rectangular into his free hand, and Titus had just enough time to push her to the ground, the blade catching him across his upper arm before he threw the heavy implement. It hit the assassin's chest dead in the centre, sinking deep enough he staggered back, hand releasing his sword. Titus threw himself forward, taking them both down in a tackle. With his entire weight he knocked the object deeper, realising it was one of his table's wooden legs. The assassin stilled beneath him, and Titus didn't wait for him to wither in death to his true age before he launched to his feet.

"Come on," he grunted, running through the hallway, Rae tight on his heels. "Stairs."

Rae shoved through the emergency exit, racing down as footsteps and shouts rattled above. Shots echoed, whizzing past to leave holes along the wall millimetres above their heads.

Titus ignored his car when they emerged in the garage, pulling Rae along when she hesitated by its side. "What are you doing?" she asked, hand curled around another table leg as if it were a bat. The edge had been splintered, creating a sharp weapon perfect for both stabbing and striking.

"Leave it, we don't know if it's been compromised," he replied, stepping out into the street just as the garage door was kicked open. Rae turned at the sound, holding her new weapon out in warning.

"Gerald?" she shouted across the distance, not even flinching as the wall crumbled next to her from another bullet. "Fuck off, you prick!"

"Gerald?" Titus pushed her through, closing the heavy metal door behind them. "Gerald a Vamp?"

Rae faced him, anger darkening her eyes. "Vamp? No, mage I think. Maybe a witch. One with a tiny dick!" she shouted louder, as if the insult could carry through the solid metal.

"Good. Give me that." He reached for her makeshift spike, using it to wedge the door closed. A weight hit it a second later, the wood groaning, but holding. "That'll give us a few minutes."

Metal clanged, the wood cracking under the pressure. "Or not." Rae pulled at her t-shirt, exposing her rash covered stomach, and the scars that slashed along her ribs. "What's the plan?"

Titus already knew exactly where they were heading.

"This way." He led the way, knowing Rae had no choice but to follow.

The train station was still open despite the late time, but quiet as they climbed over the ticket barriers, much to the lone staff member's anger, his fist bashing against the glass of his booth. White tiles paved along the entire tunnel, beneath their feet, the walls and even the ceiling as they followed it deeper beneath the city. The wind whistled behind them, bouncing against the sharp turns to follow them down the escalator several stories. Music played softly, and it took Titus a second to pin it to a busker hidden in the corner, between the north and south platforms. A few women huddled around him wearing short dresses tight enough to be painted on, clapping along to the guitar while their equally dressed dates chatted a few feet away.

Rae didn't give the busker a second glance, looking up at the board before heading towards the southern tunnel. The wind turned into a roar, a train pulling onto the track just as they reached the empty platform. Both Titus and Rae jumped on, not caring where it was heading.

"You think he followed us?" Rae whispered, moving down the train, checking every window with such frustrated intensity, only relaxing when they left the platform behind and the outside blurred into a darkened smear.

"Possibility." The first three carriages were empty, and only a handful of people sat on the fourth, loudly giggling and sharing a bottle of cheap wine. "Gerald part of your guild?"

Rae tugged at her shirt again, rubbing her hand across her stomach. "No." Her brows pulled together. "The Knights, I think. From down south, they're not usually working in the city."

Titus glanced down at the red marks on her skin, her nails irritating the rash with each scratch. His own itching had finally subsided, thanks to his fast healing. He'd have to remember to tell Kace that his powder mixture was fucking terrible.

"I met him on a joint assignment once, right arsehole. The client didn't trust either guild, so hired both."

Titus paused at the end of the carriage, gesturing for Rae to take the aisle seat. He sat on the opposite side, his voice a whisper that couldn't be heard above the laughter from the drunken group a few seats down. If Gerald had made it on the train, he wouldn't risk an attack in a carriage with witnesses. "Thanks."

Rae's eyes narrowed in suspicion. "For what?"

"You seemed concerned for my life."

A snort. "If you get killed by someone else, I'll be in some deep shit."

Surprised laughter burst from him, the chuckle a rumble that echoed through his chest. "You do realise they weren't targeting me?"

Rae scratched at her skin once more, mouth pinched in irritation. "Of course they were."

Titus rested his arms on his knees, leaning forward. "The Vamp grabbed you."

"Yeah, to get me out of the way."

"Those bullets were aimed at –"

A frustrated sound, Rae yanking her shirt down, which only drew his attention to her nipples pebbling beneath the fabric.

Fuck's sake.

"You're impossible," she grunted, thankfully not noticing his attention dip.

"And you're a Rae of fucking sunshine. Now, where are we going?" At her frown, he continued. "We've just been attacked by not one, but two assassins –"

"Contractors."

"Contractors," Titus growled in correction. "Which means whatever timeframe you thought you had has already run out. So we're going right to the source."

"The source?" Rae asked, hand reaching down to grip her seat.

"That's right sweetheart, you're taking me straight to the fucking guild."

CHAPTER 13

RAE

"Yeah, no." Rae wasn't taking him back to the guild. No way in hell. It just wasn't happening.

She scratched harder against her stomach, the itching driving her mad. Her skin was becoming sore, but still she couldn't stop, the urge to scratch growing stronger, the area expanding until her side and part of her back crawled too.

"We don't really have a choice," Titus said in his voice like fucking silk.

"The guild isn't an option." *What the fuck is wrong with my skin?* "I can't take you there."

Titus reached over his shoulder, gripping his t-shirt in one hand, and pulling it off over his head and shoulders in one, slick move. "Here." He shook out his shirt, white powder jumping off to land on the floor.

Rae bared her teeth at him instead. It wasn't a dignified response, and nothing like the curse she wanted to shout. But the itchiness was starting to really override all her sane thoughts. If she'd been given the option to peel her skin off with a knife, she'd likely have accepted it right at that moment.

"Stop being stubborn and take the fucking t-shirt. It won't be so tight on your skin." Titus shoved the fabric across the aisle separating them. "That Vamp was covered in the powder, which transferred to you when he –"

"Grabbed me. Yeah, yeah." She eyed the t-shirt like it was a venomous snake. It wasn't lost on her that it was the same bloody t-shirt that he'd thrown a hissy fit at earlier. "Why aren't you itching?"

Titus shrugged, drawing her eyes across his damn shoulders. "I didn't hug a vampire assassin."

"Contractor," Rae growled, but from the twitch of his upper lip she was sure he said it to tease her.

No! Of course stick in the mud Titus wasn't teasing her. He didn't have the emotional spectrum. He knew bland indifference, and calm fury that he hid behind a façade of that bloody bland indifference. Nothing in-between, and especially not desire that she'd sworn had been on his face when she'd stood naked before him. The single look had hardened her nipples, thighs clenching in anticipation. Except she was going mad, because no way would Titus find the woman who'd tried to kill him attractive. The same woman who'd locked a metal cuff around his wrist, chaining him to her because she still needed to kill him.

It's just stress, she reminded herself. Stress and a sexy fucking man who was watching her like she'd lost it.

Fuck. How long had she been silent? Staring at his wide shoulders?

"You can't walk around shirtless," she said through clenched teeth, voice huskier than she would've liked. "You're going to draw attention."

"Rae..." A warning.

"Fine," she grumbled, unable to take the itching any longer. She grabbed at his t-shirt, hoping he read the irritation in her expression. "Close your eyes."

"Why?" His brow arched, eyes darkening with impatience. "It's not like I haven't seen it before." His gaze dipped, and heat curled low in her stomach, her nipples reacting to the attention like the traitors they were. "Not much to get excited over."

"I swear to fucking God," she muttered. "Just close your eyes, or I'll throw the itchy powder in your face."

A shadow of a smile, but he turned to face the front of the train. "I'll keep a look out."

Knowing she wasn't going to get anything better, she hid herself behind the chairs, carefully removing her powder covered t-shirt, and replacing it with his. The itching didn't stop, but it did ease a fraction, allowing her to think straight.

Shit. There was nowhere else to go, and the only place she was going to get answers was the one place she *couldn't* take him.

"So, when are we getting off?" he asked, his head remaining forward.

Rae couldn't believe she was sneaking Titus inside the Guild like some horny teenager still living at her parents'.

Who was she kidding! They were going to get caught. No way would she successfully sneak a guy Titus's size inside without the others finding out, not when Atlas had freaky vampire hearing, and the twins liked to nosey themselves into her business daily.

Not to mention he was gloriously naked from the waist up, much to the delighted passengers of the Northern, Bakerloo and Metropolitan line. At least Gerald hadn't shown his face again, which was a bonus, she supposed.

"Just... be quiet," she said, climbing the stairs slowly.

The lift wasn't an option, not when Vivian was the eyes and ears that controlled it. There was a small possibility the others wouldn't share the news of her guest with her, at least not straight away.

The door on the ninth floor moved silently, heavy before Titus pushed at her side, opening up the secret book-shelf to reveal the shared area. The kitchenette was empty, as was the two-seater leather sofa in the corner. Reaching back to grab Titus's hand, she quickly pulled him inside before the bookshelf automatically heaved closed, the edges sealing to hide the secret door entirely.

"You have to be –" Rae skidded to a halt, Nix and Atlas sitting at the table going over a map. Nix didn't react other than a single raised brow, but Atlas jerked back in his chair, his brown hair a cap of messy waves sweeping across his surprised face. He swiped at the strands, black eyes flicking between Rae and Titus.

"I can explain," she said, holding onto Titus tighter, as if that would make him disappear.

"No need to explain," Atlas said with a chuckle, fangs peeking from between his lips. "He must have been good to break your streak. Means you owe me two Imps."

"Interesting decision," Nix added with a cock of his head. "Fucking your target."

"We're not –" Rae began.

"Your target?" Atlas shot to his feet, his fangs descending in anger. "What the fuck were you thinking Rae?"

Titus pressed against her back in silent reassurance.

"I wasn't. I'm not!" she shouted back, immediately regretting it. "Look, I don't owe you shit, Atlas. I just need to hide him until –"

"Until what?" Vivian's cool voice slithered down Rae's spine, coming from the speaker perched high in the corner.

Fuck.

"My office, now."

Rae knew not to argue, not against the woman who held her fate in her hands. Literally. She didn't bother explaining more, pulling Titus towards her room, and then pushing him inside.

"Stay here," she said, ignoring his slight smirk at her demand. "And lock the door." She didn't wait to see whether he'd followed her instructions, knowing the longer she made Vivian wait, the worse it would likely be. "Don't let him out," she barked to Atlas and Nix, who'd resumed staring at the map between them.

"You sure you know what you're doing?" Atlas asked.

Rae shook her head, following the slim hallway that was the entrance to Vivian's quarters. She'd been there only a handful of times, and only by invite. The generic blue wallpaper of the main area changed to pretty florals, the wooden floor pale with light coloured rugs to break up the clean space. Art decorated the walls, mainly flowers, but some green landscapes that definitely weren't taken in London.

"Through here," Vivian called, the door to her office open just past the lush velvet sofa in pastel pink. It would have looked ridiculous, but somehow worked with all the other soft tones and patterns. Feminine in design, but with bold bursts of solid black in bookshelves, statues, and frames. Her quarters were essentially a self-contained flat, with her own kitchen, bathroom, bedroom, living room and office. There was a reason she didn't leave much.

The office was just as pretty, the desk pure white with chrome edges. Fresh flowers sat against the fake window, giving off an artificial light that Rae wouldn't have been able to tell the difference about if the scenery wasn't trees and a grove blowing in the wind, rather than the real visual of brick, steel and glass.

"What were you thinking?" Vivian asked in a strained tone. "Bringing your target here?"

"Someone else tried to kill him," Rae said, her hands clenched at her sides. "I wasn't told the assignment was open to multiples, it complicates things."

"I know of no other contractors."

"You must know something. We were –"

"There are no other contractors, Rae. At least not from the Syndicate." A slight pause, Vivian turning away from the eye contact.

All assignments went through the Syndicate, and then whichever guild bid the most won the job. If multiple bids were accepted, every Guildmaster would have been informed. But independents weren't tracked.

"What was your plan? To protect him?"

"No." Rae ignored the clench in her gut, at Vivian's response. She was more volatile than normal, almost unprepared. "Until I can figure out what's going on, it's best to keep him close, rather than let another guild complete the assignment."

"The Syndicate isn't going to believe this." Vivian reached for a tissue, gently patting the dark circles beneath her eyes. She wore silk pyjamas, her hair up in rollers. Rae had never seen her so bare of her usual armour, tense. "You were supposed to kill him. Not bloody befriend him."

"Trust me, we're not friends," Rae muttered. "And I did kill him, sort of."

Cold calculation in the brown of her eyes when they finally turned back, her resolve fully back in place. "How you deal with your target isn't my problem. You've already cost me a lot of money Rae, giving you a contract and paying off your brother's debt. Sometimes I wonder if that was the right decision."

"I've completed everything you've asked, and according to this hit, I still have time."

"Less than forty-four hours to kill him. Or the forfeit initiates, and your life is out of my hands."

Rae's nails pressed into her palms. "I need to figure out who created the hit, I'm not going to risk losing out on the completion if there's others working against me."

"You know that's not how it works. We don't receive anything but the information to carry out the assignment."

"Surely you have –"

"That's enough!" Her voice was a verbal slap, leaving no room for argument, or excuses. "You know what needs to be done. Do not disappoint me." Vivian dismissed her with a wave of her hand, ending the conversation.

She owed Vivian her life, but right then Rae fought anger and frustration. Without Vivian intervening Rae would have been dead, or worse. She'd offered Rae a lifeline by signing her to the guild, becoming a contractor in exchange for paying the loan sharks. Ten million Ravyns her brother had owed to some bad people, and they'd gone after Rae as collateral. Each hit slowly reimbursed what Vivian had paid, and until then she didn't have a choice.

She was thankful that Vivian had helped, but she knew that woman didn't do anything from the kindness of her heart. She may have paid ten million, but she did it knowing it was an investment. She'd received a contractor that couldn't refuse assignments, and after accounting all the conditions in the contract, Vivian would make easily ten times what she'd originally paid.

"What the fuck did I hear about a man in your room, Cupcake?" a voice sneered as Rae walked down the hall, lost in her own thoughts.

She scowled at Nathan. "I'm not in the mood right –" A long, slim arm reached out to grab her, hauling her hard against the wall. The impact knocked the air from her lungs, the enchantments pulsating in the background.

"You were supposed to break your streak for me!" Nathan hissed, adding pressure on her arm against her chest before he stepped back. "I'm the one who deserves it."

"Why's everyone so interested in my sex life?" Rae kept herself pressed to the wall, Nathan giving her little room to manoeuvre.

His tongue flicked out to lick across her cheek. Rae couldn't control her recoil. "Fuck off Nathan, I'm not in the mood for your games."

"Why him? Why not me?"

"You?"

"Yes me," he growled. "I think I've been fucking patient considering –"

"Considering? Considering what?" she interrupted. "You know it's the twenty-first century right? I'm not interested in you, or anyone else for that matter. Now back off."

His pupils shifted into slits. "You owe me for helping you."

Rae's mouth snapped open. "Fuck you, Nathan. I'm not sleeping with you because you helped me." She swore it felt like fumes were coming out of her ears.

"Well, I wasn't planning on much sleeping." He brushed his fingers against her jaw, featherlight before moving down her throat, and then lower. "You're mine, I was promised –"

Rae didn't let him finish, lifting her knee and hitting him straight between the legs. He collapsed against her with a puff of air, but recovered far faster than she'd expected.

"Do not touch –"

A sharp pain across her face.

"Don't worry," he whispered against her stinging cheek, blood on her tongue. "I'll make you pay for that."

CHAPTER 14

TITUS

Titus stared at the closed door for a few seconds, amused at being shoved into the room by a flustered Rae. He'd only known her for a few hours, and not once in that time had she looked rattled. Not when he'd almost killed her, first with his fingers, and then with the chain tightening around her delicate throat. Or even when they were running, bullets echoing around them in a chaotic storm. She'd dealt with the shit thrown at her with a tenacious smile and unyielding attitude.

Which meant he'd found something she was afraid of.

Interesting.

Her room wasn't much to look at, a double bed, side table and a thin, screen door that barely gave the en suite any privacy. The bed was unmade, the sheets a pale blue colour with small daisies dotted, which, for some reason surprised him. Notes and pieces of paper littered the floor, and clothes were thrown without care onto the dresser at the foot of the bed. But what caught his interest were the guns and blades she'd carefully placed in the corner. Each with their own holster or sheath, except the sniper which was dismantled and set in soft foam.

Titus brushed his thumb over a few of the guns, recognising the 'J' mark of his brother's work. They were expensive, the clientele usually handpicked by Jax himself. Which meant Rae likely bought them from someone else, or they were stolen.

Stepping back from the wall of weapons, he reached for the scattered papers, shuffling them into a pile before flicking through each document. His assignment was on the fifth page, and just as Rae had told him, it was basic. The pictures were taken from a distance, the first one not long after his recovery. The others were of him running, the images grainier, as if taken from a phone rather than a professional camera. She'd tracked him for at least a week, according to the amount of outfit changes he'd gone through, but each one was taken on the same route. The one thing that calmed him, had almost killed him.

Of – fucking – course.

A knock on the door, Titus flicking the pathetic excuse for a lock. He tensed in the doorway, Rae pushing past to slam the door closed behind her with a quiet curse. He stopped her before she could step away, gently tugging her back to wipe a thumb across her lip. She sucked in a pained breath, the skin split, blood dripping down her chin.

Rage, so hot and vivid it blurred her delicate features for a single heartbeat. "Who the fuck touched you?"

Rae scowled, trying to pull back, but he just curved his other hand around the back of her neck, keeping her there.

"Don't make me repeat the question." His thumb continued to stroke, as if soothing the sore skin better.

"It doesn't matter, he won't do it again," she said, eyes bright with her own anger. "Now, are you going to let go? Or do I have to knee you in the balls too?"

Titus's lips curved, amusement cutting through the

intense rage until it was more of a simmer than an explosion. *Fuck.* What was wrong with him?

"So meeting with your Guildmaster went well then?" he asked, trying to ignore the dread settling on his chest. Rae meant nothing to him other than a means to an end. So why was he ready to slit the throat of whoever'd hurt her?

"She said she doesn't know anything."

"And you trust her?"

"Of course not." Rae's face screwed up, and what looked like panic flashed across her features. "Everything will be written down in her office, which we don't have access to." Her tongue shot out to lick across her bottom lip, her wince small when it touched the cut.

"We'll break in then," he said matter of factly.

"It's not that simple." Rae frowned at his chest. "She barely leaves her quarters. No way can we sneak in without getting caught. She controls the cameras on the entire floor, and..." Her voice drifted off.

He'd noticed the cameras, high-tech and hidden discreetly in the corners. They would have cost the Guildmaster a pretty penny.

"And what?" Titus asked.

"If we're caught, she could sell my contract on." She rubbed against her face, her entire body wavering as if tired. "Shit. Shit. Shit. The next person may be even worse, and I may never..." She glanced up mid-sentence, eyes narrowing under his scrutiny.

"How long do you have?" At her confusion, he continued. "How long until you have no choice but to kill me?"

Rae pursed her lips, and he knew she was debating whether to tell him the truth. "Less than forty-eight hours."

"And then what?"

A hint of irritation hardened Rae's reply. "And then I'm dead, okay?" She began to pick up her discarded clothes, tossing them into the corner rather than the dresser. "My guild contract would be void, and I'll be put on the system for any contractor to hunt me down for an easy pay cheque. Then, because I still haven't paid off the debt, Vivian will probably go after my brother. Or if not her, someone else –"

"So you're telling me," he interrupted. "That if you don't kill me in the timeframe given, you'll be killed?"

Rae pulled off her t-shirt, turning towards the small mirror on the wall. Titus dropped his gaze to the swell of her breasts peeking out from her bra, unable to stop to rush of heat down his abdomen.

Fuck's sake.

"My mark's not yet filled," she said, pointing to the stylised moon painted on her sternum, the bottom half darker than the top. "So your assignment's still active." She turned to face him, hand gripping the fabric. "But I don't have long. I need to get into that office, see if there's any paperwork I can –"

"*We*," he emphasised, noting her earlier panic had settled. She was still rattled, but somehow more resigned, as if she'd already processed and accepted the knowledge, and now was working on ways to fix it. "We both need to get into that office. But first, how did they track us?"

Rae frowned, brows pinching together.

"My name isn't connected to that apartment."

"Well, we must have been followed."

"I can assure you we weren't." He'd been hyperaware of the possibility of another assassin, made sure they weren't trailed. "Which means they're tracking us. Give me your phone."

"What?" She took a step back. "No."

"Rae." He made her name sound like a curse. "If they're tracking your phone, then they know where we fucking are."

"How do we know they're not tracking your phone?"

"Rae!" A warning.

He saw the defiance in her gaze, the need to defy. "Do you know what? Fuck you. Here." Reaching into a pocket hidden in her skirt, she threw her phone over the short space. "And here's your fucking shirt too." She tossed the t-shirt onto the bed, storming into the bathroom and closing the flimsy door.

Titus closed his eyes, praying for patience before he scanned her phone, knowing without his computer he could never be confident that her software wasn't compromised. Pulling out her sim card, he crushed the entire phone beneath his boot. If it was her phone that was being tracked, those that were hunting her already knew where they were hiding. Which meant they needed to move.

Reaching over for his crumpled t-shirt, he pulled it over his head. Peaches and cream filled his lungs, and he ignored the desire at just the simple scent, his cock responding uncomfortably beneath his jeans.

Surely none of his mated brothers ever had such vicious need dominate their thoughts? He eyed the bed, barely big enough to fit him, never mind the both of them. But that didn't matter, because no way in hell was he going anywhere near it. Not when he'd never felt so out of control, his mind and body at war with one another.

Pressure consumed him, deep within his chest, tension wrapping around his lungs, locking them in cement until every breath was a chore. He was dangerous, his power unpredictable, and right then he felt it surge through his veins, looking for an outlet.

"Titus?"

He heard his name in the distance, muffled as if wading through water.

"Titus?" Fingers on his face, running along his jaw to

scratch against the stubble. He knew it would be dark there, a shadow of a much darker blonde compared to his head. Something that was always pointed out growing up, blonde being an unusual colour for a child of his maternal heritage. His father's genes were clearly more dominant than just his Breed.

Those fingers clenched, forcing his face up until Rae appeared, concern marring her face, washed free of makeup. It brought out the delicate freckles spotted across the bridge of her nose, and also the bruise blossoming on her cheek.

Titus clenched his shaking fist, surging to his feet from where he'd been on his knees. He had no memory of getting there, but he never did, his thoughts a spiral of distorted conversations and reminiscences.

Rae stepped back, dressed in a fresh vest and not much else. "They can't touch us here, at least for tonight," she reassured him. "Tomorrow we'll deal with it. Or later today, technically."

Titus barely managed a nod, his skin damp, hands clammy. The shaking had subsided, leaving nothing but a bitter taste on his tongue. "Take the bed," he said, voice hoarse. "Get some rest."

Rae pursed her lips, glancing down at the messy carpet, and then to her guns perched neatly in the corner. "I won't be able to sleep with you here."

"You did just fine back at mine."

A frown. "That was different."

"How so?" he challenged, using her biting frustration as a much-needed distraction. The power had settled, content inside him for now. He was going to need to purge it soon, before it started eating away at his chi. Then he would puke, his body rejecting the remaining effluence.

Something to look forward to.

"It just is," she shot back. "It's weird."

"You're a difficult woman," Titus said, pressing himself against the wall. If anger were a physical manifestation, he was sure he would have been burning from the scowl she'd shot in his direction. "Why don't you just stay on your side of the room, and I'll stay here."

"Fine." A bad-tempered grumble.

He studied his phone, not looking up until he was sure she'd settled herself in bed, curling on her side facing away. He couldn't help but turn briefly, watching how her shoulders tightened.

"Stop being a creep," she muttered quietly. "Or I'll lock you in the backroom."

"Get some sleep," he shot back, shaking his head. "You'll be useless tired."

Rae shot him the middle finger.

He quickly returned his attention to his phone, logging into his account and deleting everything that held a hint of his true identify. He'd bought his apartment along with Axel in cash, neither of their names on the paperwork, and instead signed by a fake company used as a front for Storm Industries. Smoke and mirrors, the sole purpose of which was to guard their identity. Because to do what they did, to protect the weak, and destroy those that would otherwise cause others harm, they couldn't exist.

They weren't like the Lords who ran the Undercity, corrupt bastards who would sell their first born if it got them ahead. But if the Guardians wanted something, they took it, whether it was through blackmail, or force, they didn't care. Morals weren't black and white, there were no strict rules that were right, or wrong. It was all shades of grey, and that was where the Guardians thrived, in the quiet shadows, acting on behalf of those too weak to defend themselves.

He wouldn't be surprised if the majority of citizens that

called London their home lived under the illusion that the city was run by those that cared, that the politicians that smiled and waved to the crowds had their best interests at heart. It was all bullshit, those in high positions ruled either by manipulation, or were bought by those more powerful. The governing bodies were nothing but puppets to the real people who controlled the city. Even the Council of Six didn't care, letting the Lords bring their drugs, abuse and money to the streets they were supposed to protect. Because that money lined the politicians pockets. Likely lined the Council's too.

Titus easily slipped into the guild's camera feed, the security sloppy and only taking him seconds to break in. Flicking through the images, he counted eighteen cameras in total, all hidden cleverly in crevices across the area. The majority most likely undiscovered by those that lived there.

The entire building was connected to the same encrypted server, including the commands for the single lift, as well as electrical locks throughout. Titus frowned, climbing to his feet. The lock on Rae's door was shit, nothing a hard kick couldn't break. But according to his phone, every door in the Guild was remotely controlled. Frustration bit through his interest, the lack of his computer hindering his ability to override the security system. He'll still be able to do it wirelessly through his phone, but it would likely take hours.

He wasn't sure he had that much time, every moment ticking down until his hand was forced, and he'd have to kill her before she killed him. He lifted his head at the thought, taking in Rae who'd rolled onto her back, red hair fanned out like a halo around her. It hadn't taken her long for her breathing to have slowed, steady in sleep.

Seemed she could fall asleep with him there, after all. She was either too trusting, too stupid, or more exhausted by the day's activities than she let on. Titus seemed to forget she was human, someone far weaker than even one of the smallest prey shifters. Humans dominated the realm, at over sixty-five percent of the population, but their bodies were much more fragile. They lived to barely one-hundred, and had more fatal diseases than he cared to name. Yet she'd surprised him with how easily she'd handled the situation, not only with her reaction, but with how she'd sidestepped out of the vampire's reach. A human, even one trained in combat, shouldn't have as easily twisted out of the grasp.

Fatigue beat against him, the headache building behind his eyes with every passing moment. He knew he should rest himself against the wall, close his eyes long enough for his software to work, and hope the nightmares didn't howl too loud. An hour, maybe two if the Fates let him. Just anything to help ease the continuous exhaustion. Except he couldn't, his body too tight, thoughts too consuming.

A whimper, so quiet he wasn't sure whether it was in his head or not. Rae's face creased in sleep, a single tear glistening against her cheek.

What possible nightmares haunted her? he thought, reaching down to gently swipe his thumb along her skin. She pressed into his touch, seemingly calmed by his presence.

What the fuck's wrong with me?

Titus dragged his fingers through his hair, the strands loose around his shoulders. He was there for a single purpose. Find out who'd put a hit out on him, and then kill them.

Nothing else.

Her lips parted, letting out another whimper.

Titus slipped onto the bed, lying on top of the duvet to stoke his fingers back over Rae's cheeks. She sighed in contentment, snuggling closer until she curved her entire body along his side.

Fuck.

He was there for a single purpose, but right then he didn't seem to care.

CHAPTER 15

RAE

Her side was pressed to something solid, hard and deliciously warm. Rae tensed for the barest second before she forced herself to relax, to keep her breathing steady and even. Opening her eyes to slits she found herself wrapped against the last man she expected to be in her bed, her leg hooked over Titus's hip, her hand speared beneath his t-shirt to rest against the centre of his chest. He lay flat on his back, teetering on the edge of the bed as if trying, and failing to escape. Yet his arm lay beneath her head, his hand precariously close to resting on her bare butt.

Humiliation burned hot beneath her skin, disappearing as quickly as it came. He climbed into *her* bed. Uninvited. She would not be embarrassed about her body subconsciously seeking out heat. *Arsehole.*

The need to shove him was an almost violent compulsion, except when she studied the sharp features of his face, she hesitated. His hair brushed his darker brows, free from the band that usually kept it away from his face. She pictured him clean shaven, but the stubble suited him, the hair even darker than his brows, defining the sharp line of his jaw and throat. That was where his tattoos started, skin decorated in such detailed lines she ached to stroke, to study every inch of art. Then there were the rings, one in his nostril and another through the centre of his bottom lip. She'd never cared for piercings, but on him they were perfect. She knew beneath his t-shirt he had one more, and she'd done everything not to stare at his nipple when he stood before her chest bare. To ignore the spike of desire at the idea he likely had more piercings she was yet to find, because of course he would just have to be the most striking man she'd ever met.

Rae frowned, not impressed with the line of thought. He always looked so bloody composed, in control, but now she could see that was a façade. The underlying tension that was always there was gone, smoothed out in sleep.

Moving slowly, she slipped her hand out from beneath his t-shirt, ignoring the sudden loss of heat as she moved it under the pillow. Her fingers wrapped around the cool metal of her skull dagger hidden there. If she killed him, her assignment would be over. Then she could go back to ticking off her kills one at a time until she was free, pretending the entire situation hadn't happened.

The blade nicked his neck, slicing a line of red before a tight grip encircled her wrist, yanking it away. Rae grunted as she was forced on her back, Titus pinning her from above.

"An assassin," he grunted, pressing her own blade against her skin, still caught in her own hand. "A thief, and now a liar."

Rae tried to wiggle beneath him, both her wrists caught in a single one of his. He raised them above her head, knocking the knife free from her grasp. Calm rage radiated from him in waves, blistering against her skin. He'd restrained her so effortlessly, his movements a blur.

"Rae of fucking sunshine."

She licked along her bottom lip, pulse rapid in her throat, a heavy drum that echoed between her treacherous thighs. Titus traced along her lips, eyes alight with darkened flames. The colour shifted as if alive, the edges teasing what looked to be silver, only highlighting the hauntingly beautiful, yet terrifying shade of red.

Tension vibrated between them, violence making everything heightened, his anger a caress she wanted to drown in. She thrust her hips up, seeking friction, anything to quell the sudden need that surged through her blood like a herd of wild horses.

With a growl he knocked her legs wider, settling himself between her thighs and right against the place that begged to be touched. Rae moaned, actually moaned when she felt his hard length press against her pussy, hidden beneath a layer of denim.

Jesus Christ.

"That's the second time you've tried to kill me," he said, rolling his hips against hers with a hiss.

"Third," she forced out between clenched teeth, confused as fuck at her reaction. It was as if her body had a mind of its own, and was no longer listening to reason.

"You're right," he said, reaching down to pinch a nipple through the fabric of her vest.

Rae all but whimpered, her thighs unable to clench, to ease the ache that was steadily building between her legs.

Titus dropped his head, his breath hot against her ear. "Do you want my cock, Rae?" he whispered, his voice so smooth, so deliciously deep that she was sure to commit it to memory.

Rae shallowed, throat dry as she nodded.

"Words." His lips ghosted along the column of her throat, brushing against her pulse. "Use your words."

"I fucking hate you," she hissed, her body betraying her.

"It's mutual," he growled. "Now answer the fucking question."

She let out a sound of irritation. "Fine. Yes!"

Titus pulled back, his eyes no longer the deep burgundy, but a silver that swirled like liquid metal. She should have been scared, because it wasn't Titus who looked back at her, not entirely. And yet the added unknown caused trembles along her needy clit.

"Yes, what?"

Rae snarled, fighting, twisting until he pinched her other nipple, the pain sharp before pleasure radiated from the small hurt.

"Yes, what?" he repeated, rocking his hips forward.

"Yes, I want your cock," Rae cried, her thighs wet, the cheap fabric covering her embarrassingly soaked.

"Does trying to kill me turn you on?"

She was totally fucked up. "Yes."

His grip tightened on her wrists, still pinned above her head. She tensed against the restriction, at the vulnerability of being helpless. And yet rather than fight, she moaned, her body alight in sensation. His lips caught the sound, dominating her mouth in powerful thrusts of his tongue. Devouring her from the inside out. She'd never been so turned on, her hips wiggling when he pressed his thigh harder against her clit, rubbing herself against him until she felt the familiar tightening in her stomach.

Titus pulled back, the orgasm she'd been working towards fading.

"Fuck!" she cried, trying to break her wrists free. To rub herself until she exploded.

He smirked above her. "Beg me."

Rae took a second to understand his words, so worked up she couldn't think straight. Her mouth dropped open, a flush creeping up her neck as anger burned. "Fuck you!"

A rough laugh, his grip finally releasing on her wrists. A second of victory, of her hand slipping down her front to dip beneath her underwear and through her wet folds, only for him to flip her, front pressed to the mattress.

Before she could muffle a sound, he'd pulled her to her knees, yanking her fingers to his mouth and sucking her arousal clean. "Don't move," he demanded, placing her hands along the headboard once he was done.

Rae was panting, core clenched and clit throbbing painfully.

"Beg me," he said, his voice pure silk, a stark contrast to the way in which he rolled her nipples, the sensitive nubs begging for attention. "And I'll let you come."

'Please,' was at the end of her tongue, but she just couldn't say it. Couldn't give in. "No."

Her vest was torn from her body, leaving her in nothing but her underwear. A single hand wrapped in her hair, and Rae let out a cry when he pulled, bowing her back, his thighs moving either side of hers. She felt him at the base of her spine, so damn fucking hard she knew it had to hurt. That made her grin, knowing he was as desperate as her. Maybe she could make him *beg*.

His lips touched the shell of her ear, scalp stinging from the painful angle. "This is what you wanted, wasn't it?" His free hand stroked leisurely down the valley of her breasts, caressing across her stomach before his fingers teased the edge of her thong. "For me to be behind you, hair tight in my fist with your delicious cunt begging for my touch."

His fingers dipped beneath the fabric for a second, a single stroke against her engorged clit before pulling back.

She pressed back against him, his entire body

consuming hers. Her legs quaked, muscles coiling tightly. "Fucking... just..." Rae let out a strangled scream, desperate.

Teeth dug into the hollow between her throat and shoulder, followed by such a soft kiss she thought she'd imagined it, if it wasn't for the cold metal of his lip ring. "You really shouldn't be such a brat, if you don't like the consequences." His fingers teased her once more, slowly rubbing circles around her sensitive bundle of nerves.

She was going mad, the release so close, but just out of reach. "Please!" she finally begged. "Please make me come!"

His fingers stopped, and before she could scream, he sunk a single finger inside, thumb pressing against her clit. "Good girl."

She came, a powerful convulsion as he thrust hard and deep, thumb never letting off her clit. He didn't stop when she cried out from sensitivity, continuing his assault on her senses until another orgasm grew, threatening to send her to the stars.

"Please!" she begged once more, not even sure what she was even begging for. For him to stop? To press harder?

Titus added a second finger, stretching her long unused muscles, curling until he hit the spot inside her that had her trembling.

"Please Ti –"

"Sir," he growled.

TITUS

He'd never had the women he fucked call him 'sir,' but with Rae he needed it, the complete submission a gift as she clamped around his fingers, drenching the bed beneath them. He wanted to consume her, bathe in her surrender until she thought of nothing but the pleasure he forced from her body.

The fucking brat had tried to kill him, again. And rather than be angry, it had made his cock so fucking hard he thought it would break. His kiss had been nothing but a test, to see whether his beast was wrong, and she was just a passing obsession. He'd never allow his beast to be in charge, but the pressure to take her, to taste her had been something he wasn't sure he wanted to fight.

She yelped when she released his grip on her hair, her body boneless as she draped forward, perspiration glistening along her spine. She looked fucking beautiful quivering between his thighs, still encased in the fucking denim, her arse a sight he couldn't wait to see red from his palm.

He continued to stroke her needy flesh, her pussy so wet she spasmed when he flicked his thumb across her clit. "Again," he demanded, knowing he could pull one more orgasm from her. It was a torture, he knew, having so many in such a short amount of time. A punishment.

"No, no I can't."

He brought his spare hand down hard on her round flesh, the resounding smack beautiful, as was the sudden heat as he gently soothed his hand over the blossoming mark. He expected her to fight, to turn and pin him with one of her glares, but instead she clamped down on his fingers, her moan echoing around them.

It seemed his Rae of sunshine liked a little pain.

"Good girl," he said when she pushed back against his palm, her head dropping to between her outstretched arms, still holding onto the lip of the headboard.

"Please," she whispered, barely audible above her panting.

Titus smirked. "You know what to say. Please..."

"Fuck you." The words were dragged from her throat, a

feral growl that would have held more bite if it didn't end in a breathy groan. Titus brought his hand down on her other cheek, satisfied with the matching marks.

"Tell me to stop," he said, fisting his hand to stop from unfastening his jeans, and stretching her far wider than his fingers. "Tell me to stop, and I'll stop."

Rae sucked in a breath, her hips shifting as he slowed his thrusting. But she remained silent.

He dropped his voice to a rich timbre. "Say it, Rae." His fingers in her pussy had stopped moving entirely, this thumb barely ghosting over her throbbing clit. "Say it, and I'll make you —"

"*Sir!*" she hissed through clenched teeth. "I swear if you don't —"

Titus pinched her clit, and that was all it took for her body to submit to him for the second time. Every muscle tensed, her cry so loud he was sure the entire floor heard the way she exploded. Satisfaction pooled in his chest, and he finally pulled his fingers free from her pussy, sitting back on his heels as she turned her head, her face a picture. Her hair was a mess, cheeks flushed, and lips still swollen from his kiss.

Mine, his beast grumbled in his head.

No.

Titus eased back, letting her calm herself as he reached the small, compact bathroom, finding a suitable cream in the mirror above the sink. She hadn't moved an inch, still half hanging over the headboard in nothing but her thong.

"You're an arsehole."

Titus's right hand bracketed her throat, his thumb brushing over her pulse. Her eyes narrowed over her shoulder, but she didn't fight the hold. "Next time you try to kill me," he warned, forcing a neutral tone. "I won't let you off so easily." He released her, only to sit at the edge of the bed.

"Next time," she said as he unscrewed the cap of the aloe vera cream. "You'll be too dead to care." She snatched it from his hand, moving to stand.

Titus watched her struggle, her body continuing to tremble from the aftermath of her orgasms. His cock ached, every movement painful as he denied his own release. Her eyes dipped to the strained denim.

"You gonna deal with that?" she asked, brow raised.

"No." He had no interest in a mate, on binding himself to another. Not even to save him from his curse. If he fucked her, he wasn't confident he'd stop at just sex. He was scared he'd take it all, her mind, body and soul.

"What time is it?" she asked, pulling on a flowing skirt and attaching a holster and sheath beneath, one on each thigh. "Hello? Earth to Titus."

Titus blinked, realising he was staring. "Early, you only slept for a few hours."

"*We*," she muttered. "*We* only slept for a few hours, considering I found you in my bloody bed."

"What did you want me to do?" he asked, enjoying her frustration, her eyes no longer clouded in pleasure. "You were whimpering in your sleep."

Her mouth gaped, letting out an exaggerated gasp. "I did *not* whimper!"

"Like a child," he added, glancing down at his phone. "Now are you done complaining, or are you ready to break into the Guildmaster's office?"

CHAPTER 16

RAE

They were going to get caught. She knew it just like she knew the sun set every dusk, only to come back the following dawn. She just had to figure out a way to not be sold to another guild, one who wasn't as accepting of her mistakes.

"The cameras are on loop," Titus said, as if he could sense her unease. "And your Guildmaster's currently locked in her bedroom."

"With the special lock in the door?" she asked with a frown. Locks Rae wasn't even aware of existing, hidden and controlled by Vivian herself. Rae wasn't sure why the knowledge had surprised her.

"Yes," he replied with a touch of impatience. As if she'd asked the question thousands of times, when in reality, it was only three. "The locks are across the floor, but I can only override one at a time."

"With your hacking skills?"

Titus's face may have been as cool as ice, but she saw the irritation in the slight narrowing of his eyes, and subtle clench of his jaw. She would have teased him about showing a reaction other than blatant insouciance indifference if she wasn't already concentrating on not being caught. The timer aching on her sternum was a constant reminder that she was on a deadline, which meant Titus magic-fucking-fingers Liu Wood was also on a deadline.

Rae walked them down the hallway towards Vivian's quarters, hoping the Guildmaster was still asleep. "Through here," she whispered, turning back to see Titus following close behind. He was all black and sharp angles against the pink tones and soft textures, a juxtaposition that worked surprisingly well.

Or that could have been the post-orgasm hormones speaking.

"So what are you going to do about the ward?" She pointed to the carved symbols surrounding the office door in a pretty arch.

"Nothing." His hand reached for the handle, but Rae grabbed him before he could make contact.

"What do you mean nothing?" she snapped, keeping her voice barely above a whisper. "As soon as we break the ward she'll know."

"I can't do anything for the ward because we only have a short amount of time before she figures out how to override the door." He reached past her again, but she stepped forward to block.

"No, we need to –"

Titus pushed her against the door, her back hitting it with a gentle thud. Before she could react, he pressed harder, pinning her to the wood. Except it was a fraction less than he really needed to keep her immobilised, and she hated how her pulse jumped at the rough touch.

"Looks like the ward's activated," he said with a controlled growl. "We don't have the time. She's going to know we've broken in with, or without the ward. We just need to be gone before she gets out."

Rae caught the argument at the end of her tongue, swallowing it bitterly. He was right, she knew that. But she didn't have to like it. "Just so you know, when we're caught, I'm throwing you under the bus."

Titus dipped his head, and her lips opened automatically, stomach tightening in anticipation. Only for him to reach down and turn the handle. The door swung open, eyes darkening in challenge.

Bastard.

He smirked, the curve of his lips lasting a single heartbeat. "I don't expect anything else."

The office was dark, the fake window the only source of light. It showed a different scene to the one she'd seen hours earlier. The grove was long gone, replaced with a vacant beach, the sea an angry storm with the waves crashing against white gold sand. The moon glowed in the distance, a strange blue glow surrounding the orb far larger than it would have in reality.

Titus moved straight to her desk, clicking a few buttons on her keyboard to wake up the computer. He said nothing as he pulled his phone out, placing it on the desk face up, random numbers flashing across the screen.

A few papers were piled neatly on a cabinet directly behind, but after Rae flipped through the first few, she realised there was nothing but expenses and random reports that had nothing to do with her assignment. She moved to the drawers, finding only pens and other stationary.

Fuck.

"There's nothing here," she said, turning to find Titus relaxed back in the chair, watching her search the room. "Are you going to help?"

"What do you think I'm doing?" The computer screen flashed, replicating the image on his phone. Clicking a few buttons, he brought up an assignment, his name on the top.

"It came directly from the Syndicate," she said, reading over his shoulder. "There wasn't even a bid from other guilds, Vivian was *given* your assignment."

Titus clicked a few more buttons, Rae's name appearing on the bottom as the contractor selected.

"Then who the fuck hired the other two guys?"

Titus Liu Wood
Assignment No – 638273

Aliases, if known: Unknown
Gender, if known: Male
Age, if known: Unknown
Undead age, if relevant: N/A
Known areas: London
*Breed, if known: **REDACTED***
Friend and/or family, if known: Riley Storm's the best-known associate, although do not engage. Ana Liu, maternal grandmother. Axel Wood, cousin. Oscar Wood, father and Mei Liu, mother. Exact addresses are not known.

Other details that may be important to the success of the hit: Caution must be taken, Titus is classed as very dangerous, and must be disposed of from a distance. Ideally with a gun, which must destroy his heart. Head must be removed to ensure full death. Payment will not be completed without proof.

Competing Guilds: N/A
Winning Guild: Crimson Hollow (South East)
*Bid accepted: **REDACTED***
*Deposit received: **REDACTED***
Contractor assigned: Raegan Fox

Details were given freely and to the best of knowledge in reference to the above target.
GM Signed: Vivian Montgomery, Guildmaster of Crimson Hollow.

Signed: **REDACTED**

Titus clenched his jaw, a red flush touching his cheekbones.

"It's mostly redacted," she said. "If the other contractors were hired, it wasn't through the Syndicate."

Titus frowned. "Are all the contractors on the system?"

Raegan Fox (Alias)
Crimson Hollow

Aliases, if known: N/A
Gender, if known: Female
Age, if known: 25
Undead age, if relevant: N/A
Breed, if known: Human
Contracted term: N/A
Other details: Must complete 100 kills
Availability: Out on assignment, No – 638273
Guildmaster: Vivian Montgomery

"What are you looking for?" Rae asked, already knowing the details on screen.

"Do you know that assassin's full name? Gerry?"

"Contractor," Rae sighed. "And it's Gerald. Cross reference him with the Knights."

Gerald St. James (Alias)
The Knights

Aliases, if known: N/A
Gender, if known: Male
Age, if known: 32
Undead age, if relevant: N/A
Breed, if known: Mage
Contracted term: 35 years
Other details: N/A
Availability: Available
Guildmaster: Miviana Arthurian

Rae bit her lip. "He's not on assignment, so why the fuck was he shooting at you?"

Titus's phone let out a single, long beep. "Shit, we've got to go."

"Wait." Rae quickly scrolled down. "What were you looking for?"

"We have thirty seconds before your Guildmaster's lock's released. You want to risk it?"

"What were you looking for?" Rae asked again.

Titus unplugged his phone, shoving it in his pocket. "I think you're being targeted, not me."

"There's no reason for me to be targeted." Doubt twisted her stomach. "If it was under the Syndicate, the details would've been there."

"Exactly, if it was under the Syndicate. Doesn't mean Gerald didn't take a private hit." Titus clicked a few buttons on the keyboard, the screen turning black as Rae made sure everything was exactly like it had been. She didn't want to hang around long enough to be deal with Vivian, running back to her room to grab her gun, and her skull dagger which had fallen to the floor. "I promise not to shoot you," she said to Titus, slipping them both beneath her skirt.

"Yeah, like I trust your promises," he replied. "Let's get out –"

"There you are Cupcake," Nathan smiled, standing just outside her room. His nostrils flared, sickly green eyes landing on Titus. "Who are you?"

"He's no one," Rae said, pushing against Titus's side. "Come on, we have somewhere to be."

Nathan frowned, arm shooting out to block them. "I know you." He cocked his head, studying Titus like a bug. "You're supposed to be dead."

Rae shot a look over her shoulder, knowing they didn't have long. They needed to get out of the building before Vivian figured out something was wrong. "Nathan, fuck off."

"Stupid bitch, do you not think you wouldn't be caught fucking your target like some common whore?"

Nathan stood there, glowering at her and then he was crushed against the wall, Titus's forearm pressed against his throat.

"I'm sorry," Titus said. "I didn't hear you. Want to repeat that?"

Nathan struggled in the hold, nails clawing down Titus's arm, mouth open in a gasp. Titus released him as quickly as he'd struck, stepping back utterly calm while Nathan choked in a staggered breath.

"It's... it's not long before Rae's assignment's up," Nathan managed to push out between puffs. "And when it does, I'll take over." He turned his attention to Rae. "You're going to regret choosing him, I'll make sure of it."

CHAPTER 17

RAE

Rae frowned at the new phone she'd made Titus buy, the unopened box sitting on the pristine wooden table. Playing with her pendant between her fingertips, she stared at the sim glinting beside it, wondering what would happen if she simply dunked it in her coffee, and walked away from everything.

Her real name was technically dead, and the one on all her fake IDs was easy enough to erase, Raegan Fox disappearing into the night. She had some Ravyns saved, definitely enough to get a new ID with another alias, a new life. She'd have to find a witch willing to negate the pain from the mark on her sternum, the stylised moon both a visual, and physical reminder that she was Crimson Hollow's property.

She could catch a ride to the white cliffed docks, bargain her way onto one of the ferries across to mainland Europe and go somewhere warmer, where the weather wasn't mostly drizzle with random bursts of sunshine.

Except she couldn't run. Because then she'd sign her brother's death warrant, and that was something she could never do. No, she'd have to convince him to run with her.

Rae nibbled her lip, stomach in knots as she turned to watch Titus pace outside the window, his strides long and powerful as he talked on the phone. His face gave nothing of the conversation away, but she was sure he was angry, her ability to read his empty expressions improving with every passing hour they spent attached to the hip.

He turned, lips pressed into a thin line when he noticed her staring. The rain that had started as a trickle had increased to a downpour, darkening his blonde hair and sculpting his t-shirt against his chest. Why the fuck did her thighs clench at the sight?

"Here you go."

Rae jumped at the new voice, blinking up at the waitress who'd appeared from nowhere, placing two croissants onto the table. Her stomach growled at the sight, reminding her she hadn't eaten in close to twenty-four hours.

"Can I get you anything else?" the waitress asked, repeating each word slowly. "Maybe some more coffee? A chocolate muffin?"

"No, everything's fine," Rae said with what she hoped was a reassuring smile. "Thank you."

Worry creased the waitress's brows. "Just call if you need me."

Jesus, how bad do I look? It wasn't like she wasn't clean. Her skirt was fresh, as was her top. Her hair was tied up in a high ponytail, and she didn't think she looked that bad without makeup. She couldn't even complain about lack of sleep, because between Titus's place, and hers she'd slept at least six hours. She'd survived on a lot less than that, her body trained over the years to catch as much sleep as possible in short bursts because she grew up never knowing if she was safe.

Picking at the croissant, she peeked at Titus once more, his pacing no longer as rough, his tense conversation coming to an end. Returning her attention to her plate, she bit into the croissant, the chocolate spread she added to hers heaven on her tongue.

The little bakery surrounded in fake greenery was just off the corner of Covent Garden, hidden in one of the slim pathways just off the hectic centre. It was mid-week, so not as busy with tourists than it would have been at the weekend, but it was enough. They'd both agreed to surround themselves with a crowd whenever possible, hoping it would force any contractors to hesitate. At least until they'd found somewhere else secure, because she still had to decide what the fuck she was going to do, and the time was running out. But until then, she couldn't risk someone else taking her assignment. Which meant she was sticking to Titus like glue.

Rae glanced back at the phone, quickly unwrapping the device, and shoving the sim inside. Her finger hovered on the power button.

"Come on," Titus said, appearing by her side. "We've got to go."

Rae looked up. "You look like a drowned rat."

Titus brushed his hand through his hair, fingers coming away wet.

"I haven't even finished my food," she continued, "And we need to figure out our next step."

Titus gestured to the waitress, grabbing Rae's coffee and taking a mouthful. "We can do that on the move, now get up."

Rae purposely took another bite of her food, chewing leisurely.

"Are you honestly going to fight me every step of the way?" he said, his tone a deep timbre. "Because I'll just leave you here to be taken out by another assassin."

"Contractor." Rae jerked her chin up, meeting his eyes.

"And I'm not the one being hunted." She set the rest of her croissant down just as Titus slipped into the seat opposite. "I think we need to make a deal."

"A deal?" He rested his arm along the spare chair to his right, raising a single brow. "You called truce last time, and yet still tried to kill me."

"This'll be different." She stole her coffee back. "It'll benefit us both."

Titus cocked his head, jaw clenched with impatience.

"I won't try to kill you," she said, dropping her voice. "As long as you help me break out of my contract." Titus had been able to read locked files on Vivian's computer within minutes, If anybody could help her, he could.

"How do I know you'll keep your word?"`

Rae sat forward, emphasising her words. "Because I want to be free, more than I want to kill you."

"Should I be flattered?"

She couldn't read his expression, his impassive mask in full place. "Do we have a deal?" She held her breath, his answer the difference between being free, able to do what she wanted with no repercussions, or be forced to murder people. She knew she could continue to take side jobs, slowly earning enough money to pay herself out of her contract. But that could take almost as long as fulfilling her one-hundred kills. Three years she'd been under Crimson Hollow, and not including Titus, she'd only managed thirteen.

"Deal." He stood, placing some cash on the table. "Now get up. We're going."

Relief, so strong she swore her hands trembled. "Stop ordering me around."

His voice was as smooth as chocolate when he lowered his head. "You know what happens when you disobey me, Rae."

Heat rushed through her blood at the reminder.

"Now, are you going to get up like a good girl?"

Good girl. Rae ignored the way her insides tightened, instead allowing her lips to curve. "Yes, sir." The change was instant, his pupils dilating, and the red of his irises swirling to that beautiful liquid silver. He blinked and his response was gone, but she took those few seconds as a win. His body reacted to hers, just as easily as his manipulated hers.

Which made them both as fucked up as the other.

"Where are we?" Rae asked, looking around what looked to be a bar. The tables were yet to be set up, the chairs stacked against the dark walls and framed photographs of artistic, vintage cocktails. The stage appeared to be a gentle wave, surging seamlessly from the wooden flooring with a sound system that looked like it cost more than her car.

The bar itself was decorated with shapes and curves, each line glowing from within like a crackling white flame. Bottles lined the shelves directly behind, light shining through the glass to create a stunning backdrop of colour.

"It's a bar."

"I can see that," she said, unable to stop the roll of her eyes. "I mean, why are we here, specifically?" They hadn't walked far from the bakery, the bar disguised beneath scaffolding.

"I need to meet with a few of my brothers, and I think a public area is safer, don't you agree?"

"More brothers?" His lips were pursed when she turned, the need to know more about him strong. She wasn't sure why she asked the question, knowing he wouldn't answer it anyway.

"Go sit by the bar," he said, face schooled into his usual composed expression. "Sam will keep you company."

"Babysit me, you mean?" Rae grabbed the last remaining stool, pulling it out slightly before taking a seat. She'd already noticed the two men watching her, their attention prickling since the moment she stepped inside. One was pale blonde, with eyes of amber and the other dark, with irises similar to Titus.

"Aye, but I'm a great babysitter," the one who must have been Sam said, his smile infectious. "Besides, I need someone to help me pick out the new name."

"I told you, Drunken Beasts is the winner." The darker one snorted, turning to Titus. "They're waiting for you in the office."

"Thanks," Titus said, facing Sam. "Don't let her out of your sight."

Rae smacked her palm down on the top of the bar. "Hey, stop talking about me like I'm not here."

Sam's smile grew, and something feline danced across his features. "Feisty, I like her."

Titus shook his head. "Of course you fucking do, you like everybody." He turned to the man with similar red eyes a shade similar to his. "You coming?"

The man lifted a dark brow, upper lip curved into a smirk. "I'll follow once I've met the delicious redhead."

"Careful Luce," Titus warned.

A taunting pause. "You've got to be fucking with me." He jerked between Rae and Titus. "You have some serious timing."

Titus narrowed his gaze, turning to Rae. "Be good."

She glared at his retreating back, not looking away until he and the dark-haired man disappeared up the twin staircase hidden in the corner. There was a smaller floor above, a balcony as well as a large, mirrored wall that replicated the unfinished bar below.

"So you're the mysterious Rae that Titus texted me about a whole hour ago," Sam said, pulling her attention to him. His head was cocked, hair wrapped in a single plait that draped over his shoulder. "I thought you'd be taller."

"I disappoint myself sometimes too," she muttered, studying the bottles at his back. "So how come you're the one who has to babysit me?"

"Just lucky, I guess." He laughed. "I'm Sam, I'm mated to Titus's cousin."

"Mated? So you're a shifter?" She knew shifters mated, similar to how humans married. Except she'd heard that once someone was mated, there was no divorce. Her parents weren't married, her father refusing the human custom. Instead he'd bound himself to her some other way.

"I am," he said carefully. "And you're Titus's human."

Rae scowled. "What has me being a human got to do with anything?"

"Really?" Sam grinned. "That's what you got from that statement?"

Rae tried to relax, but she couldn't. "Does that mean Titus's cousin is also a shifter?"

Sam's smile was warm, but his silence was loud.

"Right," she said, her laugh forced. "I guess he's asked you not to share personal details, I get it." She ignored the strange disappointment. "I'm not going to do anything. I don't need to be watched like a child." She dragged a hand through the end of her hair, trying to brush out the knots.

Sam frowned. "He doesn't think you're going to do anything, he's making me watch you because he's worried you'll get hurt."

Rae took a second to register his words, realising Sam wasn't aware of who she was. Which meant he was mistaken, as no way did Titus give a shit whether she was hurt or not. Because just like her, he was only there until he got what he needed.

A mutually beneficial relationship. One where she received orgasms, apparently.

Rae drummed her fingers against the bar. "I don't have time for this." Anxiety wrapped around her chest, pressing against the strange warmth that she hadn't been able to clear in the centre. It was strange, but not entirely unpleasant.

"I'm not stopping you from leaving," Sam said, leaning back against the bar. "But we both know you won't."

His comment bristled. "You don't know me."

"No, and yet I'm not wrong." He tilted his head, cool gaze assessing. "So until Titus is done, you may as well sit and talk to me."

"I can possibly spare five minutes." A reluctant smile touched her mouth. "So, what is this place?"

"It's our new bar, considering the old one burned down." He shrugged, not elaborating anymore.

"And you're calling it Drunken Beast?" She had to admit, the name was memorable.

"No," Sam snorted. "Well, maybe. The name's under consideration."

"What was the old name?" she asked.

"Blood Bar."

"Oh, I remember that place." She'd seen in the news the place had been hollowed out from fire, as well as the adjoining units. "So why can't you just rename it Blood Bar?"

Sam's smile was tense. "The place needs a fresh start, which means a new name."

Rae noticed his eyes darken with memories, ones Sam clearly didn't want to share.

"Phoenix," she said. "Don't they rise from the ashes or something?"

He eyed her with curiosity. "What about Liquid Dreams?"

Rae smirked. "Sounds like it should have a red light outside. Is that something you guys offer for extra?"

"Hilarious," Sam said dryly.

"Okay," Rae continued. "Well, what does the bar offer? Karaoke?" She tried to hide her excitement.

"No..." Sam's eyes brightened in enthusiasm. "But we should definitely have a karaoke night every week. I could create a special cocktail, one that makes you so drunk you sound like the next superstar regardless of talent."

"Maybe just cut the middleman and call the place Liver Failure."

Sam raised a brow. "Loose Lips?"

"Either I have a dirty mind, or you have." She snorted. "The well hung, drawn and quartered?"

Sam burst into surprise laughter, the sound infectious.

"Okay, what about —" She jumped from her seat, her pendant burning against her skin. Pulling it from beneath her shirt she frowned, the metal stinging her fingertips.

"Hey Jax, the meeting's upstairs," Sam said over her shoulder.

Rae turned to face the one with the scar down his face, his dark navy eyes dropping to her necklace. He tried to reach for it, but she shuffled back, the stool toppling between them with a clang.

"Hey man, you okay?" Sam asked, tone bright compared to the growing tension. He seemed relaxed, elbows resting against the bar, but she noticed the slight tightening of his muscles. As if ready to move.

Jax seemed to ignore Sam entirely, his frown seeming to pull the scar. Up close she noticed the end slicing thinly through his top lip, mouth moving as he spoke in a language she'd never heard, the words somehow calming despite her not understanding.

"Where did you get the necklace?" he said, returning to English. His voice wasn't as rough, his words spoken calmer than before.

Rae clutched the pendant tighter, ignoring the pain. It took her a second to realise it had changed, lines forming in the centre stone that definitely weren't there before.

"My mother gave it to me," she found herself saying, fascinated at the change. "What happened?"

"I don't know," he said, just as confused as she was. "Has it done it before?"

"No... wait." She thought back. "It reacted to you last time, but I didn't see whether it changed."

"It's celestrial."

"Like the angels?" Rae frowned. "But my mother was a human. Why would she give me a necklace that's celestrial?"

"What about your da?" Sam asked, just as curious.

Rae shook her head. "Witch."

"Do you know what it is?" Jax asked.

Rae bristled at his tone, back to his usual harshness. "A necklace, obviously."

Irritation flashed across his face. "I think it's a relic, one that only works if you have celestrial blood. The magic is old, long dead." His eyes dipped once more. "It roughly translates to child of the gods."

CHAPTER 18

TITUS

Titus ignored his beast, the bastard growling at him for leaving Rae. He'd left her downstairs for a reason, not trusting her with any more knowledge than she already knew.

What he found on the Guildmaster's computer had turned his blood cold. He knew who'd ordered his hit, he just had to confirm it with evidence, which was one of the reasons he'd asked all his available brothers to meet.

"Ti," Riley said in greeting from his desk, with Xander and Kace standing just behind. Just like in Blood Bar, the main wall was specialised glass, with the patrons seeing nothing but mirrors, and the office having an unfiltered view of everything below.

"You move Lǎolao? My parents?"

"We're working on it," Xander answered, turning away from the view of the bar below. "Your grandmother's fuming. Apparently she didn't want to leave her place, and Axel's currently coaxing her as we speak. We found your parents in Greece. Mykonos, specifically."

Titus's head jerked to the side. He wasn't sure why he was so shocked, it wasn't like his parents ever updated him on anything to do with their lives. Only calling when it was convenient for them, or when they needed something. "They moving to a safehouse there?"

Riley sat back in his seat, the office space taking up the right side of the room. "No, I'm flying them in where we can keep a closer eye on them, at least until the threat's been removed."

Titus clenched his fists, surprised at how easily they'd hopped on a plane when he'd barely seen them as a kid, and even less now he was an adult.

"Which will be in the next five, six hours or so," Lucifer added, leaning against the lip of the large poker table to the furthest left. "I'll pick them up from the airport."

Kace sniggered, moving to sit in the chair closest to the glass wall. "You can't drive, Batboy."

Lucy looked over his shoulder. "Alright Psycho, I'm sure I can figure it out."

"Axel's already on guard duty," Riley said, standing up and moving to the seat beside Kace. "He'll pick them up from the airport, he's a face they'll recognise."

Xander chose the seat beside him, and Lucy slipped into the space left, the rest of the chairs yet to be unpacked.

"What did I miss?" Jax strolled in with his usual scowl, flicking his eyes between everyone.

"Nothing, Titus was just about to update us about his little issue," Lucy said, clicking his tongue.

Kace frowned. "You mean the woman?"

"Ti's been a naughty boy, haven't you?" He rubbed his hands together like an excited child.

Titus shot him the middle finger, only for Lucy to burst into laughter.

"Touchy, touchy."

Jax shook his head, moving to lean against the wall

beside the table, arms crossed. "Be careful with her Ti, she's hiding something."

"She's fine." Titus's growl erupted from his chest, a full vibration pushed from the beast. "She's a means to an end, and that's it."

"Have you seen her necklace?" Jax said. "Because it's –"

"When the fuck did you see it?" Titus stilled, power uncoiling in his gut so suddenly he held his breath. Rae wore a necklace, but it was usually hidden beneath her t-shirt, and the unsolicited image of her stripped bare for another man flashed across his mind.

Jax blinked, taken back by the hostility. "Fucking hell Ti."

"Answer the fucking question." He knew the idea was ridiculous, but he couldn't seem to drop it, the intrusive thoughts a violent hurricane in his mind.

"The necklace's an old relic that can only be worn by the blood of a celestrial," Jax said carefully. "When I approached her, it reacted. There's more to your human than she's letting on, brother."

"Stay the fuck away –" A dark essence bristled against his skin. He could feel it, the black magic growing the angrier he felt, like a glass bottle cracking from inside, ready to burst.

Lucifer's smile slipped, the chair screeching as he stood. "Ease down, Ti."

Titus clenched his fists, trying to control the pulsating surge along his arms. He'd gone from calm to an intense craze in seconds. He hadn't lost himself in years, and there he was, about to shift into his beast, or combust into flames. At that point, he wasn't sure which would be worse.

Arcane burned his fingertips, growing fast until his entire hands and forearms were encased, and there was no way to stop it. *Fuck.*

Lucifer appeared in front of him, smoke teasing his legs as he drifted the short space. With a loud rip, wings erupted from his back, taking up almost the entire span of the office, and blocking the view from his brothers.

"Concentrate on me," he said, voice low enough to only reach Titus. "You need to ease down, or it's going to consume you."

Titus's hearing was a vicious hiss, the oxygen in his lungs nothing but flames. Lightning burned through his veins, pulsating with a power so dark he could taste it.

"You're losing," Lucifer said, his tone like a whip. "Is that what you want everyone to remember you by? A loser who accepted death?"

Titus clenched his fists, concentrating on every breath going in, and out.

Breathe.

Memories of pain struck, so vivid he swore he was experiencing it again. Except he knew he wasn't. He'd survived that pain. He'd survived the bastardised version of the Rite. He'd survive this.

"Accept the change, Titus," Lucifer said, face etched in panic and anger. "Accept the summoning name and balance the fucking power. Trust me."

The strange heat inside his chest spread until it touched the arcane, settling the power enough that Titus could smother it. The arcane disappeared, but the intense warmth stayed, a welcome diversion.

Lurching to the side, he found the paper bin, dropping to his knees just as puke erupted like a violent volcano.

"Ti?"

"Fuck man, what happened?"

"You okay?"

So many voices, all concerned, but he couldn't concentrate, not until his stomach stopped twisting, the nausea settling to a chunk of solid coal in his gut. Spitting the last of the vile taste, he stood, wiping his mouth with the back of his hand.

It was Riley who stepped forward, moving around his desk to grab a bottle of water. "You want to explain what just happened?"

Titus accepted the bottle, taking a swig before answering. "The Order paid for my hit."

Riley froze at the information, supernaturally still, his beast flashing behind his eyes. "How sure?"

"I need to confirm with a data trace, but I'm confident. I found the original paperwork, and other than you guys, no one knows the names of my direct family."

"The Order would have records, considering all our fathers were once members." Riley swore, gripping the edge of his desk hard enough to leave an indent.

"Fucking Archdruid," Xander growled. "He's wanted us gone for years, ever since we wouldn't jump to their fucking demands anymore."

"Except he hasn't done anything until now," Jax added. "So, why now? And why Titus?"

"I think the answer's obvious," Lucifer said. His wings were held tight against his back, a dark silhouette against the light from the glass behind.

"No one knows what happened," Kace said. "We've made sure of it."

"So you believe in coincidences?" Lucifer chuckled, the sound hollow.

"Lucy's right," Riley said. "No way, out of all of us, it's a coincidence Ti's been hit. But we can't make a move against the Order, or the Archdruid without solid proof."

"That's why I've called you all here. I need access to my computers, my apartment's been compromised."

Riley frowned. "You always have access to –"

"I would never risk the family, so I wanted permission to take Rae with me. Wherever I go, she does."

"What aren't you telling us, Ti?" Xander asked.

"Rae isn't a risk to anyone." *But me,* he silently added. "And I only need my computer, we won't stay because you're right. Wherever I am, it's dangerous, at least until I sort the hit out."

"She's the assassin," Kace said, swearing low beneath his breath. "She's the one who shot you."

Jax's head snapped to the side, eyes glowing.

"Fuck the Fates, right?" Titus's humour fell flat. "Because I think she's also my mate."

Four pairs of eyes widened. It was only Lucifer who reacted, bending over with laughter, shoulders shaking. "Fucking hell, and I thought I had bad luck."

"That's why you almost exploded earlier," Riley muttered. "She's your fucking mate."

Unease flowed through him, putting him on edge. "My beast could be wrong."

"Wrong?" Xander dragged a hand down his face. "We don't really get to choose our mate's, Ti."

"I don't believe in this mates shit. Shouldn't I be able to choose? Not my beast? The curse can go fuck itself."

Xander smacked his hand against the table. "That doesn't make it any fucking less true."

"That's enough." Riley demanded the attention. "Right now we need to confirm who paid for the hit, nothing else matters."

"Unless his assassin kills him," Kace muttered, arms crossed. "That'll fucking matter. Do you trust her?"

"Of course not," Titus said, the words causing a strange ache in his chest. "But we have a truce." *Sort of.* "She won't move against me, because I have something she wants."

"What the fuck do you have that she wants?" Xander asked.

"Freedom from her contract."

Xander raised a pale brow. "And you think you can do that?"

"I have no idea, but she doesn't know that. So until we take out whoever hired her, I'm going to keep her close."

"You should've told us immediately," Riley said. "We're a team, Ti."

Titus looked away, clenching his jaw.

"As soon as you've confirmed who paid for your hit, you tell us, and we'll figure out what happens next. Do not make the move without us, do you understand?"

"I wasn't aware I'd lost your trust," Titus said between gritted teeth. "But yes, *Sire*. I understand." Not waiting for a reply, he turned back towards the hall, needing a second to calm himself. He knew he'd reacted unfairly, but he was tired at being treated like he was broken.

Titus paused at the bottom of the stairs, watching as Rae laughed casually with Sam. Her head was thrown back, uninterrupted happiness pouring from her, and Titus felt jealous.

Which was fucking ridiculous.

There was something about her that just crawled beneath his skin, her attitude and disobedience something he wasn't used to. Yet the memory of the way she submitted. *Fuck.* It wasn't even the submission, it was the fact she'd fought him the entire time, despite her body betraying every word she'd snarled over her shoulder. Her submission had been a gift, one he planned to take advantage of. It made him want to tie her up, turn her pretty skin various shades of pink. He knew it would too, his hand leaving the perfect mark.

Titus felt Jax approach from behind, his brother's attention on *his* assassin.

"I'm sorry about earlier." *At losing control.*

"I worry about you, brother." Jax's eyes were hard when they met his. "You're bottling everything inside, and then you say shit like that?"

"I'm –"

"You're not fine," Jax said, voice sharp. "A blind hound can see you're not fine."

"We don't have the option to be anything but fine," Titus said. "I'm dealing with it my own way."

"By locking yourself in your room? To come out when you're on rotation, and then to go back inside? What are you, a fucking teenager?" Jax shook his head. "You're always so calm, Ti. Content to hide every emotion, but you're allowed to lose control every now and then."

"Yes, because earlier when I almost combusted it was very beneficial, thanks."

Jax sighed. "What did you tell me when we were kids? When I was attacked, and realised I would forever bear the memory on my face."

He was unable to stop himself studying the harsh scar that sliced down Jax's skin. "I said, 'at least you weren't pretty to begin with.'" Titus smirked. "And that's still true."

"I was eight," Jax said with a shadow of a smile. "I dealt with that trauma because I had you, and the others to help ground me. Don't shut us out because you think it's weak to ask for help. You don't have to deal with this alone."

Titus shut his eyes, wanting to shut him out. But Jax was right. "I think I've bonded to her."

Jax froze beside him. "Does she know?" He kept his voice a whisper.

"No," he said hesitantly. "I don't think she does." He felt an intense warmth, tugging him in her direction. But she showed no signs of feeling the same. "It wasn't meant to happen."

"Your beast took over." Jax let out a breath, hand coming up absently to run across his top lip, rubbing the rough skin. "He's chosen an assassin trying to kill you, to be your mate. I guess your beast wins the idiot of the century award."

"I prefer it when you're silent," Titus muttered.

Jax chuckled, the sound alien. "If I've learnt anything from the others, is that there's no point in fighting instincts. There's a reason your beast chose her. Maybe she's your salvation."

Titus swallowed. "Why would I need a salvation?"

"Only you can answer that." Jax gripped Titus's shoulder. "Whatever your assassin's necklace was, the magic that the stone held has dissipated to almost nothing. I'm surprised it even reacted to me."

Titus nodded, Rae's voice echoing around them, and he couldn't help but glance back over. She played with the new phone, a charging cable attached to the bottom, and draped over the bar. Her smile dropped when she read whatever was on the screen.

Titus closed the distance within seconds. "What's wrong?"

"It's my brother." The colour had drained from her face. "They're going to kill him."

CHAPTER 19

RAE

This wasn't the first time she'd received a panicked message from Miles. In fact, he'd done it a few times over the last few years. He had a knack for getting himself into dangerous situations, whether it was for money, drugs or his favourite vice, gambling. She didn't really care what it was, her job was to bail him out. That was what family was for, and he'd done it enough for her when they were kids. Taking the brunt of the punishments from their father, trying to shield her as much as possible.

She'd sent him to rehab so many times, and still he'd always come out telling her he was changing his life, only to fall right back to where he started. Worse even, because last time she'd been forced to give her life over to Vivian, in exchange for his. There was never much choice, not when it came to Miles.

"Fucking idiot," she cursed. "I'm going to kill him if they haven't first."

Titus scanned the street, taking in the vandalised cars, shut down shops and overflowing bins. "You checked your gun?"

"Of course." She always made sure it was ready, her dagger a backup in these situations.

"Good, you may need it. Just don't shoot me."

He moved a step behind, and for some reason she was comforted at his presence. She'd always had to deal with her brother's issues alone, and it was strange to have someone at her back. A partner, even if she didn't trust him.

"I tried that before, didn't work out well for me," she said, and she swore he smirked.

It took them longer than necessary to find the grungy club, hidden down a side road with its windows smashed and covered haphazardly with wood. A burst of neon pink broke through the shadows, the club's logo a flamingo holding a snooker cue while standing on one leg. The light flickered every few seconds, creating a low buzz as Titus knocked his fist against the metal door.

A section slid open, a man scowling through the gap, large enough to see half his face. "What?" He barely gave Rae a cursory glance before settling on Titus.

"We're here to see Miles," Rae said, but the man wasn't listening to her. "Hello?"

Titus remained silent, simply crossing his arms across his chest as he waited.

"Your kind's not welcome here," the man growled, "Fuck off." The metal section slid closed.

Rae's mouth snapped open. "What a prick!"

"My kind?" Titus frowned, his knock against the door hard enough to leave a dent.

The gap slid open. "I said your kind –"

Titus reached through, gripping the man by his throat.

"Fuck, fuck, sorry. I didn't realise, I thought you were one of them Breeds."

"What made you think I was Breed?" Titus asked, squeezing enough that the man's eyes bulged.

"The wrists man," he gargled. "We've been told to look out for tats on the wrists, the way those druids like them. I didn't see your eyes!"

Rae frowned. *His eyes?*

Titus released his grasp, the heavy metal door groaning as it unlocked. The man stepped out the way as they entered, keeping himself an arm's length away from Titus at all times.

The large room was empty but for two people, both playing on one of the five snooker tables. They didn't look up, continuing to play their game. "Through there," the one on the left said, carefully lining up his shot.

"Thanks," Rae muttered, looking at the old guns and knives decorating the walls, along with taxidermy heads of boars and ducks. Another flamingo neon light was behind the bar, but unlike the one outside, it had no head, the space replaced with dramatic blood squirts.

Cries of pain echoed down the slim corridor, the smack of flesh on flesh.

"Where's his money, Miles?" someone growled. "You know he doesn't like to be kept waiting."

A groan, followed but what sounded like spit. "She's coming. She always comes, I promise."

"You better not be lying, you won't like what I do to liars."

Rae took a second to compose herself before she stepped into the room, her brother refusing to look at her as he kneeled on the floor. A man stood over him with the smoothest caramel eyes, an unusual contrast against his, dark, messy hair. His smile was crooked, a dimple in his right cheek as he slowly appraised her body.

"Well, hot damn. Looks like you really do have a sister, and she came with her own bodyguard. Cute." He looked at

163

Titus before returning to her. "You bring Angel his money, darling?"

A low whistle from the blonde behind him, a snooker cue held over his shoulders, arms hooked over. "If I'd known she was this hot, we would have broken your face earlier, Miles. You know how I have a thing for redheads."

Titus stiffened behind her, but he continued to let her take control of the situation. "I would like to speak to my brother. Alone," she added.

"No can do, darling," the caramel eyed one said. "You see, Miles here owes Angel a ton of fucking money, and I can't risk him making a run for it."

Rae kept her tone sharp. "You won't see a penny if I don't speak to him alone."

The blonde chuckled, swinging the cue over his shoulder. He threw it onto the snooker table, knocking the balls together. "What a shame, looks like I'll just take it from his flesh instead."

"Please, just give them what you have," Miles begged, finally turning to look at her. His left eye was swollen shut, the right side of his face a pattern of bruises. His nose was broken, recently if she went by the fresh blood still pouring from it.

She'd seen him a mess before, and each time it made her heart ache, her stomach clench. "What happened?"

"He thought he could borrow from Angel without paying him back," the blonde said. "With interest, of course."

"Fucking loan sharks, Miles?" Rae barely controlled her anger. "How many times are we going to do this?"

"Just fucking pay them!" he growled, climbing to his feet. He favoured his left leg, leaning to the side. "You fucking owe me, so pay them."

"I owe you nothing!" Her voice rose to a scream. "When

will it be enough, Miles? When you've killed me? Will you forgive me then?"

"Fuck you, Rae," he said, spitting blood to the floor. "Just pay them."

Her slightly enraged smile tightened. "How much?"

Miles swallowed, his Adam's apple bobbing at the motion. He looked to the side, voice a mumble. "Fifty thousand."

Rae fought the manic laughter bubbling up her throat. "Pounds?"

"Ravyns," Caramel eyes added. "We can't have it traced now, can we?"

Something dark and volatile twisted deep within the pit of her stomach. "And you think I have that?" she whispered. She was sure it was more than everything she'd saved, the jobs she took on the side few and far between.

The blonde sniggered. "There's other ways to pay, beautiful. You'll look real pretty on your knees."

TITUS

He knew his face projected a lethal calm, nothing but muscle at Rae's back. Not that Rae needed protecting, but in their world of violence having someone bigger, and scarier caused people to hesitate before attacking, and that hesitation could be the difference between life and death. Rae, with her startling hair and curves didn't look like she could shoot someone between the eyes, even though he knew she could while smiling the entire time.

Her brother, on the other hand, clearly wasn't built for their world, whimpering and crying as he begged his sister for money. *Pathetic.*

165

He wasn't sure what he'd expected when he'd first stepped into the snooker club, but the small flame painted onto the wall definitely wasn't it. Church of the Light, extremists who hated anything Breed. Nor did he expect Sythe to be one of the guys beating the shit out of Rae's brother.

He was a shadow, able to infiltrate anything with enough time and patience. He was the Guardians spy. The executioner.

So what the fuck was he doing there?

"Ravyns," Sythe said, barely taking his attention off Rae. "We can't have it traced now, can we?"

Of course, Titus thought. *It would have to be the currency of the fucking Undercity.*

Rae stiffened, her spine rigid. "And you think I have that?" she whispered, rage dripping from every word.

The blonde sniggered, clearly enjoying himself. "There's other ways to pay, beautiful. You'll look real pretty on your knees."

Something inside Titus snapped, his beast roaring to the surface, tearing to get out. It took every ounce of willpower not to leap forward, and rip the blonde's head clean from his shoulders.

"Come near me," Rae said with an eerie calmness, "and I'll cut your fucking dick off."

Sythe finally looked at him, his expression not changing. *'Calm the fuck down, dude,'* he said, connecting mentally. *'You're going to mess everything up.'*

"She'll do anything you ask," Miles said, holding his hands out in surrender. "Won't you, Rae?"

Titus clenched his fist, his chest aching from the power surging between his ribs. He wanted to repel it, the black magic vile on his tongue, but instead he used it to centre himself. He was always the calm Guardian, never losing his temper. But, yet again he found himself on the edge. All because of her.

"Fuck you Miles!" she hissed.

Sythe chuckled, continuing in his character. "As amusing as this is, we still haven't seen any Ravyns."

Rae let out a frustrated sound. "I don't have that sort of money!"

"How much to keep you off his back?" Titus finally said, Rae turning to him with a frown.

Sythe's expression hardened. "Angel wants all of it."

"And I'll get you all of it," he growled. "So how much to get you off his back until we find that sort of money?"

Sythe cocked his head, looking towards the blonde with a raised brow.

"We'll take half now," the blonde said. "Half tomorrow."

"We don't have –" Rae began.

"Three days," Titus interrupted. "Half now, and the other half in seventy-two hours."

'What are you doing?' Sythe asked, his face smooth, giving no indication they were communicating. *'He's a piece of shit. We caught him beating a woman unconscious.'*

'This isn't for him,' Titus said. *'Take the deal, Sy.'*

"How can we trust you?" Sythe said aloud. "I don't know you from Adam."

"You haven't got much choice, have you?" Titus reached into his back pocket, pulling out three Ravyns. They were cold in his palm, around twice the size of a normal pound coin, but rather than metal they were made from solid onyx. Two were engraved with a detailed image of a sphinx, while the third was a unicorn. "Twenty-five now, another twenty-five in seventy-two hours. You either take the deal, or you don't get anything."

"Twenty-Five now, thirty in seventy-two hours just for

the inconvenience of us having to wait." Blonde held out his hand, accepting the deal. "Maybe next time, beautiful," he chuckled towards Rae. "I'm sure you'd be a decent ride."

Miles was visibly relieved, dropping his chin towards his chest. "You'll get your money."

"We know," Sythe agreed. "Otherwise you'll be dead."

The blonde gestured to leave. "Don't worry, we'll send Angel your regards. May the light guide you."

Miles bowed his head. "And give sanctuary from the darkness."

CHAPTER 20

RAE

Tears burned her eyes, but she refused to let them fall as she followed Miles back out into the street.

"Where were you?" he said, beginning to pace. His nose had finally stopped bleeding, but he'd need to reset it soon if he didn't want it to heal crooked. "I called you eight times and it went straight to voicemail!"

"My phone was –"

"Look at me!" he screeched. "Look at my face! That's your fucking fault."

"Careful what you say next," Titus warned.

Miles snarled. "I'm sorry, who the fuck are you again?"

"Enough!" Rae shouted, stepping between them. She was both angry, and confused at Titus's intervention. Why the fuck would he offer to help? What did he want in return? "I can fight my own battles."

His eyes flashed, but he stayed silent.

She turned towards her brother. "Fuck you, Miles. Why did you borrow money from a guy like Angel in the first place? The Church of the Light? Really?" She wanted to knock some sense into him. They were an extremist group hiding in plain sight as a recognised religion. They openly preached that everyone non-human was inferior, and therefore lower than dirt.

"That's none of your business." He wiped his sleeve across his face.

"You're not even fucking human! Why would you join –"

"I know I'm not fucking human!" Miles barked, stepping until he was barely an inch away. "Dad always fucking reminded me that I wasn't witch enough for him, and wasn't human enough for mum."

"What's wrong with you?" A single tear burned down Rae's face. "I had to sell my soul to keep you alive, and now you're trying to give me over to some shitty thugs like I'm a piece of meat?"

"You know it's the least you could do." Miles spat. "You know –"

"Please," she whispered. "Don't."

"– for killing mum and all," he continued.

Titus stepped forward, but Rae stopped him with a palm to his chest. His face was calm, but the muscles beneath her hand were rigid. "I need you to give me a minute." Her voice wobbled, the agony of her brothers words hard to hide.

"Oh look," Miles sniggered. "Perfect little Rae's going to cry. You know what happened when you cried? She was beaten even harder."

"Please," she begged Titus, who remained solid beneath her palm. "Wait over there."

He finally tore his attention away from her brother, his irises silver rather than the usual deep burgundy. Without a word he turned, leaving her alone with Miles.

Rae took a deep breath. "That was cruel," she said, closing her eyes. "Mum's death wasn't my fault."

"She took your beatings," Miles snarled. "As soon as he

raised a fist to you, she intervened. She suffered because of you."

"I never asked her to do that!" Rae said, trying to swallow the pain until she felt nothing at all. "I tried to stop him, but I was just a kid."

"So was I!"

"Exactly!" Rae screamed. She absently reached for her necklace, gripping it tightly. Miles had been the first to find their mother on the kitchen floor, blood a hot pool around her head. "Her death wasn't my fault, and it wasn't yours."

"You keep telling yourself that." His eyes dipped to her pendant. "Do you remember when she tried to set us on fire? The voices told her it would cure us."

"She was sick."

"She was fucking crazy," he cried. "And she only got worse over the years, her episodes lasting longer until I barely recognised her."

"She didn't mean it, Miles. She needed help, she needed –"

His laugh was wet. "She never stopped him from beating me, you know?"

"Miles –"

"You were always the favourite. Even when she wasn't our mum anymore, the voices taking over, she still chose you over me." He shook his head, stepping back.

"That money's everything I have, Miles. Everything. It was supposed to help me buy out this fucking contract. But that doesn't matter, does it? Because you know I'd spend my last penny on you."

"There you go again, always protecting me." His smile was cold, empty. "Guilt's a powerful emotion, isn't it?"

His words cut as deep as any knife. "Go home. Put some ice on your face. I'll deal with your fuckups, just like I do every time."

"What would I do without you?" he chuckled, the sound hollow.

She didn't watch him leave, folding her arms around her chest, tight enough to hold herself together. Their father was the perfect husband and dad on the outside, a highly respected officer, friend, and neighbour. But behind closed doors he was anything but, disciplining his kids, and his wife with frequent outbursts of violence. Rae couldn't recall everything, sure her mind was suppressing most of it, but she remembered crying, her arm broken at just five, maybe six. Miles had been only three years older, and he'd cuddled her on the floor, wiping away her tears. His face had been black and blue, and yet he sat with her until their mother came back. After that she'd stepped in whenever she was home, taking the beatings instead of Rae.

But she wasn't always home.

'She needs some respect.'

Her father's voice flowed across her mind, and fear speared through her heart much the same as when she was small. It had taken her nine more years to gain enough courage to stand up to him, and as a result he'd lost it. He'd killed their mum in a rage, and because he was a corrupt cop, he'd gotten away with it. He'd told everyone she was crazy, planting a knife in her hand despite him having nothing but defensive wounds. His skin beneath her nails as she fought until her last breath.

Strangely, one of the things Rae remembered in vivid detail was the time directly after, the media circus surrounding the 'crazy' mother who'd attacked her police detective husband. She remembered every face of the force members who'd investigated, and quickly swept evidence under the carpet. Almost everything before then was a blur, pops of colour in a history of black and white.

Her father had gotten away with it, and Rae had taken

great pleasure in pulling the trigger less than a year later, watching her father's brains explode from the back of his head. She'd used his own gun, the same one he'd trained her with. It had been easy to set it up as a suicide, typing a note admitting everything, from the beatings to losing control. How he couldn't live with himself anymore. The same people who'd failed her mother, didn't give a shit about her father.

Guess she was a result of her upbringing. Nature versus nurture, and all that.

"Why do you put up with him?"

She'd felt Titus approach, a comforting warmth who'd given her the space she needed. The same man who she'd tried to kill, and yet helped her without question.

Rae turned, confused why the ache in her chest calmed at his presence. "He's the only family I have left."

"You can choose your family, you know."

"Like you did?"

Titus didn't smile, and she wasn't sure why she was disappointed.

"You shouldn't have done that," she said, clearing her throat. She'd cried too many tears over her parents, and then Miles. There would be no more.

He blinked, expression empty. "Done what?"

"Stop playing fucking games." Rae moved forward. "I can't, not right now. Just..." She wasn't sure how to react right then, her emotions raw. "I don't have another seventy-two hours. I'm not sure I even have half that." And unlikely the money to pay him back anytime soon, which meant if she somehow survived timing out, she'd owe him.

"We better keep working on who fucking hired you then."

Rae licked across her bottom lip. "We need to keep

moving. I can't risk you getting yourself killed before I decide whether to collect on my assignment or not."

A break in his mask, a slight curve of his lips. "Such a Rae of fucking sunshine."

Rae waited for Titus to unlock the door, pulling the fabric from her face. "I don't think a blindfold was necessary."

"I don't trust you."

Okay, fair, she thought, taking in the large house that had an amazing amount of natural light, and the grand stairwell that led to the floor above. "But with your t-shirt? You keep trying to get naked around me, it's alarming."

Titus shot her a look over his shoulder, guiding her to what she'd assumed was his room. "We can't stay long."

"I know, we have to keep moving." She had just over forty hours left, and she needed to make a move before it was too late. "If my phone *was* being tracked, you took care of it."

"You can never be sure."

Titus's bedroom was similar to the one back at his apartment, decorated in various shades of black, grey and white. Although it was at least twice the size. And just like his other place, everything was perfectly straight. His computer, which had three screens, and a computer tower which was directly to her right, and not one cable was out of place, each one pinned straight. His bed looked like it had been ironed, not a single wrinkle in the sheets, and she was sure the framed photographs on his walls were all angled at ninety degrees.

Titus sat, still shirtless, at his desk, leaning to plug his phone into the computer. Throwing his t-shirt onto his bed, she looked around the room.

"Don't touch anything," he said, not even turning away from the screens.

Ignoring him, she opened the top drawer, and everything inside was painstakingly folded. "I think you have a problem," she muttered, wanting to mess something up and see whether he exploded, or just reprimanded her with his calm voice.

"What part of 'don't touch anything,' didn't you understand?"

"The part where you opened your mouth."

Her phone vibrated, and pulling up the conversation, she typed out a reply.

> There's a fake bottom in the bottom drawer, and inside will be the black bag I need you to get. xx

A pause, Rae waiting.

> Got it, where am I dropping them off at? Also, Viv is raining HELL. She thinks you did something to the locks? Since when did we even have those locks? xx

> I'll update you when I can, but drop at the usual place, I'll get there as soon as I can. Thanks for this, Winter. I owe you, big time!

> Give me that blade with the serrated edge you never use, and we're square. xx

> Deal.

> I'll let you know when I've made the drop. There's no word on a forfeit yet, but I'll give you a warning if I can. Be safe Rae. xx

The Ravyns she'd been saving were hidden back in her

room at the Guild, somewhere Rae couldn't risk going to until her assignment was done and Vivian had calmed down. She wasn't sure how much she had, but prayed it was enough to cover the entire amount. She was running out of time, dread forcing her hand.

Titus continued working on his computer, the screens moving too fast for her to read even if she were closer.

"Why did you bring me here?"

He clicked a few buttons before he sat back, arms relaxed on the rests with his legs slightly spread. He looked like a tattoo covered god, his nipple piercing glinting in the light as she hungrily took in the sight. His hair was wrapped into a messy bun, with a few strands framing his angular face that was covered in a delicious stubble several shades darker. He bit at the ring in the centre of his bottom lip, watching her too closely. As if he could see beneath her skin.

"Well?" she asked, heart racing as if she were being hunted. "Like you said, you don't trust me."

His chair squeaked as he stood, and Rae tipped her head up to meet his gaze. "Keep your friends close –"

"And your enemies closer," she finished for him. "Is that what we are? Enemies with benefits?"

"What else would you call us?"

"I don't know," she said, irritated at how her voice had become huskier. "You're the man I'm forced to kill, and yet you just helped my brother. I don't like owing people."

"What do you want me to say, Rae? Would you have preferred they'd killed him?"

"No. I just..." She let out a sound of frustration. "I didn't ask you for help."

"You don't owe me anything," he growled, hands slapping against the wall beside her head. "I don't need, or want anything from you."

His attention on her was both infuriating and addictive, confusing her emotions that were a violent storm beneath her skin. She wanted to hit out, push him away, and at the same time drag him closer.

She was drowning in him, and she wasn't sure which way was up.

"This would've been easier if you'd stayed dead."

His eyes flashed, but she didn't let him speak. Curving her hand around his neck she pulled him down the few inches until his lips touched hers. He quickly jerked from her grip, the spike of disappointment disappearing as he forced her harder against the wall. His lips crushed against hers, his tongue devouring, dominating.

She was losing control of her life, everything falling apart. Maybe she wanted him to break, to lose his constant fucking calmness until he was a mess too, just like her.

"Please," she begged when he moved to nibble against her throat, his hand lifting to wrap in her hair.

"Please what?" His fist tightened, a sharp ache along the back of her skull. Use your words, Rae. Want me to stop?"

"No!" Her pussy clenched, already embarrassing wet. "Don't you dare stop."

"Good, but I'm not going to fuck you." His voice was smooth compared to the roughness with which he stroked. His fingers heavy, unforgiving as he flicked hard at her nipples. "You're not ready for what I want."

She would have shoved him, clawed at him. But he sucked the sensitive space between her throat and shoulder, biting down until she was pinned, completely at his mercy. The slight pain shot straight between her legs, and she groaned, needing more.

"What... what do you want?" Only he'd ever brought this reaction from her body, as if she'd combust if he didn't touch her.

His breath was hot as it caressed the edge of her ear, his hand still holding her head at an angle. "Complete submission."

Her thighs went to press together, but he'd shoved a leg between hers, stopping her. "Fuck you," she hissed, finally shoving against his chest. He didn't budge, and that infuriated her further.

"You and this bloody short skirt," he said, hand disappearing beneath the fabric. "Drives me fucking crazy."

Rae was panting, his finger slipping straight past her underwear to spear between her slick folds. She let out a cry, clenching as he thrust inside. He pulled her underwear, letting it fall to the floor. There was no teasing, no build up or prep. She had no choice but to stretch around two of his thick fingers, both expertly rubbing against her g-spot, punishing her with such intense pleasure she was going to explode.

"Easier... easier to reach my gun," she managed to say, his thumb flicking against her clit, bringing her closer and closer to a release.

"That's right," he said, pulling away. "Your gun."

Her thigh holster drooped, the cold press of something metal touching her seconds later. It was an extreme sensation, forcing her to gasp as he moved her own weapon back and forth through her folds, the barrel touching her clit on every stroke.

"Oh, God." It was too much, the cold against her heat, Titus pushing her beyond her limits. He still hadn't released her hair, keeping her exactly where he wanted, unable to move with arousal dripping down her thighs. Completely at his mercy, and she fucking loved it.

He dipped his head, kissing a line up her throat before coming to her lips. "You're cunt's mine, Raegan Fox."

Another thrust of the gun. "Not your God's." The barrel slipped to the opening of her core. "Mine."

Her pussy contracted around the cold metal, both pain and pleasure.

"I didn't say you could come yet," he whispered against the skin of her throat, teeth biting down. "You have to beg."

Rae tried to roll her hips, but Titus simply pulled away, leaving her aching. "I'm going to fucking kill you," she hissed.

"You've tried that," he chuckled, smearing her arousal along the inside of her thighs. "And look where we are?"

"Please," she growled, her release so close, she could taste it.

"Please what?"

She was going to kill him. Something painful. "Please Titus, or I'll finish myself!"

The gun brushed against her clit, so cold and heavy that the orgasm tore through her so hard she almost collapsed.

Titus's caught her cry with his tongue, his hand continuing to stoke in precise movements, drawing out her release until her legs shook, bones aching from how intense she'd exploded.

Rae sagged when he released her hair, head dropping back to rest against the wall. He pulled the gun from beneath her skirt, bringing the barrel, slick with her cum up to his lips. Slowly, his tongue flicked out to lick along the entire length, and Rae was sure she could come again just from that sight alone.

She wanted to hit him, but instead she reached up on her toes and kissed, tasting herself on his lips. She kissed him like he was the last man on earth, as if they weren't enemies, but normal lovers lost in each other.

She pulled back, entire body flushed. "Forty-three

hours," she whispered, knowing her decision had been made for her.

She didn't have the time left. One of them was likely to die soon, so she figured she would be as well having a little fun before then, and teasing Titus seemed like a great way to spend it.

She'd wanted him to break apart for her, the same way she'd shattered at his touch.

He watched her beneath his lashes, body solid below her palm as she stroked across his chest, tracing along the tattoos, and over every ridge of his abs before sinking lower. He caught her wrist before she could touch where she wanted.

"Please," she said, knowing it was what he wanted to hear. Her begging, pleading on her knees. She'd never done it for any other man, but with Titus it was raw, unfiltered lust.

He threw her gun onto the bed, and she expected him to stop, never taking it further. Instead he held her still, locked in his grip while he released his cock, and Rae held her breath in anticipation.

Fucking hell.

A pearl of arousal glistened on his tip, veins pulsating down his thick shaft. But what caught her eye were the metal studs, piercing each side of the head. Titus said nothing as he guided her on how to wrap around his girth, his own hand pressing down, using her as his own, personal toy. He controlled the strength in which she held, the length on which she stroked.

She wanted to take charge, but watching him use her to get himself off was something she never thought she'd enjoy. It was the power of his hold, the rough movements as he stroked himself, all while watching *her*. Using *her*.

The cords along his neck strained, his body held

painfully still. He grunted as thick ropes of cum covered her hand, and still he kept her stroking, forcing more and more out of him until he was done. Her fingers ached when he finally released, but the entire situation had been an experience she wanted to repeat.

Which made everything more complicated, especially when she still had to kill him.

CHAPTER 21

TITUS

That wasn't supposed to happen.

And yet, as he listened to the shower run, he wanted to repeat it. But this time with her on her knees, large green eyes looking up at him. Begging.

He dragged a hand down his face. He shouldn't have kissed her. He never kissed any of the women he played with, and yet he couldn't seem to stop, Rae being a drug that he needed like his next breath. He'd heard his brother talk about their mates, but he'd never expected to experience it himself.

The instinct powerful, violent.

And she wasn't even aware.

Mine.

"Fuck." He couldn't even distinguish between his voice, and his beast's anymore. She was his, their souls bonded on an intimate level that she likely wouldn't understand. Would probably never understand, which meant she could walk away.

That was if she didn't kill him first.

Mine.

Making sure he was using an encrypted server, Titus

logged into the trojan he'd hidden on the Guildmaster's computer. It allowed him to explore not only the guild's files, but everything connected to the Syndicate in a central database. He knew he wouldn't have long. Their cyber security was impressive, even if he hadn't designed something similar himself. There were thirty-three guilds connected through the Syndicate, all across the world. Too many to manually search, so Titus simply typed, *'contractor; vampire,'* localising the result to only show the UK.

Michael Gordon – The Knights
Kelly Turner – Dragonborn
Antonio Melendez – Silvertooth
Atlas Wolf – Crimson Hollow
Nicholas Williams – Black Talon – DECEASED

Nicholas Williams (Alias)

Black Talon
Aliases, if known: N/A
Gender, if known: Male
Age, if known: 19
Undead age, if relevant: 321
Breed, if known: Vampire
Contracted term: 100 years
Other details: Deceased
Availability: ~~*Available*~~
Guildmaster: Malic Jael

The vampire who'd attacked them was available at the time of his death, which meant he'd been hired privately, just like Gerald. Frustrating, considering it left no trail for him to follow. Which only left his own assignment.

Aliases, if known: Unknown
Gender, if known: Male
Age, if known: Unknown
Undead age, if relevant: N/A
Known areas: London
Breed, if known: **Daemon**
Friend and/or family, if known: Riley Storm's the best-known associate, although do not engage. Ana Liu, maternal grandmother. Axel Wood, cousin. Oscar Wood, father and Mei Liu, mother. Exact addresses are not known.

Other details that may be important to the success of the hit: Caution must be taken, Titus is classed as very dangerous, and must be disposed of from a distance. Ideally with a gun, which must destroy his heart. Head must be removed to ensure full death. Payment will not be completed without proof.

Competing Guilds: N/A
Winning Guild: The Shadow (South East)
Bid accepted: **5 million**
Deposit received: **2.5 million**
Contractor assigned: Raegan Fox

Details were given freely and to the best of knowledge in reference to the above target.
GM Signed: Vivian Montgomery, Guildmaster of Crimson Hollow.

Signed: **Archdruid Bartholomew Edwards**

He deleted the entire assignment, the history of his hit forever lost. He thought there would be a sense of relief as he slipped free of the database, leaving no evidence of his interference behind. Except, he felt nothing.

"Is it confirmed?" Riley asked over the phone.

"I copied everything before I wiped it clean." The chair squeaked when he leaned back. "But yeah, it's Edward's signature." But something bothered him, because no way would Edwards sign Archdruid over his higher position of Councilman.

"What's your gut saying?"

"That there's only a handful of people who know my history, and even less who would class me as a Daemon." His chest clenched at the name, a sour taste coating his tongue.

Riley swore, the word more of a growl. *"You think one of us leaked the information?"*

Titus heard the strain in his voice. "No." He'd lay his life down on that fact. "But I don't trust this. The Order's behind the hit, I'm sure, but I don't believe Edwards signed it himself. Not under his name, anyway, and definitely not as the Archdruid." Edwards was smart enough to have not left a trail.

"There may be more people behind it than simply him, which means we need to figure out who, and take them out," he said. *"What would've happened when the hit against you expired?"*

"Someone else would've been assigned to kill me."

"And what would've happened to your assassin in that situation?"

Titus turned towards the open door, listening out for Rae. "It doesn't matter, because I won't let it happen."

"Ti –"

"Sire," he interrupted, using the title knowing it pissed Riley off. He didn't like to be reminded of the hierarchy, one that was forced on him. "I'll deal with whatever happens."

A grunt. *"You bonded yet?"*

"Does it matter?"

A heavy pause. *"He'll be at a charity event tomorrow night,"* Riley said, allowing the subject to drop. *"Storm Enterprise's still a patron from when my father was the Archdruid. I'll get us in, including your assassin."*

"Good." Titus closed his eyes. "Ri, when you first met Alice, what was it like?"

"It felt like I'd been hit by a truck, and that was before I'd tied her to a chair."

Titus smiled.

"I accused her of putting a spell on me, because no way could my beast be so enamoured by this bloody witch who couldn't even control her own powers." Another taut pause. *"Sometimes we aren't even aware we're looking for something, not until we find it."*

Titus opened his eyes to see Rae there, her hair damp, loose around her shoulders. She'd put on her bra, but it dipped low enough at the front that he could just make out the moon mark peeking above the fabric, the colour almost full.

"Do I have permission to take Edwards out?" he asked Riley, but never taking his eyes off her.

"Do not touch him without speaking to me first. Being a Councilman complicates things."

Titus swallowed his frustrated growl.

"I'm not saying no," Riley continued. *"I'm saying not yet. We need to find his accomplices, if any."*

Rae looked up, a flush darkening her skin at his attention.

"Fine," Titus bit out. "I'll update you soon." He said goodbye, throwing his phone onto the desk as he waited, knowing from the way Rae nibbled her bottom lip she was about to share her opinion.

"You're an open book, you know," he said, taking his time to study the dark lace that cupped her breasts, matching the sliver of underwear between her legs. She'd added her thigh sheath and holster, and the image of an almost naked Rae armed with the same gun he'd made her come with was one of the hottest things he'd ever seen.

"If you know who hired me, why aren't we killing them?" she asked, reaching up to tie her hair in its usual ponytail.

"Because it's complicated."

"How?" She frowned. "A bullet between the eyes will nullify the assignment, surely? No guild will carry out a hit when there's no money involved."

"Not when it's a Councilman."

Rae's eyes widened slightly. "Fuck, like from the actual Council?"

"There's a charity gala tomorrow night, he'll be there."

"That doesn't leave me many hours before my assignment times out." She bit her lip. "I can't time out, Ti."

Titus stood, enjoying how Rae's pupils dilated at his approach. "Let's hope everything goes to plan."

RAE

"You okay?" Titus asked, scanning the surrounding crowd. "You've been quiet."

She'd brought him to the market, people coming from miles around to shop amongst the vintage stalls and boutiques. It was one of her favourite places, the colour and sounds something she enjoyed. But for some reason when she looked at all the colourful stalls, the art installations and restaurants, she felt... bleak.

"I'm fine," she said, brushing her fingers against a brass tankard, yanking her hand away when she realised the guy selling it wanted over fifty quid. "There's a pickup spot not far from here. I've had someone grab my Ravyns from the guild, hopefully enough to cover Miles's money."

He hitched his rucksack higher on his shoulder, brought from his place. "I've already moved your brother to a safehouse."

"You've done what?" Rae stopped to stare at him. "Why would you do that? You keep doing shit like this, taking charge of a situation you have no right to control. You need to release him. Now."

"I'm not going to hurt him." He looked disgusted at the idea.

"And how do I know that?" she asked, realising she'd raised her voice when a few people turned in their direction. She tugged on his t-shirt, pulling him to the side. "This is supposed to be between us, he's not collateral, Ti. I don't want him in a safehouse organised by a man I've tried to kill."

"I've already said that I'm not going to hurt him."

"Yeah, *you're* not going to hurt him. But what about your brothers?" Anxiety wrapped around her lungs, filling them with cement. "I'm not going to believe you helped me from the kindness of your fucking heart. Everything you do is for a reason."

His brows pulled together. "Not everyone is against you."

They stood beside the open-air pub, the large projection screen strung between two trees displaying a live football game. A goal was scored, and Rae waited until the roar of the supporters died down before she continued.

"Actually, they are." She dropped her voice to a whisper. "Look, just because you're great with your fingers doesn't mean I trust you."

"What exactly have I been getting from this arrangement? Considering I'm doing everything for a reason, apparently."

"You're such an arsehole. Is that really what you're getting from this conversation? If you didn't want to take what I offered, that's not my problem, doesn't change the fact I can't trust you."

"You're a fucking brat," he growled, fire in his eyes. "You have no idea what it's like to keep calm around you."

"I never asked you to keep calm, in fact I *begged* you not to."

That fire glowed, the red in his irises brightening like embers. "Enough, Rae."

"I'm sorry, *sir*. If you don't want to fuck me, that's fine. I can get it somewhere else."

She didn't see him move, at first he was standing there, and then she was trapped against the tree, hands framing her face.

"I've already told you," he said, his lips so close to hers she could almost taste him. "You're mine. Let anybody else touch you, and you'll see why you were hired to kill me in the first place."

Rae ignored the heat throbbing in her lower belly, angered by the response. "You need to stop doing this shit."

"Doing what?"

"Pretending like you're this fucking hero." Rae controlled the growing panic. "I'm not a damsel, Titus. I live with my choices."

He released her, and she instantly mourned his touch. "Let us do what you need, and then I'll take you to see him."

"How? We can't risk going to a safehouse. But that doesn't matter, because Miles may be safe now, but what about next week?"

"We'll make it work."

"Again with this *we!* Just tell me where he is Ti, I need to know where he is."

"Rae, look at me." He tilted her jaw. "Miles will be safe, I won't let anything happen to him. I promise."

"You see, this is why I can't trust you. Why would a man I'm assigned to kill do that?" Her voice cracked. "Winter should have made the drop off by now." She wanted to run, the urge growing. He made her feel exposed, weak, something she couldn't afford to be.

He seemed to sense her change, not pushing her for more. "Lead the way."

Rae choked down the emotions, moving towards the edge of the market once more. "I just... I have to pay off the loan sharks, I'll figure out everything else after."

"How many times has he done this?" Titus asked when they'd come to the edge of the market. The area quieter, the surrounding restaurants and shops swallowing the crowd.

"Enough." More times than she'd cared to count. "But he's my brother."

"That's not an excuse for him to treat you like shit." Titus easily kept pace, walking beside her as she found the small gap between the bollards, descending the concrete steps into the underground multi-storey car park. The lights above flickered eerily, if they worked at all. The majority of the space was covered in shadows, the security strips, along with the cameras long broken. Only a handful of cars were parked on the level, the lack of light uncomfortable for many, and the exact reason the guild used it for drop-offs.

"He's family." Rae stopped walking, spinning so fast he almost bumped into her. "You don't turn your back on family." She ignored the sour taste settling on her tongue. "He's all I have."

Titus looked like he wanted to say more, but instead she crouched, counting the bricks along the wall until she reached her favourite number. Gently removing the correct one, she found a black bag hidden behind. Every Ravyn she'd earned through the guild wasn't hers, and even after three years since she was first contracted for Crimson Hollow, she'd only ticked twelve kills against her one hundred.

But there was the money she'd been able to take from private hits she'd kept, hiding it from everyone. She was paid mainly in pounds, giving her a little sense of independence along with her small allowance. But some were in Ravyns, and those were the hits she sought after, even if they were few and far between.

Opening the bag, she counted each small, black opal coin carefully. Thirty-five thousand Ravyns, that was all she'd been able to save when her contract was ten million, not including interest. She was stupid to believe she'd ever have been able to buy herself out.

"If I don't break out of my contract soon," she whispered, more to herself. "I don't think I'll ever be free of it."

"We're going to figure it out." Gentle fingers along her jaw, tilting her head up. "I promise."

"Again with the *we*," she said, hating the vulnerability. "Why? You don't owe me anything."

"Because we all make bad decisions, and you don't deserve to be punished for protecting your brother."

Rae closed her eyes, opening them when Titus squeezed slightly. "I'm not a good person."

"Neither am I." Titus shook his head. "But 'good' is a

perspective. The choices I make are for what I believe is good, but someone else might consider cruel. We don't live in a world of black and white, Rae. There's no such thing as good or bad, only grey."

"Why do you have to make this so fucking hard?" she snarled. "Jesus Christ." Stepping back, she quickly scanned the stairs. "You only have a few minutes."

His eyes hardened. "Rae, what have you done?"

"I wasn't thinking straight, I just –"

A bullet hit the car, shattering the rear window.

They both ducked, Titus dropping his rucksack to pull her beneath him before returning fire.

"Please," she said, lifting her skirt for her own pistol. "Run."

He crouched low, barely reacting to the bullets that buried themselves in the wall.

"I fucked up." Guilt twisted her into a knot. "Please, just... I'll distract her so you can get away."

"There's no assignment." Titus concentrated on whoever was shooting, jaw clenched. "I've removed myself from the system. I'm no longer a paid hit."

His words echoed in her ears. "Impossible. My mark's still active." Something cold and solid settled in her gut. "Wait, why didn't you just delete me?" Her heart hurt, the ache of being left behind. Again. "You could've fixed it, fixed all of it. That was the deal."

"What fucking deal, Rae? Look where we are." His eyes were harsh when they settled on hers. "Now, are we running, or fighting?"

Rae squeezed her gun, aiming it at his head. "I should shoot you," she said, utterly calm despite the rage surging through every muscle. "It'll give me time."

Titus didn't even blink. "Yeah, but you won't."

Her hand wavered. "Why not?"

"Because you don't want to be the monster you think you are."

CHAPTER 22

TITUS

Titus remained perfectly still. His mate had been backed into a corner, and just like an animal, she was acting on pure instincts.

Mate. He'd called her his mate. *Fuck.*

His heart boomed inside his head, blood a rush in his ears. He needed to return his attention to the contractor, but he knew he couldn't drop the eye contact. Not until she'd decided.

Death had looked him in the face more than once, but he'd never witnessed such devastation. She was feral. Powerful. Beautiful. And if she decided to shoot him, choose herself, he'd die knowing his mate was fucking incredible.

"I hate you," she whispered, lowering her arm, only to direct her gun over the car. "I'll keep him distracted, you go around the back and take her out. Don't kill her." She didn't wait for a response, bursting to her feet.

Titus shoved himself in the opposite direction, the bullets following Rae who'd moved from behind the car a fraction faster. Thirteen, that was how many shots were fired in total, and from the sound of the discharge, and the size of the holes, Titus guessed a pistol. Which meant there were likely only a few more left in the magazine before whoever was fucking shooting would need to reload. If they didn't have a second gun at their disposal.

Using the parked cars as cover, Titus made his way around, turning the darkness to his advantage. The underground carpark was poorly lit, and unless the contractor was a vampire, they'd struggle to see either of them in the shadows.

"Stop!" Rae shouted, her voice echoing off the concrete. "I call it off!"

Titus moved closer, his boots silent. He recognised the fucking witch crouched behind the half wall, his back pressed to a parked van. He didn't sense Titus approaching, not when Rae was shooting every few seconds each side of where he was hidden, pinning the witch to the spot.

Titus lifted his gun, putting the barrel to the side of his head. "Drop it," he said calmly, gesturing to the weapon. "Now."

As soon as the witch had followed the order, he hauled him to his feet by the scruff of his jacket.

"Gerald?" Rae gasped, clearly not who she expected. "How did you find us?"

Titus grunted, muscles tensing as Gerald tried to pull his chi. It felt like a thousand scorpions stinging at once, the venom acid through every vein, spreading to the nerves. His beast roared, ravaging against his mind, desperate to get free of the pain.

"Try that again," he said, pressing his gun harder into the side of Gerald's head. "And I'll redecorate the concrete with your brains."

The excruciating sensation cut off, his chi aching as it recovered.

"What the fuck are you?" Gerald gasped, his body held rigid. "Your aura tastes wrong."

Rae whipped her pistol across his face. "Don't make me repeat the question."

Gerald spat blood. "I was given a –"

"Hey there, Cupcake."

Titus tightened his grip on the witch just as Rae twisted around with a frown.

"Nathan? What the fuck are you doing here?" She dropped her gun slightly. "Where's Winter?"

"Winter's indisposed." He grinned, vivid green eyes settling on Titus. "Got your message though, loud and clear."

"It's been called off."

"That's not how it works, Cupcake." His pupils narrowed to slits, tongue snaking out to taste the air. "But the plan's changed." Quick as a whip he grabbed her arm, pulling her against him with a knife to her throat.

Titus stilled, even his beast going quiet.

"Do you know how much you're worth, Cupcake?" he said intimately against the side of her face. "Isn't that right, Gerald?"

"Fuck off Nathan, she's my assignment," Gerald sneered. "You gave me a bad tip."

"*Our* assignment, but did you really think I would share the fee?" Nathan began to back up. "You're the diversion, you fucking idiot."

Rae grunted, crimson beginning to dribble down her delicate throat, the knife biting into her flesh with every step.

"I told you," he said, nuzzling against the side of her face. "I'd make you pay."

Titus hadn't even realised he'd lifted his arm, not until

he'd pulled the trigger. There was no hesitation, not when he never missed.

Rae didn't flinch when blood splatted across her face. "Ti!" She shoved back, Nathan collapsing with a hole between his eyes.

He heard her voice seconds before a sharp sting throbbed through his thigh. With a grunt he turned, catching Gerald before he could run. Rearing back his fist, his knuckles connected with a crack. The witch slumped, and Titus dropped him to the hard concrete.

Rae stepped over, blood adding to her freckles. Ripping the bottom of her t-shirt, she tore the fabric into strips before using them to wrap around his wound. His blood pumped dark, almost black, soaking the fabric within seconds.

"Fuck, it's bad." She looked up, a panicked edge to her expression.

He knew it would heal, could already tell the bullet had gone clean through. His eyes dipped to the cut along her throat, a growl rumbling up his chest at the sight. Rage pulsed violently through his body, hardening every beat of his heart. The wound wasn't deep, and had already stopped bleeding, but he couldn't stop himself from pulling her closer, wiping the blood from her face, fingers featherlight along her neck. It smeared when she looked down at the snake shifter, a frown marring her brows.

"They were after me, not you."

Titus couldn't find his voice, not while he was fighting the black magic steadily growing inside him, along with the pressure of his beast. He could feel them both, two entities at war with one another, and neither with any hope of winning.

Rae lifted her gun, aiming towards Gerald. "Fucking –"

Titus caught the barrel. "No," he said, his beast projecting a deep rumble.

Her expression was calm when she faced him, waiting.

"We need him alive," he managed to push out. "You can't kill him. Yet."

Titus watched with amusement as Rae shoved her car door open, a frustrated sound leaving her lips.

"You shouldn't have driven," she said for the thousandth time. "You've bled everywhere."

"We stole the van, and that's what you're worried about?" The wrap had loosened, but he could already tell it was beginning to heal. The skin was itchy, tight.

Rae's scowl didn't fade. "Stay here, I won't be long." Slamming the door shut before he could respond, he watched her walk towards the entrance to the shop, his grip on the steering wheel tightening when a man stopped her.

He didn't need to hear the conversation to know what he'd said, his smile sleazy as he took in Rae's short skirt, and bare midriff from where she'd torn her shirt. His beast pressed against the inside of his skin, pushing near to his limits. He hadn't shifted since before the Rite, and he wasn't sure how much longer his beast would give him before he forced his way out.

Even from that distance, he could see Rae's reaction, her head held high as she replied with something harsh enough the man's smile slipped, expression tightening.

Smirking, Titus released the wheel, the leather wheezing. His thigh ached, and he made a mental note to make sure he repaid the same injury to Gerald before he killed him. Resting back in his chair, he tried to stretch his leg, but even with the seat pushed back to its furthest point there wasn't enough room.

They needed to interrogate the witch, and though he

was no longer at risk, until they knew exactly the extent of the hit against Rae, they couldn't stay in one place too long.

A knock on the window, Rae gesturing for him to get out. He slipped from his seat, testing his bad leg on the solid pavement. The muscle protested, but was able to hold his weight just fine as he followed her to the back, and opened the doors.

Gerald lay folded uncomfortably, face pressed against the back of the seats with a sheet covering his body. They'd found plenty of stuff to tie him up with, considering it was a painter and decorator's van. Including a few dirty rags that went straight into his mouth.

"Sit," she demanded with a tone that made him want to bend her over and decorate her perfect arse with his handprint. "Please," she added through gritted teeth.

Sitting himself on the lip and stretching his leg, he waited as she rustled inside the plastic bag and handed him a bar. Accepting it silently he tore into it, the chocolate delicious, the sugar exactly what he'd needed.

Without asking, Rae ripped the makeshift wrap off, revealing the hole in his thigh. The skin looked angry and red, but the wound was definitely smaller already. Not even Riley could heal that fast, another reminder that something inside him had changed.

Each of her movements were angry, rigid as she pulled out bandages, vodka and a clean cloth. He expected to feel her fury when she touched him, but when she took out scissors to open the denim wider, she was gentle.

"You should go to the hospital," she whispered, carefully lining up everything on the plastic. "You could get an infection."

He reached forward, cupping her cheek with his palm in reassurance. It was clear she wasn't used to this, the panic clear in every jerky movement.

"I'm sorry if this hurts." Splashing the vodka onto her hands, she carefully poured it straight onto his leg. He didn't flinch, didn't utter a sound, even as the alcohol burned, sinking into the wound to set it ablaze. Her eyes were desolate when she looked up, vulnerable. He wanted to kiss her, to remove her dark thoughts until there was nothing left but his lips on hers. He didn't enjoy seeing her so exposed, not when he was used to the fire.

"I'm trained not to feel pain," he said, giving her something personal. "It was beaten out of me as a kid."

Rae's expression softened. "Your parents?"

Titus chuckled, the sound empty. "My parents aren't bad people, but they should never have been parents." He'd spent almost his entire life needing their validation, and it had taken him until he was in his early twenties to stop searching for it. "They didn't want me, didn't want the responsibility, so they gave me to an organisation to be trained as a solider." Like an unwanted dog.

"To train you not to feel?" she asked, looking up. "How old where you?"

"Three when they signed me over, but it wasn't until I was seven that they the Order enforced it. Until then it was my grandmother who raised me."

"I don't think I believe it was a grandmother who raised someone like you." Rae laughed. "She must be a lady made from iron."

"Not only me, but my cousin too. He wasn't even blood to her, and she opened her arms as if he was."

"Sam's mate?" At Titus's nod, she continued. "Your grandmother sounds amazing. I'd love to meet her."

He knew she didn't mean to let the second part slip, her eyes widening slightly.

"What about you?" he asked, welcoming the warmth spreading inside his chest.

200

Rae pressed one of the clean cloths to the top of his thigh, leaving it to balance before holding another to the back. "What about me?" she replied, holding both pieces in place. "You heard what Miles said, he thinks I killed our mum."

"He's a prick."

Rae pressed her lips into a thin line. "Can you grab the bandage?" She gestured to the bag.

"Pink?" He raised a brow.

"It was the only one they had left," she said, beginning to wrap the bandage around his leg.

He watched her work, brows furrowed in concentration. He didn't think she would answer, so he made sure he focused on every word when she finally spoke.

"My mother was kind," she said, sorrow frosting her words. "Quiet. She was the sort of woman who'd bless the sun, and then mourn the moon. She wasn't well, hearing voices that scared me as a girl, but she was never cruel. My father, on the other hand, was a monster hiding in plain sight." She checked the bandage, making sure it was tight enough without touching the denim. "The only good thing he ever did was teach me to use a gun."

"Is he dead?"

"Yes." Rae smiled, enjoying her fire that was just on the edge of sanity. "So where are we heading? Or are we sleeping with Gerald tonight?"

Gerald took that moment to groan, the sound muffled through his gag.

Titus moved to stand, the pressure from the bandage helping. "We're dropping your friend off somewhere first, and then we'll figure something out for tonight."

Rae nodded, swiping everything into the plastic bag before moving around to the passenger side. She didn't argue about him driving this time, content to sit there.

"So where exactly is 'somewhere?' Are we not just going to kill him?"

"Not until he tells us what we need." He eyed Rae, her body turned, back against the door so she could watch him openly. Streetlights flashed across her face as they passed, throwing her features into sharp relief. "Do you trust me?"

"No."

Titus smiled. "Good."

CHAPTER 23

RAE

By the time Titus pulled over, it was dark.

Rae eyed the nondescript building, the brick generic and giving no indication what could be inside. The windows were boarded up, a latticed grate covering the wooden planks.

"This would be a great place to kill someone," she said around a mouthful of chocolate. "It's quiet, secluded, and already screams death."

Titus grunted. "My brother's waiting."

"The one with the scary face scar?" she asked, turning in her seat. Titus gripped the steering wheel, his profile highlighted from the dash. "Yeah, he doesn't like me much."

Titus smiled, just a slight curve of his upper lip. "Jax's complicated, but he's someone I'd have protect my back without question."

"That must be nice, to have such loyalty." She nibbled her bottom lip, remembering how Nathan had taken a knife to her throat. *Prick.* "I've never had that, not really. Atlas, Winter, and even the twins were cool, but they were in it for themselves, just like me. Fuck, I can't even trust my own flesh and blood."

A knock on the back of the van, her pulse jumping. She'd never felt so unsteady, not since she was a child at the hands of her father.

"Ready?" he asked, only pulling himself out of his seat once she'd nodded, and even the softening of his face pissed her off, as if he knew she was rattled.

Grabbing his rucksack, she pulled it onto her back, her hand dropping close to her hip, just above her gun. *How times have changed,* she mused to herself. Following the man who she'd tried to kill several times, because he was the only one who could help her.

Desperation was making her stupid.

"Neither of you are Jax," Rae said when they met two guys at the back of the van, already opening the door to reveal Gerald.

The redhead raised a brow, looking to Titus before returning to her. "Kace. He's Marshall." He pointed to the large guy beside him, a cigarette hung between his lips. "Now what the fuck happened?"

"Looks like your boy's been shot," Marshall said, smirking at the bandage. "Pink suits you."

Titus flipped him the finger. "Hudson okay with this?"

"The boss's fine, as long as we clean up after and don't let the kids know." Marshall rubbed his hands together. "Plus he wanted you to take a look at his cyber security. Free of charge, of course."

"Marsh is going to keep your man comfortable until you're ready," Kace said, pulling Gerald out by his feet, only for Marshall to haul him onto his shoulder, the witch groaning.

"Right... comfortable," Marshall snorted. "He'll be singing like a canary soon enough."

Titus reached out for Rae, and rather than pulling away, she pressed into it.

Kace noticed the connection, his irises swirling silver, the same as Titus.

"So you're the brother," Rae said. "Can you all do the creepy eye thing?"

Kace didn't comment, guiding them into the scary building. "Come on, we've set up a side room for you both. The kids aren't due until tomorrow, and Hud's keeping the others away until morning just in case."

"In case what?" Rae asked, following through the large room. Benches had been stacked at the sides, leaving the area open apart from a metal cage. "I'm not going to hurt anyone." What looked like a booth was at the back, partially obscured by a metal shutter.

"In case you're still being tracked," Titus answered. "Not many people mess with Hud, but we still can't risk the kids that live here."

Rae paused by the cage, the inside stained with blood. She'd heard of the cages, how people willingly entered into unsanctioned fights for the chance to win serious money.

"Through here," Kace said, pointing to the door just beyond. "It's not much, but it'll do you for tonight. Riley's organised a room at the Conservation from tomorrow."

"How the fuck did he manage that?" Titus frowned. "It's notoriously membership only, and usually reserved by the dark elite of the Undercity. So how the fuck did Riley get us a reservation?"

"His name." Kace shrugged. "How the fuck am I supposed to know? I've never been interested in staying at that snobby place. He's sent a tux too, and a dress." His eyes briefly touched hers before returning to Titus. "We're going to lock down the unit. You need anything, call. Marsh will be downstairs keeping the witch company." He left without another word, leaving them alone.

"Well, it's bigger than my room back at the guild." Rae

placed Titus's rucksack onto the pull out bed, moving to touch the dress hanging beside the jet black tuxedo. The fabric was stunning, the beading subtle, and she already knew it would hug every curve. She'd never worn anything like it. "You really think they're still tracking me?"

"It's possible." Titus leaned against the wall, arms folded. He watched her move around the room, his attention warming her skin. "It's why we can only stay here tonight, and then tomorrow –"

"Tomorrow we give the Ravyns to my brother," she finished for him. "You release him from the safehouse, and only then do we chat with the Councilman."

"He's not a prisoner, we're not forcing him to stay there."

"Promise me." She turned to face him fully, her shoulders rigid. "I'm giving you my trust, so promise me I can give him the money before anything else. I need to know he'll be okay. Just in case something happens to me."

"Nothing's going to happen to you."

The mark on her sternum ached, the pendant cold against it. "Promise me."

"Fine," he said, the word laced with a growl. "I promise."

Rae nodded, some of the tension leaving her shoulders. "The Councilman, are we going to kill him?"

"Not yet."

"Then what's the point of going if we're not even going to take him out?" she asked, an ember of irritation sparking to life. "Why the fuck am I here, Ti?"

"What do you want me to say, Rae? I didn't plan any of this."

"I want you to tell me why you didn't delete me when you had the chance!" A pressure was building, one she

206

couldn't seem to contain. "This could've been over. A simple button and I could've been free."

"You think I didn't want to?" Titus moved until they were toe to toe. "You know if I'd deleted your information, it would've only caused you more problems. It's not as simple as removing the data, not when you're bound to your guild through some type of magic."

Panic made her tone harsh. "I have nothing left. Everything I have, everything I've worked for I have to give to those fucking arseholes." Her eyes closed, bottom lip trembling. "Why is everything always taken from me? My mum? My childhood? My fucking life? When do I get a choice?"

Titus gripped her jaw, forcing her attention back on him. "We're going to figure it out."

"Again with the fucking 'we'?" She was struggling to breathe, Titus seeming to swallow up the surrounding oxygen. "Why do you even care?"

"Because –"

"Because what? We're nothing, you're just an assignment." Her words sounded weak, even to her.

"I'm not going to let anything happen to you."

Rae hated the single tear that burned down her face. "What are we doing here, Ti?" He seemed so calm while she was steadily breaking apart. She wanted to hurt him, to make him feel the same pain, the helplessness. "I've tried to kill you so many times. I've lied, and yet here you are. So tell me, why do you care so much?"

A slip of his mask, something flashing across those beautiful, unique eyes.

His voice was a growl, a deep rumble that surprised her at its harshness. "Because you're mine."

CHAPTER 24

TITUS

He didn't expect to kiss her, not until he caught her breathy moan, lips crushing hers in desperation. Her nails scraped down his arms, and he was sure she was going to push him away, her anger vicious when she wanted it to be, but instead she pulled him closer. The answer was there, the truth of why the idea of her hurting sent jagged claws though his soul. She was his, and he was finally ready to accept it, even if it meant the end of them both.

"Look what you do to me," he said, lifting her until her legs wrapped around his waist, her pussy pressing against his painful erection. "This wasn't something I wanted."

She cried out, rubbing herself against him. Her pupils were blown, lips parted as she sought out his next kiss. But he wasn't going to give it to her, not yet.

He wanted to devour, tease her until she cursed his name and then begged for more. She pushed him beyond his limits, and yet eventually bowed at his demand in reward of his touch.

"I never wanted a fucking mate."

Desire carved harsh lines into Rae's features. "Not your mate." She yanked at her t-shirt, pulling it off her head as he gripped her hips. "Humans can't mate." Her bra went next, and before the fabric even hit the floor he'd sucked a hard nipple into his mouth, rolling it between his teeth.

She'd look perfect tied up, bent over and spread open. At his mercy. But he didn't have time to do what he really wanted, the need between them intensifying until it seeped beneath his skin.

"Not yet," he said against her breast, scratching her delicate skin with his stubbly cheek.

He knew he should stop, Rae emotionally fraught. But the thought evaporated when her hand sunk between them, stroking his length against the denim. He pushed against her hand, seeking the friction. He'd used her hand to get himself off last time, but it wasn't enough.

Not when the hunger between them was so unyielding.

"Don't I get a choice in this?" she asked, squeezing hard enough he saw stars.

She cried out when he smacked her against the wall, grip loosening until he pulled her hand away. "I've always given you a choice, but it doesn't make it any less true."

He'd never allowed a woman to touch him during sex, not seeing the point when he got off on the domination, but with Rae he craved it. He wanted her fingers through his hair, her lips pushing against his while he spread her around his cock. Fuck, he found he'd started to love her attitude, because it meant he could punish her for it later. And with that pain, came the most intense pleasure.

Mine, his beast rumbled, and Titus finally agreed. There was no more denial, no more excuses. Not when it came to her.

"Please," she begged. "I need more."

He dropped her to the floor, watching how the skin on her breasts flushed pink, how her nipples hardened. "Take the skirt off." He wanted to worship her totally bare, exposed while he remained entirely clothed.

He froze at her teasing smile, at the way she hooked her thumbs in the waistband. She wiggled the fabric down her hips, moving so slowly his body ached from how tight he held it. Her underwear was soaked between her thighs, and before she could remove them he lifted her over his shoulder, smacking her arse with the palm of his hand.

She yelped, legs clenching as they hung down, and he could feel her arousal soak into his t-shirt. As quickly as he'd picked her up, he threw her down onto the bed, her body bouncing for a single second before he was on her, pinning her hands above her head.

"Keep them there, and don't move an inch."

Mischief flashed across her eyes, but biting her lip she nodded. He knew she wasn't going to stay still, not without restraints. The visual alone was enough for his cock to twitch, Rae's fair skin bound tightly in black rope, tight enough it was an abrasion. Every time he moved, every thrust and it would rub her raw, each rope tied specifically for her pleasure.

"I can't wait to see you bound, completely at my mercy."

Rae moaned, pushing her head back against the bed.

He wanted to consume her, revel in her surrender. "Imagine all the ways I could take you, my Rae of sunshine. The ways I could make your body explode, and you couldn't do a single thing except take my cock like a good girl."

She gasped, skin quivering beneath his touch, rippling.

"Use your words," he said against her lower stomach.

"I need you naked," she panted. "Please."

Titus leaned down to lick straight through her fabric covered centre, only for her hips to bow off the bed, seeking more friction. Her cry was beautiful as it echoed around them, and Titus was thankful Marshall was staying with the witch below, that no one else could hear her screams. They were for him, and him alone.

"Don't move." Reaching over his back he pulled off his t-shirt, leaving him in just his jeans, his cock aching against the zip. His second lick was harsher, tongue seeking the wet heat beneath.

"I swear If you don't –"

Her underwear tore, his tongue delving deeper as he licked her with quick, hard strokes. He didn't stop, not giving her a single second's break as he devoured her needy pussy, sucking her clit into his mouth as she cried out, drenching his face.

Her body was coiled, ready to explode, but rather than stroke her through her orgasm, he pulled away. She wasn't allowed a release, instead flipping her over until she was on her front, pushing her up onto her knees. He pressed his denim covered cock against her, leaning over until he could whisper in her ear.

"Be a good girl, and maybe you'll get my cock." Last time he'd forced several orgasms out of her in quick succession, but he knew if he edged her enough, she'd explode so hard she'd forget about everything else but him. Just for the moment.

She panted, pushing back against him. "I said naked."

Titus wrapped her long hair in his fist, bending her back. "Since when were you allowed to make demands?" he whispered against her ear. "You'll get whatever I give you."

She released a sound between a growl and moan, wiggling against him. She was ferocious, chest moving with shallow breaths. He was losing it, the demand to take her growing, his beast insistent about solidifying their union.

He was mated to her, the bond there, a connection that had snapped taut between his soul, and hers well before he'd accepted it. Except she couldn't feel it, feel him. It was driving his beast to violence, fur pressing beneath his skin.

Releasing his erection, he hissed out a breath at the zipper's teeth biting against his swollen flesh. He'd never been so hard, the entire length throbbing as he pressed it between her legs, rubbing his cock along her glistening slit. His head knocked against her clit, his piercings cold against her hot. She stilled at every touch, her body absorbed by the sensations.

"Mine," he said, pinching her nipple tightly between his fingers. "Tell me, Rae."

He slipped his hips back, teasing her entrance with just the tip. He knew the piercing felt good, especially when he angled his hips a certain way, making sure each stroke rubbed against her g-spot. It could bring a woman to orgasm within minutes, but his goal wasn't to let her come. Not until she was a wet mess. Not until she begged.

She tried to thrust back, and he chuckled, dropping a kiss against her shoulder. She wouldn't be Rae if she'd submitted so easily. But when she did, it was a fucking gift. One he intended to thank her for, over and over.

He sunk an inch deeper, listening to her whimper as she stretched around him. He tightened his grip on her hair, angling her head to better wrap his spare hand around her throat, feeling her pulse react to his rough touch.

"Such a pretty pussy," he whispered against her, pulling his hips back, only to sink slightly deeper inside. "And it's all mine." His piercing scraped against her delicate spot, her breathing rapid as he did it again, and again. "Let anybody else touch you," he said to her fevered flesh, her body quivering as it waited to take his entire cock. "And I'll kill them."

He sunk to the hilt, her scream of pleasure placating his beast, at least for that moment. He wasn't gentle, not giving her another chance to get used to his size before he began moving, the zipper of his jeans cutting into her sensitive skin on every thrust, adding a little bit of pain. He'd never been held so tight, her body made to fit his.

"Say it," he said, feeling the first ripple of her impending orgasm. "You're mine."

"I'm yours!"

He waited until she teetered on the edge of bliss before pulling out, releasing her throat and hair at the same time. She fell forward with a cry, hands slapping down onto the mattress. "Titus!"

He loved her like this, hair a mess from where he'd pulled, her face flushed and lips parted. Her thighs were slick with her need, pussy swollen, and there was already a slight mark from his palm. He stroked against the blossoming bruise, knowing he wanted to do it again. Harder. But not then, not when he didn't have the right aftercare.

He had to rip the rest of the denim off, wary of the bandage that still wrapped around his thigh. He palmed his cock, stroking down the length as she pressed her legs together, seeking the final touch for her release. She watched his hand move with a hungry expression, and he had to squeeze to stop himself from coming.

"When you come, it's with your eyes on me." He wanted to see how beautiful she was when she finally broke apart around his cock.

Pulling her back down the bed, he hooked her legs over his arms, opening her to him. She stretched her arms up over her head just like he'd pinned her before, a knowing smile curving her lips.

Bending her in half, his cock so close to where she needed it, he whispered against her lips. "Good girl."

He gave her no warning before he thrusted, her pussy taking him whole. He watched her every expression, felt every twitch of muscle, and gentle ripple around his cock. His hips pistoned in a brutal rhythm, angled perfectly with every lunge. He knew exactly what she wanted, her moans and cries telling him what her body needed.

Her body seized beneath him, her scream cut off from how tight she clenched. She drenched his thighs, the stupid fucking pink bandage and the bed, and still he didn't slow, drawing out her orgasm until she'd found her voice once more. There was no stopping, not until he'd forced at least one more out of her before giving into his.

"Please," she managed to push out, her cries primal as she accepted every inch, and still her pussy begged for more.

"Fucking beautiful." Dropping her legs, he moved to kiss her in a clash of lips and teeth. He pressed a thumb over her clit, chasing the second orgasm straight after the first. His own release coiled at the base of his spine, and only once she'd pulled back, screaming into his ear, did he finally allow himself to fill her.

The sight of Gerald bleeding, face a mess of swollen flesh and dark bruises would've usually pleased him. Except he'd left his naked mate upstairs in bed.

"Let's try this again," he said, holding the hammer between his hands. "Who hired you to kill Rae?"

Gerald coughed, the sound wet. Probably from the collapsed lung. "I've told you all I can, I can't say anymore."

"Can't, or won't?" Marshall asked, smoke from his

cigarette billowing over. "Because the night's young, and we haven't even gotten to the fun equipment yet."

The first thing Titus had discovered was that Marshall gave no shits. He'd happily tortured the witch without a second of hesitation. He'd also realised that after he'd pissed himself, that Gerald wasn't likely to talk.

"Can't!" Gerald cried, saliva and blood dripping from his cut lips. "Please, I can't. If I go to say anything, it doesn't come out!"

Marshall leaned over, pressing the heat of his cigarette to the end of his nose. Gerald screamed, wrists pulling at the metal cuffs attached to the chair. Surging forward he puked, emptying his stomach onto his own shoes. Puke and piss, just two of the reasons Titus never enjoyed interrogation.

"Please!" he said, "I'm telling the truth."

Marshall went to burn him again, but Titus lifted a hand. "You ever heard of anything that could stop him from talking?"

Marshall shrugged, crossing his thick arms across an even thicker torso. "I deal with fuckers who hurt kids, not this. But I guess the idea's not impossible."

Titus thought on it. "Hold his head."

Marshall followed the instruction, Gerald's eyes widening as Titus crouched down in front of him, just out of reach of the puke.

"We're going to play a game," he said calmly, knowing his face revealed nothing of the rage he felt. A break in his armour, but one he wasn't interested in repairing. "I'm going to ask a question, and then a series of answers. You will say yes when I get to the correct one, understood?"

Gerald blinked, letting out a hiss of pain when Marshal pressed his fingers into his skin. "Yes!"

"Good. Now are you magically restricted from speaking?"

Tension bled from his shoulders. "Yes!"

Titus made sure each word was clear and precise. "Was it by a witch?"

"Yes."

"Did this witch hire you?"

A gargled sound, panic widening his eyes. "Can't."

"Do you know how many assassins were hired to kill Rae?"

A hesitant nod. "Yes."

"How many? One?" He waited, Gerald remaining silent. "Two? Three?"

"Yes!"

"Three assassins?" Titus confirmed. The vampire, Nathan and him. And all were indisposed.

"Yes."

"Progress," Marshall snorted. "You think he's telling the truth?"

Titus kept eye contact with Gerald, knowing how uneasy it made people when he showed no emotion. "If he wasn't, I'd let you cut off his cock and feed it to him." Sometimes showing nothing was scarier than showing rage. Rage could be predictable, but a complete void of emotion was the unknown. And the unknown, was fucking terrifying.

Gerald visibly paled. "I'm not lying, please, you have to believe me. The bitch isn't worth it, she's not worth –"

His voice shut off when Titus stabbed down into Gerald's thigh, twisting the blade. Physically having to tell his fingers to release, he stepped back into his original crouch, leaving the knife where it was.

"Now," he began, trying to calm himself. "Were you hired privately?"

A whimper. "Yes."

"To kill her?"

Gerald hesitated, face turning red when Titus stood. "Wait!" He licked at his broken lips. "Not just kill. I had to –" He let out a strangled sound.

"It wasn't just to kill her?"

"No."

"To rape her?" Black rage hazed his vision, Gerald flinching at the change. Arcane burned from his fingertips, the power unrepentant and out of control. He immediately wanted to recall it, struggling to pull the flames as they licked against Gerald's skin. The once white magic had darkened, the black heart spreading.

"Please, stop! It wasn't that! I don't do that!" He began to cry, and Titus finally managed to cut the power, keeping it coiled tightly inside. "Please, no, something else. Ask me something else. It's to do with an... object."

"Object?" Marshall asked. "You had to steal from her?"

Gerald squeaked. "Yes!" His eyes dipped to Ti's throat.

"To steal her necklace?"

"Yes! Fucking hell, yes!" Gerald's cries turned to sobs, breathing frantic as he sucked in large gulps of air. "He... the neckl –!" Gerald spasmed violently, his eyes rolling into the back of his head.

Marsh released his grip, and Gerald tipped forward, silent. "I think he's done, unless you want to go again?"

"No." Titus dragged a hand over his face, stomach churning with nausea. "Keep him alive for now, only Rae's allowed to kill him."

"Understood."

Titus left Marshall to deal with it, queasiness growing until bile bubbled up his throat. Using the bathroom by the cage, he reached the toilet just in time, crashing to his knees as the effluence erupted from his body.

"Fuck the Fates," he said, spitting into the bowl. Moving

to the sinks, he washed the blood from his knuckles before splashing water across his face.

Three assassins were after her, all for a necklace that held very little power.

Frustration made him grip the edge of this sink, the porcelain cracking. "Fuck." Forcing his fingers to release, he stood back, averting his eyes from the mirror. Ignoring the time, he dialled. Xander answered after the third ring.

"You better be dying," he growled down the line. *"It's three in the fucking morning, Ti."*

"I need to speak to Kyra."

"Did you not just hear me? It's fucking –" Rustling, angered whispers before Kyra's familiar voice came on the line.

"Titus, are you okay? What's wrong?" He could hear her concern through the phone.

"Have you heard of a spell that could stop someone from talking about certain subjects?" Kyra was one of the two witches he trusted.

"Like a binding spell? Yeah I've heard of them, but I haven't done one." A pause. *"I think it would require a pretty big sacrifice, you'd probably get more info from Lucifer than me."*

Titus gritted his teeth. "Is there any way to break it?"

"It's not that simple. It depends on the original spell."

Titus eyed the bright pink bandage on his thigh, his back pressed against the cool tile. "If I was able to bring you to the person, would you be able to figure it out?"

"I don't know. It's not something I specialise in, and I don't think Alice does either."

His skin was hot, his stomach rolling. Lurching forward he dry heaved, bringing nothing up but spit.

"Ti, are you okay?"

Titus pushed himself to his feet, wiping a hand across

his mouth. "Fine. Just, can you speak to Lucy about the spell and get back to me?"

"I'm worried about you. Dark magic's difficult to regulate without an anchor, and you haven't been training –"

"Thanks Kyra," he interrupted. "I appreciate it." He hung up before she could continue, not needing to be reminded that he wasn't strong enough to handle the magic. He'd attended the training, did everything that was asked of him and more. He'd proven himself stable enough to go back on rotation, even if it was with babysitters. He didn't need to be constantly monitored, everyone waiting with bated breath for him to explode.

He'd survived the ritual.

He'd survived the Rite.

He would survive the power imbalance.

Waiting until his gut had stopped doing somersaults, he made his way back to where Rae waited. The noxious magic was still there, just beneath his fingertips. It polluted his very essence, constantly fighting against him.

She was exactly where he'd left her, fast asleep on her side with her fiery hair wild across the pillow. She was gloriously naked, just a thin sheet covering her hips. He paused by the side, her face relaxed, content.

He shouldn't have reacted so violently with Gerald, not when he was always cold, calm. Able to close off his emotions until he felt nothing. It made him perfect at his job, able to detach himself from any situation. Even after he'd recovered from the Rite, he was still able to recall his arcane, even if it was more powerful than he'd ever held. And even though his earlier rage had been biting, he shouldn't have lost the grip on his magic again.

But he had lost it, and in that split second the black magic forced itself through his chi, pushing past his mental barriers with an ease that terrified him. He hadn't called his power, and yet he'd lost control.

He didn't lose control.

Except when it came to her.

Rae was his weakness, and as he slipped between the sheets, her body warm as she pressed against him with a gentle exhale, he found he didn't care as much as he should.

CHAPTER 25

RAE

Rae twisted her hands in her lap, feet resting on the bench as she perched on the back. "How much longer?" she asked, probably for the second or third time.

"They're still on their way," Titus said, scanning the area.

Rae nodded, pulling her bottom lip in between her teeth, fiddling with her pendant. She knew they couldn't go to where Miles was staying, not being able to risk the safehouse until they were one hundred per cent sure it was safe. But she couldn't control the biting nerves, unable to calm herself until she'd given Miles every penny she had.

Titus didn't understand that she couldn't simply choose her family, not when Miles was her blood, her brother, and if he left, she'd be alone. It'd been just them since even before their parents died, forced to look out for each other. Whether it was simply a warning for when their father was on his way home, or having to take care of their mum when she was having one of her episodes. It was always the two of them against everything else.

Their relationship had been struggling since she'd

moved into the guild, a growing bitterness between them that she couldn't seem to fix. But that didn't mean she didn't love him.

Her mother's necklace cut into her palm, but she still held it tight, like it was a lifeline. The wind wrapped around her bare legs, leaving goosebumps in its wake. It wasn't like she had a chance to pack spare clothes, and she didn't want to ruin the dress before the gala. At least Titus had given her one of his t-shirts, the look close to obscene considering it almost hid her skirt. The fabric was warmer, but not enough against the cold.

Moving the bag closer beside her, she watched Titus constantly searching the area, always alert and on watch. She'd slept like the dead, waking to find herself draped against him. She wasn't sure what had happened last night, something changing between them.

His head turned, eyes meeting hers. He didn't move, but the tension grew strong, hot to the point she no longer felt the cold. Something had definitely changed, and she wasn't sure if she was ready for it or not.

"Get the fuck off me!"

Rae jumped up at her brother's voice, grabbing the bag just as he appeared.

"I said get the fuck off me!" Miles snarled, his arm held by a man who looked like he belonged on a high fashion magazine cover. Except his lips were pinched, expression frustrated.

He released his grip, and Miles stumbled before regaining his balance.

"You fucking –"

"Miles!" Rae ran the short distance, wrapping her arms around his middle. "You okay? Are you hurt?"

His arms tightened around her for the shortest time before he shoved, creating a cushion of air between them.

"What's the –?"

A sharp sting across her cheek. Her fingers hovered over where he'd slapped her, not the first time he'd resorted to violence. But the first in front of Titus.

Miles cried out, pinned to his knees with a gun pressed to his head. He looked at her expectantly, his tone on the edge of desperation. "Rae, stop him!"

The slap had been audible, but unlikely to leave a long-term mark. "Let him go," she said, meeting the unflinching gaze of Titus. "Please."

He released her brother, and Miles launched to his feet. "What the actual fuck?" he hissed. "Why did you get your barbarians to kidnap me?"

"I never –"

"You didn't seem to be complaining at the time," the man with the model face said, taking his place next to Titus. "In fact, I remember you being relieved, weeping like a child."

"Fuck you," Miles growled, pointing his finger and moving until he'd placed her between the two men. "Rae, what have you done?"

"Me? I'm just trying to keep you safe!" she said, taken back by his hostility. "What else was I supposed to do? You keep messing with the wrong people."

Miles bared his teeth. "Don't treat me like a child!"

"Then stop acting like one!"

His face twisted, bloodshot eyes flickering between Titus, the other man, and then Rae. Licking along the bottom lip his attention dropped to the bag. "That my money?" He reached for it, but Rae stepped back, just out of reach.

"This is everything I have."

His expression hardened. "Give it to me, I have to pay Angel."

"I know." A weight settled on her shoulders, so heavy she was almost crushed beneath it. "There's thirty-five thousand, take it all and use the extra to help yourself." She held out the bag, and he snatched it out of her hand. "Please, just stop making stupid decisions."

He shoved the bag into his coat pocket, folding his arms over his chest. "You're not better than me, so stop acting like you're on some pedestal. Do you know how many people I've had to pay off who wanted to use you like a common whore?" His eyes dipped to her bare legs, and then towards Titus. "Although, looks like you're doing it fine by yourself."

"Careful," Titus warned, but remained where he was.

Miles's gaze could cut glass. "Do you even know who they are, Rae? What they're capable of?"

"Miles –"

Forced laughter interrupted her. "You're fucking everything up, but I don't think I give a shit anymore." He rocked back on his heels. "You say it's me who makes stupid decisions, but I'm not the one who so easily agreed to kill people."

"That was for you, I didn't have a –"

"Choice? You left me, Rae. You have no idea what I've done to protect us over the years. The shit I've had to do, the sacrifices I've made. And yet as soon as you were offered a way out, you took it without hesitation."

"They were going to kill you!" she screamed, no longer caring who overheard. "What did you want me to do? Sit back and watch them murder you? You're all I have!"

Miles shook his head, taking a step back. "It should have been me who joined the guild, not you. You took that from me, because you're a selfish bitch who doesn't think about anyone else but herself. That was my way out, a way for me to take back my life, and instead the golden child stole it from me."

Rae had never felt so numb. She could no longer feel the wind, or Titus pressing a reassuring palm to the small of her back.

"That's enough," she said, her tone obstinate. "I love you, but I'm not your punching bag. Go give Angel his money, and then I'm done."

Miles's shoulders tightened, jaw set. "What do you mean you're done? I'm your brother, you can't just be done!"

"I can't do this anymore." Her voice was soft, gentle compared to the fury simmering inside. "I don't think there's anything I can do to convince you that I'm anything but evil, and do you know what? That's on you, not me."

Miles looked younger, weak when his green eyes met hers. "You'll regret this." There was no threat in his words, just arrogance. "Mum would be disappointed."

"Maybe." Rae clenched the pendant, her arm trembling. "But she's not here to ask, is she?"

His eyes glistened, wet, only to harden when they looked over her shoulder. Without a word he turned on his heel, and Rae watched as her brother left.

TITUS

His mate was in pain, and there wasn't anything he could do.

'Her brother's a real pain in the arse,' Axel said inside his mind. *'I swear I'm never doing babysitting duty again, not even if its family.'*

Titus allowed Rae a minute to recover her emotions, her body trembling slightly as she watched her prick of a brother walk away. She'd held herself with such strength, his beast beaming with pride.

"How's Lǎolao?" he asked, wanting to bring her into the conversation. She turned her head at his voice, face composed, but he saw the fire there, simmering gently.

Axel eyed her, but dropped the mental link. "Being difficult. She hasn't said a word to your parents. But they want to speak to you."

"They'll have to wait." It wasn't like he'd ever been their priority.

"Your parents were at the safehouse too?" Rae asked, eyeing him curiously. She was always asking him questions about his life, about his family. Before he didn't want her to know anything more about him, but now it was different. Now, she was his. "And Lǎolao, our grandmother."

Rae flicked her eyes to Axel, and Titus found himself tensing, wondering if she noticed how perfect his face was. How he was used to people begging for his attention, even if he wasn't interested. Jealousy twisted his gut, but he shot it down before it could grow into anything else.

"So you're Sam's mate," she asked with a small smile.

Titus pulled her against his chest. He expected some resistance, but instead she pressed her cheek against him more firmly, right above his heart.

Axel blinked, lips pursed. "Fucking hell, I've only been gone a day. How much have I missed?"

CHAPTER 26

RAE

It wasn't lost on her that the only time she'd ever had to dress up and attend a posh event was under a false pretence.

The dress she'd been given was jet black, a size too small with a slit on the left side that was a few centimetres shy of indecent. The neckline was high, modest, and paired perfectly with the floor length, bare backed design. It hugged every single curve, and while it was beautiful, she'd never felt so fake in her entire life.

She wasn't someone who wore evening gowns, definitely not with such pristine makeup and hair elegantly styled around her shoulders. Well, she wasn't until she'd noticed Titus's expression. She'd stepped out of the small room to find him waiting, eyes hungry, ruthless in their thoroughness as he'd leisurely took in every inch of her. As if she was a temptation he could barely resist.

So clearly evening gowns were now her thing.

"You ready for this?" he asked, his profile obscured by the shadows in the limousine.

She'd never been in such a long car, either. She

suspected the night was going to be full of firsts. "Born ready."

Titus had been quiet for the majority of the ride, turning only to respond to Riley who'd given them a brief rundown on what was to happen. They were allowed to approach Councilman Edwards, but they weren't allowed to kill him. Not tonight, at least.

Rae wanted to protest, but Titus had been edgier than usual, even though his expression revealed nothing of the sort. She was slowly learning to read his subtle cues, the slight tightening of his lips or jaw, the narrowing of his eyes or the grip in which he held her.

He was about to find his answers, and then whatever was between them was coming to an end. Because she wasn't his mate, and no cock, even one as magnificent as his, was going to change that.

The cool steel of her favourite dagger was the sole comfort as they pulled up after an hour to white flashes of cameras, each so startling in their brightness. Her dress was too fitted for a gun, but the knife was fine against the front of her thigh, the delicate beading concealing the outline, and with the high slit she'd have easy access.

The door opened, and Riley stepped out to the thunder of the paparazzi. Titus was next, the photographers just as excited despite not knowing his name. She couldn't really blame them, not when Titus was hot with a capital H. His dark blonde hair framed his freshly shaved face, bringing out his sharp cheekbones and beautiful eyes. Add the tattoos that swirled up his throat and covered his hands, the metal rings through the centre of his bottom lip and nostril, plus his uninterested expression, he was bad boy personified.

Rae paused when it was her turn, not used to the attention. Titus held out his hand, sensing her hesitation. Taking a breath, she stepped out of the car, thankful the heels she wore fitted perfectly. His hand slipped to the bare skin of her back, and she wanted to think she only allowed his possessive touch because they were in public. But in reality, she was beginning to crave his skin against hers. He was a warmth against the hollow void left by her brother.

Salty wind whipped at them, the shouts and calls nothing but a wild buzz as Titus guided her down the red carpet, Riley by her other side.

"Lots of media for a charity event," Rae said, eyeing the sea of men and women waiting behind the rope.

"Normal for this particular gala. Children of the Moon's a large charity, and the yearly event always brings the top elite and celebrities. It's usually at the Grande Hotel back in the city, but this year they've moved it to the coast," Riley answered before turning to Titus over her head. "Xander and Kyra are already inside."

"Who's Kyra?" A camera snapped right in her face, capturing her frown for eternity.

"Someone who shouldn't be here." Titus's clenched his jaw, the only sign of aggravation. "I don't need –"

"She insisted," Riley growled, his smile revealing nothing as he continued to nod towards the photographers, clearly an expert compared to her. "Said she had something to give you."

Fingers pressed against her back. "Titus?" she whispered his name in question. He simply shook his head, guiding her to the restaurant at the very edge of the cliff.

The gala had stripped back the décor to reveal meticulously cleaned oak flooring, ostentatious gold edged tables and matching chairs, all moved to the sides, allowing a large space in the centre. A stage had been set up by the large windows overlooking the cliff, a podium along with a speaker waiting for the event to start. Two posters and a single pop-up stand were displayed for the charity, including a sign on how to donate.

"How much is it to attend this sort of thing?" Rae asked when she noticed the thankful notes left on each table.

"Six thousand per plate."

Fuck. Me.

"What are those?" She subtly gestured to the large orbs that clearly didn't match the decor, one in each corner of the restaurant.

It was Riley who noticed. "They're anti-magic devices designed to block your connection to your chi."

"Which means..." Rae waited.

"It means magic bearers cannot call their magic," Titus said. "It feels like a pressure, more annoying than anything."

"Oh." Rae couldn't feel that, unable to connect to her chi anyway. "Well, they're eyesores."

Rae expected more from a charity as widely known as the Children of the Moon. The organisation was one of the largest in Europe for helping young children who suffer from life-threatening illnesses caused by the vampira virus, and one of the richest if she was remembering correctly. Not that her knowledge in conditions caused by freshly turned vampire daddies fucking human mummies and causing sick children was particularly vast.

The view was the best part of the entire thing, the sun setting in a burst of pink and orange, reflected against the vicious waves that crashed against the cliff below.

Titus stiffened beside her, his head cocked towards Riley. They didn't speak, but their eyes were fixed, direct.

"What?" she asked, nudging him in the side.

"We didn't expect the entire Council," he said, leaning down to whisper in her ear.

"Does it matter? We're only here for one."

His breath was hot against her face. "No, it doesn't. As long as we play this carefully."

Rae pressed her lips together, biting back her retort. She scanned the crowd of snobs, stopping at a young girl not much older than fourteen. Her hair was a dark curtain that fell to her mid back, skin paler than even herself. She stood so effortlessly still, a statue who watched everyone with a dark gaze. A man stood at her side, equally uncomfortable.

"Valentina and her Soldier," Riley said when he noticed her line of sight. "She holds the seat for the vampires. The man beside her is Danton, an Elder." He stopped a passing waitress, grabbing three glasses.

Rae frowned. "She looks like a child."

"Don't let that fool you," Titus said, his grip tightening on her. "She's old, and has had her seat the longest. Don't ever meet her eyes."

"I thought that was a rumour?" She'd asked Atlas about it once, and he'd simply laughed, explaining he'd never been able to hypnotise anyone.

"There's usually a grain of truth in rumours and myths," Titus said, pulling Rae against his chest. "You think there's disruption amongst the Council?"

Riley handed out the glasses, and Rae tipped half it down her throat before they'd even taken their first sip. "When is there not?" He gestured to a tall faerie with lavender eyes. "That's Liliannia, she holds the seat for the entire Fae."

"The guy hiding in the corner's Xavier," Titus added. "He's –"

"For the shifters." Rae could see it in the way his body was tightly coiled, the barely controlled predator behind his single eye. The other was permanently closed, a ragged scar across the lid. Every few seconds claws would pierce through the end of his fingertips before being retracted.

"Xavier never comes to these, not unless he gets something out of it." Riley pursed his lips. "Cassiel's the guy with the wings, and I'm yet to meet the new woman who represents the witches and mages."

"Okay." Rae quickly looked over Cassiel, his presence loud and boisterous as he soaked up the flattery. Her pendant warmed against her breast, but she ignored it. "Don't you think it's weird that humans have never been represented on the Council?"

Titus frowned down at her. "Humans have a separate governing body."

"That's my point." Rae finished her champagne, placing it on one of the tables. "The peace treaty's over three-hundred years old. You'd think by now we'd all be seen as equal."

"Humans out populate us six to one," Riley said. "Does that seem equal?"

"Says the guy represented, and not seen as inferior, or weak just because we can't light a birthday candle with a finger. It's stupid supernatural society bullshit." She frowned, biting her bottom lip. "So which one of these lucky fuckers is Edwards?"

"Yet to make an appearance." Riley lifted his hand, a man with the palest blue eyes she'd ever seen walking over with a beautiful woman on his arm, her brown skin kissed by the sun. Her long, dark hair was tied tightly in a braid, gently draped over her shoulder to blend into the black of a dress not too dissimilar to Rae's.

Her smile was a little forced when she approached, the man beside her not bothering with any friendliness. Those pale eyes assessed her as if she were a venomous snake, only skirting away when Titus growled.

Guess he knows who I am, she thought. *And what I do for a living.*

"And who are you?" Rae asked, surprised at her own hostility.

The woman flipped her braid over her shoulder. "I'm Kyra, and this is Xander."

Xander said nothing, his eyes set hard on Titus. "I'm Rae."

"I've been looking forward to meeting you." Kyra's smile widened, the sentiment more genuine. "So, I've spoken with Lucy," she continued. "And he agreed that without knowing the original spell it would be difficult to break."

Rae frowned when Kyra rustled in her small clutch bag, pulling out a small disk. A dried red smear darkened the wood, and Rae knew exactly what it was.

"Why do you need a charm?" she asked, turning in Titus's grip.

Kyra flicked her eyes between them. "It's for the witch? The one with the bound tongue?"

"Witch?" Something cold and hard settled against her chest. "You spoke to Gerald? Without me?" She stepped out of his reach, knowing the only reason she could, was because he'd let her. "When?"

Titus frowned. "Rae –"

"When?" she repeated, heat burning against her cheeks. It must have been when she'd slept. "I need a minute," she whispered, the anger so palpable she could feel it spread like wildfire.

Titus reached out to her wrist.

"Touch me again, and I'll make you regret it." There was no emotion behind her threat, just honest truth.

He released her, and she immediately made her way to the outside terrace that wrapped around the side of the restaurant, needing to feel the cool air against her fevered cheeks.

The sea crashed and spluttered, the rhythm of the

motion the only thing able to calm her down. Titus seemed to be the only man who'd ever really understood her, the only one she'd shared her history with, and yet, he still went behind her back. The pain wanted to bury deep, until it settled against her soul and festered into something dark and unforgiving. It hurt, more than it would have if he were anyone else. And that terrified her, that he had that power.

Curving her hands over the barrier, she stared out into the distance, the metal cold beneath her palms. Solid. She counted in her head, knowing he wouldn't give her the minute she'd asked. He wasn't used to anyone like her, someone who'd fight his every demand, who wouldn't step back and let him take charge. His response was actually something she loved because it made him easy to tease. His expression rarely changed, but she lived for his biting words, said with such velvet authority she wanted to see how far she could push. How far she could take him before his calm façade cracked. Because it was a façade, his anger running so deep she felt the ache. He was fighting against himself, even if he wasn't ready to admit it.

A presence behind her, and she didn't need to turn to know who it was, her body attuned to him like a fucking stalker.

"You had no right," she said to the wind. "He was after me, not you."

"I left him alive. I thought you'd want to kill him yourself."

She waited for him to step beside her, but instead he pressed against her back, one hand settling beside hers, and the other stroking up her arm, over her shoulder until it palmed the side of her throat.

"You think that makes it better?" she asked, pressing back against his heat. She hated the way he made her body feel, the way she desired his touch. Even his fingers pressing against her pulse. Pushing. Possessing.

"No." His voice was a deep rumble, his grip tightening beneath her jaw to angle her head, lips pressing against her skin. "You fucking confuse me, Rae. I don't know whether to fuck, or punish you most of the time." His hand eased against her throat, and hers slipped beneath her dress.

"You shouldn't have done it." She spun, her dagger pressed against his cheek. It didn't break skin, but she was tempted, wondering what he'd look like with one of *her* marks on him instead. "You didn't see me as an equal."

He pressed closer, a line of red glistening along the blade. "I was protecting you."

"From who?"

"From me."

Rae didn't release the pressure, knowing if she gave an inch, he'd take a mile. "Bullshit."

"I almost killed him before I could finish the interrogation. I lost my temper. I don't lose my temper. Ever." He pressed against the sharp blade. "Ask me why, Rae."

She thought about disobeying, and in that split second, she could tell he thought she would too. "Why?"

"Because my fucking heart seems to beat for yours, despite everything."

"Ridiculous," she whispered, the wind whipping her hair, the violent crash of the waves below a perfect metaphor. "How can you forgive me so easily?"

"What's to forgive? You do what you have to, to survive." His expression was intense. "But the thought of him, or anyone else hurting you makes me want to destroy the fucking earth." His eyes swirled liquid silver, the colour fascinating and beautiful at the same time. Except in a blink something else looked out, something dangerous, predatory.

"I'll torture, maim, and fucking annihilate anyone who thinks they can hurt you."

Rae tried to swallow past the rushing emotions, her lungs under strain each breath a struggle. "You think that scares me?" She finally pulled the blade away, studying the straight scarlet mark down his cheek.

"Yes." The cut stopped bleeding instantly, and within a few seconds it had healed entirely. "I think it terrifies you to let someone close, because all you've known is disappointment."

"Stop it." Her voice cracked.

"But that doesn't matter." Titus pushed forward, backing her up against the barrier. "Because I've already told you, you're mine."

CHAPTER 27

TITUS

He'd fucked up. He knew he'd fucked up from the way Rae's face had hardened, eyes empty when she'd turned away. She was always so open, her every emotion clear like one of his favourite books. So raw in her reactions, so chaotic that seeing her close down like that had panicked him. Panicked his beast.

"Not yours," she said, tone not so acerbic. "This is just sex."

He'd fucked up by interrogating Gerald alone, taking that away from her, and it wasn't a mistake he'd repeat.

"Mind blowing sex."

Her upper lip quirked, painted a startling red, the same shade as her hair. "You have a high opinion of yourself."

"You're not denying it though."

A laugh, her usual fire returning. "Men and their egos. You think I'd drop everything for some good dick?"

No hesitation. "Yes."

Her eyes narrowed, seemingly to wait for him to continue. "Hilarious," she finally said, dragging her fingers though her hair, trying to tame the strands against the wind.

"This is fucking crazy," she muttered. "This was never supposed to happen. *You* were never supposed to happen."

"And yet here we are."

"You're just an assignment. Once this is over, you'll be gone, and I'll be right back to where I was. Well, with less money, and probably a different guild."

"You really believe that this has an expiry date?" He forced himself to give her space, to not bracket his hands on the barrier, trapping her in between. "I say we need a new truce, one where we don't try to kill each other."

"You want another truce?" She shook her head, flipping the dagger in her hand. "You sure have a death wish." She was teasing him, he knew it from the way her eyes glistened, the way her lip twitched.

Titus couldn't keep himself back any longer, reaching forward to cup her jaw. "I'm sorry about interrogating Gerald without you. It won't happen again."

She pursed her lips, disbelief darkening her eyes.

"You're not some princess to keep locked in a tower." He tilted her head, thumb sliding between her lips. "You're not even the knight. You're the fucking dragon, queen of the ashes."

She bit his thumb, not hard, but enough for him to feel her teeth.

"Do that again," he whispered, lips feathering over her ear. "And I'll bend you over my knee in front of everyone."

His cock hardened at her reaction, her tongue licking against the small hurt as her pupils dilated simply from his words. She may have protested at being his mate, but he knew she was addicted to him, as he was to her.

She pressed her ridiculous blade against her red lips, still stained with his blood. "Try it Mr Liu Wood, and we'll see who survives this dance between us."

Taking the dagger from her fingers, he dragged the flat

side against her leg, drawing it up her thigh until he placed it back into its sheath.

He hated to break the tension between them, the intimacy and trust that was slowly building. But they were there for a reason. "Ready to meet the man who hired you?"

Rae blinked, her earlier arousal disappearing beneath a burst of fierceness that tightened his chest. Reaching for her hand, he walked them both back into the venue, the event having already started while they'd been outside. The guests had grouped together, waiting as the presenter finished setting up on the stage.

He found Riley immediately just past the crowd, Kyra and Xander waiting in one of the corners. But it was the man he spoke to that held Titus's interest, their eyes meeting over Riley's shoulder. Councilman Edwards tensed for the briefest second, professional smile slipping before he recovered.

"Edwards," Titus greeted when he reached their side.

"It's Councilman Edwards," he said with a cutting edge before returning to Riley. "I was just asking Mr Storm where his wife was."

"Mate," Riley corrected him. "Alice's working on a big case, so couldn't attend, unfortunately."

"Mate," Edwards repeated with a look of disgust. "I forget. How barbaric of you. Must be from those beasts of yours."

He felt Rae glance towards him, her hand squeezing his gently in curiosity. He squeezed back, but didn't remove his attention from Edwards.

"I've requested a meeting with you several times," he said to Riley, deciding to ignore Titus entirely. "But you've never responded."

"I've made you aware of the increased activity, that's all I'm required to do."

"I'm your Archdruid –"

Riley bared his teeth. "And I'm not one of your dogs to be called to heel. We don't work for the Order, or for you."

Anger flashed in Edward's eyes, disappearing as quickly as it came. "Thanks for reminding me," he said with cool contempt. "The Guardians seem to have gotten out of hand, you were created by the Order, and yet do not follow your duty."

"We do exactly what we've been designed for," Titus growled.

"And yet," Edwards said with a flash of irritation. "I've heard of the evil you've invited amongst your men." He looked directly at Titus, eyes widening a fraction before stepping back.

'*He doesn't know about you,*' Riley said through his mind, placing himself between them slightly.

Titus kept himself composed. Edwards had noticed the colour of his irises, surprise darkening his own eyes. '*Which meant he likely didn't set the hit.*'

'*Then who the fuck did?*'

'*Someone wanting to use Edwards against us.*'

"I expected decorum from someone of your prestige," Rae said, seeming unable to keep quiet any longer. "Not a pompous prick with superiority syndrome."

"And who exactly are you?" Edward's expression hardened.

Rae's smile was deceptively sweet. "Your worst nightmare."

Edwards went to respond, but a man appeared by his side, the silver 'V' pendant of a Vector glistening on his breast pocket. His head dipped, whispering directly in Edwards ear.

Titus's beast stilled, claws prickling at his mind.

Riley's voice was sharp. '*You sense that?*'

"It seems I'm needed elsewhere," Edwards said, his professional smile slipping back into place. "Until next time."

Heart pumping fast enough to ache, Titus felt his muscles lock, his breathing quickening. The Vector turned his head, and something inside snapped.

There was nothing but crackling, a white noise of incoherent screams that changed in pitch. The face that looked back at him was all wrong, eyes brown rather than crimson, face soft rather than sharp. But it was the same leer that had plagued him for fucking months. The same nightmare repeating, reliving the pain over and over. The man stood, wrinkles creasing his face, and hair peppered with greys. But Titus blinked, his memories merging with reality as he saw someone else, the face angular, auburn hair a straight curtain over his shoulders as he spoke to the Councilman.

Bishop.

One of the fucking Daemons who'd forced him through the Rite.

Destroy him. His beast a snarling monster, locked in his incorporeal state. He had no body, nothing but pure animalistic rage that shot through every muscle, nerve and bone. Urging him to react. To Fight. Kill.

And yet he couldn't.

"Titus?"

His voice was called through water, faraway, muffled. Nothing compared to the cacophony of noise that was assaulting his ears, memories and thoughts all distorted together.

Pain shot through his centre, his heart ready to break from his ribs. And yet he still couldn't move, couldn't breathe.

"Titus?"

A blink, and it was Rae who stood there, her fingers

pressing to his face and directing his notice. Everything surrounding her was a blur, but that didn't matter, not when her lips opened, a sensual wave that moved silently. A strange warmth spread through his chest, quietening the noise until he finally could concentrate.

"Look at me."

Destroy him.

"You need to get back!" Another snapped. "He's unstable."

Rae shot a baleful look to her right, but remained exactly where she was, and his beast released a feral grin at her strength.

She will destroy him.

Power thrummed beneath his skin, lightning at his fingertips as black magic wrapped itself around his throat, constricting, choking until it polluted every struggling breath.

And still, he couldn't move.

"Riley, you need to force an anchor, or syphon his excess before it kills him." A familiar voice, but again not from his Rae. Kyra, his brother's mate.

Xander's harsher tone broke through. "His power's surging, he's about to blow the fucking orbs."

Peaches and cream, Rae's scent calming. He concentrated on her eyes, on the gentle slope of her brow, and on her delicate freckles, peeking through the base of her makeup.

"Come near me again, and I'll cut your pretty face," she hissed over her shoulder, and Titus felt his lips curve. He wanted to sink his fingers into her hair, press his nose against the side of her face, but the arcane had crept up to his elbows, the magical flames dancing against his skin.

Rae didn't care, reaching forward to brush the hair from

his brow. "I thought you didn't have access to your chi? Or are you just showing off?"

"What happened?" he asked, pulling his arms back, away from her.

"I think it was a panic attack," Riley said, touching his shoulder. "If you don't level down, or anchor to someone, I'm going to have to syphon you chi."

His blood iced, not knowing how his beast would react after the sudden episode. "No." He recognised Riley as their Alpha, but that didn't mean he wouldn't just tear through his body in defence of them both.

"Titus –"

"You don't touch him," Rae said, her tone leaving no room for argument. She'd turned to face the others, her hand hovering over the slit in her dress. "I won't say it again."

She was defending him against his own brothers.

Mine.

"I'm fine." Titus tried to recall the power, ignoring the swift queasiness that always accompanied it. It stuttered, a tap he struggled to turn off. But it finally did, the effluence coiling itself back into his chi.

"How long have you been having these attacks?" Riley asked, grey eyes hard. "Why the fuck didn't you tell us you needed support?"

"I've been dealing with it," Titus said through clenched teeth, realising they'd somehow moved him to a quiet corner, the guests all watching and laughing at whatever was happening on stage, none the wiser of the possible explosion beneath his skin.

"Your beast's strangled, Ti. What do you think'll happen when he pushes for fucking dominance? We may not be able to get you back."

Titus bristled at his tone. "We have mutual respect."

His beast understood why they hadn't switched, knew Titus wasn't ready. Not yet. "I didn't exactly expect –"

A loud pop, followed by three more in quick succession.

Titus instinctively twisted to protect Rae.

The orbs had exploded. All of them. Titus had been able to call his magic, but it hadn't been strong enough to shatter one orb, never mind four.

"What the fu –" Both Xander and Riley turned with him at the same time, the floor in the centre of the room breaking, fracturing. Silence, nothing other than the crack moving like a bolt of lightning across the floor, splitting the venue in two.

"Everybody get outside!" Riley shouted, the fissure opening, widening with every passing second.

The crowd finally reacted, shocked out of their stasis. Many scrambled back, screamed, the hole continuing to grow until it swallowed a table, and then began taking the stage.

Rae grabbed at the back of his jacket. "Cliff! We're on a cliff."

Fuck.

"Bishop," Titus managed to push out, fists clenched as he tried to recall the fucking magic. "The Vector was Bishop." He was sure of it, even if he wore a different face.

Something dark brushed across his senses, familiar.

Riley sensed it at the same time, calling arcane to his own hands while Xander pulled Kyra away, pushing her towards the exit.

"Xee!" she shouted, but he'd already exploded into a burst of colour, his powerful beast standing there a heartbeat later. He tore towards the fissure, tackling the hound that had pulled itself from the hole.

"Get everyone out," Titus shouted at Rae, who'd already pulled out her dagger. "Go!"

"I'm not leaving you!" Her expression was severe, and so fucking beautiful in its defiance. She would fight beside him without question, but even she couldn't deal with a Shadow-Veyn.

"Please! Go." He couldn't focus with her there, his beast's concentration already split.

"I swear, if you fucking die," she cursed him, reaching up to slant her lips over his.

He waited until she'd stepped back before summoning his power, the black flames crackling with their intensity. The magic swelled, fighting against him, his stomach rolling from the assault.

He tensed for his own power to attack him, eating away until it left him raw. Magic came from the extension of an aura, the chi, and his was fucking trying to destroy him.

He'd sensed the next hound, it's claws huge as it dragged itself from the fissure. It was twice the size of the first, its usually sleek canine form stockier than expected, pure muscle covered in jet black fur. Its ears were clipped short, spiked with a barb that was repeated along its exposed spine.

It was covered in more fur than any he'd ever seen, even having a complete snout with a nose rather than just an exposed skull with gaping holes. It was as if the Shadow-Veyn were evolving the longer they survived up in the light, compared to being imprisoned down in the dark.

Red eyes rolled loose around their sockets, connecting to his. Titus didn't hesitate, releasing the arcane in a powerful strike that hit true. It seared through the hound, disintegrating everything it touched, killing it instantly. The hound was a Veyn that would usually take two, or even three guardians to take down so quickly, and yet died within seconds using the same magic in which it was likely summoned.

Bile threatened, and Titus swallowed the nausea.

Riley had remained the man, a hound on his back while he fought another at his front. Xander took down the first who'd appeared with his powerful jaws, tearing the hound to pieces as Titus spotted another trying to crawl from the debris.

Four hounds, which meant it was a fucking pack.

The building creaked, tilting. There were a few guests left, a couple dead, their bodies crushed in the panic. They were caught on the wrong side of the fissure, their expressions terrified, flicking between the beasts, the hounds, and the growing gap that would soon leave them stranded.

A flash of red, Rae appearing at their side along with Cassiel. He seemed to freeze when he noticed her, reaching forward with his copper wings held high above his head. Titus was already moving, ready to leap across before a weight knocked him to the side, a hound's teeth snapping at his throat. He caught its bottom jaw, razor-sharp fangs slicing into his fingers as he pulled with all his strength, its breath rotten carrion.

Caught beneath the hound he turned his head, finding Rae exactly where she'd been a moment before, threatening the Councilman for the celestrials with her fucking dagger. She seemed to turn to face Titus at the same time, eyes widening as the hound fought against his hold, shaking his head from side to side.

Cassiel gripped the blade, pulling it from her grasp with little effort and throwing it to the side as if it were a toothpick.

The hound whined above him, skin and tendons stretching before they finally snapped, the jaw hanging loose. Blood splattered across Titus's face, each drop burning as black vapour floated from its exposed ribs to try

246

and repair the damage, the freezing mist leaving pins and needles everywhere it touched.

Rae's face was like thunder, her words not carrying across the distance as she faced off against the large angel. His wings lifted, spread before he disappeared out the side door that led to the terrace. Rae returned to helping people over the fissure, screaming at them when they simply stood there, immobile.

The last person passed safely before there was another creak, electrical cords snapping, sizzling as the floor tilted further, the cliff collapsing beneath them. Rae slipped, sliding until she crashed against one of the windows overlooking the water with her entire weight. The glass spider-webbed around her, blood dripping from her elbows from where they'd hit.

"Rae!"

Titus called his arcane, pulling the black magic that was slowly imbedding itself in his soul to his fist. There was no light left in his magic, the flames pure obsidian. He shoved the arcane through the partially exposed ribs at the hounds side, tearing through bone, muscle and flesh with ease. The hound stilled above him, allowing Titus to throw the fucker down into the crack, the edge crumbling.

He rushed to his feet, but the gap was far too large to jump.

"Don't move!" he shouted, the window beside her cracking further as a table hit.

Rae remained where she was, stuck against the weakening glass. She let out a scream as the far side of the restaurant dropped, the angle so sharp it almost faced the raging waves below.

His heart stopped, knowing that even if he was already shifted, he wouldn't make it, not before the window collapsed.

A white beast at his side, Xander's claws sliced into the wood. Three of his seven tails tried to snap against the fissures edge, but even with his strength, he wouldn't be able to stop the descent. The cliff was collapsing, and there was nothing they could do to stop it.

"Rae, look at me!" She couldn't hear him above the whistle of the wind, the creaking of the building and the fierce sea below.

Black magic tore through his chi, a wrath so hot it scorched, acid burning through every vein as it tried to finally settle against his soul. He needed to stop thinking as if the black magic was a separate entity. His beast wasn't just the one fighting it, he was too.

Riley called his name, shouting from somewhere behind. He'd used his Alpha voice, the one designed to make their beasts respond, but Titus couldn't obey, couldn't look away from his mate.

'Give me a summoning name,' he shouted through his mind. *'Now!'*

Riley's response was instant. *'Are you sure? There's no going back.'*

'Do it.' Titus was no longer terrified of the power that had corrupted his ancestors.

'Then Titus Lui Wood, by the Fates and those who watch above and below, I gift you your new name, Theltuz.'

Titus accepted every dark tendril of power, his entire body seizing under the influence, the rush.

Everything moved in slow motion as the glass finally shattered, little glistening shards a halo around Rae as she began to fall. Titus roared, his body pricking with sensation that pulled him from where he stood, his molecules moving space with a static pop. One second he was standing, watching, and then the next she was wrapped in his arms, both of them soaring towards the stormy sea. The cliff thundered as

248

it began to slide down, half the restaurant separating from the edge to fall along with them.

An intense ache tore from his spine, skin splitting before two weights erupted from his back. Something black in his peripheral, slowing their decline. Gritting his teeth Titus tensed his back, trying to use muscles he didn't have before.

There were no natural instincts, no instant knowledge about what to do. The ache deepened, muscles and tendons straining as he tried to angle their fall, attempting to control their descent. Something snapped at this back, causing them to both twist violently towards the ocean.

He gripped her harder, wrapping his body around hers before they could hit the water.

She was his darkest temptation, and if she was going to fall, he was going with her.

CHAPTER 28

RAE

The ocean was silent, black.

Peaceful until something crashed into the water beside her, a chunk of concrete that sunk deeper as she kicked wildly, not knowing which way was up. Her head breached the surface, and then she was sucking in a great lungful of air.

"Titus?" she choked, a wave crashing against her back, forcing her under, draining her energy with every kick of her legs. "Titus?" she shouted when she resurfaced once more, the sun almost set in the horizon.

The salt burning her eyes, she saw a blurry figure in the distance, closer to the cobblestone beach. Rae used every last bit of strength as she swam towards Titus, his body lifeless despite the sea trying to churn him away. She reached him, the waves pushing them both towards the shore.

Her heels were long gone as she scrambled onto the beach, her dress barely enduring the plunge, never mind the water. She had no idea how she'd survived, the impact should have been like hitting concrete. And she was perfectly fine other than a few bruises, and scrapes. Titus had somehow reached her, protecting her from the fall.

She choked up the seawater she'd swallowed, back arched as she expelled it from her stomach. "Titus?" she managed to cry out, pushing against his shoulder. His eyes were closed, limbs limp against the waves lapping at him. "Don't you dare fucking do this!" She checked his pulse, wary of the twisted lump of flesh and exposed bones jutting from his back.

Wings. He had wings, except the right was almost torn off. They were dark, slick feathers a jet black at the edges only softening to a slate grey closer towards his spine.

A screech tore through the air, and Rae looked back over her shoulder just as the cliff finally fell, crashing into the sea. She watched the building drop, almost moving in slow motion before it hit the water, causing a powerful wave. She waited, the wall of water rushing towards them. She covered Titus's body with her own as it hit with the force of a train, knocking the breath from her lungs as it tried to pull her back into its depths.

She was doing her best to hold on, but failing. The sand was disappearing beneath her along with the water, sucking, pulling with far more strength than she had. Her fingers scrapped against his jacket, trying to find grip before...

Titus gripped her hand, angling his back against the water. "I've got you," he said, his voice several octaves deeper than usual.

Relief almost made her cry, her body shaking as she gripped him harder. "I thought you'd died," she whispered against his salty skin. "You can't do that to me." She never expected such despair at seeing him lifeless, at his face so still. The panic as she tried to find a pulse.

A shadow in the sky, Cassiel landing with a crunch of sand.

Rae clutched the pendant, her palm burning. "Back off," she growled, not caring that she had no weapon.

"Daemon, I see you survived your first flight," he chuckled, jumping to perch on a large rock.

Titus jerked his head up, eyes so bright red it was startling. The wings at his back twitched, beginning to lift.

"It's broken," Rae said, hand hovering over the high arch. "Stop, you're going to make it worse."

Cassiel's own wings rustled, pulled tight to his back to not touch the sand. "I wonder how your line survived the culling?"

Rae crouched in front of Titus, hair slick against her face. His eyes, the same copper as his wings, were steady on her breasts.

"My eyes are up here, arsehole," she hissed, releasing the pendant to drop back against her dress.

Cassiel jumped from his rock, moving closer.

"Stay back," she warned him, holding her hand up in threat. Her other slipped behind her back. "Come any closer and I'll shoot you." She was bluffing, but he didn't know that.

"A gun won't kill me."

"Want to test that theory?"

Titus moved beside her, wings a dead weight behind him. The right was hanging on by a single piece of flesh, and he reached around and tore the entire thing off, the wing landing with a thud.

She didn't know how he was standing, never mind walking.

"Fuck," she whispered, rushing to his side, she placed her arm around his back, trying to keep him steady. "What do you want Cassiel?"

"I'm not here to harm, just curious," he said, warily eyeing Titus, his assessment taking in the width of his broken wing in one, quick sweep. "I didn't exactly expect the night's activities."

"Curious about?"

"You, Child of the Gods." Cassiel cocked his head. "Who gifted you the relic?"

"Relic?"

"Pendant," he corrected with an impatient huff. "Your pendant's a relic from when celestrials were revered as gods. Humans were gifted them as an honour for their services."

"It was a gift from my mother."

A sharp nod. "It can only be gifted from a parent to a child, but that still doesn't answer my original question of how your line survived the culling. You, and that relic shouldn't exist."

Titus tensed, a flash of blinding colour that pushed Rae back. The light lasted only a second, then something heavy wrapped around her waist, tugging.

A large beast stood where Titus once was. He was as black as the wing that had doubled in size, arched high over his left side. Patterns identical to the symbol tattoos mirrored in his thick fur, with quills jutting from his spine, sharp needles that raised when he growled towards the angel, the sound like metal grinding.

"Titus?" she whispered, pressing her hand into the beast's nape, the fur strangely soft. The markings that replicated his tattooed symbols brightened through the dark fur, giving off a pale white glow.

Tails, that was what wrapped around her middle, seven furry ropes that kept her to his side. His large head turned slightly, a silver eye blinking at her once before he returned his attention to Cassiel.

What the fuck.

The angel stood as still as a statue. "I meant no harm," he said slowly.

Rae gripped her pendant once more, the metal no longer hot to touch. "Tell me why it shouldn't exist?"

253

Cassiel warily watched Titus. "The blue stone holds a reminiscence of power long gone, a power that corrupted over time. Human minds are so delicate, weakening over generations, causing a sickness. It was why those of the line were culled, before that sickness could be passed onto my ancestors."

"What sort of sickness?"

"Of the mind." His eyes were direct when they met hers. "It was a different time, neither realm understanding mental illness as we do today. But the humans were, I guess in your language, worshippers of my people, believed we were gods. So they were gifted stones taken from the heart of the great mountain in Aetherna, beyond the veil to the sky. It protected the human worshippers, and then their children, from death so they could better serve their gods."

"Death as in not getting my head smashed in when I fell into the sea?"

Titus growled once more, a deep grumble that she felt vibrate through his tails.

"Not entirely. It won't stop you from suffering injuries, they'll just be less likely to kill you." Cassiel smiled, just a slight curve to his lip. "It's designed to keep you alive, to never suffer from infections, or disease. To heal mortal wounds at a faster rate that would otherwise kill someone without the stone. Your essence became locked to the relic as soon as you wore it, giving you an extended lifespan, only to be removed if you wish to pass the gift to your child, one who also has celestrial blood."

"There's the catch," Rae spat. "Human baby makers in exchange for slower aging. Fucking perfect."

"Do not degrade such a gift." Cassiel flung the words like an insult. "It was an honour to receive."

"If you say so." Her tone was harsh. "What happens if I remove it without a kid?" She'd not taken the necklace off since she first found it in her music box, and she didn't plan to.

"You won't be able to unless you bear a child, or if you're killed in such a way the stone cannot protect you."

Rae nibbled her bottom lip. "So how long will I live for if I can't ever remove it?"

"It's old, the magic almost dissipated. I could only sense it because of who I am."

Rae rolled her eyes. *Of fucking course only* he *could sense it,* she thought.

"If you don't suffer from an extreme injury," he continued, undeterred. "Or succumb to the sickness. Possibly two, three hundred years."

"Jesus Christ." Rae stroked along the tails around her waist, trying to sooth the beast that rumbled beside her, so tense it was if he was ready to strike. "So the pendant only works for me? It's useless to anyone else?"

"Other than your child, yes." His wings flapped, spreading. "It's a priceless treasure from a time that no longer exists. Protect it with your life."

"I don't –"

Cassiel shot into the sky, the wind generated from the force causing the sand and stones to move. Darkness spread across her vision, Titus's single wing moving to block the onslaught. With a shaking hand she reached out to touch it, the feathers small, not entirely covering the black skin stretched between the bones.

"I need the man to come back," she said, Titus loosening his tails enough she could twist free. The beast turned to look at her, tongue falling out the side of his snout like a grin. "Seriously?"

There was no fear, not even when she studied his fangs, or the serrated claws that dug into the sand. He was beautiful in a terrifying way, his body sleek enough for speed, but covered in muscle, with powerful front legs that reminded her of a lion despite the head being closer to a wolf. He stood almost as tall as her, she'd guessed the size of a bear or a small car.

The wind whipped at her hair, reminding her she was soaking wet, and the sun had set. Wrapping her arms around herself, she eyed the large beast "What the fuck am I supposed to do with you?"

CHAPTER 29

RAE

"You sure they're not going to have an issue?" Rae asked, eyeing the Conservatory Hotel, the white columns framing a grand entrance edged with chrome and gold. Gargoyles protected the double story glass doors, the large stone creatures grumpy and snarling in their frozen positions.

Riley shoved at Titus's side, who was trying to lay on her lap like a big dog, ears flat to his head. "They'll be fine, just don't let Ti harass anyone."

"You think I'll be able to control him?"

Titus had remained as his beast, his large body barely able to squish into the limousine. His single wing that seemed to have a spike on the upper curve, had awkwardly scraped the ceiling, taking out the strip lights and the sunroof. She was thankful Riley had found them shortly after Cassiel left, because she had no fucking idea where she was supposed to go next. Titus had held her phone, and everything he'd worn vanished when he shifted. Or maybe it was when they'd hit the sea.

Riley eyed the great black beast, mouth pinched. "You

have some explaining to do," he said, but Titus just pressed harder against Rae, crushing her against the seat.

"Oomph," she exhaled, trying to wiggle out from under him. "Ease up, big man."

The limousine pulled up out front, the doorman opening her door as soon as they'd stopped.

"Here, you'll need this." Riley held out what looked like a gold coin, around the same size as a usual pound.

Rae went to take it, but Titus's growl stopped her short.

"Titus, enough," Riley snarled in return. "I'm not going to hurt her." He stared at the beast, and Titus stared back, unblinking.

"It's rude to have a silent conversation when someone else's here," Rae muttered.

Surprise flashed across Riley's face, and it confirmed her suspicion. She'd caught Titus staring at his brothers a few times, and now she knew they were communicating in some silent sort of way. Seems it still worked when Titus was in his beast mode, too.

"Is that how you found us on the beach? Titus told you?" She tapped her head.

He tossed the coin in response, and Rae caught it.

"Thanks," she grumbled, turning it in her hand. It was heavy, with both sides printed with a sigil of a jawless skull. "You guys secretly pirates?"

"It's a —"

"I know what it is," she said, crushing the coin into her palm. "I kill people for a living, you think I've never been to the Troll Market? The question is why do I need the token here?"

"Same owners, and just like the Market the hotel's neutral territory. Not many people would risk being black-listed from the Faerie Boys, you should be safe."

"The key word there is 'should.'" She shoved at Titus,

the great beast finally releasing her to slip out of the car. "Thanks again."

"Rae," he said as she followed Titus, grabbing the rucksack Riley had the sense to bring. "It doesn't matter what you've done, it's what you *do* that's important."

"Well, that's fucking cryptic. I'm not planning to kill him, if that's what you're worried about. Not that I could, have you seen the size of him?"

A shadow of a smile, quickly returning to a concerned frown. "Look out for him, Rae. He's been through some shit, and deserves someone who accepts him for who he is."

"A weird statement considering you were just worried about me killing him." An impatient paw against her knee. "Thanks again."

Rae glided out of the limousine, Titus tight to her side as they approached the doors, held open by a severe looking gentleman in a full black suit. The notorious Faerie Boys owned the Troll Market, the leading place to find black magic and illegal services in the northern hemisphere. The hotel did not match that vibe.

The Conservatory was grand, much posher than she expected with marble flooring and gold features. Murals were painted between the panels on the walls, soft artistic landscapes in pastel pinks, yellow and blues. A bar took up the right side of the atrium, what looked like a selkie serving drinks to those that sat on the tall stools, again, edged with gold.

Not one person turned, gawked at the wolf/lion creature the size of a bear. They all remained absorbed in their drinks, newspapers or conversations, keeping to themselves.

Rae's bare feet ached, her body shaking as she walked towards the front desk, head held high, as if she was meant to be there. Riley had lent her his jacket, but Titus had quickly shredded the fabric to ribbons, using his body heat instead. It didn't change the fact her dress was still wet, clinging to her with every movement.

"Do you have a reservation?" the receptionist asked, his face just as severe as the gentleman who held the door. Vampire, she would have guessed from the lack of whites in his eyes, and the way he stood so still it was unnerving. Yet his black slicked back hair revealed pointy ears, which meant he was part of the Fae.

He didn't even blink at her wet clothes and smeared makeup, or the fact she was walking beside a fucking beast. He'd lost a few of his feathers, the wing now closer to that of a bat than a bird.

"Yes, Liu Wood."

The receptionist didn't look away, didn't move a single inch. "Token?"

Rae unclenched her hand, placing the coin onto the pure white desk. It was entirely unadorned, not a single piece of paper, computer or pen.

"No weapons, magic, fangs, or claws to be used to cause damage to the rooms, or other guests," he said politely. "Doing so will cause a violation. Do you understand?"

"Yes."

A beep, the wall panels to his right opening.

"Your lift, ma'am."

Rae frowned, the lift operated by a small women in yet another black suit. "What about the..."

The receptionist held out a gold card.

"Key," Rae finished. "Thank you."

He didn't nod, or acknowledge her expression. "Enjoy your stay, Mrs Liu Wood."

She was too tired to correct him.

The lift barely fit all three of them, Titus pressing himself between her and the small, straight-faced woman.

The card was metallic in her hand, a mirrored finish with the number thirteen scratched in the centre.

"Lucky number thirteen," Rae whispered, amused as she waited until the lift stopped before stepping out. The woman hadn't made a sound, her back ramrod straight the entire time. The corridor was much the same as the atrium, the wallpaper white with beige stripes, the doorframes all edged in even more gold. The sconces were the only other colour, a matt black that faced each room.

The door clicked open when Rae pressed the card against the little infrared box, revealing a four-poster bed, chaise lounge and dressing table. Candles were placed on the end, three tall, twisted columns with crackling flames.

"What a surprise," she muttered as Titus pushed past to check it out, his wing tucked neatly to his side. "More gold."

Locking the door behind her, Rae took in the room, the colour scheme warm, and comforting. Titus jumped on the bed, three of his seven tails wrapping around the wooden frame. Her body continued to gently shake, goosebumps pricking down her arms.

"Are you going to stay like that the whole time?" she asked him, checking out the side where he'd ripped his wing clean off. There was no evidence of anything beneath his fur, no mark or wound that she could see. "Because if you are, you can sleep on the floor."

She dropped his rucksack by the door before turning her back, checking out the bathroom, the bath big enough to fit a football team, with luxurious bubble baths, soaps and shampoos presented on the side. She caught her reflection in the mirror above the sink, her makeup smeared, but not too terrible. Her hair had started to curl as it dried, and there was a slight cut on her cheekbone as well as one on her lip. She sure as hell didn't look like she'd fallen from a cliff, and then almost drowned.

Reaching down her side she found the zipper, easing it down the teeth. The fabric sagged at her waist, sodden, uncomfortable. Wiggling it down her hips, she stepped out of the dress, leaving her in nothing but a thong and her pendant. It glistened blue, beautiful with the adjoining stones as it lay flat against her skin. She tried to remove it from her throat, but it didn't matter what angle she tried, an invisible block stopped her.

She wasn't sure why she'd never tried before, years of wearing the pendant and chain, and not once had she wanted to remove it, a gift from the person who'd loved her unconditionally and without motivation.

Dropping the pendant, it landed just above her sternum, the guild mark almost black, her time essentially up.

"Beautiful."

Rae flicked her eyes up, catching Titus in the reflection. He'd changed back to the man, leaning against the doorjamb, a living work of art with his arms crossed. His wing arched high above his shoulder, the muscles strained as he held it poised.

"Turn around."

She debated on disobeying, but decided she needed to see him properly, to convince herself he really was alright. His eyes remained on her face, her nipples pebbling at the hunger etched across his features. He didn't move, staying exactly where he was.

"I thought you'd died." She swept her gaze across his body, finding nothing but perfect, unbroken, tattooed skin. Not even a single mark.

His mouth curved, and she realised his lip, as well as his nose rings were missing. "You think I would let anything but you kill me?"

"You can't do that again." Rae held her pendant

between her fingers, hard enough to sting. "You can't make me feel things and then almost die."

He finally moved, and she found she'd held her breath until his palm cupped her jaw. "You drive me crazy," he whispered against her skin, lips brushing along her shoulder. "Who would have thought I would jump off a cliff for a woman who's tried to kill me three times."

"Four," she said. "Don't make it five."

A chuckle against her throat, teeth biting down as his hand swept up her side to cup her breast. "I haven't felt fear like that since I was a child. The utter terror of watching you fall, so much so that I grew fucking wings."

Rae brushed her hand across a few feathers, Titus flinched at her touch, pulling away until her fingers dropped. "Let me see."

His face tightened. "Rae."

"Please." She didn't think he would, so she waited as he fought an inner turmoil she couldn't comfort. He finally turned, revealing the slope of his back. There was no gaping wound like she'd expected, just perfect skin where his right wing should have been. "It's like they were always supposed to be there." His tattoos had shaped themselves around his left wing, his muscles solid when she stroked against the edge with her fingertips.

His wing snapped open, knocking everything off the sink to crash onto the floor. Several feathers fell, the largest the size of her forearm. "Shit." He pulled it closed, but she could tell it took effort.

She walked around until she faced him once more. His expression had closed off, almost cold. It was an emotion she wouldn't allow, not after everything. "So you're this sexy warrior that has magic, telepathy, a beast mode, and now wings?" She stroked across his chest. "You're just trying to make me feel inferior."

Titus lifted her under her thighs.

"Ti!" she squealed, automatically circling her legs around his waist. "What are you –" The hot water hit her skin, the shower steaming up around them. He held her against him, not letting go even when her shivers stopped, her back arched against the stream. He couldn't fit himself inside too, his wing too tall, too big.

His lips feathered along her ear, and she quivered for an entirely different reason. "Trust me, my Rae of Sunshine. No one could ever see *you* as inferior."

Her breath caught, and she tipped her head back as he dropped his head to kiss her. His lips tasted of salt, his grip tight on her thighs as he devoured her with deliberate strokes of his tongue.

"You said I wasn't ready for what you want," she said when they finally released for air.

His voice was soft. "Rae – "

"There's no more fighting this. Fighting us." She curled her hands around the back of his neck. "But I'm ready for everything with you. I want you to punish me."

CHAPTER 30
TITUS

I want you to punish me.

Six words, and he had already forgotten that he'd blurred the lines between druid and Daemon. It was a fear he'd never admitted out loud, not even to himself. It was never about the horns or the wings. It was the magic, so powerful, so addictive that it had terrified him.

Not many could survive such power without losing themselves, and yet that same magic that he'd feared, had saved Rae.

"It's never been about punishment," he said, placing her on the bed. His cock already rock hard, the urge to mark, to show everyone that she belonged to him such an overwhelming compulsion that he was willing to ignore the fact he'd just grown fucking wings, despite the extra weight at his back.

He couldn't deal with that right now, not when Rae's skin was flushed a beautiful pink, her eyes darkening until her pupils nearly swallowed the green of her irises. She lay complacent on the sheets, a goddess surrounded in fire. "Then what's it about? Submission?"

"Pleasure." The women never came to him to be hurt, it

was about balancing pain and pleasure, and finding a release in other ways. "Giving yourself over to someone you trust, to let them take care of you." It was a gift for anyone to offer their body, but it was even more so with Rae, the trust that he wouldn't hurt her intoxicating. It was what he enjoyed, the dynamic of giving his partner exactly what they needed, even if they didn't know what that was. The ability to control their body, their orgasms.

Her lips twitched, legs clenching together before he settled between them, palms pressing her thighs apart. "You like to be in charge."

"Yes." There was no point denying it. "I found I needed the control. Needed the power that came with someone tied up and begging for my attention. I discovered it was cathartic for me, healing I guess." He paused, wanting to elaborate, for her to understand a part of him he couldn't change, but not right then. "They were never allowed to touch me, and I usually didn't even fuck them."

"You didn't?" Rae frowned. "Then why?"

"I got off on their pleasure, on what I could force from their body."

"And that comes with pain?"

"Sometimes." His fingers found the edge of her underwear, the fabric digging into her hips before snapping. "Some came to solely be punished, releasing them from their guilt, a penance. With pain comes pleasure, but only if you learn your partner's body. Is that what you want, Rae? For me to learn your body, to know exactly your threshold for pleasure and pain?"

"I want you to punish me."

He placed a kiss on her inner thigh, watching how her breathing quickened. "Why?"

She cleared her throat. "I need it. I need you."

"That's not enough." He made his voice stern, authoritative. He'd never be able to do what he truly wanted, not without the right equipment and planning. But he could give her a taste. "Tell me why?"

RAE

"Because I want to be released." Rae barely controlled the rising guilt, and the tears that chased it. The guilt of her mother's death. The guilt of her brother's relationship. She wanted the punishment, and the forgiveness that came with it. She trusted Titus, more than she'd trusted anyone.

She found herself craving him, and that alone should have scared her, and yet it didn't. Because there was just something there, something that clicked. It was as if she'd always been looking for the other half of her soul, the person who knew about her past, knew about her present, and wasn't afraid of her future.

He understood what she needed, before she even realised herself.

"Are you going to be a brat, or a good girl?" he asked, and Rae melted at the rough silk of his tone.

Rae trembled, his face stern as he watched her, his single wing a great shadow at his back. "What will you do if I'm a brat?"

His smile intensified the tension, the air electric between them to the point static tickled along her skin. "Put your hands above your head, and keep them there. Now."

Rae didn't move, desire pooling between her thighs at his command.

He stepped back, and Rae cried out at the loss of his heat. A rip, him tearing the bottom of her sodden dress into strips.

"Wait, what are you –?" Rae released a squeak when he pulled her towards him, his movements precise as he wrapped the ribbons of fabric around her wrists separately before attaching them to the posts of the bed. It was tight enough her arms were spread, but loose enough she could wiggle, still be restrained , her butt perched on the end.

Titus said nothing as he flipped her, her arms crossing beneath her breasts as she found herself on her knees, head pressed into the soft duvet. His breath was hot along her spine, his body covering hers.

"This is nothing compared to what I want to do to you," he whispered, nibbling at her throat. "I can already imagine you stuffed with toys, begging me to let you come."

"Titus." Rae tried to clench her legs, but he'd slipped his thigh between them. "Please."

"You wanted this, remember."

She shivered as he gently stroked along her skin. "We're going to use colours. Green is good, amber is okay, and red is stop. Do you understand?" When she took too long to answer he slapped his palm across her butt, the sting sharp. "Do you understand?"

"Yes," she wheezed, trembling, her thighs already embarrassingly wet. She'd tensed before the smack, but as soon as his palm hit, adrenaline had heightened the sensation, her skin sensitive when he gently brushed his fingers over the sting.

It felt... amazing, even the slight after burn. It made her feel alive, anchored to reality. Connected to Titus.

He pressed his erection against her hip, so thick and heavy she ached to have him inside, to stretch her to the very edge. She wanted to feel the cool hardness of his piercing, but that was absent too.

"Don't move," he said, his heat disappearing from behind her.

Rae turned her head, her arms pulled, trapped beneath her breasts. She couldn't see where he'd gone, body twisting as something hot scorched her skin, cooling quickly.

Wax, he'd poured wax from one of the twisted candles.

"Colour," he demanded, and it took a second for her to gather her thoughts over all the sensations. Another drop, just above where her skin still stung from his palm. "Use your words, Rae."

"Green," she said, panting into the sheets. "Green."

The wax had already hardened, his fingers pressing it further into his skin. "Good girl," he breathed, and she relaxed into his voice. The next drop slid between her cheeks, burning a trail that had her panting, his fingers chasing the wax. He dipped between her legs, circling her clit, but not touching.

She was already close to an orgasm, body quivering with anticipation just from the situation. "Titus," she moaned, trying to thrust her hips, only for him to pull away. She yelped when he smacked the other side of her butt, the wax extra hot on the fresh sting as he tipped the candle immediately after.

"I told you not to move," he said, fingers returning to her clit, but again, just teasing. "Only good girls get to come."

"I'll be a good girl," she begged. "Please, just —"

Two fingers slipped inside, thumb brushing gently against her clit and she exploded so fast a cry was torn from her throat. Her pussy convulsed, his fingers continuing to thrust while his thumb pressed harder against her pulsating clit. He didn't relent, even when she cried out raucously. He seemed to know her body, know every cry and moan. He brought her to another orgasm painfully fast, only to pull away as she was just on the edge. Her body ached from where she'd tensed, muscles jelly as she relaxed forward, hair sticking to her face.

"You're so fucking perfect." He rubbed the wax against her skin. "But you don't get to come again unless it's against my cock."

He nudged her further onto the bed, sliding behind her, thighs spreading her legs wider. She felt his head nudge at her entrance, and she wanted to shift back, needing him inside her, but she knew he would deny her if she did. Probably force another orgasm out of her, before finally stretching her in punishment. So she stayed perfectly still, stomach tense as she waited, his cock pushing in so slowly she cried out.

"Colour?"

"Green," she whispered, wanting him to hurt her. "Harder, please."

Titus stilled inside her, cock pulsing, stretching her to the edge of pain. "What was that?" He pulled out, only to sink in just as slowly as before. "You don't get to make demands."

He stroked along every nerve ending, driving her crazy. Pulling his hips all the way back, his left hand stoked over her shoulders to circle around her throat.

"Such a good girl," he whispered at the same time he thrust himself to the hilt, and pulled her upright.

Rae choked out a cry, his fingers constricting, controlling her breath with every thrust of his hips. She groaned when he stopped moving, just keeping her impaled, her back pressed to his chest with his hand gripping her throat. The move had forced her arms tighter beneath her breasts, still crossed.

She tried to swallow, the effort harder with the restriction.

"Colour?" he asked, bringing the candle around the front so she could see it. He gently tipped it, the hot wax landing on her right nipple.

Her pussy clenched, and he groaned.

"Colour?" he asked again, this time sterner.

"Green," she managed to say.

The wax hit her other nipple, her body flinching at the shock of heat, and then the quick cooling sensation. She'd never felt anything like it, her body so sensitive, that just his fingers pressing against her pulse felt as if he were stroking her clit.

"Ready?" he asked, voice a rumble against her spine. At her nod he released her neck. "Keep your head rested against my shoulder, and don't move."

She wasn't sure if she could even move, so following the demand wasn't hard.

His spare hand brushed across her breast, the wax already hard, flaking off with every breath. The candle dipped, splashing against her inner thigh at the same time he pinched her nipple. Rae thrust her head back, pussy so wet she soaked his thighs and the bed beneath. His cock remained exactly where it was, buried so deep she'd began to ache at the stretch, praying for friction.

"Please," she begged.

"Please what?" He pinched her other nipple, the pain sharp, followed by an intense heat that had her sagging against him.

"Fuck me, please. Make me come." She needed it. She needed him.

"You can take more."

"No!" she was ready to sob, do anything he asked just to find the release she needed. "Please, just –"

Before she could finish, Titus had pulled his cock out, only to impale forward in a powerful thrust, stealing the air from her lungs. The momentum would have almost pushed her forward, if it wasn't for his hand returning to her throat.

"Mine," he growled against her skin, fingers rubbing her clit.

Rae couldn't speak, couldn't think but for the cock pistoning through her slick folds, drawing out so much pleasure she was sure she was going to pass out. Titus moved like a dancer, his hips gyrating in a brutal rhythm, his fingers knowing exactly how hard to touch her. To stroke.

It was what Rae needed, for her pleasure, and even her breath to be controlled while he fucked her like she deserved. Raw. Hard. Titus had a way of getting under her skin, making her forget about anything but him. Every thrust, every slice of pain was like a weight off her shoulders, the guilt of her choices evaporated by the man who so easily possessed her. And she fucking loved it.

Her orgasm was being pulled out of her with such force she screamed, her body convulsing around his still hard cock. He continued to rub her, drawing out the pleasure until she was nothing but a pathetic mess, and only when he stiffened behind her, his cock releasing deep inside did she finally let her tears fall.

CHAPTER 31

TITUS

R ae rested back against his chest, the hot water lapping at her breasts. The bubbles scented of lavender, the water milky from the oils he added.

"This is my favourite part," he said, gently brushing the sponge down her left arm, and then her right. She'd relaxed against him entirely, her head resting against his chest, the bath big enough to fit them both, as well as his bloody wing.

"The bath?" she asked, turning to look at him.

"The aftercare." The wax had burned her pretty flesh, marking her everywhere it fell. He knew it wouldn't last, but he loved seeing her skin marked.

She was like a cat, rolling her body towards his strokes of the sponge, moaning in the back of her throat. She'd cried when she came the final time, but when she'd looked at him he didn't see sorrow, he saw relief. Freedom.

He smiled, pressing a kiss to her cheekbone, and then one on her lips. He hovered there, loving the way she reacted to him, her breathing quickening before her brows drew together, creating a delicate line on her forehead.

"I have to re-pierce them after every shift," he explained, already knowing where her thoughts were.

"So you have to keep re-piercing your cock?" she winced.

"I do." Titus chuckled. "Would you prefer I didn't?"

"Oh, I'm one hundred per cent on team cock piercing."

The sponge brushed over her sensitive nipple, and she sucked in a breath through her teeth. So he did it again.

"Ti!" she groaned, reaching up behind her to thread her fingers through his hair.

"Would you let me pierce your nipples?"

She bit her bottom lip. "Maybe. Do I get a special prize if I do?"

He buried his nose against her neck. "You'll have to wait and see." The idea of him piercing, permanently marking her sent blood straight to his cock, and it wasn't like he could hide it while she was currently sitting on him. But the bath wasn't about sex, it was about her. "Drink your water."

"I'd rather sit on your –"

"Rae." His tone left no room for argument.

She sighed, sitting forward to grab the glass he'd poured for her. She was all talk, her muscles like marshmallow as she swallowed several decent gulps before placing it back down on the side. He'd had to carry her to the bath, her legs trembling in the aftermath.

"Turn," he asked rather than demanded, nudging her hip. She followed the instruction without an argument, straddling his thighs. "You're much more agreeable after an orgasm, I've noticed," he said with a smirk.

She stuck her tongue out, but her eyes glistened with amusement. Her attention drifted to his chest, hands reaching over to touch against the large skull tattooed there. "What do they mean?" she asked, fingers brushing along the dark lines and swirls.

"They're called glyphs. Unlike witches, who use all five

elements within their magic, druids can only use arcane. The glyphs are traditionally tattooed onto young druids' wrists. They're used to syphon their chi, because without them what little magic they have would be too much, and could kill them."

"Yet you're covered in these glyphs," she commented, meeting his gaze. "And Cassiel called you a Daemon, not a druid."

He raised a single brow. "So you're on a first name basis with the Councilman now?" he asked with a slight teasing note.

She smacked him against his pec, the water sloshing around them. "Is that what you are? A Daemon?"

He'd been waiting for the question, and still he didn't know how to answer. "I don't know."

"Tell me about them," she asked. "Are they like what I learnt as a kid? An eternity of suffering my sins in hell, with horned men poking me with pitchforks? Because not going to lie, sounds like a good time to me."

"I sometimes forget you're human." He shook his head.

Rae's eyes narrowed, but her upper lip twitched. Titus gently grabbed the shampoo bottle, Rae moaning when he began to lather it into her hair.

"Tell me," she said huskily. "Please."

Titus didn't stop, enjoying the way her eyes closed in bliss. "Daemons are druids who choose to accept black magic, and in doing so it corrupts them in both mind and body. Many became monsters, but they're not like the stories you grew up with, at least not entirely. They're a Breed not yet recognised by the Council, despite being as old as time."

"What makes them so bad?" she asked, eyes opening to slits.

"The same as everyone else. Their choices. Black magic

can change you, the power that comes with it obsessive, and the only way to gain more is with sacrifices." He cleared his throat. "All magic requires balance, a sacrifice for power. In exchange for the magic, Daemons became chained to a realm called the Nether through a summoning name, which is where the scripture for Hell came from. While the name is still used for balance, Daemons are no longer trapped to live in the dark."

"And what about you?" she asked softly.

Titus pulled his hands free, and she immediately dipped her head back into the water, washing away the bubbles. He waited until she'd finished before continuing.

"I was recently forced through the Rite, which is the ceremony in which a druid can ascend into that black magic."

"Forced as in... no choice?"

Titus watched her expression, finding no disgust or pity, not even when he nodded. He only saw strength, almost pride.

"I was fighting the change."

"But you accepted it, and you grew some pretty cool wings, not to mention you saving me." Rae cocked her head, expression pensive. "Were your eyes the first to change? Is that why you don't look in the mirror?"

He tensed beneath her.

"Your eyes are beautiful. Unique." She moved forward, legs straddling and her hands coming up to stroke along his jaw. "You said yourself, it's the choices they make which makes them bad. Your eyes don't show you as the monster you believe you are. They show you as a survivor."

Rae kissed him, and Titus pulled her even closer, her breasts flush against his chest with her pendant biting into them both. He needed to continue bathing her, worshipping her. He still had to rub oil into her skin, massage every single mark he'd left on her body.

"Not many people are as amazing as you, Titus-fucking-Liu Wood," she whispered, pulling back. "Not that I would ever admit that to anyone else. We can't have your ego growing any bigger, now, can we?"

Titus welcomed the warmth spreading in his chest, his beast content.

"You need to tell me what happened at the gala," she asked gently, his hands exploring her skin beneath the water. "Who made you react like that, so I know who to kill."

Titus smiled at that. "I was hurt when they forced me through the Rite, badly. The man who spoke to Councilman Edwards reminded me of one the Daemons."

She stilled beneath his palms. "Was it him?"

"Yeah, although it wasn't the same face." He was sure it was Bishop. His beast was never wrong. "And I suspect he's behind the hit against me. I don't believe the Councilman knew anything about it."

"So, are we going to kill him? The Daemon who wore a different face?"

He stroked up her arms. "When we find him, yes."

"Good." She nibbled her bottom lip. "So then what's our next step? How *do* we find him?"

Titus sat up, his wing sopping behind him, uncomfortably heavy against his back. How the fuck did he make it disappear?

His eyes dipped to between her breasts, past her pendant to where the guild moon was entirely black. "Rae..."

They'd run out of time.

"Oh, I guess it timed out." She sounded unsure, her shoulders slumped. "It's weird, I don't feel any different."

She pressed her palm to the mark. "It's supposed to hurt, ache. But all I feel is this warmth."

Titus pressed his hand over hers. "I'm not going to let anything happen to you."

Her smile was sad. "Even if the worst happens."

"You're –"

"Even if I'm so glad you didn't die, despite me trying."

Titus pressed a single finger beneath her chin, tipping her head back. "I'm glad you're a shitty contractor." He hadn't wanted a mate, his beast making the decision for them. And now, he couldn't imagine his future without her.

Pulling her arms around his neck, he lifted her out of the water. She didn't protest, clinging to him as he walked them both towards the towels he'd prepared. His wing dragged against the cool tiles, shoulder and back stiff as he tried to figure out which muscle did what.

Rae spread her fingers through his hair, yanking slightly. "Titus, I –"

A shrill ring echoed through the bathroom.

"Is that... a phone?" she asked.

Titus followed the sound, placing Rae on the edge of the bed while he searched, finding a gold-plated rotary phone in the top drawer.

"Evening Mr Liu Wood, sorry for disturbing you," a smooth voice said on the line. *"There's been a slight problem that we wish to bring to your attention."*

"What happened?" he asked, Rae frowning as she waited.

"Well Sir, the problem has been detained, and as per the policy for staying at the Conservatory we leave the decision to you. They violated the rules, and are therefore void of our protection."

The receiver groaned in his ear, Titus having to physically relax his fist. "Where have you detained them?"

CHAPTER 32
RAE

The dress hadn't dried, the fabric still too wet to wear comfortably, so she'd opted for the complimentary white dressing gown, the middle knotted to stop any accidental flashes as they'd made their way to the reception desk.

Titus had offered her his spare t-shirt from his rucksack, but even though it reached to her knees, it was arguably even more indecent than the gown, without the option for trousers, especially considering he'd snapped her only pair of underwear. So white dressing gown it was.

"Mr and Mrs Liu Wood, if you would follow me," the receptionist said before they'd even approached, turning to guide them behind a wall panel. "I would like to apologise again for this inconvenience. I would like to assure you, not many people risk a violation here at the Conservatory."

"Not unless they're stupid," Rae muttered, her bare feet cold on the hard wooden floor.

"Or desperate," Titus added, pausing to let her walk in front. He wore no shirt, neither of them figuring out how to get the fabric over his wing without ripping the entire back. "Can you tell us what happened?"

The receptionist turned, raven hair not moving a single strand at the gentle movement. "One of our security found this person entering the premises through a window, armed with a gun. It didn't take us long to apprehend the intruder." He gestured to a small lift, the style Victorian, old with a metal gate sliding open. "After you."

Titus and Rae walked into the tight space, the receptionist closing the lattice behind him before pulling on the lever at his right. The lift descended slowly, the light growing more limited the further they descended.

"They have been tied up for ease, and we have provided you with some equipment. Please note any clean-up will be sorted in house, we just ask you to let us know when you're done."

With a heavy whine the structure came to a stop, the metal door squeaking as it opened. The golds and beiges were nowhere to be seen, the floor hard concrete beneath her feet, the walls stone with cracking flames lighting the way. The air was bitter, so cold it stung with every breath.

Sobbing echoed, bouncing off the hard stones.

The receptionist came to a stop outside a thick wooden door, unlocking it with a key card. "I will leave you here. Again, I offer my sincerest apologies for any inconvenience, and will send champagne to your room once you are done." Without another word, he turned back towards the Victorian lift, leaving them alone in the concrete basement.

"This is so weird," Rae whispered, the chill teasing her ankles. "Does he creep you out? Or is it just me?"

"Faerie," Titus said in explanation, pressing his palm to the door.

Rae didn't immediately recognise the person bound to the chair, their head covered in a black fabric hood. A single light shone above, the rest of the room covered in shadows.

The person cried out, pulling against the ropes around

their wrists and ankles, arms bulging with the effort. Titus reached into the room, clicking something on the wall. Three sconces, one on each wall flickered on, revealing a metal table with a selection of perfectly presented scalpels. The floor was concrete, stained a dark brown with a drain directly beneath the chair.

Rae let out an impressed whistle. "These guys mean business." She had purposely ignored the person in the chair, a man, she guessed by the body shape.

She knew from practice the longer she made them wait, the quicker they cracked. So she took her time looking over each blade, amused with how neatly they'd been placed. She suspected Titus would have done the exact same, her man liking everything perfectly straight. Neat.

She was going to enjoy introducing him to a little mess.

"What do you think we should do with him?" she asked Titus, reaching for one of the smaller scalpels. "Should we cut him up a little first?" Rae straddled the man's legs, making sure he felt her entire weight.

The man flinched, his cries muffled.

"Or just gut him like a fish, and be done with it?"

She reached beneath the hood, drawing the edge of the scalpel against his throat. It wasn't deep enough to do damage, just enough to feel the scratch.

Titus allowed her to play, an encouraging presence at her back, allowing her to take the lead in any situation she owned.

"It's not much fun when they can't speak back," she sighed dramatically. She grabbed the top of the fabric covering his head. "Hmmm, let's see what's behind door number –"

Rae dropped the fabric, staggering off his lap until her back hit the wall with a crack, the scalpel jumping from her hand to clatter onto the floor.

A block of ice settled against her chest, spreading like icicles until her entire body stung.

"Miles?" she choked out, her brother's eyes full of feral panic.

A gag had been shoved into his mouth, tied around the back of his head, but he still managed to give her an ugly sneer, a coat of sweat glistening beneath the harsh fluorescent lights. Blood was a neat line down his throat.

Titus unclipped the gag, and Miles spat it out instantly. Snot and tears stained his face, the colour around his right eye darkening with a bruise.

"Let him up," she said, her voice cold, empty. "I said, 'let him up.'"

The bonds sagged, Miles watching her before he launched forward, hands curved into claws. His fingers brushed against the lapels of the dressing gown before he was hauled back, Titus pinning him to the chair once more.

"Careful," he warned, and Rae could hear the beast through his tone, his voice dropping to a growl. His hands were planted on Miles's shoulders, her brother no longer fighting the restraint.

"It was never yours!" her brother sneered. "I'm the eldest, it should have been mine!"

The ice cracked, her heart a jackhammer that hurt, ached. "Miles," she asked, not recognising her own voice. "What have you done?"

Angry tears burned down his face. "Mum told me it was for me, but then she fucking gave it to you. That should be my necklace, my fucking money."

Rae tried to control the rising fury. "Money? There was no money! When dad died he left us nothing!"

"Not that, you stupid bitch." Miles winced, Titus digging his fingers in. "The necklace is worth hundreds of millions, and it's supposed to be gifted to the first born!"

Rae reached beneath the dressing gown to hold the pendant, her hand shaking. "It was you, you're the one that paid for the hit against me." Everything clicked into place. "You borrowed the money from Angel."

Miles sobbed, snot dripping beneath his crooked nose. "He said he'd give me two weeks to give the money back. But the fucking liar only gave me a week. Why couldn't you have just died Rae? Everything would have been so much easier if you'd just fucking died instead of dad."

"Miles –"

"Everything's always your fault," he spat. "You were the reason dad starting taking his anger out on us. It was perfect before you were fucking born." He laughed, but there was no humour in the sound. "Then you came along and everything changed. You look nothing like him, you know. I wonder why that is?"

"Enough –"

"You really are fucking stupid." His eyes dipped to her necklace. "All this time, and you had no idea what you had around your neck. Give me the necklace, Rae. It's mine."

"I can't. It doesn't come off."

"You're such a selfish bit –"

Titus yanked his head back, cutting off the rest of his words.

Rae struggled to breathe, the anger so vibrant it burned. "So what, you came here to steal it from me?"

Titus eased his grip, and Miles hung limp, hatred burning from his expression.

"I know it can't come off, I've tried to remove it before, when you were asleep. I've even tried to cut it, but no scissors or knives have ever been able to break the chain."

Rae blinked away the tears, not allowing them to fall. "You really believe you could have killed me, Miles?"

She knew from his desperation he could, the way he

met her gaze without flinching. Everything she'd ever done for him, for them, meant nothing. She'd sacrificed her life for his mistakes, and in return he was the one who'd tried to kill her. All for a necklace that was never meant to be his.

A smile cut across her face, cruel and devoid of any warmth. He must have seen something in her expression, because all the colour had drained from his face, his mouth gaping like a fish.

"Please," he begged, eyes bulging as she reached for another scalpel, picking the largest one in the line-up. "Please, don't do this. I'm your brother!"

Rae tested the blade against her finger, a bead of blood appearing with just a single prick. "You've proven to me that it means nothing." A hopelessness weighed heavily on her bones, making every movement an effort.

She settled herself on his lap just as Titus yanked his head up, pinning him in place and exposing the column of his throat.

"Don't do this," Miles hissed, teeth bared in desperation. "I'm the only family you have left."

"You're wrong." Her voice cracked, but she was beyond caring. "I've chosen a new family." She made the cut quick, precise as she moved the blade from ear to ear. For everything he had done, she couldn't see him suffer.

A light spray hit her face, but she didn't wipe it away, instead watching as her brother choked, gargled before finally stilling beneath her.

And just like that, the last of her relatives were dead.

Her hand opened, the scalpel clattering audibly to the hard concrete.

Warmth against her cheek, Titus pulled her up to her feet. He wrapped his arms around her, crushing her against his chest. She expected tears, even grief, but nothing came.

She wasn't sure how long they stood there, long enough

for the blood on her face to cool, for her legs to shake from exhaustion.

Titus said nothing, just held her, comforted her.

His eyes were calm when she looked at him, proud.

"I'm good," she said, and meant it. There were many things she'd have forgiven her brother for, but trying to kill her wasn't one of them. "Really, I'm fine." She shouldn't have been, she knew that. The fact she wasn't confirmed she wasn't normal. But then again, her life had been anything but normal.

Titus's lips pressed into a thin line, but he nodded. Taking her hand, they walked out of the room, leaving her brother behind. Only when they were back up to the main floor did she adjust her dressing gown, hiding her pendant back beneath it. She was aware the white had been stained pink, and blood was still smeared across her face. Never mind the large half naked man with a single wing who walked beside her, and yet no one spared them a second glance.

"Excuse me, Mr Liu Wood. I have your guest's personal items here." The receptionist waved in the direction. He placed a small gun on the desk, and beside it a mobile phone. "Your champagne will arrive at your room shortly."

Rae ignored the gun, instead grabbing the phone. It was basic, with buttons rather than a touch screen. "It's a burner." Clicking through the menu, she read the last text message.

'Is it done?'

"Who else knew about your pendant?" Titus asked, taking the phone from her fingers. He scrolled through the recent call list, clicking on the last number called.

The phone rang once. Twice.

"Miles? Is it done?" the voice said from the speaker. "Did you get the necklace?"

285

Rae quickly pressed disconnect. "That fucking lying bitch," she whispered. "I'm going to kill her."

She knew there had been something amiss the last time she'd spoken to her, Rae's instincts very rarely being wrong.

"You recognise her?" Titus asked.

Rae grabbed the gun, comforted by the cold weight. "That was my Guildmaster, Vivian."

CHAPTER 33

RAE

W hen Titus suggested he could get them back to his place far quicker than a car, she was sceptical. Was even more sceptical when he grabbed her around the waist, and her whole body felt like she'd been stuffed through a hole a quarter of her size.

Rae crashed to her knees, head spinning as she tried to regain her equilibrium.

"We're not doing that again," she said, groaning as she looked up through her hair, to find Titus on the floor, eyes closed. "Ti?" Rushing over, she tried to lift him up, but he didn't budge. "Shit."

The bedroom door crashed open, and she immediately jumped up, holding her hands out in defence. "Back the fuck off!" she warned.

"Rae?" Sam appeared in a pair of undone jeans, and nothing else. His eyes widened as he took her in, and then Titus passed out on the floor.

"What the fuck was... Ti?" Axel rushed in behind him, bare chest pumping, similarly decorated in the glyphs. "What happened?" he asked, crouching beside Titus.

"I don't know," she began, talking quickly in her panic. "We were at the hotel, and then we were suddenly here."

Sam came to Titus's other side. "Baby, did you see the fucking wing?"

Axel paled, but lifted Titus up off the floor. There was a crunch when he placed him on the bed, and everyone paused.

"His wing!" Rae cried. "You crushed his wing!" She knew it must have caused him pain, but he didn't react. Not even a single muscle twitched. "He's okay, right?" She'd never seen him so still. Not even when he slept.

"Fuck. Sam, go get Lucifer," Axel said.

Sam didn't need to be asked twice, shooting into the hall to leave them alone.

Rae brushed the hair from his forehead, the skin clammy. "Is he sick?"

"We need to wait for Lucifer," was all Axel said, hovering on the other side, panic and worry carved into his expression. "Was he okay before he drifted?"

Rae frowned. "Drifted?"

"He jumped you from the hotel to here, right?" Axel asked slowly.

Rae bit back her snarky retort, knowing Axel was reacting to the stress of the situation. "He was fine earlier."

Axel crossed his arms, fingers digging into his upper arms. Sam reappeared, followed by a tall male she recognised from the bar. His eyes glowed, and she finally recognised them for what they was. A Daemon. Just like Titus.

"What the fuck happened?" Lucifer asked. "Is that a fucking wing? Where's the other one?"

Rae stood guard beside Titus, wary. "He kind of pulled it off."

Lucifer jerked his head to her, mouth snapping open. "Fucking hell."

"Is that bad?" Axel asked, Sam wrapping his arms around him from the back. They were mates, Rae remembered. He was comforting him.

"Well, it's not fucking good, is it?" Lucifer rubbed his jaw, his wrist covered in around ten different beaded bracelets. After a second he shrugged. "Idiot's passed out from the drift. You can't just fucking drift without preparation, otherwise your molecules might go missing." Reaching over, he rolled Titus onto his side, manhandling his wing out from beneath him.

"Will he be okay?" Rae asked, cringing at the clicking sound his wing made as Lucifer stretched it out beside him.

"He'll be fine in a few hours, just takes a while to get used to." Stepping back, he eyed his handiwork. "He received a summoning name, but I didn't think he would get wings, or even fucking drift."

"Does that mean the Rite was completed?" Axel asked.

"Looks like it." Lucifer clicked his tongue. "I wonder what his beast will look like now he's more like me."

Rae cleared her throat. "He... he keeps the wing."

"Well, that confirms it." Lucifer clapped his hands together. "Titus is officially my favourite Guardian."

"Wait, you've seen his beast?" Axel turned his attention to her.

Sam tightened his arms, pressing his jaw against Axel's shoulder. "Easy, he'll be okay," he said to his mate.

"Can you feel him?" Axel asked, gaze direct. "In here." He slapped a hand against his chest, just under where Sam held him.

Rae wasn't sure how to answer that, the scrutiny under the three men too much. "He needs his rest," she said instead. "I'll watch over him."

Axel looked like he wanted to argue, but Sam pulled

him back. "Come on, we're only next door." His lips brushed Axel's ear, and whatever Sam said, he softened.

"You'll call us if he needs anything?" Axel asked. "Please."

Rae nodded. "Of course."

"Right, I'm going back to bed." Lucifer yawned, stretching his arms up above his head. "Unless he's dying, don't call me. It takes at least eight hours every night to look this good." With a wink he left, Sam and Axel following quickly after. Rae stood there for a few minutes, not sure what to do.

Titus looked so still, too still. Climbing onto the bed, the opposite side to where his wing lay, she pressed her body against his. As soon as she'd settled, the earlier panic came back with a vengeance.

"You need to stop doing this," she whispered against him, knowing he couldn't hear her. "You're going to give me a heart attack. Do you think the relic will bring me back to life if that happens?"

His breathing was soft and even, and she pressed her hand against his chest, just feeling his heart beat steadily. The relief was instant, easing the tightness in her lungs.

"I don't know how to feel about it," she continued. "It's weird to think that I'm going to live a few more hundred years. That this whole time my mum had kept this a secret. Do you think the pendant was what turned her mad?"

The pendant lay against her skin, the dressing gown gaping slightly.

"I'm jealous of your family. I thought Axel was going to explode when he saw you, he was so scared." She smiled against his arm. "Must be nice to have that, for someone to care so much. But then again, I've haven't felt real fear in a long time, not until I thought I'd lost you."

She tried to relax her body beside his. "You scare me,

Titus. Other than my brother, I've never had to care about anyone else in a long time."

Rae yawned, her body fatigued, drained. They hadn't slept at the hotel, instead deciding to head straight back to the house. His home.

"I can feel you, you know," she whispered, as if she was confessing a sin. "I didn't realise what it was before, but you're there, this warmth that I couldn't explain." Lifting her head, she looked down at him. "Does that mean we're mated? Like you said?"

She knew he couldn't reply. And yet, she still found herself talking, unable to stop the verbal diarrhoea.

"I don't know why I'm surprised. You're always taking charge in these things." She continued to talk, telling him stories of her childhood, the few happy ones, and then tales of her assassinations in glorious detail. She wasn't sure how long she simply whispered to him, baring her soul before she finally closed her eyes, and sleep finally dragged her under.

TITUS

His back fucking ached.

"Fuck the Fates," Titus muttered, turning on his side to find it empty. "Rae?"

He sat up, wincing at the pain in his wing. It lay limp beside him, a large, black, useless piece of flesh. He was tempted to rip that one off too.

"Rae?" he called louder, panic sour on his tongue. He remembered convincing her it was safer at the house, and then nothing. "Rae!"

"In here," came her reply, voice drifting from the bathroom.

Titus settled on his legs, satisfied that they'd hold under his weight. Other than his fucking wing, he felt fine, good even.

Rae stood by the mirror, her dressing gown caught on her elbows, her breasts exposed. She was staring at the moon, her smile sad. "You've been asleep for eight hours straight," she said, turning to look at him over her shoulder. She was beautiful, her hair holding a natural wave and the morning sun highlighting the freckles along the bridge of her nose. "You even snored."

"Did I?" he asked, her smile turning teasing.

"Hmmm. Like a train. Is this what I've signed myself up for?"

Titus couldn't not touch her, his hand curling around the back of her neck. "Plus orgasms."

She tipped back her head to better meet his gaze. "Oh, like I could forget about the orgasms." She smirked. "You feeling okay?"

"Better once we kill your Guildmaster." He wouldn't settle for anything less.

Rae pursed her lips. "Axel knocked about an hour ago. He loves you, you know. As do the others."

Titus nodded. "I know. They're my family –"

"Chosen, I know." She brushed the hair from his eyes. "They're waiting for you. I know how little you sleep, so I convinced them to wait a while longer."

A hint of amusement touched his face. "You threatened them, didn't you?"

"Maybe." A grin.

A knock on the door, Lucifer opening it without waiting. "Yo, where are you?"

Titus groaned, pulling Rae back into the bedroom with him. "Couldn't even give me five minutes, could you?"

"Ah, there he is!" Lucifer bounded over with a spring in his step, his t-shirt black with silver spikes decorating his shoulders. A bright pink headband pulled his hair from his face, complete with a little glittery heart. "If it isn't Mr Wonky Wing. You feeling better?"

"Grand," Titus muttered. "You able to help me get rid of this thing?" He rolled his shoulder in emphasis.

"Oh, sure." Lucifer touched his arm, and a burst of magic tingled against his skin. Titus sucked in a breath through his teeth, the weight at his back disappearing. He expected a burst of nausea, but there was nothing, no feedback, and no throbbing like when the magic fought against him.

Rae gasped, her hand brushing against the space where his wing once was. "It just disappeared."

Lucifer whistled. "I'll teach you how to hide it, but if you get too angry, they just kind of explode out. Well, one will. Your other will take a while to grow back."

"So it will grow back?" Rae asked.

Lucifer shrugged, taking a seat on the bed. "Eventually. I wonder if you'll grow horns?" He leaned back on his hands, head cocked. "Guess we'll find out. So, are you going to kill the Councilman?"

"No."

"Yes." Rae turned to face him. "If he hurt you, he's dead," she said, matter of factly, pulling the dressing gown tighter against her.

"The Councilman wasn't behind the hit," Titus reassured her.

Rae pursed her lips. "He's an arsehole, we can kill him anyway."

Lucifer hollered in excitement. "We're keeping her, right?"

Rae shook her head. "I'll get changed, one of the girls brought me some spare clothes, Eva, I think her name was." Eyeing Lucy, she closed herself in the bathroom.

"So... you're officially mated," Lucy said, crossing his leg over his knee. "Soul bound and everything. Congratulations, or condolences?"

"Fuck off."

"Congratulations it is," he said with a smile. "You do know you owe your beast for that. I suspect he was fighting against the black magic just as much as you were."

Mine, his beast growled right at that moment. Titus had suspected it was why his beast pushed for the mating more violently than the others, because he felt Titus needed the anchor.

"My beast has great taste."

"That's what you all say, but it's going to be entertaining to see how having a beast is going to change you from the black magic." He looked pensive. "Anyway, the reason I'm here is because I spoke to Riley, and I have the address of a certain Vector you may be interested in."

Titus stilled, heart a rabbit against his ribs, trying to break out.

Lucifer shot to his feet. "Breathe."

Titus swallowed, realising he'd started to panic. "Shit."

"It's cool, you're fine." Lucifer hovered his hand, but didn't touch. "I can feel you've merged with the black magic, which means you're no longer likely to just keel over and combust. It takes a while to get used to, the power overwhelming at first. It's reacting to your emotions."

"This address, you sure it's the same guy?" His voice croaked when he spoke.

Lucy nodded. "Riley confirmed it. I've been waiting for

your lazy arse all morning. Thought we could just pop over and give the guy a friendly visit." Lucifer grinned, his teeth a little too sharp.

"Visit who?" Rae came out dressed in jeans and a vest, her hair tied up high on her head.

"A guy we're gonna kill," Lucy said. "You wanna come, assassin lady? It'll be fun."

"The guy from the Gala?" she asked, excitement brightening her face.

"We're not dealing with him right now," Titus said. "Not until we sort your Guildmaster."

"Vivian isn't going to get paid anymore, but your guy's still out there. We can't wait for him to strike again."

"I'm not arguing over this Rae, you will always come first."

Rae made a sound of frustration. "I'm not some damsel –"

Titus pulled her towards him, gripping her jaw in his hand. "I never said you were." A flush crept along her collarbone, the way it did when she was angry. "I'm saying that you don't have to do this alone anymore."

He watched her face twist, but she didn't bite back. "Truce."

Titus released her jaw. "Rae –"

"This is the weirdest relationship I've ever seen," Lucy snorted. "Carry on arguing, it's not like we haven't got things to do, places to see."

Rae shot him a dark look over her shoulder, which only made Lucifer laugh.

"You're not thinking strategically," she said. "You want to go in all guns blazing when we both know that won't work. Vivian very rarely leaves the guild, which will be made even less likely when she doesn't hear from Miles. She's surrounded by a ward that prevents her from harm, not to mention she controls the entire building's security. We need time to prepare." Rae placed a hand against Titus's chest, above his heart. "This is what I do, I plan and prep. You need to trust me about this."

"Rae –"

"So what you're going to do, is you're going with your creepy friend here, and you're going to take out the fucker who dared hurt what's mine."

"Creepy?" Lucifer muttered.

"And what are you going to do?" Titus asked her.

She bit her lip. "I'm going to do what I do best."

Lucifer slapped a hand against Titus's back. "So, she's going to try and kill you again, mate."

CHAPTER 34
TITUS

"You're acting like Kace when he first mated," Jax commented, sitting sideways.

"It's called being pussy whipped." Lucifer pulled the sun visor down, pouting at himself in the mirror. "They seem to only be able to think with their cocks."

Titus crushed the steering wheel beneath his palms, praying for patience.

"No pussy can be that –"

"And what's your excuse? Considering you only date your hand." Titus reached over and closed the visor. "You're beautiful princess, stop staring at yourself."

Jax chuckled in the back. "Now you sound like Xee."

"Damn, you're mean now you're mated." Lucifer cocked his head. "She'll be fine, she's a big girl who literally kills people for a living. I think leaving her for a few hours will be okay."

Titus opened his door, slamming it shut behind him. He felt normal in his fighting leathers, the weight of his guns comforting, but he still couldn't shake the feeling that he might return home to find Rae gone. They may have been mated, but she could still walk away.

"If she was going to run, she would've last night," Jax said, coming to his side.

Titus glared at him. "Stay out of my head."

"Then stop projecting, you're making my beast anxious." He checked the knife strapped to his thigh. "I'm not going to pretend to understand, but she wouldn't still be there if she wasn't committed."

"You guys finished being all romantic? Because I must say, we look positively terrifying," Lucy commented, pulling at the tight black material on his stomach. "Yet incredibly sexy."

"I can't believe you're allowed to come hunting with us," Jax muttered, but his lips curved into a shadow of a smile.

Lucifer rolled his shoulders, knives crisscrossing his chest, just as a guy crossed the street with his dog. "We're going to get the cops called on us," he said, winking at the man.

Titus began to move. "Then we better make this quick." They'd parked on a different street, but there wasn't much they could do considering it was a built-up residential area in the middle of the day.

The house was like every other suburban home, detached with sky blue painted cladding on the first floor. A white picket fence surrounded it, the bushes overgrown, but still reasonably neat for the street.

The door opened without any resistance, the latch broken. "Fuck." The stench escaped quickly, the air thick, musky.

"Smells like something died," Lucifer said, face creasing when he stepped inside. "Shit, something did die."

The Vector lay on the floor in the centre of the living room, his mouth gaping open, tongue black and eyes misted in death. He was pale, much paler than he was the night before, his skin mottled blue. Blood splattered around him in a perfect circle, yet he had no open wound.

"Lawrence Wallace," Lucifer mused, kicking the dead guy in the side. "Looks like he's been a naughty boy."

"You think this was a possession?" Jax asked, bending down. The left side of Lawrence's face was crushed to the carpet, his right arm bent back at an impossible angle. He still wore the robe he'd worn the previous night, the pale fabric covered in dirt.

"He shouldn't be this decayed," Titus commented.

Lucifer shrugged. "Can depend on how long he was possessed for, and whether it was forced, or welcomed." Reaching for Lawrence's arm, he pulled him onto his back, the bones clicking as he moved, broken. "You see, this is why I never practiced this shit. It's disgusting."

"Didn't you used to eat people?" Jax asked.

Lucifer hmphed, placing his hands on his hips. "Look, do you blame lions for eating gazelles?"

"Yes, because that's the same."

Titus frowned. "There's been an impact at the back of his head." Lawrence's eyes were bulging, the left almost out of its socket. A cut sliced his left cheek, the surrounding area red and puffy. Likely infected. "He didn't look like this last night. How long do you think he was possessed?" he asked Lucy.

"How the fuck am I supposed to know? It's not like I can ask him now, can I?" Lucifer sighed. "He looks like shit, it's possible he's been frequently possessed on and off for some time, he may have not even known."

"Horrifying thought," Jax muttered. "We usually notice the longer the Daemon controlled them, the more they start to deteriorate."

Lucy kneeled, a frown pinching his brow. Tugging at

the robe, he tore it straight down the middle, exposing Lawrence's chest.

"What the fuck are you..." Jax began, cutting off when the bloody marks were revealed. Lawrence's chest was a mess of runes, both old, scarred, and some fresh. A few bulges were shown beneath his skin, and Lucy whistled happily as he cut one of them out.

"Charms," he said, holding up the blooded disk, a simple wooden circle with a slight dome. "I would say he's been a passenger in his own body for a few months, at least. The charms would've hidden the deterioration."

Titus grunted, crossing his arms. "Plenty of time to infiltrate the Order, and –"

"Use the Councilman's details to hire a hitman," Jax finished for him. "Bishop's trying to put a wedge between us and the Order."

"I don't think you guys need the help," Lucy snorted. "What?" he asked when they both turned to him. "The Councilman's a prick, and clearly dislikes you all."

Titus grunted. "We're causing a problem for them, so they're trying to get us cut off."

Jax leaned against the wall, his shoulders shifting beneath the black leather. "But what they don't know, is that we're not reliant on the Order."

"Which we could use to our advantage." Titus nudged Lawrence. "Is there any way to track Bishop?" He knew the answer before Lucifer even answered.

"Not without his summoning name, no."

Jax cleared his throat. "Kyra summoned a Daemon without his name."

"She had a coven, and it almost killed her. It's not worth the risk." Titus shook his head. "Bishop and Gideon are going to make a mistake, and when they do, we'll be there to take them out."

CHAPTER 35

RAE

To be a hired contractor, you needed patience. Rae had planned her assignments over days, weeks, and even months before. And yet as she sat at the kitchen counter, pencil in hand, drawing the guild layout from memory, she was out of her comfort zone.

She enjoyed the planning, but her patience was waning the longer she waited for Atlas to reply to her message. She couldn't risk anything against Vivian without knowing all her options, and until he answered, she was stuck.

Eva peered over, her arm moving at lightning speed as she stirred the batter in her big red bowl. The entire situation was weird, being surrounded by Titus's family, as if she were a part of it. Eva had welcomed her into the kitchen without hesitation, offering her a seat and a drink, and seemingly ignoring the fact Rae had tried to kill one of her family members numerous times.

Rae wasn't sure what to feel, the pencil held so tightly she risked breaking it.

"Hunter, are you going with Kace to the Vault tonight?" Eva asked the boy sat beside her.

"Maybe," Hunter sighed, drawing the hood further over

301

his face. "I don't want the attention, and you know what Marshall's like. He'll go overboard." He sat in the stool beside her, seeming content to watch Eva bake.

Eva turned, and despite looking around the same age as Rae, she'd gotten the mother stare down pat. "They just want to celebrate, you only turn fifteen once."

Hunter tensed beside her, hands curling into his lap.

Rae nudged him gently on the arm. "Fifteen huh?"

Hunter looked at her from beneath his hood, his eyes blue, guarded.

"I think I stole my first car at fifteen," she continued, nibbling the end of the pencil.

"Really?" Eva muttered, but there was amusement there. "That's the story you're going with?"

"What? I was acting out." Rae grinned, winking at Hunter. "My aunt tried to send me to some boarding school for deranged kids or something." The idea hadn't lasted long, not until Miles had threatened her for even the idea of sending Rae away. The thought of her brother soured her mood.

Hunter touched her hand, breaking her out of memories she would rather forget.

"You should celebrate every birthday. Eat every slice of cake, and surround yourself with people that love you enough they want to celebrate your life. I didn't get that."

Hunter's nose wrinkled. "Where were your mum and dad?"

Rae looked towards Eva, but the vampire just leant against the kitchen counter, waiting as much as Hunter for the answer. "Dead," she answered.

"Did you kill them?" he asked.

"Hunter!" Eva gasped. "That's not —"

"Only my dad."

Eva turned to pin Rae with a stare, fangs punching down to pierce her bottom lip.

Hunter burst into laughter, and the sound seemed to calm Eva. "That isn't funny," she said.

Rae shrugged. "He was a bad person who shouldn't have ever been a parent."

"And your mum?" Hunter asked, and Rae suspected there was more to the question.

"I didn't kill her," she said, ignoring the twinge in her chest. "But from what I remember, she was good. But sometimes, even good people shouldn't be parents." Her mum hadn't been well, and could barely take care of herself, never mind two children.

It was Eva who broke the silence. "I'm sorry."

"Don't be." Rae placed the pencil down to cup the hot chocolate, the phone still empty of notifications beside it. "I get to blame all my mental issues and poor personality traits on my upbringing, so it's a silver lining."

Hunter thought on her words for a moment. "My mum's like that. Good, I mean." His voice quietened to a whisper. "But she shouldn't have been a parent."

"Maybe, but at least you have something I wished I had growing up." Rae leaned in as if it were a secret. "You have a family chosen."

Hunter's eyes glowed, changing from blue to green. He licked across his lips before pulling the hood further down his face, shadowing his features. When Rae cut her attention back to Eva, her smile was soft. Rae didn't know Hunter's history, or Eva's for that matter, but she knew they cared for each other.

It caused her stomach to tighten, jealousy blossoming.

"How long are we to be here?" a voice echoed down the hall. "It's been days, and he hasn't bothered to even visit us.

What type of son forces us from our home, and then disappears?"

Hunter perked at the new voices, turning towards the doorway just as Axel burst through, expression like thunder, followed by three adults.

"We were supposed to fly to Athens yesterday," the woman whined, her jet-black hair a straight curtain across her shoulders. "Our friends are expecting us."

"We had scuba diving booked," the man snapped. His hair was a dark blonde, and between them both, she could make out Titus's features. "Axel, you said it was an emergency, but this is ridiculous."

"It *was* an emergency," Axel said through gritted teeth.

The man scoffed. "Clearly everything was exaggerated, otherwise Titus would've shown his face."

"He probably just wanted attention," the woman added. "You know how he was when he was young."

The older lady watched, her dark eyes narrowed. She burst into a barrage of Mandarin, her words sharp before the younger woman replied in the same language.

"Fates," Axel muttered, dragging a hand through his hair. "Kill me now."

Rae couldn't help but stand from her stool. "So you're Titus's parents?" she asked, not understanding a word said between the two women. They both turned to look at her, their features identical even with the age difference. Titus had inherited the delicate angle of their eyes, but everything else was from his father, the sharp jaw, high cheekbones and blonde hair.

"I'm sorry, who are you?" he asked with a sneer. "This house is like a bloody circus. Why did you bring us here, Axel?"

"Oscar," the older woman scolded before turning to the

woman, clearly her daughter. Which made the woman Titus's grandmother. "Mei, if you do not care. Leave."

"We never said we didn't care," Mei snapped. "But we're busy people, and whatever this is, it's interrupting our plans."

"Interrupting what plans?" Rae asked, meeting Titus's mother's eyes. She wondered if that was his original colour, before the beautiful red. "What plans are more important than helping your son?"

Oscar's face darkened. "How dare you –"

"Tell me, when was the last time you asked how Titus was? Whether he was struggling? Or happy?" She noticed Oscar and Mei look at each other, foreheads furrowed. "When was the last time you even called him?"

"That's none of your business," Mei said with a regal tip of her head. "Our son put us in this situation in the first place, putting us in danger, and for what?"

"For a situation that he had no control over." Rae could feel the anger bubbling. "Your heads are so far up your own arses, that you haven't even bothered with your son."

Oscar's chest puffed out. "That's enough. Axel, are you going to let this stranger talk to us like this?" he asked in a fittingly pompous tone. "This is ridiculous, we're getting on the first flight out of here."

Rae laughed, the sound hollow. "I honestly have no idea how such a strong, amazing man came from you two."

The old woman chuckled, mumbling something beneath her breath.

"See what I mean, Hunter?" Rae asked, turning back to him. "Some people shouldn't be parents."

Mei gasped, Oscar grabbing her hand and dragging her back into the hall.

"Good riddance," the older woman muttered, coming to

pat Rae on the arm. She was small, her head only just over Rae's shoulder. "Tell me, do you like dumplings?"

Axel groaned. "Lǎolao."

"Ah, you're just jealous Samion makes them better than you." The old woman smiled, brightening her entire face when she returned to Rae. "You love my Titus, I see it in your eyes. There's a fire there."

Warmth spread through Rae, cutting the earlier anger.

"I'm Ana," she continued. "But you can call me Lǎolao."

"Lǎolao," Rae repeated. "I'm so happy to finally meet you."

"I have waited so long for someone for my Titus. His soul is pure, just like my other boys." She smiled at Axel. "Titus deserves a woman who will fight for him."

Rae wanted to laugh, but couldn't seem to make a sound, so Lǎolao patted her gently on the cheek.

"You're so beautiful, you must give him beautiful babies!"

Axel seemed to choke on air. "Lǎolao!"

Rae dipped her head, skin burning as she returned to her seat. Hunter gave her a small smile just as the borrowed phone lit up, and determination tightened her stomach at the message.

> Rise & Grind Coffee, back room. 5pm.

Rae climbed off the train at Camden Town at three minutes past five, already knowing Atlas would be waiting with a scowl. The coffee shop was directly outside the station, a line already forming to get inside. Pushing past the crowd, she walked through to the back, finding Atlas sitting behind a circular table with his back to the wall.

"Thanks for meeting me," she said, not taking a seat. The room was private enough, with only beads separating their section to the main seating area. The coffee shop was busy, the noise loud enough to drown out their conversation.

"You carrying?" he asked, dark brow raised.

"Yes." She knew there was no point in lying. "A gun." She'd taken it from Titus's room, finding an entire wardrobe full of weapons. She'd had to put it inside the back of her jeans, stealing a leather jacket from Titus to hide it. It drowned her, but hid the bulge of the gun beautifully.

"Why did you message me Rae? You've been flagged as AWOL, and Vivian's having a fit. She's doubled down on protection at the guild."

"That's why I asked to meet you, because I need to get back inside."

His pupils swallowed his eyes, until they were entirely black with no whites. She hated when he did that, reminding her that he was a predator as old as time. "Stop it," she said. "I've seen you puke because you drank too much alcohol from Winter's blood, it's hard to act tough after that."

A thin circle of white appeared in his eyes, but he smiled. "She hadn't told me she'd taken Acid."

"That same night you were sobbing into your own sick."

"Fucking hell, Rae." He blinked, eyes returning to their dark brown. "What do you want?"

"I need help, Atlas. You know I wouldn't ask if it wasn't important."

He leaned back in his chair, waiting. She explained everything she knew, from figuring out her brother had hired assassins, to Nathan, and then to their Guildmaster.

Atlas was uncharacteristically serious. "Would you go on the stand with your accusations? Knowing the consequences of slander within the Syndicate is punishable by death?"

"On the stand?"

He stood, his eyes passing over her shoulder. Rae tensed, reaching for her gun at the same time she turned. She held Titus's gun at the stranger's head, a man who didn't even blink at a weapon an inch from his nose.

Atlas cleared his throat. "Rae, I would like you to meet Kyle."

The man who was Kyle stared at her, silent. His hair was thick, a dark brown that brushed his brows, drawn together in a frown. A heavy band was tattooed around his throat. She'd seen it before, similar marks found on the slaves sold at the Troll Market, and it distracted her a second before she noticed his eyes.

Rae put space between them, but didn't drop her gun.

His eyes were red.

It wasn't long ago where Daemons were just stories told to naughty children to scare them, and now look at her.

Kyle blinked, his irises turning green.

"Cool trick," she said.

"Thanks," he muttered. "But I would appreciate it if you put the gun away so we can finish the meeting."

"Atlas?" she asked, refusing to look away.

"Kyle's from the Knights. I invited him."

"Why would you invite him?" Her heart pounded behind her ribs, and she knew Atlas could hear it. "This was supposed to be between us."

"Because once we take out Vivian, Kyle will be the one taking over Crimson Hollow. Unless you're interested in the role?"

"Of course not!" Rae gripped the gun harder, her arm wavering. "Fuck." She dropped her arm, turning without giving Kyle her back. He took a seat, but Rae refused to take

308

the remaining one, instead pressing herself against the wall so the door was to her left, and both men were in her sight.

"I've been trying to get rid of Vivian for years," Atlas said, placing both of his hands flat on the table. "She's corrupt, taking side unapproved assignments. The Syndicate was designed to regulate the assignments, making sure the reasoning for the assassinations were justified."

"Protect the innocent. Slay the corrupt. Defend the realm," Kyle added.

"How would you..." Rae began. "Shit, you're a mole," she finished, the realisation hitting her like a sledgehammer. "You work directly for the Syndicate."

Atlas smiled, the emotion forced. "She's been under investigation for years, it's the reason she rarely leaves her quarters. If what you're saying is true, it's cause to remove her from her position."

She'd never heard him speak so formally. It was disconcerting. "I'm not planning to stand up at trial, I'm going to kill her."

Atlas didn't even blink. "I didn't hear that, so any consequences that she may find herself suffering don't concern me. All I care about is restoring Crimson Hollow, otherwise the entire guild will be unsanctioned."

Rae looked between the two men. "Does that mean you'll get me back inside?"

He shrugged. "The wards only repel those that aren't already blood bound, so you can pass through without problem, but you'll find it difficult to harm her."

Rae worried her bottom lip. "Do you know a way around her wards?" If she couldn't get Vivian out, she was fucked.

"Blood," Kyle said, having been sat there silent. "Powerful blood will be able to break the wards, at least for long enough to take her out."

"And where exactly will I find –"

"You'll figure it out." Kyle's face smoothed into an emotionless mask, and she knew he was hiding something. "Give me a warning, and I'll make sure to take the magic in which binds the Guildmaster to the guild."

CHAPTER 36

RAE

Rae looked ridiculous. The leather trousers and skin-tight top were fine, although she would've preferred the ease of a skirt. But the luminous pink bum bag Lucy had forced her to wear around her waist made her look like a murderous doll.

"Do you remember the plan?" Titus asked over her earpiece.

"Do you mean the one I came up with?" she whispered quietly, unzipping the bag to check the contents while she waited for his green light. Fresh runes had been carved into the doorframe, stained red.

"Brat," he grumbled, and Rae wanted to grin. *"I'm linking into the server, you're good to go in three, two..."*

Rae cautiously pulled open the door to the garage, expecting to meet an invisible shield. "That feels weird." It was like the building was trying to repel her, her skin tingling as she stepped over the threshold, shivers crawling down her spine.

"The ward feels dark. Likely blood magic, so we're not going to be able to cross it until it's been removed from the source."

The lift doors opened within seconds of her approach. She pressed the button to the ninth floor, unable to stop herself from glaring up at the camera blinking in the corner. She knew Vivian couldn't see her, Titus reassuring her he was going to loop all the footage.

"You're going to want to make this quick, there's someone trying to kick me out."

"That's probably Killian." Which meant his brother Bastion would be around too. She'd listed her colleagues into three groups, the first being Winter, Atlas and Galen who she was sure would be on her side. Probably. Then she had Nix, who she'd put in the 'stay the fuck away from' category, because he had a stick up his arse and always stuck with the rules. Then there were Killian and Bastion, who were highly unpredictable. She'd put them in the maybe pile.

"Remember you just need to get to her —"

"Office," she said as the lift dinged just past the sixth floor. "Which is where I'll set off the bomb, and bring down the ward so you and your weird friend can come save the day. Yes, I remember. Want to know why?"

She waited for his growl, was satisfied when she heard the familiar rumble.

"It's because I created this plan."

"You're such a Rae of fucking sunshine."

"Is this you two flirting?" Lucifer muttered into her ear. *"Because if so, I think you need therapy."*

Titus's growl deepened. *"What did I say about staying radio silent?"*

"This is why I work alone," Rae said. "I'm about to reach the ninth floor."

"I see you. The hall directly after is empty, and I only count four people including Vivian on the floor. The office is the only place without a camera."

The doors opened, and Rae drew her gun, clutching it with both hands. She wouldn't shoot, knowing that doing so would cause severe pain through her brain from the ward protecting the building, but it would at least make someone hesitate.

That hesitation was what she needed.

"Talk to me, where are they?" she asked, scanning the kitchen to find no one there. The enchantments had been doubled since she was last home, painted rather than carved. They pulsed, sensing the violence that threatened.

"You're clear."

Picking one of the weird balls from the bum bag, she stepped back, aiming it at the wall. The ball exploded on impact, loud enough she flinched. If they didn't know she was there, they did now.

The contents splattered across the entire wall, reaching as far as her feet.

"Is that... glitter?"

"Luce, did you seriously add glitter to the blood?" Titus asked, his voice softer, as if he wasn't speaking directly into the microphone. *"Kace is honestly going to kill you if you keep touching his stuff."*

The scent of copper was strong, the blood diluted and mixed with salt as it dripped down the walls, obscuring the runes. They pulsated faster, the engravings darkening to black. "How do I know if it works?"

"You won't really," Lucifer answered. *"Not until you hit someone."*

"I fucking hate magic," she muttered, moving quickly towards the office. "These runes are everywhere." Vivian had added them to the hall, the bedroom doors, and even to the ceiling.

"Smear the blood as much as you can, we only need a small window to break through the block."

Rae grabbed another ball, bouncing it off Winter's bedroom door, painting everything a startling red. She wouldn't be able to reach the ceiling, but she pressed her hand to the wall, spreading the sticky, grainy mixture.

"Rae, we're getting inter –"

The back of her neck tingled.

Rae spun, finding Nix leaning against a door, watching her with his crystal blue eyes. He didn't say anything when she met his gaze, his body relaxed, head cocked.

"I have to do this," she said, her voice soft. She hadn't heard him come up.

"I agreed to give you a head start," he said with his rich, deep voice.

"My assignment never timed out. It was removed from the database, voided."

Nix nodded, just a gentle dip of his chin. "This is your head start." Without another word he disappeared back towards the kitchen.

Rae gripped the gun hard enough to hurt, heart hammering against her ribs.

"Titus, you there?" she asked, hearing no feedback from her earpiece. "Fuck."

Vivian's quarters were empty, taking her seconds to throw another ball, and smearing the blood along the runes. Each time she brushed her hand against one, it burned, the blood bubbling before the enchantment darkened to black. She had no idea if that was good, or bad.

"I don't know who it is," Killian said, voice drifting, from the office. "But they're shutting down all your security protocols. Everything's locked out."

Rae kept herself tight against the wall, making out Vivian pacing through the gap in the door.

"Figure it out!" she snarled. "We're clearly being attacked, and you're supposed to be able to..."

A hand across her mouth, yanking her back. "What the fuck do you think you're doing, Rae Rae?"

Rae kept herself calm, allowing Bastion to remove the gun from her grip. He spun her until her back hit the wall, his mismatched eyes frowning down at her, one brown, the other blue. It was the only thing that distinguished them as twins, with Killian having both brown.

She waited for him to release her mouth, dropping her eyes before she accidentally challenged his wolf.

"Vivian's been unsanctioned by the Syndicate," she said quietly, hoping Killian couldn't pick up her words from the other room. "She's corrupt, selling me out to the highest bidder."

"Explain," he demanded.

"Nathan came after me, trying to kill me for my necklace, and Vivian knew. She approved it."

"Impossible." Bastion stepped back, but still held onto her gun. "The Guildmaster is bound to protect those under their contract."

"Tell that to Nathan." Rae slowly slipped her hand behind her back. "Oh right, you can't, because he's dead."

"This is –"

Rae pulled out her knife, holding it directly above his heart.

"Fuck," Bastion hissed. "I forgot you're into knives, Rae Rae."

"It's silver," she said, his skin burning red from just a single touch even through the fabric of his t-shirt. There was a slight pressure against her brain, but nothing like there was supposed to be. The little blood bombs were working.

"So you came prepared." His eyes narrowed, his upper lip twisting into a snarl.

"This isn't about you." She eased up on the pressure,

allowing him to swallow. "Bas, you need to trust me." Against all of her instincts, she stepped away.

Bastion touched his chest, his fingers coming away red. "You're breaking the ward."

She pulled out the last bomb.

His eyes dipped to her hand, and she tossed it before he could stop her, the ball crashing against the office door to explode it off its hinges. Blood splattered against her side, the impact stinging her exposed skin. Bastion crashed into her seconds later, dragging her against him and marching her forward. She flipped her knife, hiding it beneath her sleeve.

Rae grinned at Vivian's expression, Killian frowning from where he sat behind her desk. "Miss me, Viv?"

The door had slid across her pristine floor, leaving a bloody smear.

"What have you done?" she hissed, pink flames dancing around her fingertips.

"I'm here to give you a message from the Syndicate," Rae said, grunting against Bastion's grip on her upper arm.

Vivian's face paled. "Remove her Bas, she's broken the rules."

Killian flicked his eyes between everyone. "Someone want to tell me what the fuck's going on?"

"Remember I could've killed you," she whispered towards Bastion. "But I didn't."

Bastion hesitated.

"That was an order, Bastion," Vivian said, her tone leaving no room for argument.

"Where's Nathan?" he asked. "Haven't seen him in a few days."

"He's under an assignment," she replied smoothly, her shoulders stiff beneath her purple pastel suit. Some blood had lightly speckled the fabric.

Bastion growled, the sound clearly his wolf. "Truth."

"What assignment?" Rae asked. "Tell everyone Viv, who exactly is his target?"

A flush darkened her cheeks, her stare promising death. "You're his target, Raegan. You timed out, and as we all know that makes you fair game."

Bastion's grunt echoed in her ear. "Rae, you need to give me a little more here. She's the Guildmaster, we're bound to her word."

"I can't time out, because my assignment was voided. Look for yourself, it won't be in the database."

"Do not touch that computer!" Vivian held her hand out.

Killian was already typing.

"I said do not —"

"Rae's right," Killian said. "Her assignment's closed."

Bastion released his grip.

Vivian looked like she'd swallowed a lemon. With a snarl she gripped Killian's hair, yanking his head back. "I'm the Guildmaster, you do as I say."

"Not anymore, they're replacing you." Rae flipped out her knife.

Vivian smiled, her fingers touching Killian's forehead. His eyes rolled, body convulsing. "Step out, or I'll kill him."

"Rae? Can you hear me?" Titus's voice flowed in and out.

Bastion tensed beside her, claws piercing through his fingertips. He still held her gun, but it was forgotten at his side. Not that they could use it, not knowing whether the ward was weak enough to allow harm to Vivian, or whether the bullets would simply bounce off and hit them.

"What are you going to do?" Rae asked, keeping calm. "I have the entire building surrounded." Technically a lie, one Bastion scented by the gentle shift of his head. "Your ward's compromised, and your corruption's been exposed."

Vivian's face had cooled to a lethal calm, but behind those eyes was fear.

"There's still resistance."

Resistance? The runes were black, dead, and yet something was stopping them from getting inside. "You shouldn't have come after me, Viv. No amount of money was worth it." With a small smile, Rae threw the blade.

She wasn't practiced in throwing, preferring to be up close and personal with her knife skills, but it skimmed past Vivian's arm, enough for her to jerk back, releasing Killian. Bastion jumped to beside his brother, shoving the desk to the side hard enough that it crashed into the digital window, the glass shattering.

Pain seared across her brain, forcing her to her knees. The ward was still protecting Vivian, the scream torn from Rae's throat echoing before the pain finally subsided. Rae sagged forward, hands slapping against the floor.

"If you need something done, do it yourself," Vivian snarled.

"Rae? Can you hear me?" A bang from her earpiece. *"Fuck!"*

Rae screamed, agony blinding down her arm, arcane licking at her skin. Smoke swelled, the digital window sparking.

"Killian!" Bastion growled, trying to pull his unconscious brother towards the door. "Get the fuck –"

A pop, the digital window exploded into flames, exposing the runes hidden beneath.

Pressure built around her throat as a warmth spread from her breast. Vivian yanked the chain from behind, but it wouldn't break, cutting into her flesh.

Rae's back arched backwards, her fingers barely slipping beneath the chain before it cut off her oxygen.

"Why couldn't you have just died?" Vivian snarled, flames crawling up the wall.

A shard of glass glistened, just out of reach. Rae swung her leg, foot touching, stretching. Vivian pulled tighter, cutting off circulation to the end of her fingers, and making every breath a struggle. "You always have to make everything difficult."

Rae kicked the shard back, catching it as it slid across the wood. It cut into her palm, but she didn't care, her blood as hot as the crackling flames. With a cry she twisted, slamming the shard down into Vivian's leg.

Vivian's grip loosened, allowing Rae to throw herself forward into a coughing fit. It burned to breathe, the smoke excruciating, filling her lungs. Something cold knocked against her hand, something familiar.

Rae didn't hesitate, didn't think as she turned, holding the gun.

Vivian's eyes widened, Latin exploding from between her lips.

Rae pressed the trigger just as the spell hit her, and she smiled at the perfect hole between Vivian's eyes, something heavy pressing against her head, swallowing her in darkness.

CHAPTER 37

TITUS

H is beast was violent, pressing against the inside of his skin.

Lucifer smacked his hand against the side of the screen. "Stupid bloody thing."

"Stop that!" Titus growled, trying desperately to get the video feed back. Something hadn't just kicked him out, but fried the whole damn server too. He couldn't even get a signal to Rae, as the connection was lost. "Fuck this, Axel and Xee just rolled up outside. Let's jump."

Lucifer pulled the headgear off. "You got the visual?"

He'd memorised the entrance to the guild, pulling the image to the forefront of his mind. He still didn't know how it worked, but first he was standing in his bedroom, and next his entire body felt like insects were crawling all over it.

Shaking the sensation away, Lucifer appeared beside him. "Not bad," he said, nodding to Xander and Kace. "You made it in one piece."

Titus grunted, his stomach threatening to expel its contents.

Slight buzzing in his ear, Rae's voice quiet, broken.

"We can't get in," Kace said, fingers brushing down the throwing knives he had strapped across his chest.

Titus tapped his ear, hoping Rae could hear him. "There's still resistance." He could barely make out any sounds, just muffled static. "Rae? Can you hear me?" He hit against the door, the runes that surrounded the frame pulsating red. "Fuck!"

He hit it again, but the magic was strong, repelling every effort.

"Step back," Lucifer barked, his hands clapping together to create a large ball of arcane. It hit the door, dissipating on impact with an audible bang. The enchantment throbbed, the red flickering.

Xander dropped to his knee, touching the edge of one rune. "Hit it again."

Lucifer's arms danced with arcane, the flames thick. "This is gonna –"

The ward stuttered, the red darkening to black with a fizz.

"Do it," Lucy finished, the arcane fizzling out. "Huh."

Titus didn't hesitate, pulling up his memory of Vivian's office, and forcing himself through the sensation of insects, his body tearing apart only to crash back together piece by painful piece. A single blink, and the door changed to a wall of flames, the roar of the blaze deafening, eating away at anything exposed.

"Rae?" he called through the smoke. His heart thumped heavily inside his chest, the panic overtaking every thought. A wolf whined in the corner, a man with mismatched eyes trying to grab his scruff.

A flash of red hair, her hand cupping a gun. He scooped her up, pulling her to his chest and dragging in her scent of peaches and cream. She was limp, head rolling on his arm to reveal her pendant cracked down the centre.

"Rae?"

Burns blistered down her arms, her skin splitting from the heat.

Mine.

Her eyes fluttered, and Titus almost collapsed from relief. "Vivian's dead," she said, voice hoarse.

Titus only tightened his hold, not caring that her Guildmaster was dead. He'd had twenty minutes of not being able to feel her, the ward cutting everything off. Twenty minutes of not knowing whether she was alive, or dead. His beast had gone mad, and it had taken all his strength to remain as the man.

Intense heat licked at his side, the ceiling whining as it began to crumple.

"We need to get out of here," he said, ready to drift them back outside.

"Wait!" Her arms shook, likely the adrenaline. She hooked them around his neck, better stabilising herself as she turned to the man and wolf. "Bastion, you need to get out of here."

Bastion snarled, canines much sharper than they should have been. "I'm not leaving –"

The air shifted, and a man with piercing blue eyes and dark hair appeared.

Titus immediately called his arcane, the power vicious compared to the wild magic that tingled against his chi.

"Nix?" Rae called, the Fae turning with an expressionless mask. He grabbed Bastion, and disappeared with a static pop. "What the fuck!"

The wolf snarled, his eyes showing nothing but feral instincts. If a man remained, he wasn't present.

Rae reached for him. "We can't leave –"

The Fae appeared once more, glaring down at the wolf

who tensed as if to pounce. He grabbed the wolf by his scruff, and disappeared with him too.

Titus wasted no more time, holding onto Rae, he recalled the image of outside, and pulled them both through a drift. On his own, it felt like waving through water, but with Rae it was like moving through mud.

The sunlight blinded, the air crisp compared to the heat of the flames.

Rae groaned in his arms, taking a second to shake the drift's effects.

"You piece of shit!" Lucifer growled, his wings spread and horns curling through his hair. "You honestly think you can just disappear, and never fucking call?" His hands were fisted at his side, sparks slipping between his fingers.

"It wasn't about you," came the smooth reply, and Titus had to shift to the side to see past Lucifer's wings. A Daemon, one who barely looked at him before settling on Rae. Titus didn't bother to hold back his growl, gripping his mate tighter.

Lucifer's wings snapped tight to his back. "Fuck you, Kyle. People cared about you, you selfish prick." With a snarl he stepped away, fury apparent in every line of his body.

Xander's voice flowed through his mind. *This might be a problem.*

Is that who I think it is? Titus asked, Axel and Xander appearing beside him, positioning themselves as guards.

Yep. Xander crossed his arms. *What are we going to tell Alice?*

The truth, Axel said, the connection spreading to include all three of them. *She deserves to know her brother's back.*

"Is it done?" Rae asked, wiggling in his grip. He gently

323

set her down, making sure her legs fully supported her weight.

Kyle nodded, his expression cautious.

"What about my contract?" Rae pressed herself against his chest. "I was forced into my contract, I want to be set free."

Kyle's smile was sad. "It's not possible, the magic's complicated, and must be fulfilled one way or another once signed in blood." He cocked his head. "But as the new Guildmaster, you'll be given as much freedom as possible."

"So I don't have to stay at the guild?"

A heavy whine, something crashing inside the building, the fire gutting the inside.

"No," Kyle said. "You only have to return when assigned a hit."

Rae turned, looking up at him with wide eyes full of hope. She looked beautiful even covered in blood and soot, an open book with every emotion flashing across her features like his favourite story, and he loved her for it.

Cupping her jaw, he tilted her head better to meet his lips. She tasted like everything he'd ever wanted, and without a word he pulled up an image of his bedroom, and drifted them both back home.

CHAPTER 38

EPILOGUE

TITUS
THREE WEEKS LATER

Titus walked quickly through the labyrinth of entwined corridors and halls, ignoring the druids who came to sneer or gawk at his mate. Many kept a wide berth, expressions a mixture of anger, fear, and indifference to a woman gracing the abbey. Others tried to approach, but quickly scattered once they met his gaze.

Rae had been furious at having to wait, suffering more damage than they'd originally realised, ripping several muscles as well as a few severe burns. Nothing permanent, her relic doing its job at healing her at a faster rate than a normal human, but now she was almost entirely healed.

Excitement vibrated her every single step, and he couldn't wait to get her back home, to place the collar around her throat while she dropped to her knees. She laughed when he revealed the leather piece, but eagerly fastened it tight. It marked her as his, but that was something private between them. He still wanted something she could physically wear in public, warning everyone that she was taken.

The door to Councilman Edwards office opened with a strategic kick, the Councilman himself jumping to his feet as they strode inside.

"What do you think you're doing?" he sneered, eyes settling on Rae. "Why would you defile our sacred place with a *woman?*"

Rae turned to the druids who came to Edwards aid, ready to fight.

"Did you honestly just complain that I'm a *woman?* Jesus Christ, your priorities are seriously wrong." She looked around the room, seemingly unimpressed with all the white.

"What's the meaning of this?" Edwards asked. He settled back in his oversized chair, his hands clawing over the edge of the armrests. "You've entered uninvited."

"I came to discuss your recent problem with Vector Lawrence Wallace," Titus said, his tone empty. "Seems even you couldn't sense the Daemon within your precious abbey."

Edwards growled, the leather squeaking beneath his grip.

Rae brushed her hand along his desk. "Poor baby, having a Daemon fool you like that."

"He infiltrated the Order," Titus added. "And used your name to hire a contractor."

"Everyone leave," Edwards barked, dismissing the druids behind with a dismissive flick of the hand. "Now."

Rae pouted, moving to stand behind his chair before producing a small knife, only to stroke it against Edwards's cheek. Titus smiled, Rae loving to tease her prey with a blade.

Edwards remained calm, his eyes anything but when they met Titus's. "Tell her to back off."

"You seem to think I have any control over my mate," he said with a chuckle. "But you failed as the Archdruid, and because of that you're compromised."

"I cannot be held accountable for a Daemon's trickery," he snarled, Rae reaching around to hold his head still. "It will not happen again, I have already made arrangements to fix it."

"Your mistake almost cost Titus his life," Rae said, dropping her voice to an angered whisper. "Maybe I should take yours instead?"

There was no fear in Edwards's expression, not for Rae, at least. "I cannot absolve you of your choices, you ascension is a disgrace to our Breed," he snarled, gaze direct. "The Order was created to neutralise threats to keep the world safe, and you've become a threat."

Rae pressed the knife hard enough it pierced his skin, but still Edwards didn't react, not daring to look away from Titus. Edwards thought he was the only threat, but clearly he didn't know Rae.

"Are you saying you were aware of the hit?" Titus asked, holding his breath for the answer.

"No, I wasn't aware. But that doesn't matter." A frustrated response, his mouth pinched. "Druids are taught from birth the consequences of choosing dark power, and yet you stand before me with red eyes and a dark chi. Your presence alone tells me the Guardians have become a liability."

Titus cocked his head, a familiar presence walking the halls behind him. "Rae." He nodded to his side, a hint of desire darkening her eyes at his command. She smirked, leaning closer to Edwards ear.

"Be very careful who you threaten, Councilman

Edwards." With a last pressure of her blade, she stepped back. "You're not immortal."

Edwards didn't touch the blood that dripped down his cheek, his jaw clearly clenched. His eyes returned to the door, which opened as if on command. Titus didn't bother to turn, knowing who it was who'd entered.

"I'm not your dog," Sythe growled, the scent of copper, death, and rot flowing along with every step. He gripped a head in a tight fist, the hair auburn as he dropped it with a thud onto Edwards's desk.

Titus expected panic, maybe even a full-on attack at seeing the head of Bishop, his face frozen in death. But with Rae beside him, her hand pressed gently against his heart, he felt nothing but grim satisfaction.

'Looks like you've been busy,' he commented, connecting mentally to his brother.

Sythe turned, meeting his gaze. *'This one's for you.'* He raised his brow at Rae. *'And your new mate?'* Titus nodded, and Sythe grinned. *'Fucking hell, what else have I missed?'*

Edwards recoiled from the head, the chair scraping as he pushed it back. "Is this the Daemon that murdered Vector Wallace?"

"The very same, your highness." Sythe bowed, a sarcastic dip of his waist. "But this wasn't done for you, it was for my brother."

"He's not your brother," Edwards snarled.

Sythe shrugged, not seeming to care. "And you're nothing but a sperm donor."

If Rae recognised Sythe as one of the men who beat up Miles, she didn't let on. "Are you telling me, Mr 'scared of anything with breasts' has touched a woman?" She snorted. "I don't believe you."

"That's quite enough." Edwards clicked his fingers, the doors opening, and the security returning. "I ask that you all leave the premises immediately, and son, I expect an answer soon."

Sythe shook his head. "I've already given you an answer, it's go fuck yourself." He flipped up his middle finger. "You can tell the Fates that too."

Edward's skin flushed angrily.

Titus reached for Rae, following the security out of the abbey, back through the twists and turns until they'd been kicked out into the surrounding green, Sythe chuckling behind them.

"Such a pompous prick," Rae said, biting at her lip. "Should have let me kill him."

Titus laughed, tugging her against his chest. She was everything he never knew he wanted, needed. Her smile, her laughter, and even her attitude.

"So, are you going to introduce me before I go back?" Sythe asked. "Or are you going to make me beat it out of you?"

Titus brushed his fingers along Rae's jaw. "Sythe, I'd like to introduce you to my mate."

RAE

The pendant was cracked, what looked like lightning shooting through the centre of the blue stone. It didn't matter to her, not when the celestial relic had likely saved her life. The spell Vivian had thrown had been a black curse, at least that was what Kyra had said, explaining there was a residue on her aura.

Not that Rae could see, or feel her own aura, so she had to trust the witch.

"Are you ready yet?" Eva called with barely constrained

excitement.

"Perfection takes time!" she shouted from the bathroom, applying a sweet-smelling cream to her skin. It created an extra protective layer, helping the burns heal with minimal scarring.

Eva, Alice and Sam waited impatiently, ready to hit a karaoke bar on the other side of the city. Rae couldn't contain her excitement, but Titus had delayed her by a good thirty minutes. She had no regrets, that man a professional with his fingers.

"You're already perfect," Sam chuckled, his knuckles racking against the closed door. "But if you take any longer, we're going without you."

Rae shook her head, eyes dropping to the new guild mark between her breasts. There was still the moon, but beside it was a stylised sun, indicating the new leadership for Crimson Hollow. It could have been worse, but Kyle already seemed a much fairer Guildmaster, even paying her for her hits, rather than keeping the money.

She'd asked for freedom, and he'd given it as much as he could.

Yanking on the shirt, and zipping up her skirt, she pulled the door open to find three of her new friends grinning.

"You guys are terrible," she muttered, unable to fight her own smile. "I'm almost ready, and then we can head out."

Eva blinked innocently. "Look, I know you're freshly mated, but making us wait isn't cool when we're celebrating."

"What are we celebrating?" Rae pursed her lips, yanking her hair into a high ponytail. "And wait, didn't you lock us all out the kitchen the other day because you were busy with Kace?"

Alice laughed, perched on the end of her bed beside

Eva while Sam had draped his entire body over the armchair, legs kicked over the side.

"Don't get us started on Kace and Eva!" Sam chuckled.

Eva crossed her legs. "Hey, we're not talking about me!"

"Actually, I'm pretty confident I saw Kace with fang marks only a few minutes ago..." Alice added.

Rae laughed as they teased each other in the way only friends could, attaching the gun holster to her thigh. She may have been only going to a karaoke bar, but she never left unarmed. It had only been a few days since Titus had agreed she was well enough to be back on her feet, and had already taken her to a gun range to practice her shooting.

She was good, but he was better.

She'd made it her goal to beat him, just once. She had hundreds of years to practice, but she was content at the moment to just tease him, knowing that the punishment he delivered was delicious.

"Okay, I think I'm ready." Rae slipped her gun beneath her skirt, the fabric hiding it perfectly. She missed her dagger, but she was yet to find a suitable replacement. She'd borrowed a few from Titus, and even one from Jax, but it wasn't the same.

Sam jumped to hit feet. "Come on my lovely ladies, the bad cocktails and even worse singing are just moments away."

"Speak for yourself." Rae reached for the door, pausing when she noticed the candles, along with black petals carefully laid out in the hall. Someone had turned the lights off, the candles and fading sun the only light.

"Oh, you should probably follow that," Alice said, appearing by her side. "Looks important."

Rae thought she was hallucinating. "What's going on?"

"Well," Sam drawled. "The off-pitch singing is going to have to wait."

"What..." She was pushed into the hall, her own bedroom door shut behind her. Rae could hear them laughing behind the wood, but she was too confused to do anything but follow the candles.

They guided her down the stairs, past the kitchen and towards the dining hall. She could tell which petals Titus had placed, each one perfectly spaced from another, compared to someone else who'd just left them where they fell. The candles too were evenly placed, protected by glass as they flickered gently against the impending night.

Rae didn't stop following them until she found Titus standing beside the large windows, the sky behind various shades of pink. He'd moved the table and chairs, the petals and candles directing her straight to him.

"What's going on?" she asked.

"I have something to ask you," he said, and she could sense his nerves despite his face reflecting calm. His Adam's apple bobbed, his gaze not leaving hers even as the double doors closed behind her, leaving them both alone.

"Ask me?" She walked slowly towards him, eyes bouncing off the petals, to the candles, to the window showing the sun setting, then back to Titus. He was the most gorgeous man, dressed entirely in his signature black, with kohl smudged beneath his eyes, and fresh rings through his nose and lip. "Should I be scared?" she teased.

His smile was strained. "Truce."

Rae reached him, butterflies assaulting her stomach. "Truce," she agreed, still confused.

Titus nodded, and then very slowly dropped to one knee.

"Jesus Christ!" Rae laughed. "What do you think you're doing?"

He produced a black velvet box. "Raegan Fox," he began. "Will you marry me?" The lid flipped open to reveal a solid silver ring. It was perfectly sculpted, the left half a skull, and the right looking suspiciously like Titus's beast, merged beautifully together with eyes of obsidian.

"That's..." Rae laughed, the sound wet. "But we're already mated?" She could feel him in her heart, a comforting warmth she never wanted to let go.

"I know," he said, knuckles white with which he held the velvet box. "But our mating wasn't exactly ordinary, my beast forcing the connection before either of us were ready."

"Do you regret what happened?" she asked.

"No. I'dll happily suffer through the Rite a thousand times more, if it meant meeting you."

Rae bit her bottom lip, wanting to tease him a while longer. "Hmmm, do I really want to spend my extended life with you?"

"Rae," he growled, the sound sending tingles between her thighs. His eyes darkened, upper lip twitching.

"Hmm, but you're so –"

His lips captured hers, pressing, possessing her in every way possible. She melted beneath the touch, his hand curling around her throat to lay against her pulse. His entire body consumed hers, and she fucking loved it.

"Of course I'll marry you, you idiot," she said, voice embarrassingly husky.

Titus grinned, slipping the ring onto her finger. "There's more."

"More?!" She wasn't sure her heart could handle it.

With a wink he reached behind his back, and pulled out a dagger, the same size as the one she'd lost. And just like her ring, it had half a skull and beast on the pommel, as well two more sculpted on each side of the guard.

Throwing her arms around his neck, she jumped into his arms. She'd never met someone who understood her the way he did. The butterflies had died down enough for calm to settle into her bones, a sense of security that she never believed she'd ever achieve. Rae didn't believe in fate, or destiny. But she believed they were always meant to be, because Titus was the calm to her chaos.

She smiled, happier than she'd been in a long time.

"You're mine, Raegan Fox," he whispered against her ear.

"It's Raegan Liu Wood," she said with a defiant tilt of her chin. "And only if you're mine too."

Want more of Titus & Rae?
Sign up for my newsletter and get a bonus (sexy) epilogue!
Download!
https://BookHip.com/WANJQSK

Thank you for reading Heart of Crimson, the fourth in The Curse of the Guardians series. If you enjoyed this book and would love to see more, I would be forever in your debt if you could leave a review on the platform(s) of your choice!

Reviews are super important and help other readers discover this series.

Much love,
Taylor

P.S. Want a fun, safe place to chat about my books with others? Join my exclusive reader group, Taylor's Supernatural Society!

"Can't get enough of me, can you?"
Sythe and Harper, coming soon!

Keep in touch with Taylor Aston White

Instagram
@tayastonwhite
TikTok
@taylorastonwhite
Facebook
/taylorastonwhite
Website
www.taylorastonwhite.com
Bookbub
www.bookbub.com/profile/taylor-aston-white
Goodreads
www.goodreads.com/taylorastonwhite

Sign up for Taylor's newsletter mailing list to receive updates, exclusive content, giveaways, early excerpts and much more.
Plus there's a free short story!
www.taylorastonwhite.com

About the Author

Taylor Aston White loves to explore mythology and European faerie tales to create her own, modern magic world. She collects crystals, house plants and dark lipstick, and has two young children who like to 'help' with her writing by slamming their hands across the keyboard.

After working several uncreative jobs and one super creative one, she decided to become a full-time author and now spends the majority of her time between her children and writing the weird and wonderful stories that pop into her head.

Printed in Great Britain
by Amazon

26909111R00200